Oneiro III

Illusion of Chaos

by

John Stuart Goldenberg

ONEIRO III: ILLUSION OF CHAOS

Cover designed by Telemachus Press, LLC

Cover art:
Copyright © iStock 000034164596/Atypeek

Digital design by Telemachus Press, LLC
http://www.telemachuspress.com

Visit the author website:
http://www.John-Goldenberg.com

ISBN: 978-1-942899-58-7 (eBook)
ISBN: 978-1-942899-59-4 (Paperback)

Version 2015.12.02

10 9 8 7 6 5 4 3 2 1

By John Stuart Goldenberg

Oneiro I
Anumen

Oneiro II
Gauntlet

Oneiro III
Illusion of Chaos

Oneiro IV
Apotheosis

Daughter of Pallas
A Tale of Cold War

Shadow Fade
*A Dilettante's Guide to
The French Language
Provençal Culture
& Murder*

With Sincere Thanks:

Mme. A. M. Zender

Author's Note

Oneiro is a teratology, of which this is the third volume.

Many of the expressions in this book are inherited from previous books in the series.

Such may consist of character names, acronyms, accepted scientific terms, or speculative frivolities conjured in the mind of the author.

Some fanciful spelling from time to time compounds these transgressions.

The author freely admits, when the right word does not exist, he cobbles one together.

Therefore, should you detect perceived misspellings or malapropism herein, such is probably by intent.

A Glossary of Names and Terms is provided at the end of this book to hopefully help mitigate these shortcomings.

To
Mark Osojnicki
Who insisted on Gauntlet's log
Detailing her prodigious voyage
Thereby greatly enriching this epic.

&

For
Marion Nelson,
Always wondering:
Why doesn't he just tell the damned story instead of writing
All that 'stuff'?'
We miss you Marion.

Oneiro III

Illusion of Chaos

Prologue

God be between you and harm in all the empty places you walk.
Blessing of the 18th Egyptian dynasty

WE BEAR MANY titles in the course of our lives.

Mr. Philip Carr, formerly of New York, bore more than most. Certainly the strangest and most diverse: President, Chancellor, Councilor, CEO, Proprietor, Ambassador, Captain, Consul, Qadyme, Questor, and ultimately, Verteror.

Verteror: The most dangerous job in the universe. Dangerous for the Verteror and dangerous for the universe.

Many titles, many roles, many places, ranging from the killing pressures at the bottom of Earth's numbingly dark oceans, to the freezing hard vacuum of deep space light-years from the scorched cataclysmic charnel that had once been planet Earth.

Phil's incredible odyssey began with a seemingly innocuous mandate handed down by his law firm in Manhattan:

Travel to an island in the Aegean.
Give the island's Directors whatever they want.

The fees involved beggared all other concerns, so Phil caught a plane. On arrival he quickly determined their want.

They wanted him.

After an intense familiarization, he accepted, assuming command as Chancellor of the University, CEO of the island's governing corporation and ultimately as President of a new and soon-to-be autonomous island state.

Philip christened the new nation and the hitherto nameless island, drawing upon the Greek term for *DREAM*: *Oneiro*

Oneiro: A rugged Greek island rising dramatically from the sea, hidden amidst the thousands comprising the Aegean Archipelago—resplendent isolation at the confluence of the Mediterranean, Ionian and Aegean Seas.

Oneiro was founded specifically to home a lavishly funded university and its laboratories. A university unique in human history, staffed with exhaustively vetted experts, drawn from all academic disciplines, united in the single-minded pursuit to actualize human ANUMEN.

The Founders, faculty and students of Oneiro are united in the commitment to human ANUMEN, convinced it equates to no less than survival of the human species itself. Incipient humans purged of their inherent predilection for self-destruction, capable of adaptation and survival on a celestial scale.

Their ultimate goal:

A human genus no less immortal than the heavens themselves

Remarkably, they began to succeed. At its apex, Oneiro's population amounted to some 24,000 souls—the best educated, happiest, physically and mentally well adapted, and gifted population in all of contemporary man's 250,000 years.

Not delusion.

Not gasconade.

Empirical, observable, provable fact.

In terms of evolution—predicated upon brood inception series, genetic drift and gene adaption, as well as intelligence, fitness and psychological testing—Oneirons were conservatively gauged to be from one hundred and sixty thousand, to nine hundred and fifty thousand years advanced beyond Earth's anthropic population. Such was not overtly self-evident. Instead it was exhibited in a hundred diverse ways.

Phenomenal leaps revealed themselves in exceptional manifestations of ANUMINA; and Oneirons were only beginning to plumb their limits. A complex hybrid of all extant human specie evolved as their congenital ANUMINA expanded at a near exponential rate.

Perhaps the most stunning, and disturbing phenomenon was the spontaneous eruption of a totally alien language, far beyond the grasp, or even the vocalization of non-Oneirons. This strange language ultimately insinuated nearly every aspect of Oneiron life: art, music, design and far more—in forms capable of imparting madness and even death to non-speakers. In fact Philip Carr nearly died the first time he witnessed one such painting; and stringent steps were taken to insulate non-speakers from dangerous contacts. Oneiron science finally hypothesized that non-speaker attempts to follow the convoluted patterns inculcated in these works generated an intense feedback loop in the frontal cortex of the viewer. Should a viewer's mind prove insufficiently robust to end the loop, an agonizing, mindless, drooling death would soon result.

Oneirion developments in human learning, syncretism, food production, energy and genetics inevitably acted to the perplexity of world powers—their hegemony suddenly threatened from a mysterious unknown source. Accordingly, Oneiro maintained strict anonymity throughout their development and philanthropic dissemination of aid and technologies hitherto unknown on Earth.

With their power and wealth slipping away, leviathans of industry, government, and most especially religion, erupted in smoldering ire. To their great frustration there was no distinguishable cause, or identifiable entity to condemn or attack. No defense or offense against a phantom benefactor.

All dressed up and no one to kill.

No sanctioned target.

No target at all.

Inevitably they did identify their nemesis and they struck out with an unspeakable reprisal. This was but the savage dawn of Earthly horrors.

In those dark days, Phil was forced to engage in acts of hideous barbarism—his only recourse, given the survival of Oneiro and perhaps mankind itself. Blood poured like water through Phil's crimson fingers and he prevailed for a time, despite the monstrous cost.

Lofty motivations notwithstanding, his acts cost him dearly, driving him to a disconsolate inner retreat, where he would forever seek a solitary refuge from memories so distressing as to threaten his sanity. The noblest purpose, regardless of import, despite repugnance, is never immune to self-loathing borne of its execution.

Meanwhile Earth emerged a seemingly happier, safer, more prosperous, albeit bewildering world. Even sea creatures exhibited bizarre behavior. Despite widespread improved quality of life, many cultures found this new world immensely unsettling. Unable to adjust to a world of intriguingly curious anomaly, life became a fragile time of precarious transition. A new world. Not a brave new world—a tediously old and timorous world—unworthy to confront the daunting new elements within, or the wondrous future materializing before them.

***

Oneiro was founded by a brilliant scientist: Dr. Craig Webber. He sought an anonymous retreat for his studies in human development, devoting the majority of his energies, personal fortune, and ultimately his life to the project. His vision was very straightforward: create a University where his cadre could freely advance human development based on the processes he innovated, without intervention by sectarian governments. Webber had developed an inculcāt that allowed him to compress generational years into months, ultimately days and even hours under certain conditions.

Of equal import, he was able to incorporate, with absolute equity and mathematical precision, proportional representation of all extant races of modern man. A stunning achievement in congenital eugenics. The absolute abjuration of the genetic bigotry that had poisoned mankind in the 19th and 20th centuries. A profound departure from man's monstrous past perversions of the science of eugenics and the quasi non-sense-science practiced by murderous bigots and charlatans throughout contemporary history. An unequivocal validation of his genius and vision.

It was his hope such advanced and enriched Homo sapiens would demonstrate superior abilities, the ability to quite literally survive the ages: ANUMINA.

Indications thus far: his vision was flawlessly brilliant.

***

Unknown to anyone save Webber himself was his ultimate dream. Removed from the ANUMINA project, a project Dr. Webber labored upon in solitude. A super secret project imbedded within the already secret ANUMINA project:

> *To foster a mitotic cell capable of immediate and independent evolution, extending to whatever advanced degree it and only it desired. Single celled self-determinism.*

Such a vision appeared utterly fanciful until he happened upon a journal which described a discovery that certain cancer cells could literally modify their form and signature, adapting to a new environment within its host, thereby avoiding the attack of specialized topical antibodies. The trigger, method and mechanism were unknown. A single, deterministic 'intelligent' cell.

What could provoke such a wonder?

Webber believed the critical element lay at the moment such a cell migrated the blood barrier to a specialized organic ambience. At these sites an adaptive immune response was activated by the incursion of a foreign body. The answer seemed straightforward:

> *Parody the ambient chemicals used to mask such cells from the immune system.*

This indeed proved to be the key, the starting point and ultimately the solution. He developed a 'wash' of the desired enzyme catalyst, simulating the chemicals unique and resident in that area. In effect, he was 're-masking' localized chemistry to fool the healthy mitotic cells into an adaptation of the cell it would be compelled to affect.

Although the solution was straightforward, it needed many long years to perfect a wash capable of imparting:

1) *Genetic intelligence supported at various levels in specialized base pairs*
2) *The ability to radically modify its form*
3) *The ability to repeat and modify this process ad infinitum, and*
4) *Manipulate peripheral quanta in a sort of micro-twisted-pair.*

As it turned out, when he had achieved 1), the cell itself demonstrated self-realization of 2), 3). Certainly 1) was the most difficult, in fact impossible, until he looked to quanta. If he could chemically organize quanta in such a manner it could store information at a deep sub-atomic level. It would process such information. It would draw conclusions from it and act upon it at any level of granularity. If he could accomplish these things, he might just succeed.

He succeeded. At least partly. He had yet to coax 4) from his new super cellules. The solution was elusive and probably far beyond the grasp of even Dr. Webber. Some other stronger, far more advanced agent was needed; and Webber could not begin to fathom the nature of such a catalyst. Among other difficulties, Webber refused to subscribe the concept of a twisted-pair. He suspected that inadequate instrumentation led to the logical trap of false cause. Instead he believed that immensely tiny sub-atomic objects indeed exist both as particles and waves (eg: photons), thus lending some credulity to his hopes for 4).

Even Dr. Webber was unable to project the implications of such an organelle. It would represent a totally incipient life form, unpredictable and uncontrollable, with unimaginable potential.

He designated this once and future life form: *Eos*

***

With each achievement, each breakthrough in language, philosophy, religion, art, science, music, nutrition, communications, the Oneirons found themselves immersed evermore within their deepest sub-particulate Numina. A profundity undreamt of by contemporary physics, or even metaphysics.

University cadre suspected the prime catalyst provoking these wondrous attainments was the new language borne in the span of a single day, perhaps a single instant. Confined only to native Oneirons, commencing with a given generation, they called the new language Oneirion—a language soon to be re-named *Kosmas*—under extraordinary circumstance.

A simple carrier wave. An amazingly focused, narrow band EM pulse 2,620,000 kilometers distant, directed precisely at Oneiro's communications center. A race called the QAVL. The QAVL had maintained a synchronous solar elliptic relative to planet Earth for more than 2,000,000 years, observing and studying Earth both on-site and remotely. Time and location having quite literally no import for the QAVL, they were content to hold their position for an indefinite period, chronicling Earth's myriad life forms as they duly passed their allotted measure from incipience unto extinction—among their innumerable other occupations. The QAVL have maintained such studious vigil at millions of planets for millions of years. They await one prime event: the achievement by any indigenous life form of the cosmic language, *Kosmas,* on behalf of their protégée planet, *Kosmas Kentrikos*

Inhabited by: *Kosmasians*

Kosmasians: Hundreds of thousands of advanced beings from throughout the galaxy united in a common abstruse quest.

Their mission: *Kosmas Nisus*

Kosmas Nisus. Their ultimate goal: comprehension of existence itself

Oneiro, and ostensibly Earth, became the newest constituent of an emergent consciousness, as transcendent as the universe itself.

There was much to learn and much to do and much danger—from Earth itself. A vast journey. An infinite voyage without respite.

The ascension of humankind into galactic congress.

***

vii

Well removed from either Oneiron or human genotype is Philip Carr.

Equally well adapted to aquatic and terrestrial environments, capable of achieving ocean depths well beyond the reach of but a few marine creatures, invulnerable to killing pressures and numbing temperatures. Neither Philip, nor his doctors, nor the scientists of the University of Onerio have explained this phenomenon to anyone's satisfaction. Although a reasonably credible working premise had been advanced.

Phil commands a memory capable of summoning previously unknown information, deeply cached at sub-cellular and infinitely granular subatomic levels. Despite the extraordinary abilities of the Oneirons, their prowess is dwarfed by those of Carr. And his talents continue to reveal themselves. The critical skill he lacked was mastery of the universal *lingua galatica*: *KOSMAS*, spoken in innumerable ways by sufficiently advanced species throughout the galaxy. Using Oneiron technology, the assistance of the QAVL and his own strange abilities, Phil acquired *Kosmas* at great risk and great suffering, nearly at the expense of his life—the only non-genetically-inherited being to ever accomplish such a feat in all of human history, perhaps all galactic history as well.

Oneirons ultimately suspected their imponderable micro-corporeality held the great common *anima mundi*, the great *anima universitas* of the cosmos themselves. The ancient link between the animate and the inanimate. Philip Carr the first and most accomplished of their kind. An insight as old as the universe itself.

CREATION'S AWARENESS.

They were right.

The tiny island of Oneiro was now the center of the Earth and soon to be central to the entire galaxy.

Granular Flow: The Cosmic Cue-Ball

THE QAVL WERE extraordinary beings: incorporeal in form, tripartite in their mature bonded form, immortal and indestructible. Infinitely scarce respective to protonic life. They were also profoundly wise and gentle, as well as ostensibly much given over to humankind. Their true allegiance lies with *Kosmas Kintrekos* however, the galactic center for study and amalgamation of knowledge. The most advanced such foundation in the galaxy.

Eons ago *Kosmas* embraced an unambiguous axiom:

The universe is infinite in infinite ways. Its depth and reach are infinite.
Matter is composed of particles that unendingly wane to the infinitely small—
dwarfed unto forever by the perception of quanta, elegantly expressible
mathematically—progressing forever to the infinitely large, dwarfing the
known universe itself.
Such particles were created and set in motion by the immense inauguration of
existence.
Every particle and anti-particle is undeviatingly impelled in its ballistic
trajectory, set at the explosive creation of space and time itself,
*Entropy & Uncertainty Principles notwithstanding $\neq$ [/\X * /\P ≥ h /*
*(4 * pi)] **
*Exacerbated by Schrodinger $\Psi(x, t) = Aei(kx{-}\omega t)$ ***

* Heisenberg's original equation expounding his uncertainty principle

** Schrodinger's equation describing the transience of waves and ultimately matter

***

Hence:

All actions, objects and thoughts are manifest of the precisely predictable interaction of these particles. And as the movement and interaction of particles were—and must have been—predetermined at the birth of the universe, then it must follow that all events in the universe are predetermined.

All movement, the accretion of nebulae and stars and planets, the rise and fall of immense civilizations, the end of the universe itself. An individual's tiniest thoughts, actions, emotions. The blink of an eye, the twitch of a finger, the taste of an orange, the pirouette of galaxies. All these things—everything cumulating upwards and cascading downwards—unalterably predetermined by the immutable velocity, direction, azimuth and interchange of particles ascending and descending to the infinite—in unwavering compliance with immutable astral-mechanics.

The normal interaction of particulate mass—magnetic, gravimetric, chemical, fission, fusion, inertial and so on—is entirely consistent with this model. Were there to be deviations from this model (chaos) then what could be the source?

Certainly nothing in our universe.

Is causality embodied in something external to our universe? Nothing in our known universe is superior, or exempt from the model's implications. Therefore, it is reasonable to conclude the model is a universal absolute. The same axiom applies to physical laws. In fact, they are one and the same.

To date no external or supra-universal force has been detected, or even remotely conjectured. Hence no object, real or imaginary, would account for an intervention capable of propagating an anomalous (i.e. random) deviation from a particle's 14 billion year old trajectory. All things considered, a Draconian cosmic reality the QAVL describe in human terms as the *Skuldian-Ballistic* (Skuld, after the three Norse goddesses of destiny). Accordingly:

> *Chaos is illusion.*
> *Randomness is fiction.*
> *Free Will is delusion.*
> *Such can not, does not, nor will ever exist.*

Initially humans railed against these realities, arguing that phenomena such as weather were truly chaotic; a specious argument which is easily rebuffed simply by demonstrating if all variables were known (down to individual atoms), weather behaves with a precision equaling the contact and subsequent angle of deflection from the impact of two billiard balls, factoring in the effects of the sun, the moon, the solar system and even the cosmos. The human inability to create a coherent paradigm in no way equates to chaos. This same absolute applies to astral bodies, the seas and the planets themselves … in fact, the totality of the universe.

Such revelation was crushing for those humans *au courant*. The bitterest pill. Beyond belief or comprehension. Beyond faith. Beyond philosophy. Beyond human reason.

This monstrous truth brought forth in such humans a profound despondency and a dark premonition of submissive, meaningless death and non-existence. An oppressive shroud of futility. Submission to the universe itself. Submission to physical laws and destinies conceived eons before man's rise. Submission to the cruel reality of man's very existence. A reality over which man has no ascendancy.

Submit.

Relinquish control, honor, courage, faith, hope, goodness, and any responsibility for man's own actions.

Conceivably this might reflect the manifestation of a creator, or whatever entity set this colossal precision in motion. Kosmians equivocally refer to this icy transcendent force as *GENITOR*.

A dispassionate creator indeed.

Don't drop in ardor.

Just drop.

***

As with all inhabitants of this universe, any given process may be reliably observed only from without. Denizens of creation that we are, regardless how advanced any may be, all look from the inside out. All creatures in this universe exist as goldfish in a glass bowl, struggling to understand the incomprehensible, invisible boundary that confines it and isolates it from comprehension of the transcendent wonders lurking just outside its aqueous thralldom.

The Kosmians, despite a vast body of unparalleled knowledge, are eons from achieving such understanding, if ever. In this respect they share a common deficiency with humans.

However, emanating from studies spanning millions of years, the Kosmasians have deduced a meager few thousand individuals—so rare as to statistically approach a zero sum. These unique life-forms appear to possess the ability (albeit empirically unproven as yet) to effect deviation in the preset movement of a given particle. Were this true, the implications would be shattering.

Chaos and free will would be wrested from the rigor of space/time, and sentience itself would cast off its hitherto perceptive predestined bonds. Beings throughout the galaxy would ascend another step toward understanding. Another step towards a universal sanctity, approaching the dominion of the gods themselves.

Eventually a few such specimen were encountered.

Accordingly, such beings were prized beyond reckoning. Sadly they are thus far tragically short lived. With every attempted particle deviation, a digressive impulse is propagated known as Resumptive Reticulation (explosive restoration). Essentially the particle in question resumes its speed and trajectory, with unimaginable resumptive power. These unfortunate individuals are referred to as Verterors. Kosmas dispatched a race uniquely qualified to comb the galaxy seeking potential Verteror, which they have done eons before man strode the Earth.

The QAVL

AMONGST UNCOUNTABLE OTHER worlds, the QAVL studied Earth. After two million years they happened upon Mr. Philip Carr. Perhaps *happened upon* is a misnomer. The QAVL had expended great time, energy and method in the assiduous search for Philip. The *Kosmians* had deduced the arrival of Phil as an immensely promising Verteror long before he was born. Accordingly they closely observed and even discretely manipulated his genesis in the laboratories of Dr. Webber, along with every aspect of his life since long before he relinquished his swaddling.

The QAVL delegated an Ambassador to Earth. QASI. Charming, gentle, wise and constant. QASI and Phil became fast friends. QASI had ensured from orbit that Oneirons were equipped with The QAVL DOCUMENT. Twelve million pages containing some of the most advanced information in the galaxy. Among their vast repertoire of information, the QAVL provided the plans for a fabulous sphere capable of carrying some two hundred Oneirons seven light years to *Kosmas* at a maximum speed of .77 light-speed in great comfort and safety, housed within a lavish Earthly domain, a round trip journey of well over one hundred Earth-relative years.

The ostensible objective of the voyage: carry the first contingent of humans to join with the legendary world of *Kosmas*.

Work on the vessel began almost immediately and was completed (with extensive help from the QAVL) in a remarkably short time.

Phil accepted the title: *Captain*

The vessel they christened: *Gauntlet*

Gauntlet: The most fantastic vessel in all of human history

Preparations progressed at a frenetic pace and launch was soon imminent.

In the midst of this tumult, an old love of Phil's, Aiyana ATSILA (Aiy for short) inveigled herself into Oneiro, for reasons unclear and potentially sinister. In truth her father was colluding with and ultimately fell hostage to those powers wishing to destroy Oneiro. She herself would soon become prey to these same elements, suffering unimaginable torture and mutilation—leaving her at the very point of death or endless catatonia.

Based on reports submitted by their operatives on Oneiro, these powers astutely concluded that a skillfully engineered release of the hitherto unknown QAVL DOCUMENT, with all its implications, would incite worldwide insurrection. Their plan worked beyond their wildest expectations.

Man's world caught fire and man was immolated.

A savage war arose. This was truly the war to end all wars. Ending mankind as well.

Phil ordered the immediate launch of *Gauntlet*, never to see the Earth he knew again. In fact no human would ever stand upon that same Earth again.

Thus began the most epochal voyage in human history, aboard the Interstellar Star-sphere *Gauntlet*.

Lift Off

THE PLANNED LAUNCH of Gauntlet was rushed forward at breathtaking speed. At nearly the exact moment the war reached Onerio, they launched a submersible colossus—the most advanced underwater vessel in history—equipped with nearly any manner of propulsion—intended for advanced scientific study. She was also deadly capable in combat.

The submarine was named JAEKEL. Her mission commander was Captain Philip Carr, acting in the stead of her permanent Captain, Hicky. Phil would lead her through the hazardous and violent crossing from Oneiro to Anastasios Island, as vicious attacks roared in from every direction and JAEKEL proved herself a extremely formidable war-boat.

Anastasios Island was the home, construction site and launch-point of Gauntlet.

"The boat's yours now Captain. Treat her right. We may need her back someday."

"Aye Captain. She'll be waiting for you."

After a smart salute Phil found himself descending JAEKEL's portside gangplank. His shadow long and sharply etched as the submarine's blazing onboard lights backlit his passage down the offload ramp into the darkness. Before stepping onto the beach he turned and saluted again, this time her stern. A time-honored gesture of respect not lost on those few submariners crowded onto the conning tower. As he began the long walk to Gauntlet's entry-point, the corner of his eye informed him the crewmen had smartly returned his salute, heightening an already poignant departure.

His walk across the beach was surreal. It had the forlorn feeling of crossing a tarmac, or a platform, or a pier to board a plane, or train, or ship late on a dark lonely night. Now he was crossing a rocky beach on a moonless night to board a craft no man had voyaged before. Factoring in relative time and time to be spent on Kosmas, they were leaving for more than a century, yet they carried little if any baggage. Phil carried nothing.

Having traversed the beach, Phil made his way through the enormous on-load tunnel entering the colossal sphere's monumental access hatch.

He examined an imposing brass plaque he'd ordered installed above the giant hatch:

> *From this day to the ending of the world,*
> *But we in it shall be remembered,*
> *We few,*
> *We happy few,*
> *We band of brothers,*
> *For he today that sheds this Earth [sic] with me this day …*
> *Shall be my brother.*

> William Shakespeare
> Henry the Fifth

His reverie was interrupted by a youngish voice. "Captain Carr?"

"Yes … ah, Ensign?"

The man was in Class-A uniform. His rank designated by one pip on his tunic. He smiled "Ensign Nelson sir."

The Lieutenant stood in rigid expectancy. Phil continued. "Permission to go aboard sir."

"Permission granted sir." The man smiled broadly and saluted.

Phil returned the salute. *I hope we won't have to endure much of this. It could be an unbearably long voyage.*

Naval protocol that had seemed so natural aboard JAEKEL minutes ago—a deadly underwater war-boat—was now nearly anachronism. There was more of country club than combat vessel in this mammoth sphere.

"Am I to accompany you?"

"Yes sir, if you would. What with all the recent installations and changes, we were concerned you might have problems finding the bridge; and you haven't been issued your new DIT/Com bracelet, which I have right here sir."

Phil slipped his unit onto his wrist.

Contrary to any sort of intuitive logic, QAVL gravity engineering facilitated their way up the path, defying gravity with each movement. Fighting vertigo with every step. Behind him, Phil heard the huge entry hatch being dogged and sealed. Moments later profound vibrations rumbled through the ship underfoot as explosions destroyed the huge access tunnels. Strangely, he hardly heard a sound other than an extremely low frequency rumble that seemed to be the basso lowing of a gigantic bull. They were now irrevocably committed to their voyage. The only exit now lay light-years in the future.

***

The sphere was vast. Thus, in conjunction with minimal anti-grav emissions, they were allowed to move as a fly up the wall, without disorientation and progressively lessening vertigo. Soon walking about the sphere would seem as normal as a morning stroll on Earth.

Arriving the Gauntlet's capital city, they QAVL-Gated to its largest building, home to the ship's most critical command functions. The official designation of the building was Gauntlet Central Command—lovingly referred to as GEECEC. Each floor was dedicated to a specific command function, Tactical, Engineering, Navigation, Communications and Strategic Command.

The top floor housed the huge open-air, therefore weather exempt, Command Bridge. The floor just below the Command Bridge housed the Captain's quarters, skillfully engineered to ensure the Captain's total privacy. Nothing interior or exterior to his residence was visible from either above or below.

Phil's quarters on Onerio were specifically designed to officially portend the residence of a head-of-state, receiving and entertaining other heads-of-state. The Captain's Residence on Gauntlet had an even more important mission to serve. Accordingly, private VIP entrance(s) were accommodated at the prestigious leeward side of the building. Size and ambience being demanding requirements, special efforts were made to facilitate such needs within feasible human and rational non-human proportion.

Lightening the feel of the massively imposing building, the ground floor was given over to shops, bars, restaurants and such, out of the view of future visiting VIPs. None knew how such mercantile might be viewed by alien eyes.

Adjacent to GEECEC, sharing the enormous Onerio Plaza, were buildings housing the Gauntlet Medical Center and an array of Science Centers specializing in nearly every branch of human research.

All seemed pretty much unchanged to Phil. He could have found his way alone easily, but all the same a little help this one time was not altogether unwelcome. They entered the immense lobby, taking a gravity chute to the Command level. Phil was initially surprised not to find the standard lift he'd used on his first visit.

Among many improvements made by the QAVL prior to launch, they replaced the many elevators throughout Gauntlet with what they termed *gravity chutes*. The chutes had several advantages over elevators. They were lighter and quieter, literally maintenance free, velocity adjustable by user. They could transport a nearly unlimited number of passengers. They consumed nearly no energy and were immune to ship's turbulence.

Phil assumed his station at the center-stand on the immense Command Bridge as sixty sets of eyes followed him from some thirty duty-stations, surrounding his command console in an enormous, perfectly circular amphitheater.

He was well aware he had the expertise and technology to Captain *Gauntlet* through any situation. He had consumed his GAUNTLET Bar (an advanced version of the JAEKEL Bar, imparting total expertise in the operation of each vehicle respectively.) He was also confident his unique mental abilities could be relied upon to react with their normal alacrity. All the same, for some reason he felt the need to drill himself over and over on procedures. It occurred to him he was actually nervous for the first time in many years. Accordingly he intensively reviewed pre-launch protocol. A launch every three decades or so seemed to merit its fair share of due diligence.

Pre-launch preparations: Manual and automated pre-launch check out. Gravity propulsion systems up to full standby. All open waters sealed or gravity secured. Internal grav increased to 110%. All crew seated and secured. All non-essential systems off. All galleys powered down by Central Engineering. All unstowed objects confirmed secure. Bussard Systems on emergency standby. Spheriscope 100%. Running lights inactive. Internal lighting down by eighty percent. Escape systems fully prepped and powered on hot standby. All bridge positions manned reporting respective instrumentation nominal. Master at Arms and staff standing by, fully armored, side arms loaded. Defensive systems on full standby. Full radar scans active.

To ensure launch security, the QAVL will be orbiting Gauntlet at distances of from one kilometer to five hundred kilometers. DAR (Detect-Analyze-Respond) will be active as well.

Then we break out: Full power. Heading Right Ascension, Declination 185.63325 29.89598611 (This will break out of Mount Anastasios and commence our journey out of the solar system.). Fully extend DAR Systems. Gravity drives to one hundred and fifteen percent. When we have passed the Kuiper Belt, bring gravity drive systems to one hundred and bring Bussard Drive to one hundred. At that threshold we will switch to QAVL celestial course and velocity navigation.

***

"This is the Captain. We are in final countdown. Sixty seconds to breakout and lift-off."

QASI's DIT lit up. "Our QAVL sentries advise there are unfriendlies in range. Given sufficient acuity on their part and our immense radar signature, it is reasonable to assume they will engage when we emerge from Mount Anastasios."

"Acknowledged. Thank you Ambassador."

How did the bastards know we were here? We must have, or had, an informer in our ranks.

"Twenty seconds to lift off …"

"Final countdown …"

Phil began issuing the orders initiating the launch sequence.

"Confirm course. Right ascension, declination 185.63325 29.89598611.

"Activate DAR Systems.

"Gravity drives to one hundred and fifteen percent."

Phil forced himself to filter out the background noise of Nick's repetition of orders and subsequent echoes from respective duty positions.

When all orders were acknowledged and ready to execute …

"*ACTIVATE.*" Phil's order dramatically resounded throughout the vast spherical ship. He and all aboard and those on Oneiro felt the galvanizing drama of the moment.

***

Nothing.

No sound. No movement. Nothing. A thundering anticlimax. Why was the greatest moment in Earth's history suddenly a momentous non-event? A cosmic pie-in-the-face.

Phil discreetly brought his DIT to his mouth. Very quietly "QASI?"

"Patience Philip." QASI's voice a calm digital whisper audible only to Phil. "Cold-start gravity drives require a few moments to develop sufficient fusative-contra-mass, in particular when we must break through the flank of a large volcano from the inside. There will be some perturbations that could be disturbing. Were you not advised of this? Did you absent yourself from various prelaunch briefings for some reason?"

As Phil was formulating a suitably acerbic response, a deep resonant vibration permeated the ship commencing at an inaudibly low frequency. Phil could feel it in his bones and teeth, and it was painful. He heard nothing and he felt as if he had a severe sinus headache. Breathing began to feel close and slightly labored. He could see signs of alarm around the bridge. Blood seeped unnoticed from a few noses and even the occasional eye or ear.

Then it began as a titanic, booming foghorn, thrilling, deafening and awesome.

Next a barely perceptible lurch. Millions of tons brought to bear against the majestic basalt face of the huge volcano. An orange/white glow began smoldering in *Gauntlet's* 'sky'. Suddenly the Spheriscope exploded into stars and moonlight and fury. Huge storms of vapor and dust. Superheated glowing boulders exploded outward with thunderous power.

A raging white-hot holocaust as magma was impelled towards the summit, graduating to lava as it burst out of the enormous aperture blasted by Gauntlet. Towering incandescence flared from the summit of Mount Anastasios howling in an enormous pyroclastic flow racing down to the sea. Vast clouds of steam rose from the sea as Mount Anastasios waned, and undersea Anastasios advanced. High above the clouds of steam billowing thunderheads of super-heated ash spawned blinding lightning reverberating thunderously out to sea and across the island. The entire sphere rang a deafening *basso profondo*. Phil was momentarily paralyzed by sight, vibration and sound. Every muscle in his body rigid, as though electrified, as was the entire crew. Phil breathed deeply and forced himself to regain control.

Everything proceeding normally now. Somehow Phil hadn't focused on the cold start interval, but he was …

QASI's voice erupted from Phil's DIT. Phil had never heard him so loud; and he thought he detected *excitement* in his voice. "Philip! Metallic object. Ejected two hundred meters above *Gauntlet* as we broke free. Extreme danger. Evasion! Evasion!"

Phil jumped to his feet. "Helm! Emergency dive! *Dive!*"

The helmsman's head jerked spasmodically towards Phil. A look of confused disbelief as he paused for the merest instant.

"*Emergency dive helm.* Submerge. Maximum speed. *Immediately!*"

Reacting instantly now, the helmsman frantically applied full power, pushing the helm harness straight forward to its limit.

Phil stepped towards the helm. "Helm, descend to four thousand. Mind any undersea magma outcroppings. Sonar, 180° bottom scan. We may have a …"

Too late.

Gauntlet's sky burst into blinding incandescence. The enormous Spheriscope reacted instantly, filtering and suppressing the blinding white light. Otherwise Phil and half the crew would have been blinded. As it was, they were only momentarily dazzled.

Then it hit. *Gauntlet* resounded with an explosive boom. A titanic gong, deafening, pervasive and inescapable.

Then the enormous sphere smashed into the sea with explosive force.

Phil was suddenly airborne. Then slammed into the flooring, grav systems momentarily overtaxed. Then he blacked out.

He was out for less than two seconds. When he opened his eyes he saw they were submerged in a sea brighter than daylight. Looking up at the watery, blinding sky he first thought the sea was on fire. A thousand shades of red, yellow, ochre, and purest white—dancing madly in all directions. Slowly he began to make sense of the dazzling chaos.

Caught between the nuclear blast and the conflicting impact of *Gauntlet*, the sea had been driven insane. Waves larger than office buildings crashed and flagellated in every direction backlit by the residual incendiary bloom of the bomb. Phil was pressed into his armchair as the ship was drawn upwards by an immense water jet propagated by the impact recoil.

Anastasios must be a smoking ruin now. They'll have seen the flash from a hundred miles. Are those fish on the surface? Thrashing madly in the mêlée? No. My God! The ocean is boiling!

He roused himself. "XO. Report."

"We are attempting to assess damage now. Were it not for that fiery sea we would be in absolute darkness. That was a nuke that detonated above us, a small one. I suspect it was one of the new dirty little micronukes, so popular with terrorists these days. I estimate its yield at no more than five kilotons. All electronics are out. A massive EMP hit us just as we submerged. Thankfully the QAVL drives and navigation systems are unaffected. I suggest we go to station keeping and begin repairs. Ambient controls are out. We have air, water and food for years. But it's going to get very cold and very dark, very soon."

"Casualties?"

"Just bruises and a few broken bones sir."

"No radiation burns?"

"Thankfully, no, sir. Gauntlet's a rugged little planet."

Gauntlet's aurulent sky slowly faded. After a time they were in total darkness. Suddenly, over two hundred shoulder-strap-porta-lamps activated throughout the huge vessel, lending the darkness a festive air, as seemingly disembodied lights moved about the ship like so many fireflies on a warm summer's night.

The situation turned out to be far less grim than Phil had feared.

With the aid of QASI and his QAVL it required less than two hours to regain nominal status.

***

Gauntlet broke the surface in seemingly slow motion, with a roar, casting white water and huge waves in all directions. Its original speed and preset course was unaffected in the least by the surrounding tumult.

Phil directed his personal viewer aft to examine Mount Anastasios. It was gone. Everything was gone. Only huge roiling waves remained. Phil zoomed back bringing the far horizon into view. From his perspective he saw the sleek oblate silhouette of a deadly tsunami spreading in all directions at great speed. It had already hit Onerio and was swift approaching landfall at points throughout the sea. Phil estimated its speed as close to 1,600 KPH. He pondered the fate of the many craft close to shore and in Onerio's enormous mooring cave. He thought about his Uncle Herb.

How many must die because of these bastards? Yet he knew this was but the beginning. The body count would soon end into billions.

When Gauntlet had attained sufficient altitude "Helm, Con. Confirm heading."

"185.63325 29.89598611, as ordered sir."

"Very good. Steady as she goes, course and velocity."

"Aye sir."

"Skipper, XO here. Bogies incoming. There's a combat wing of forty-three in attack formation at four o'clock low. They look to be old-style F-14's carrying AIM-54 Phoenix missiles, but we can't make out any markings."

"Take them out XO."

"They can really do us no damage sir."

"I realize that. I want these creatures to understand the futility of any attack."

"Acknowledged Captain."

Both men sounded almost bored, as the fighters futilely fired, to be effortlessly vaporized in response.

This is not aerial combat. It's a goddamned turkey shoot. What sort of Neanderthal pig orders men to certain death, knowing there is absolutely nothing to be gained?

Within minutes the sky was clear and Gauntlet smoothly continued on her uninterrupted heading.

***

Having achieved Earth/Moon trajectory, following its tumultuous launch, passengers and crew busied themselves familiarizing with their new world, confirming its status and effecting any remaining repairs.

Captain Carr devoted hours at the Captain's Command Console exercising the various controls and status displays, testing analytical tools and tactical systems. Aside from command, his duties included maintenance of the Ship's Log and optionally, the Captain's Log. Phil was never one for reports, diaries and logs and detailed daily accounts. He was militantly the opposite in fact. So he was greatly pleased when he learned that *Gauntlet* scrupulously maintained the Ship's Log as a byproduct of its monitoring and operational systems. This applied to the Captain's Log as well, augmented with observations from *Gauntlet's* sentient systems. All that was left for Phil to do was approve the logs, and add any comments he cared to make.

Phil suddenly realized he had stayed well beyond his shift, as others patiently waited to assume their posts. Clearing his throat he arose somewhat stiffly, arching his back, discretely stretching.

"Mr. Piper you have the Con."

"Acknowledging Con Skipper."

<u>*Recommendation of the Seekers*</u>
The Bayronatae Cycle: Seasons of the Beast
Journal Reference: 3jdj567
Presiding: Quaestor SOTC

Salute Quaestors.

All here in this consortium have longstanding and rigorous understanding of the subject presently under deliberation. However, this being the first occasion, in the Quaestor's long history, of abandoning a course of study without positive conclusion, we propose to test your forbearance by briefly reviewing materials so well known to us all. We do this to ensure we all share a precise and common understanding of Seeker findings and conclusions.

The overwhelming majority of life forms generated within solar array are neutron based Bayronatae. Most of us, and the QAVL Seekers themselves as Mesonatae, represent notable exceptions.

Per Contra, planetary independent environments, as well as a very few, very unique planets, yield vastly different forms. Diaphanous, non-Bayronatae, statistically approaching non-existence. Many are long lived to the point of literal immortality. As you are well aware, the majority of forms in this concordance are such.

In making these observations, we offer *in provectus* profound atonement to those highly treasured and most rare Bayronatae present in this Concordia. *Present company excepted.* Including myself.

A bizarre rumble emanated throughout the vast hall. Polite chuckles or some semblance thereof, in thousands of forms.

Bayronatae life, save in its basest forms, is congenitally incapable of sustaining itself through direct matriculation of energy in its various forms, or unlocking energy bound in inanimate matter, in whatever state. Instead it relies on intermediary lower forms to incorporate matter with energy, binding the two in a form esculent to the Bayronatae. As we are all aware, the lowest forms of Bayronatae life normally represent their nascent emergence as well, dominating the biomass for the duration of such life on those planets.

Simply stated: Bayronatae must consume Bayronatae, save at the most granular level and often with a savagery that defies ration.

Integral to such a system is the endless realignment of intra-temporal equilibrium (a common Bayronatae term equates to 'Supply & Demand' factoring in long term equilibrium). Inevitably and quite logically this inevitably foments *COMPETITION*. In turn, such competition fosters *ADAPTATION*, a cycle both fascinating and brutal. As ambient forces drive Bayronatae into ever more advanced *EVOLUTION*, a strange and tragic contradiction invariably emerges:

As such creatures develop greater and greater abilities to survive, they also develop corresponding competencies leading to their own EXTINCTION. In the end, they simply cannot master the truculence seething within them borne of eons of fierce, relentless phylogeny.

Compounding this, Bayronatae life is under relentless pressure to reproduce. Excessive procreation invariably emerges as a Bayronatae survival strategy. Breed sufficiently and nothing can consume an entire species. Failure to do so inevitably results in EXTINCTION.

Compounding this, when such life achieves sufficient survival proficiency to render this stratagem superfluous, Bayronatae cannot, or will not shed their compulsion to reproduce. Thus when predation no longer acts to control their numbers, their population expands exponentially. In turn, their prey is often hunted, or exploited unto EXTINCTION beyond any remedy of husbanding, not to mention the increased burden on conventional resources and increasing adulteration of their biosphere. Thus a hitherto promising species is EXTINCTED as a direct, or indirect consequence of its own success.

Employing a human expression we learned from the QAVL Seekers:

They foul their own nest.

Compounding this, any creature that achieves such apex predation status endures extreme danger and death frequently unto extinction, FROM THEIR OWN KIND.

With particular emphasis upon Terrestrial Homo sapiens, these creatures engage in the capricious random murder of the males, females and juveniles of their own race for no particular reason. Not for food. Not for protection.On occasion such acts appear to be pure indulgences simply for perverse pleasures. Other times the motivation may be greed, or fear, or lust for political or religious power, jealousy, sexual gratification, or simply mindless hate.

The preposterous list goes on and on—as does the carnage. Is it any wonder we long to leave these bestial creatures to their own purgatory?

In effect they suffer the legacy of the primordial savagery that predicated their very existence. A dismal cycle indeed.

Our primary Seekers, the QAVL, have encountered these dolorous species with great frequency, all sharing the same lamentable fate.

Consequently they now recommend we terminate Bayronatae studies altogether.

We find this conclusion extraordinary. We also find it justified. Their report elaborates this recommendation:

Bayronatae life comes and goes in a twinkle. Its nature demands one or more life be forfeit in favor of another, repeatedly and endlessly. The mechanism driving this process is simple brute force, whether flora or fauna. Such savage competition is their basis for adaption and development. However, after having achieved sufficient advancement, Bayronatae seldom demonstrate the capacity, or even the predilection to overcome this tragic and deadly facet of their nature.

We estimate 1:108 Bayronatae survive. A ratio that intriguingly is reflected in Kosmas Concordia's composition. The ensuing *epulae mortis* [death feast] permeates every element of their lives:

Their art, philosophy and religion, mating habits, laws, government and certainly their cuisine. Perspectives totally distorted by and predicated upon relentless death clash and predation.

Such life forms lack the robustness to withstand the elemental forces of the cosmos, or even the natural fierceness of their own planet's geo-dynamics, and most especially, the geno-suicidal torrents raging within themselves. They often evolve to sentience with a speed unique to such intense competition, only to find themselves in a desperate race to evolve beyond their own brutishness. By comparison and without exception, every species represented in this Concordia is the production of untold millions of years of methodical, exacting evolution.

We know that cosmic forces throughout the universe destroy the most robust of planetary environments. These creatures do not lack the intelligence to survive or escape such cosmic catastrophes. Instead, they lack the leadership, the will, and a common bond. Tribal mentality, so necessary to evolutionary survival, instills adamantly aggressive instincts, totally adverse to global realization.

Thus nearly all fail. They fall prey to their own rapacious tendencies. Tendencies, when compounded by tribal mentality and technology, foment a deadly competency inflamed by dogmatic tribal, theological, or ideological frenzy. Beyond doubt, the overwhelming majority of such creatures are inevitably resigned to extinction.

Such life forms rise and fall at dizzying speed. Rotating, fleshy crops responding to the cosmic seasons of creation, form and function constantly reassembling. Trial after trial through the eons. Few able to achieve constancy. A dismal cycle of ruination.

Such fatal flaws might be considered aberration and anomaly were not nearly 100% of such life forms throughout the cosmos fellow sufferers. As with two giant Klasarian scorpions scouring each other unto death under the blistering binary stars of KlasariaWB, there is little to be done and less of interest.

Simply stated, none of this brutishness is their culpability, nor can it be remedied.

We recommend all observations and studies be abandoned as redundant and fruitless. We do recommend it be augmented by occasional samplings throughout the galaxy. The QAVL, as you know, possess the resource to observe these specie remotely, far removed from their native environments.

A sample size of .0001% is recommended. Considering the population size of such specie, this should yield an acceptable confidence interval.

***

The <u>Recommendation of the Seekers</u> is herewith submitted and recommended for passage, with the following exclusion:

    Star System..: Sol (K12999SY)
    Planet………..: Terra QaSol3
    Domain: Eukaryota
    Kingdom: Animalia
    Phylum: Chordata
    Subphylum: Vertebrata
    Class: Mammalia
    Subclass: Theria
    Order: Primates
    Suborder: Anthropoidea
    Family: Hominidae
    Genus: Homo
    Species: H. sapiens
    Subspecies: H. s. sapiens

Subject......: Philipp Carr
Designation..: Oneiron

"Questions?"

"What of our quest to locate Verteror?"

"As you know, Verteror are extraordinarily rare to the point their very existence remains dubious. Bayronatae Verteror would be infinitely more so. Almost beyond imagining. In point of fact, none have ever been found. The QAVL have honed their skills in detecting Verteror, even at extreme distances and they believe they can continue their search without dwelling near to or upon Bayronatae planets."

"Further questions?"

"You do realize this human. This Philip Carr. It may become problematic as to its mortal propensities and its hopeful competence as a Verteror."

"Elaborate Questor."

"We are all aware of the outstanding leadership and combat skills a Bayronatae being can bring to a conflict."

"Conflict Questor?"

"Yes. In some respects we may stand in the purview of a potential struggle with the recently discovered Kpzmik-Dast. We have yet to confirm our inability to resist them, nor have we proof that their nature is as benign as hoped. It is highly possible such a being would be of great use. Paradoxically, they exist always in the shadow of death, yet they can be quite audacious. Such lies at the heart of their leadership."

"Acknowledged Questor. This be journal stuff."

"Further questions?"

None.

"Objections?"

None.

"Proposed?"

Agreed.

"The motion is passed and adopted herewith. The Seeker, QASI, QaQAYdun46—Ambassador to Earth—Planetary Designation QaSol3A— is herewith appointed as the sole remaining Seeker to the Bayronatae. Most specifically to Philipp Carr, an extraordinary anomaly. Ambassador QASI is directed to apply all pressure, by any means, as the Ambassador sees fit, upon Captain Carr in order to achieve Verteror. Hopefully these measures will provide a Bayronatae leader, who may also prove to be Verteror given sufficient episodic pressures.

"Anticipating inevitable objections to a direction that could prove malefic. We appreciate the degree of ruthlessness this may engender. Consider though, we stand in the purview of potential galactic Armageddon.

"The Homo sapient Carr will pursue his designated studies, presently en-route to Kosmas per our original plan, of which you have been exhaustively pre-briefed.

"Assuming Carr can achieve Verteror he would represent the single extant entity with such capacity presently known to us in this Galaxy. We suspect Captain Carr may actually possess the inherent capability to transcend his heritage from Bayronatae to Mesonatae. This may render this single life form the most unique in our galaxy, possibly the entire universe.

"Thusly his value is beyond reckoning, if we can push him far enough, fast enough, no matter the cost, or the suffering."

Sweet Home à-la-Bomba

PHIL AIMLESSLY RAMBLED Gauntlet's Captain's Quarters, which were every bit as grand as his Consul's Residence on Oneiro. They were identical in fact. So much so, Phil found himself at loose ends, rattling about the vast endless rooms.

They should have changed the joint just a little. Then I wouldn't have this eerie déjà vu of being back on Earth.

Surprising himself, he realized he actually missed the old crew. Quite a departure for the Philip Carr who was never lonely—never missed *anyone*.

Rachael Stone was long dead. Mike Auslander had remained on Oneiro to preside over the besieged island nation. Anne lived in the sea now with Aiy, fighting for her life. Edward remained on Earth. God knows what Uncle Herb was up to. Phil was experiencing one of his extraordinarily rare lonely moments. It didn't trouble him though. It would soon pass. It always did. Then he would …

"May I get you something sir?"

Edward!

Phil whirled about, the beginning of a radiant smile lighting his face, which as quickly faded—replaced by a quizzical, rather comical expression. A strange man stood before him, dressed roughly as a butler. Yet he certainly didn't have the polish of Edward—stout and barrel-chested, a prize-fighter's gnarled nose and ears, ruddy faced, thinning reddish hair, big raw bones and rugged muscular hands.

"Sorry if I startled you sir. My name is Jacob Whitecap. Please call me Jake. I have been assigned as your butler."

"Hello Jake." Both men extended hands and clasped in staunch greeting.

"I was unaware I had been assigned a butler."

"A last minute request from Mr. Edward McKnight sir. He felt you might be at loose ends in these extensive quarters."

"Good idea." Phil frowned. "But Whitecap, if you don't mind me saying so, you are much too mature to be a native Oneirion, and frankly you just don't strike me as a butler."

Whitecap grinned good-naturedly. "I don't mind a bit sir, and you're quite correct on both points. I am a *lander*, as Oneirons like to put it. Actually I am a retired Senior CPO from the American Navy; and most recently I was the Oneiro Manager of Internal Security, reporting to Margaret Harris. When Edward suggested this position, I jumped at it. Internal Security on Oneiro will be a non-job for the foreseeable future, not that it ever amounted to much, and this was an irresistible opportunity to fare the stars. To be honest, I know Edward rather well, and his stories about working for you ... well they intrigued me." Jacob took on a thoughtful look. "Perhaps you might favor the title 'Bat-man' sir?"

Phil smiled with a slight frown and tilt of the head. "I'm not sure a *Caped Crusader* is exactly what I had in mind."

"Caped Crusader?" Then Jacob chuckled good-naturedly. "Oh. I understand. You're quite right sir, and very amusing I must say." Although quite aware Phil was fully aware, he felt compelled to explain. "The correct pronunciation is closer to *batmin*. In the British military a bat-man is a soldier who is an officer's personal assistant. The term comes from Medieval Latin *bastum* 'packsaddle & man.' I would prefer bat-man over butler. It meshes much better with years as a seaman."

"Then bat-man it shall be."

His aspect explained: rugged years at sea, knocking about the world, port-to-port, war-to-war, woman-to-woman, bar-to-bar and fight-to-fight.

Phil liked him already. He imagined his many stories of ships and battles, dangerous ports, raging seas, rough bars and rougher women.

"I uh, suspect your duties probably extend beyond those of simple butlership, or ah bat-man-ship?"

"Quite right sir. I am also your bodyguard and erstwhile advisor. Praetorian and Paladin to the Consul as it were."

"The title is Captain now Jake. And what makes you think I need a bodyguard or a councilor for that matter?"

"Excuse me, Captain. Everyone needs a bodyguard, whatever physical prowess they may possess. Extra eyes and arms all round. Danger passes everywhere."

"Strange days aboard the inter-stellar-sphere Gauntlet?" Phil's brow raised in frowning inquiry.

"Indeed sir."

"And councilor?"

"Everyone, no matter intellect, needs another mind at their back."

Peering at Jake for a time without comment, Phil finally rendered a brief nod.

"Well Whitecap. How are you with a Martini shaker?"

"Legendary." Smiled Jake.

"Great. How 'bout a pitcher for us out by the pool?"

Phil noted Jake's eyebrows gradually elevating. Clearly he was taken aback at the thought of sharing drinks with Gauntlet's Captain and his superior.

Phil moued understanding.

"Look Whitecap. We're facing a very long time together. Let's not burden ourselves with some kind of manservant bullshit. Neither of us knows how to handle such a relationship anyhow. And I suggest you get rid of that ridiculous livery. What I do need is someone who acts, as you put it, as Praetorian and Paladin. You're a retired SCPO, so you must know the ropes. I need opinions. A head's up if you see an error in judgment, or see something I overlooked. I need that one hellofa lot more than my underwear laid out in the morning. Okay?"

After brief consideration, Jake smiled. "I'll bring *our* drinks to the pool sir." He lent conspiratorially towards Phil. "To be honest sir, it hadn't occurred to me to lay out your underwear."

Phil laughed and strolled out to the terrace.

Ship's lighting had readjusted to daytime normal once again and it felt good. Onerio's mission psychologists had concluded that decades of life under artificial lighting would severely impact morale and even crew health; so they decided to direct specific frequency photonic waves along the periphery of Gauntlet's inner shell. These propagated a phenomenon referred to as *airglow*. With help from the QAVL they were able to perfect Earth-type lighting at any time of day, solar aspect, season, or atmospheric condition. In this case a warm, late summer afternoon. Airglow light derived elements of ultraviolet allowing one to maintain the sort of good health dependent on sunlight, and even safely achieve a tan.

Spread below was the town of *Gaunti Kato* (Greek: 'Gauntlet Down' as in throwing down the gauntlet.). QASI had enthusiastically approved of the name. The crew already referred to it simply as Gaunti.

Gaunti Kato was far and away the most beautiful city Phil had ever seen. Breathtaking. Classical squares, wide, flowered and tree-lined boulevards, fabulous architecture, rectangles, pyramids, domes, arches, all fashioned in shades of stone, quarried or spun, running from purest white to light rust, to pinks, to deep browns, beiges and grays.

A striking feature from his lofty vantage point was the total absence of motor vehicles. Phil had hardly appreciated the incredible impact of those insatiable machines on the countenance of cities. He considered Paris, London, New York, New Delhi, Mexico City, Bangkok and more. Nearly half the land mass was supplanted, diminishing the uniqueness and beauty of the cities, and utterly destroying their openness. Claustrophobic congestion. Not to mention the noise, danger, dirt and pollution.

Gaunti Kato suffered from no such leprous conveyances. QAVLGates and PMs were efficient and unobtrusive, lending the town a classically distinguished, senescent countenance—pristine and unspoiled. From this elevation Phil might have been looking back seven thousand years to the legendary Phoenician empire of Byblos.

Phil squinted beyond the city to the world of *Gauntlet*. Parks. Lakes. Sporting Grounds. Forests. Beyond these: mountains and lakes and tiny hamlets. The lee side of the mountains cascaded down to fields and marshes and streams that found their way to the sea. White beaches, rocky shores, dizzying cliff lines, small islands and sand bars and reefs festooning bays and peninsula, leading to craggy fractal margins demarcating land from sea.

In cubic and square kilometers it was vast. In aspect: endless

The single drawback Phil could detect was his neck. It ached from looking up and even backwards. He could happily devote decades to this compendious miniature world.

He toyed with the idea of designing a specialized chaise lounge that was raised and flat and tilted, allowing the reclining human to look down, out, up and backwards with a tilt of the chair. *One could even …*

"Your drink sir."

"Thank you Whitecap. Have a seat. I was just taking in the view. Incredible!"

"Indeed sir. Looking at the sky is disorienting though. I can look at the sun. And I can look *past* the sun."

"As you know there really is no sun. It's an airglow illusion. You'll get used to it. By the way, call me Phil, or Philip."

"As you wish sir. Please refer to me simply as Jake." He solemnly raised his drink, as did Phil.

Phil toasted "To exist is to change."

Jake countered. "To change is to grow."

They tipped glasses and drank deeply.

"Oh Jake! We're going to get on famously. This is a *perfect* Martini."

"Thank you sir." He raised his glass to the 'sunlight' savoring the icy zest. "It *is* good isn't it?"

Phil squinted at his drink, pursing his lips, savoring his palate. "Let's see … two-thirds Gin, one-third Vodka, a splash of Vermouth and?"

"… the tiniest trickle of Triple Sec, a 3 jiggers of Scotch and a few drops of fresh grapefruit juice, shaken with ice and cracked lemon. I make it a quart at a time. In future I will arrange for a pitcher in the freezer at all times."

"Anyone can pour gin over ice, throw in a twist with a splash of Vermouth, and call it a Martini. This is is art."

***

It hit an hour later as Phil was dozing in the warm sunshine.

The sun was beginning to set and colors were emerging in deep reds and golds when a deafening boom thundered on the outskirts of Gaunti Kato, followed by a deep rumble, echoing throughout the ship. Suddenly it was midday again and sirens were wailing throughout the town. Phil was on his feet tapping his interface before he was truly awake.

"Command Bridge."

"Bridge, Captain."

"Report."

"An explosion at the water recycling facility at coordinates 32:15:12:22. No reports of casualties. The building was undamaged, but we believe the interior works were totally destroyed. Emergency teams are en-route. No danger of fire, or structural damage to *Gauntlet* as far as we know at this time."

Phil appreciated the manner of the man's report. Crisp. Factual. No histrionics. No lavish description.

"Whom am I speaking to?"

"Sub Commander Talbot sir."

"Put me through to the Sergeant at Arms, Talbot."

"Aye sir."

"Chief Burns here Captain."

"Chief, what the hell's going on?"

"A bit early to tell sir. I'm en-route to the site now. May I call you back when I've reviewed the situation?"

"Make it fast. We may have to consider aborting."

"Acknowledged sir."

Phil sat weighing the situation and its implications, looking off to the slowly rising smoke-plume and the dozens gathering to see and understand.

Jake looked on in concern.

"Philip, the latest release of the com unit allows you to simply state the person's name and will put the call through. As Captain it breaks through any current traffic on the line."

"Thank you Jake."

Nothing to do now but wait.

Five minutes later his unit beeped. "Carr."

"Sir this is Chief Burns. This was a bomb detonated with a digital timer and a simple mechanical detonator imbedded in a cyclotrimethylene trinitramine compound. Very basic. Very reliable."

Insurgents aboard? A fucking bomb! A goddamned bomb just hours from launch? Who in hell's responsible for this?

"I believe this may have been planted for some time sir. It is probable the perpetrators are no longer on board. I recommend a building-by-building, room-by-room search for any other devices."

"That's one hellofa job Chief. Stand by and I'll get back to you."

Phil said "Commander Farrow."

"Farrow here sir."

"I want an immediate priority one alert. The deputy Sergeant at Arms is to issue weapons to those crewmembers you designate. Post them at every intersection. Get on the horn and instruct all crew to get to their quarters and remain there until the all clear is sounded. Put out the word that anyone found outside five minutes from now may be shot on sight, but I want no casualties. Got it?"

"Got it."

Seconds later Nick's voice echoed through the hills amidst flashing strobes and wailing sirens. Minutes later Gaunti Kato was a ghost town. Shortly afterwards Phil watched armed troops fanning out in all directions.

"QASI?"

"Yes Philip?"

"Suggestions?"

"Give me three minutes."

"Fine."

I suppose if transited solid matter at the speed of light I could do it in three minutes as well.

Precisely three minutes later QASI responded.

"Your crew has between twenty-eight and ninety-six minutes based on the settings of each mechanism. Similar devices are planted in Power Station Number 5, the QAVLGate Piazza-Roma storage room, Spice Storage Bin 15A1d and in the apartment below you—the guest bathroom, in the towel closet. I suggest you target the minimum setting for all munitions."

"Thanks QASI."

"Commander Farrow."

"Farrow here."

"Listen closely Nick. Your people have exactly twenty minutes. Dispatch disposal teams to Power Station Number 5, QAVLGate Piazza-Roma storage room, Spice Storage Bin 15A1d and the apartment below me, the guest bathroom in the towel closet. Evacuate all personnel in the vicinities immediately, and keep me posted."

"Aye sir. Farrow out."

Phil could hear announcements booming all over the city. He watched security teams moving in formation at top speed mounted on what were clearly PMs especially adapted for emergency work.

Who thought of this stuff? Emergency PMs? Despite the educational wonders of the Gauntlet Candy-Bar, Phil began to appreciate just how much there remained to learn. Clearly a great deal of work and thought had gone into this vessel.

Twenty minutes later Nick contacted Phil.

"All clear. We got 'em all without incident and they're being analyzed now. Three things are clear now however."

"Yes?"

"Every bomb was of identical manufacture, which should indicate a single bomber, or single team in any event. The explosive material could easily have been produced on Oneiro. It's essentially old style C4.

"The detonators are another thing altogether. They were definitely not manufactured on Oneiro."

"Where?"

"As the fuses were not detonated, *MADE IN TAIWAN* was clearly stamped on each. Even serial and batch numbers and manufacturer's logo. Very sloppy."

"Sloppy indeed. Unbelievably so in fact, unless they had a little misdirection in mind."

"That would seem an obvious and clumsy attempt at deception. Perhaps they were simply so certain their bombs would detonate they didn't bother to neuter them."

"… Which raises another issue. Why they didn't set all the devices to detonate at the same time?"

"I wondered about that. It would seem there were several saboteurs involved and they didn't coordinate well."

"Possibly. Or perhaps they wanted to panic crew and compliment with multiple explosions."

"If that was their tactic, they certainly don't know us very well."

"Agreed."

"The second explosion would have taken you out by the way."

"Odd I wasn't slated for the initial kill."

"It is strange isn't it? Are you aware Howard Doyle is now on Oneiro sir?"

"I assumed as much. I authorized his transport just as we cast the off aboard JEAKEL. I see where you're going with this. You want Doyle to track this stuff down."

"Yes sir, the sooner the better. Since we have so much information, he might be able to locate the exact source. Maybe even the buyer."

"I'll get back to you Nick."

"Put me through to Mike Auslander on Oneiro."

Mike appeared on Phil's personal screen, flushed and clearly exuberant.

"Phil! Congratulations! We wanted to get through but we thought you guys would be busy as hell." Mike's voice exuded enthusiasm. A torrent of words poured from the unit. Phil elected to let him get it out before he dampened Mike's spirits. "I've been standing by to hear from you. I'd have contacted you myself, but I figured you were up to it in problems."

Phil graced Mike with a shallow smile. "Less than you might think actually."

Mike continued "We're popping Champagne down here and celebrating despite the attacks." Phil could hear revelries in the background. "We couldn't be more thrilled. I hope to God there's going to be a human history to record this. Our remotes captured the entire launch in great detail. We're sending you a copy. I never imagined anything like it.

"I saw *Gauntlet's* colossal sphere break out of its new caldera and then splash down seconds before the nuke detonated. It would never have occurred to me to *dive* at that point. I'm sure that was your doing. You saved the mission. Hell, you may have saved humanity."

The line was quiet for a moment, save the sound of Mike gulping his drink and taking a breath.

"Then the sea literally began to boil. And in the midst of all that hell-fire, *Gauntlet* erupted from the sea at unbelievable speed. We watched the attacks on *Gauntlet* on the way out. It looked like a flock of mosquitoes attacking an elephant. They also appeared terribly uncoordinated—flying every which way. We assumed their systems were scrambled by the EM Pulse from the nuke."

His voice softened to a whisper. "What a show! Then you were just … gone." Mike cleared his throat. Phil could sense the suppressed emotion.

"How did Oneiro fare the tsunami?"

"Our elevation easily saved us; and Oneiro has no shallows run-up. But the harbor is a wreck. We'll be months putting it back together. There were no casualties, so in that respect we were damned lucky. Your uncle is fine by the way. How about Gauntlet? The QAVL here report everything went perfectly. How are you?"

There was a silence on the line for a moment.

Mike suddenly sobered. "What's up Phil?"

"We have a problem."

Phil could see Mike moving into another room. Sudden quiet.

"What's happened?"

"We've had one bomb detonation and located four others. Unexploded."

"Damn! Anyone hurt?"

"No. And the damage is minimal."

"Did you get them all?"

"Yes. I'm certain. QASI made the search personally."

"Do you have any idea who is responsible?"

"Not as yet. Based on the locations of the devices I would surmise the bomber, or bombers, wanted to provoke an abort, more so than inflicting damage and casualties."

"Why? Where were they planted?"

"A power station, a water processing facility, ship's stores, a QAVLGate and just below my quarters. Had they been successful, the damage would have been only negligible. But it might have convinced our people to abort. I would be dead, power, stores, water and transport would have appeared endangered. This may have been enough to sufficiently discourage ship's company."

"*Can* you abort?"

"Good question. Certainly the mission plan foresaw that eventuality, but the actual mechanism was always a little sketchy. Essentially it consisted of downing the sphere in the sea at sufficient depth to avoid break up and shallow enough to allow travel to a mainland under normal thrusters, assuming we could adequately control our velocity and vector."

"Are you facing any problems with water and power and such?"

"Not a bit. As you know, that's all redundant ten times over."

"Why so puny an attack?"

"I believe this was as much as they could safely smuggle aboard. And I assume they believed the nuke on Mount Anastasios would actually do the job."

"How do you suppose they got past our security and the QAVL?"

"I believe they brought them in, in tiny increments, small enough to evade our equipment and even QAVL notice. Even the most pernicious weapons appear innocuous when broken down into its most granular components; then assemble them aboard, even down to mixing the C4 aboard."

"Where do we go from here Phil?"

"Where do we go? We go to *Kosmas*. In fact I'm planning a launch party tomorrow at ship's midday. It's highly probable the bomber, or bombers are not on board. These things were hidden aboard with timing detonators. They left some ridiculously convenient clues about the origin of the devices."

"What do you mean?"

"The goddamned fuses had *MADE IN TAIWAN* on them, along with serial, trademark and batch numbers. So what I need is ..."

"Way ahead of you Skipper. I'll get Howard Doyle on this as soon as your people give me the details. I agree with you though. This looks like they laid a false trail, albeit a clumsy one. Maybe we can turn that around.

Although, I caution you, very little remains of governments, and laws and record keeping. This could be difficult, or even impossible."

"I understand. Do your best. But I don't want you to dispatch anyone to Taiwan. It's just too damned dangerous off-island. How are things on Oneiro?"

"All quiet for the moment. We're on non-stop full alert and loaded for bear. By the way, Ian McGregor and his number two are both dead. Shot while trying to escape in one of our research vessels. Another boat is missing and that may account for the remainder of his thugs. I'm not happy we were unable to interrogate them, but they were well armed and hell-bent to get away. In all probability the tsunami took them out. We estimate it hit them at about two hundred meters from the island, so they never had a chance. Before casting off, they took out three of our people in the harbor complex. By the way, Ms Harris sends her regards and says 'she understands now', whatever that means. Care to elaborate?"

"Some other time Mike. For now, light a fire under Howard and tell him I'm sorry I missed him before launch."

"Can do Phil. We'll keep you advised."

"Thanks Mike. Out."

"XO."

"XO here."

"Nick, we'll see what Howard comes up with. Have your people supply him with all I.D. numbers. QASI assures me no insurgents remain on board. I believe the highest probability is they were ground staff based on Mount Anastasios, part of the Ian McGregor insurgents. In fact they are already dead in all likelihood, killed during the last skirmishes. Nonetheless, let's keep our eyes open. Please put out the all clear and advise passengers and crew to keep alert, but emphasize the danger has passed."

"Captain, these are Oneirons. I doubt they need any comforting."

"Everyone needs comforting XO. Hell I could use some right now. We shouldn't confuse Fear Training with plain old human needs. Anyhow, I do generally agree. But they need status in any event. I'd also like your staff to arrange a launch party tomorrow at 1200 for the whole crew. We'll do two-hour rotations at essential duty stations. Food, drinks, music, dancing, games, sports, entertainment—the whole magilla. A party as only Oneirons can throw. What do you think about Webber Park?"

"Good choice and good timing. I'll get my people on it. They had something like this in mind anyway, so the notice is not *too* short." Phil could hear a gentle chide in Nick's voice. "And I can guarantee great weather. Even though they're Oneirons, I think morale is something that wants attention for a time."

"Agreed. Thanks Nick."

For the next few hours Phil monitored cleanup and repairs from the command center in his quarters. Much improved over the Oneirion version, much easier to 'roam around' and to use. Phil found he could watch and communicate so effectively he seemed veritably omnipresent.

Finally exhausted, he ended his long first day in Command of *Gauntlet* with a peanut-butter-and-jelly sandwich and a tall glass of icy milk.

He slept as never before on Earth. Straight through for ten hours, dreamless and unmoving. With the exception of some recurring dreams, he would sleep as well and as soundly for years to come. He suspected GAEA adjusted personal gravity to slightly lower than Earth normal during sleep intervals, giving him that little additional comfort. Conversely he assumed GAEA increased localized gravity by equal measure for a limited period to assure muscle and bone mass was not degraded.

Of course there were other factors involved. Noise, light, movement, air quality, even odors. He never discussed the matter with other members of the crew, lest they grew sleep-conscious. He did note they appeared more rested, even more energetic (if such a thing were possible) than Oneiro days.

In all his travels he had never taken such an immediate liking to a place in his life. He smiled at himself, realizing he was already thinking of *Gauntlet* as a place, not a vessel.

Perhaps more than a place.

A world.

Or more than a world.

Perhaps a home.

After the Dawn

"NICK, YOU'RE A man of your word. It's a beautiful day."

"Glad you like it Skipper. A few high clouds and a light breeze allow me to turn up the temperature a bit, which makes it seem more special. A shadow once in a while emphasizes the sun and the blue skies."

"What can weather control do now?"

"You name it. Rain, sun, fog, clouds, thunder storms, snow, dew, frost, ice storms, gales, even a small tornado, were there a reason for it."

"Sounds like you're planning on seasons."

"That's a decision for you or your crew. But I do think that four mild seasons is a good idea—a sort of a visceral mechanism for marking time. It's also helpful in rotating some crops, of course. I'm not sure about sea life. We have insufficient room for major marine migrations and such. But more than that, it motivates people to look forward to change and progression. Very good for morale, especially if we randomly throw in some really bad stuff. Blizzards, ice storms, the occasional cyclone and best of all … fog. A real pea-souper for two or three days can be horribly depressing, especially if we throw in a bit of drizzle."

Let Sleeping Dogs Lie
Prime Minister Robert Walpole

PHIL SMILED IN reminiscence. "One of my favorites is a shallow and extremely intense ground fog glowing from a brilliant sun early on frosty fall mornings. This occurs when the sky is totally clear no more than fifty meters above a dense fog. The glow surrounds you and nearly blinds you. It is very beautiful."

"We can certainly arrange that. Where have you encountered such?"

"The meadowlands of north central Europe primarily in the early autumn. It is quite similar to a *fogdog*."

"*Fogdog?*"

"Yes a glow in a fogbank that manifests itself on the horizon, normally early mornings. In some respects it's considered kin to a *sundog*."

"Okay I'll bite. What the hell is a *sundog?*"

"Remember these are Earthly phenomena Nick. Although similar luminous emissions have been observed in many other astral systems."

"May I ask how exactly you know that sir?"

Phil remained silent for several moments, then proceeded as before.

"A *sundog* is a type of aerial phenomenon which forms an ice halo arc of some 22° in an clear early morning sky, generally comprised of reds, greens and blues. It's closely related to a *moondog*."

"A *moondog?* You're serious?"

"Yes."

"Alright, what's a *moondog?*"

"The moon radiates light just as the sun does. Therefore it also casts *dogs*, along with 22° degree ice halos. They're both exceptionally beautiful."

"Have we covered all the *dogs*?"

Phil paused frowning.

"One day I hope to see a *stardog*."

"A *stardog* … and a *stardog* is …?"

Phil's voice took on an unworldly, rapturous quality. He nearly whispered "Damned if I know. They don't exist yet to my knowledge. If I want to see one, I may have to spawn it myself."

Nick scrutinized Phil intently for a time.

When he'd collected his thoughts "Can you define 'spawning a *stardog*' Captain?"

Phil slowly pivoted towards his XO, staring into his eyes with a terrible intensity, as though witnessing something totally new and measureless and terrifying. Nick tried in vain to literally shield himself from the sheer penetration of Phil's gaze.

Finally it dawned on Nick that Phil wasn't looking at him at all. Didn't even see him. Phil was in the grip of something beyond Nick. Looking *through* him. Nick wasn't even there.

Phil was transfixed by a vision of things that were and would be, or might be. Things that shouldn't be, or couldn't be, or wouldn't be in an inviolate universe.

But I would violate that universe. I would dare test its laws and its limits. I would challenge its GENITOR and tear known creation apart. And when I am finished I will rebuild. I will have my stardog and galaxadog and cosmodog and nebudog as well, after my own vision, and with them I will create a new …

Trying to stifle any skepticism from his voice, Nick unknowingly shattered Phil's concentration and his vision.

"Well Captain just let me know when and what you want. I'll commence with my own *dogstudy* immediately, although I'm not sure how many of *dogs* we can bring to bay. What *dog* would you prefer?"

Phil struggled to regain his bearings. "Say again please."

"I asked which *dog* you would like sir."

Roused from his reverie, his dream faded, Phil responded, "Surprise me."

The universe seems neither benign nor hostile, merely indifferent.

Carl Sagan

Nick stood in awkward muteness for a time and then roused himself to speak.

"Well, I'll need a little notice. The secret to making seemingly random weather truly effective is to entirely remove its control from any member of the crew."

Phil smiled grimly to himself. *'Seeming randomness'—an emergent anachronism.*

"I'm hoping to turn the whole thing over to GAEA. We might even have some fun with weather forecasting. She's fully conversant with earthen meteorology, so she can act within a broad latitude of credible randomness."

"GAEA? She was simply charged with housekeeping and crew-scheduling."

"Oh our girl's grown up quite a bit since installation. She can pretty much run the whole ship now, including propulsion, navigation and weap-ons systems."

Phil's attention was suddenly drawn to the sky. "Nick I swear I see *birds* up there."

"You're seeing O^2 samplers. They look like barn swallows, or swifts so we blend their calls into the ship's ambient sound systems. Pretty aren't they?"

"Yes indeed. O^2 samplers you say?"

"Yes. Little robotic power-gliders that constantly monitor air quality and the gaseous mix throughout the entire sphere. Their power source is Oneiro standard wireless. The last thing we need is for the air to go bad; and frankly that's the most difficult ambient balance to maintain on *Gauntlet* right now. You'd think our sheer size would make it a more forgiving system. Not true. It's actually very sensitive and unwieldy. I know we had no choice, but we really did launch far too early. When our flora matures it will not be an issue, but for the next year or so we'll be watching it closely."

"Keep me posted. We should join the party now. Looks to be in full swing."

The chilling *dog* incident forgotten for the moment, the two men moved off in two directions. As Nick fell away though he thought, *this dog business is really strange. Never saw Phil like that. What a look! I think I'll remember those damned 'dogs' for years.*

Phil's thoughts ran in a far different direction.

These people have courage. Not simply just the product of Oneirion Fear Conditioning, but inbred, natural courage as well. They can handle anything. A voyage never dreamt by man to an unheard of destination. Man's world in self-destruct mode. A launch from hell itself. A bomb yesterday. Today, laughter and music, dancing and drinking, swimming in the huge fountain, competitions around the perimeter of the square, and they were eating with their normal voracious appetite.

Phil melded into the crowd around the long buffet adamantly avoiding any deferential accommodation. Phil realized they were unaware of the old-school command practice, which stipulates that Officers eat only after their troops. He wondered if his own officers were familiar with the traditional protocol.

He inspected the dishes with interest, curious if any dietary restrictions were in effect in these early days after their hurried departure.

Poires avec sauté de porc et riz savage, Beef Bourguignon with tiny onions and carrots (all Oneirion), and poultry and fish and all manner of vegetables and dozens of fruits, wines and juices. All Oneirion bounty, all harvested (with the exception of fish) in the absence of death, or suffering by any living thing, flora or fauna.

Fish, spices, mushrooms, radishes, lettuce, carrots, spinach and some condiments were already produced on *Gauntlet*. Phil understood there would actually be a wine crop in the late 'fall.' They certainly were not going to starve. And they would have water and wine, juices and beer, and every sort of drink. And they would breathe. And they would be warm and safe from the deadly cold of deep space; and they would be protected from the killing physical and radiological forces all about them in this pernicious universe.

They had cleared the first hurdle. Despite the blood and the violence, the ignorance and hate and greed, the death and the suffering, they had cleared the first hurdle.

They had survived their fellow man. And they would know the stars. And they would marvel at the wonders of an inconceivable number of worlds.

Year One

PHIL WAS STROLLING a long powder white beach by the Webberian Sea. A warm, brisk breeze frisked through the waves, splaying tips into frothy white crests—what they used to call *whitecaps* on the Chesapeake Bay of his youth.

There was a small sailing regatta taking place somewhere out there, hence the lively winds. Tall marsh grasses danced at the margin of sea and land and were blown nearly flat by the steady winds. They thrived on *Gauntlet*, as did all life forms. Phil looked straight up at Gaunti Kato. Even at this distance it was clearly evident the capital city was totally calm. No wind whatsoever. This intrigued Phil to no end. Gauntlet wasn't *that* vast. So how did Climate Control propagate low and high-pressure systems provoking strong winds in one location and becalming another? He suspected QAVL gravity mechanics were somehow involved and resolved to find time to study their operations.

Today was his Ten-Day: a mandatory day of rest if the normal work/rest cycle was not adhered to. This cannon was rigidly imposed on all crew and compliment, Phil included. And it was a great day to be quietly rambling beside his constant friend, the sea.

As he slogged through the fine white sand, he reviewed the last few months. *Gauntlet* had found its rhythm. The vessel had developed a routine and all the elements of a living, dynamic society. Oneiron school days were over. Training was behind them. Break-in was complete. They were now a well-honed, professional crew, manning a formidable deep space vessel with competence and skill.

Crew members alternated between their ship's duties and those studies and tasks that interested them … agriculture, cuisine, sports, literature and the full spectrum of the arts and sciences. They were already producing fascinating advances. Phil was deeply involved in their work. Monitoring, evaluating, criticizing, modifying and encouraging. He was well on his way towards exhausting the *brain food* library and was preparing to confront the gargantuan QAVL Document.

He had become far more than Captain. His work was not confined to the leadership of *Gauntlet* by any means. Short of their personal lives, Phil was integral to every aspect of Ship's activities. *Gauntlet* had energized to a degree he could have never foreseen back on that dark, lonely beach below the towering caldera of Mount Anastasios. It had become an exciting dynamic society aboard Gauntlet, fully capable of housing a challenging culture for an unlimited period.

Anne and Aiy were still living under the sea—Aiy recuperating from her horrible torture with Anne in attendance. He visited them often. Anne was always excited to see him and prattled on incessantly about Aiy's progress, her personal learning and the beauty of the Webberian Sea. Phil would brief her in detail of the topside news of Earth and *Gauntlet.* Invariably, when they'd talked it all out, Phil would sit with Anne for hours in the still waters watching the sea life. Aiy remained disturbingly unconscious. Dr. Singe had generously taken to making 'house calls' rather often. He would awkwardly burden himself with all manner of gear, plunging into the depths to examine his patient. Confidentially, he advised Phil that he believed the underwater ward was having a better effect on Anne than it was for Aiy. As to Aiy's progress, she was exhibiting phenomenal signs of physical recovery. No septicemia or lingering physical trauma. The saline ambience, moderated with a constant flow of emollients and disinfectants, was proving miraculously efficacious. Phil was relieved her submerged body was almost totally covered with instrumentation, concealing the horrific butchery she had suffered. Slight movements from time to time. No mental acuity whatsoever. Dr. Singe insisted all they could do was wait.

So they waited.

With the assurances of Mike, Onerion Security had eliminated any remaining saboteurs while attempting to flee Oneiro. That chapter was thankfully, closed.

Phil spent hours communicating with Mike and Howard and Edward and many others all over the Earth, politics and surviving technology permitting. The United Nations and many governments had grown ominously silent, and remained so.

Far too soon their communications would grow asynchronously cumbersome, so they were all taking maximum advantage of the glacially slow bisynchronous communications during the time remaining them. Phil assumed he would acclimate to the intervals. He was wrong. With each succeeding day, if only by seconds, the frustrating delay relentlessly grew longer.

The wars wore on, and Oneiro was literally unharmed as wave after wave of attackers plummeted futilely to their deaths. Other than defensive actions, the US, Russia, China and the EU remained reticent to speak or to act. Frigid inaction. The lion's share of aggression advanced from the zealously murderous Middle East. World order and trade remained at a standstill, an issue of far greater interest to the leaders of the few still viable industrialized nations. The world war that couldn't was allowed to run its barbaric course, ploddingly metastasizing worldwide.

Sadly there were many other little wars that *could*. They smoldered in countries all over the Earth. Travel, as trade, was paralyzed. A berserker religious renaissance was emerging—fanatical far beyond anything mankind had ever witnessed, or imagined. Its ethos was rooted in purest hate, a relentless compulsion to kill—anyone—under any guise. It made no difference. Ultimately, some idiot amongst the berserkers who somehow had managed to read a few books cooked up a rationale comprised of one part crackpotery and one part Machiavellian trickery of the most putrid. More importantly it held irresistible appeal to the basest elements of the caliginous souls of the jihadists. As it would have to be, it was deceptively simple and compelling to believe:

Man orbits the Earth from its surface.
The moon orbits the Earth in space.
Earth orbits the Sun.
The Sun orbits the galaxy.
The galaxy orbits a colossal Black Hole.
All Galactic Black Holes orbit a titanic Black Hole in deep space.
This inconceivable Black Hole is
Allah
Satin
Jinn
Whatever it's name, it wants only one thing
DEATH.
Such is the nature of the Universe.
Such is the nature of Existence.
Such is the nature of its creator.

This mantra was to grow like a cancer and gorge itself on death and men and murder, until nothing of value, or grace, or beauty remained on Earth … except Oneiro.

***

The monsters that promulgated these horrors observed from their fortified lair in the Atlas Mountains, high above Morocco. Even they were aghast as bedlam ran wild, exceeding even their depraved machinations. Fear and hate and fortune and savagery passed everywhere as the love of death and murder grew and grew. And yet they blithely remained at the end of hell's production line, reaping power and wealth with a rapacious, bestial sort of gratification. The divinely mad Dominican friar, Savonarola, at the zenith of the Renaissance, would have been in his glory, as were these greedy businessmen, mercenaries, assassins, thugs and spurious Imams.

Where it would end was anyone's guess, for there was no leader to set a course, to find a peace, to begin rebuilding and regain control. Mankind simply could not find the courage to face down the zealots, for despairingly few reasons:

- Leadership—non-existent for decades—remained so. u Idiotic PCers and anti-profilers frustrated every defense initiative.
- Man simply could not muster the intelligence, the courage or wit to thwart the bloodthirsty ignorance that held man's world by the throat.
- Belligerence trumps lethargy.
- Gullibility trumps ration.
- Always.

***

Jake was trailing Phil's meandering passage along the sea clutching a picnic lunch. Ham sandwiches, potato salad and a large container of iced Martinis, as he struggled and slogged and splashed to keep up. Phil was at his happiest by the sea. Suddenly, Phil turned to him … an excited smile on his face.

"Jake! Come on. They're right out there. Right out *there*!" Phil was highly animated, gesticulating towards a small bay thirty meters ahead. Jake looked in the direction indicated by Phil. He saw a tiny inlet, white sand, crystal water, some nondescript coral formations and little else.

"What?"

"You see those nodules a few meters out?"

"You mean the coral?"

"*Coral?* Good grief Jake, that *coral* was sent to *Gauntlet* at great risk, with great care and unbelievable expense. One of our former Board Members was the Interior Minister of Australia until he was drawn and quartered in Perth. Prior to his death, he had secretly arranged to have these reallocated from Shark Bay, delivered to the newly constructed Gauntlet and implanted with exhaustive pains aboard this ship, in this tiny bay. The worthiest farewell gift I could imagine."

"I take it those things are not just plain coral."

"That's exact Jake. They're not coral. They're called Stromatalites. The oldest life forms extant on Earth. Very close to incipient life on Earth itself. They date back unchanged for three point five billion years. I can conceive of nothing as rare, as venerable, as *important*. It gives me great joy to come to this small bay to see them. To be near them and feel their wonder."

Squinting into the sparkling waters, Jake regarded them for a time in silence. Then he set down his bundle, removed his trousers and shoes, and waded into the water. He walked around them methodically in irregular circles several times. He lent down and lightly placed a finger on one for the briefest of moments. Then he returned to shore.

He looked a Phil quizzically. "Stromatalites you say? Three point five *billion* years?"

Phil could read the awe in his eyes. "Stromatalites. Three point five billion years."

Jake inaudibly mumbled to himself. "I'll be buggered." He straightened himself. "Ready for lunch Philip?"

Both men were reclined in the sand and the bright sunshine, leaning against a large rock, shirtsleeves and pant legs rolled up against the heat of the day, enjoying the cool of the water. Each had consumed their lunch and several Martinis. They were now deep into a discussion about the mission.

"Let me understand Philip. If we're now in the midst of the Asteroid Belt far beyond Mars, why haven't I seen one bloody asteroid? I've scanned the sky carefully and I don't see a damned thing. And why aren't we in a great deal of danger? I understand some of these asteroids are real giants. Larger even than *Gauntlet*. Some are nearly as large as moons."

"Well, first of all, it's quite difficult to see a lump of dark gray rock against a black background unless back-lit, or a frontal light-source is nearby. That notwithstanding, think of this: a neutrino can race through a mile of solid lead at relativistic speeds unencumbered, as though through a vacuum. We all routinely accept that fact."

"We do?"

"Yes Jake. We do. Aside from electronic neutrality and dubious mass, neutrinos are so small they easily travel in the space between and within atoms, even in a material as dense as lead. We are proportionally about the same size and on average it's a million miles between the big asteroids, although they come together with relative regularity in cosmic terms. So in general, we are safe and very much alone in our trajectory. Just like the neutrino."

"In an odd way that's rather disappointing. Is the same true of the Ky-kyp-ky-?"

"The Kuiper Belt?"

"Right."

"Generally yes. Although we know far less about the Kuiper. It's nearly fifty AU's out."

"AU's?"

"Astronomical Units. Nearly 150,000,000 kilometers, representing the mean average apogee/perigee distance between the Earth and the Sun. I understand the Kuiper can be quite volatile at nexial times. Remember the Kuiper Belt is comprised largely of cometary material as opposed to asteroids."

"Yes. That's always been hard to overlook."

Phil cast him a wry half-smile. "In any event, with all that cometary material churning through the solar system, we'll keep DAR Systems up and on high alert."

"There's a lot to learn out here."

"You should be metrignosiculating brain food Jake ... boning up on some of this stuff."

"I'm sure you're right. But to tell the truth, the idea of brain food gives me the willies."

"*The willies* ... now there's a term I haven't heard since I was a boy. But why Jake? Why 'the willies'?"

"Oh I suppose it's the idea of knowledge just popping into my head, having no command over it ... a kind of a fear of mind control I guess."

"Interesting. You know we are now reconvening actual classroom teaching? They will start at the high-level QAVL summary documents."

"Whatever for? There are literally millions of pages to learn."

"As they explain it, ingested learning lacks some key elements, the most important of which they term the *awe coefficient*. Learning is somehow diminished without first exposure to the teaching experience, discussion, and most critically: personal *discovery* of the knowledge. Humans need to *work* for learning. Teach, talk, discover, and then ingest. Otherwise the knowledge is simply remembered—not discerned, adduced, or shared. And I would add … *earned* or appreciated. Ingested learning is just too damned easy. Maybe you should sign up for classes?"

"Possibly. I'll consider it. That method does sound much better."

"Well, I'm certainly joining the classes in the next …"

Jake sat up, suddenly alert. "Captain Carr, I wouldn't recommend that. Perhaps you should confine yourself to metrignosiculation?"

"What? Why? Why in hell shouldn't I join the class?"

"You are the *Captain*. Larger than life. Greater than human. Less than humane. And never, ever just human. You are impervious to fear and error. You are omniscient, omnipotent and inhabit a higher plane of existence. Therefore, you cannot attend classes with your crew. Because you already know everything."

"Oh come now Jake. You're not serious?"

"I am deadly serious, sir. You ordered me to point these things out to you Philip. I am doing so now. This is a basic precept of command. You train the troops. You don't train *with* the troops. Period. This is a critical element within the aura of a leader." He added hurriedly. "With all respect sir."

"I … understand. And I agree I suppose. Surprised I didn't think of it myself. Perhaps this place is just too damned idyllic." He frowned at the Champagne cork shaped Stromatalites standing in the crystal waters of the tiny inlet. He considered the changes they'd witnessed in the last three and a half billion years.

What will this place be like in a scant twenty-seven years? What will I be like in twenty-seven years?

"Thank you for pointing this out Jake. Continue to do so. Any Martinis' left?"

***

Jake wandered off to pursue his own interests, leaving Phil alone on the beach. QASI lit up on Phil's DIT. "Would you care for a little 'sage advice and counsel' from a friendly QAVLian?"

"It seems I'll never lack for hortatory on *Gauntlet*."

"Hortatory. An appropriate word, though somewhat out of character for you, if you don't mind our saying."

"Not at all. I agree. In fact I've never heard the damned word before this moment. It just popped into my head. Funny the way the mind works. I probably heard the word years ago and it was just waiting to be used."

"Possibly. Or could it have germinated somewhere else."

Phil frowned slightly.

"Suffice to say, your opinions, or your hortative, or whatever, are always welcome and highly valued QASI."

"You are too kind our Captain."

"Have you been reading Agatha Christie again?"

"Why yes. Hercule Poirot in fact. Why do you ask?"

"It's not important. But it must require less than a second for you to matriculate one of her books."

"True. However, we are quite capable of greatly slowing the process and extending it into a great deal of ah, enjoyment."

"Interesting to learn of things you enjoy. What did you wish to discuss?"

"Jake is a fine councilor. We agree with his command assessment. Such would never be an issue with the QAVL, but human psychology is vastly different. We would therefore suggest you follow his advice, and take it even a step further."

"Okay. And that further step would be …?"

"Actually a lesser step. It would be that you do not attempt, as with your fellow Oneirons, to absorb the QAVL document during this voyage. We recommend you be very selective in what you MGL, or commit to mind, and what you disregard altogether."

"Alright. And how do I determine what to ignore?"

"We will be most pleased to guide you."

"And why exactly am I disregarding selected passages?"

"We do not refer to passages as you call it. We refer to hundreds of thousands of pages. Millions in fact."

"Why? Why should I dispense with so much of the knowledge of the QAVL?"

A lengthy silence ensued.

"QASI?"

"We will be discussing this information in depth during this voyage. We would prefer to impart these ideas to you in a custom sequence. If you would allow, we would prefer to simply state that you will acquire profound, even intimate familiarity with this information; and you will do so of your own devices."

"What does that mean?"

"It means you may already possess much, if not all of this knowledge."

"So why do you wish to spoon-feed me the QAVL Document?"

Phil stared at the little light on his DIT. He pursed his lips, and his jaw muscles rippled with agitation. He had hoped QASI would be forthcoming with further explanation. However, the Ambassador appeared to have spoken his piece and was now taciturnly silent.

Stone-faced, Phil asked "QASI. What's going on?"

For the first time there was a palpable tension between them. QASI continued, conspicuously unperturbed.

"Philip we know you too well and respect you too much to dissimulate."

"On Earth you informed me the QAVL were totally incapable of lies."

QASI pressed on. "We also know you well enough not to be fooled. You have long suspected that more was afoot here than superficial appearances would imply. We have therefore never misled you with frippery."

"*Frippery?*"

QASI ignored his query. "There are critical elements of this mission that perhaps we have deferred discussing. Withholdure of course does not of itself constitute ..."

"QASI, will you cut through it?"

"Philip, we are reluctant to 'cut through it' as you say, at this time. We entreat your trust, your patience, and your forbearance. We are sure you will agree that this request is not excessive in light of the advances we have forged together?"

A compelling, almost human argument. The tension lessened.

Phil chuckled, half to himself. He smiled acerbically. "You're good QASI. You're damned good. Were there such a thing as a female QAVL,

I'm sure you could talk her photons off. And yes, of course, you have my trust and confidence. I wish we could raise a drink to it."

"Perhaps we shall Philip. One day soon. Perhaps we shall."

Year Two

THEY WERE WELL beyond Neptune now. Beyond the Kuiper belt.

Relatively soon to be out of the solar system, out of the Heliosphere, into interstellar space, and into the Oort Cloud. The Oort extended for more than three light years. Much of their journey would transpire within this titanic, icy brume.

They were on their way. And they were accelerating impressively now. Bussard Scoops were at full gain, and they were passing eighteen percent of light speed. No longer children of the star called Sol. No longer dwellers of the rocky inner planet called Earth. The bonds of home grew more tenuous each second. In less than six months time dilation would begin its mystical slippage.

***

They now called it Mount Gaunti-Anastasios. Mount Gaunti for short. The highest point on *Gauntlet*, or the lowest, or nearest to Gauntlet's mid-point, depending on one's perspective. No one knew, or admitted to know, exactly *how* high. That would destroy the mystique, since they all knew it wasn't really very high at all. It looked high however. Its deceptive perspective was perfection itself. Hikers and climbers were invariably surprised to find the mountain was much closer than it appeared. It was snow capped in 'winter'. And it had its own tree line and steep cliffs, even a budding miniature glacier. It could be dangerous to climb, but there was some facile alpine skiing and hiking on what was generally the lee side. There were high climbing cabins, snowy passes and an exquisite little alpine lake covered in ice when the mountain was covered in snow. And, when astrophysical viewing systems were disengaged, there was an Olympian internal view of the *Gauntlet* Interstellar Earth-sphere, incomparable from any other perspective on the ship, including even Phil's commanding terrace.

A pleasing aspect of the semi-mountainous heights was its gravity. It was sufficiently tall that gravity began to approach zero towards the very top, as the summit approached the central rotational axis of the sphere. Approaching the zenith, centrifugal energy was proportionately shed. This rendered climbing easy and relatively safe, if one recognized two critical realities:

1. Gravity increases as you descend (or fall).
2. Despite its depleted gravity, one still has mass, with all that implies. A climber with near zero weight could find himself uncontrollably propelled over a towering ledge, moving too quickly and unprepared, or unable to shed forward inertia.

There was something else about Mount Gaunti. Something important. It had the most incredible view of the Universe ever witnessed by terran man. Sitting atop the diminutive mountain felt very much like sitting on the surface of an asteroid racing through space. There was something enchanting in this. Something of Antoine de Saint-Exupéry's *Petit Prince*.

If the observer so wished, the view could be modified to telescopic, microscopic, infrared, radiological, or what was termed 'particle wash'. This miraculous spheriscope was capable of 'washing' out stars and planets and asteroids and comets … any Bayronatae object … revealing only the ebb and flux of the sub-atomic dark tides that sluiced through the universe. The sight was awesome and magically beautiful. The insight it provided was totally unique. It moved Phil profoundly.

The cosmic granular flux that had alternately enchanted, guided and haunted him throughout his life. In fact he was only at the threshold of an immense journey that would finally open onto understanding of this profound aspect of himself and the cosmos.

Despite his preternatural insights, Phil remained complaisantly unaware his phenomenal insight was *the* facet of his sapience that most intrigued the QAVL. That that they prized. That that drove them to watch over him. Unbeknownst to Phil, this was in reality the reason for human admission to *Kosmas.* Phil had already concluded simply speaking *Kosmas* was far too simplistic. Command of Kosmas only opened the door. Entering could be something else entirely. Something phenomenal.

Other forces were at work here. But he had yet to make the connection between his abilities and the purposes of the QAVL. Something was blocking him. The cosmic future so graciously thrown wide for mankind while the blasé destruction of man's world was simply too damned easy.

He firmly did believe dissimulation was anathema to the QAVL. Such action would demand a rationalization that would tax even their great intellects. Is suppression of the truth to tell a lie? If it effects the perceptions and providence of an entire species, can such be justified for any purpose?

Was such duplicity necessary?

According to the *Quaestors of Kosmas:* Yes

Unknown to Phil, they had acted thusly many times. Uncountable times. More significantly, the *Kosmas* Concordia had no wish to foster a cosmic messiah. Why pull a trigger whose effect was beyond divination? That way could lead to catastrophic decline. Disintegration of cosmic sentience. The very soul of the Universe. *Kosmas Kintrecos* was the embodiment of science. The scientific method. The repository of cosmic knowledge. No room here for mysticism and galloping, ricocheting postulation. None whatsoever.

Far better to proceed logically and methodically and ensure anomaly would and could be understood and incorporated into the body of *Kosmasian* Knowledge. An eminently reasonable stance, especially for an institution with millions of years of history, anticipating a future of equally immutable longevity.

In many respects this deeply troubled the QAVL, and QASI in particular. They debated it intensely and without respite for years after Phil was discovered. In the end, they weren't entirely convinced of the risk. Nor were they bound by the wishes of the Concordia. No intelligent creature of the cosmos was ... or ever would be. One day this truth would out. They would lose a friend on that day. As a consequence they determined to avoid such a confrontation. Thus they set themselves on a potentially perilous course of action.

They would take pains to tutor Phil. Acquaint him with the veritable nature of the Universe. Help him understand the serendipitous entry of humans into *Kosmas*. Aid and encourage him to explore his uniqueness.

One key to Phil's enlightenment was the periscopic Particle Wash, which the QAVL had gone to some pains to install on Mount Gaunti. They therefore would discretely prod him to observe it at great length. To really see it. Analyze it. Attempt to understand it.

In the midst of such ambiguity they hoped to induce a revelation in Phil that would lead to Verteror.

They hit upon a novel means of doing so, and it involved only the tiniest, inoffensive lie: *QASI would regularly meet Phil atop Mount Gaunti for 'cocktails.'*

***

"Do you see that object Philip?"

"At 15-29-178 QASI?"

"That's correct."

Phil huddled over the miraculous new viewer on Mount Gaunti. The viewer was installed as a gift from QASI.

"Yessss … Yes I believe I do. What is it? It's enormous. Light-years in length, I think. Like an unbelievably huge *tornado* of all things. Almost the classic funnel cloud."

"That's correct Philip. This class of object was first observed by humans on Earth from your Spitzer Space Telescope, in 2006. A very tidy bit of Astrophotography by your scientists. They chose to designate the phenomenon a Cosmic Tornado."

"Right. I remember. Quite a stir at the time it was discovered. But that was across the galaxy. This behemoth is right next-door. Why wasn't *this* one discovered?"

"This specific event was obfuscated by the Kuiper Belt and your intervening solar system, not to mention this particular one has an albedo coefficient of roughly six percent—slightly more visible than a lump of coal. These events generate massive electrical charges, so were it closer to Earth, or any such planet, it would produce quite dramatic auroras when they come into contact with your magnetosphere/ionosphere."

"What does this represent? What sort of astrophysical event?"

"Essentially it consists of a simple gyration of cosmic dust and gasses. We assume there could be several causal forces. To my knowledge no being has ever observed the formation of a Cosmic Tornado. Many cosmic forces are capable of generating such an object. The hypersonic rotation of a neutron star, the backwash of a black hole, echoes of a long past super-nova, perhaps a Gamma Ray Burst, or simple nebulae accretion at a certain phase. Essentially a magnetic or Bayronatae shock wave, articulating extant celestial material. Cosmic Tornados are interesting in form, but they do not represent a significant celestial event, although they comprise the stuff of stars eventually. We enjoy them due to the exotic low level radiations they emit, if close enough, or boosted."

The tiny QAVL lie was embedded.

"I've never heard you refer to a celestial object as a source of QAVL *enjoyment*."

"Very much as humans enjoy imbibing Ethel alcohol, we enjoy selective radiological eruptions."

"Would this be the same type of emission you consumed during your introductory address under Mount Anastasios?"

"Not at all Philip. That was simply lunch."

"I see. So uh, you're getting 'high' on that thing are you?"

"Not from this distance. Nor does the term *getting high* apply, these are extremely low level emissions."

"So you need some sort of a magnifier? A radio lens?"

"That is correct Philip; and we do not get high as you state it. We do find the emissions relaxing, soothing, and well … enjoyable."

"You don't lose control? Do foolish things? Say things you regret? Experience diminished physical and mental agility? Distorted visual acuity? Memory loss? Hangovers? Liver damage? Delirium Tremens?"

"In our experience all creatures, no matter what their form, crave some form of escape from the nettlesome harshness of reality. Such is a form of mercy, which can become addictive. However, we experience none of the symptoms you elucidate. We never have. Not remotely. Nor do you Philip."

"From time to time I wish I could. Sometimes I miss those days. A good knee-knocking-commode-hugging hangover would bring back some great memories. Might do me some good too."

"Our enjoyment is benign and harmless and immutably so. As is yours."

***

Later, Phil requested QASI leave him to his own devices, mumbling something about a gorgeous blonde girl in Biochemical Nutrition. And he was alone.

"Put me through to the Astrophysics Lab please."

Brief pause.

"Yes sir?"

"Can you build me a radiographic lens?"

Phil smiled to himself. *A nice reciprocal for QASI's gift of this incredible viewer.*

"A radiographic lens? I'm afraid I don't understand."

"Are you aware there is a Cosmic Tornado at 15-29-178?"

"Yes. We discovered it yesterday. Fascinating isn't it? We delayed reporting it until we were certain of the nature of the object."

"I see. This Tornado emits a low-level radiation field. I need a digital lens to boost its signal. If it's feasible, I'd like it installed atop Mount Gaunti."

"Atop Mount Gaunti?"

"This is a sort of a gift for Ambassador QASI. Can you do it?"

"May I get back to you in about thirty minutes Captain?"

"Certainly."

More than an hour later "Captain Carr, this is Doctor Gunawardene in the Astrophysics Lab."

"Hello Doctor."

"That was an interesting request you made, Captain. We are working on something similar for our people in Quasar Research. The technology is loosely based on Subatomic Washing—Electron-Spectrography. The essential difference being that we cannot connect it to the exterior of the ...”

"Can you build it Doctor?"

Phil could hear the smile in the man's voice. "It is being installed as we speak Captain. The unit is roughly the size of a shoebox with a small projection node mounted to one side. Power is based on *Gauntlet* wireless power transmission; and we're retransmitting to it from our spectral antenna, enabling it completely mobility. We're installing it on a targetable gimbaled pedestal permanently fixed to the Mountain. But that's purely optional; and it's easily removed. We lack only your specification for a receiver."

"Receiver?"

"Yes. The unit we've assembled gathers wave transmissions, enhances or modifies them based on user resonance adjustments, a simple knob, and then focuses the output to whatever target you designate. We have included a set of instructions with the unit. So I simply need your specs for the receiver."

"I see. We don't need a receiver, Doctor."

"Sir?"

"Ambassador QASI is the receiver."

"Oh I see. We weren't aware of that Captain. I'm afraid Ambassador QASI may have difficulties manipulating the apparatus we have assembled."

"I will be the Ambassador's 'bartender' Doctor."

After a hushed interval, the Doctor, thoroughly confused, blurted, "Well, we're all set then."

As the Doctor's voice trailed off, Phil stepped in to avoid further questions.

"I appreciate your help. I'm sure the Ambassador will appreciate as well. Thank you Doctor."

Cocktails for Two

PHIL AND JAKE faced each other in Phil's conference room, quite atypically at odds, regarding a trivial issue at that.

"Nonsense Jake. I'll backpack it up. It's not a problem."

Jake was adamant. "No sir. I must refuse. The Captain of the interstellar Terra-Penate Vessel *Gauntlet* mustn't be seen carrying Martinis' about his own ship. Especially if this is to become a regular gathering."

"*Terra-Penate* Vessel? What the hell is that?"

"Actually Terra-Penate *Class* Vessel. That's what the crew's calling her now. I find it catchy myself. They've been debating our vessel's class for weeks now. I think they had a bit of a competition in fact, and Terra-Penate won out."

"Mm … *Terra-Penate* … Terra, Earth … Penate, the Roman gods who protect home and hearth."

"Right. I believe the classification is intended to describe an Earthlike Home-World, without connoting nationalistic affiliations, including Oneiro. They tell me the term literally translates to something like 'Earth Hearth' or 'Planet Lair', similar to your interpretation. They'll be presenting the classification for your approval. If you approve, they'll christen her and log her The TPV *Gauntlet*."

"The TPV Gauntlet. Not bad." Phil nodded thoughtfully.

"I surmised you'd probably approve, so they're making some appropriate preparations."

"Kind of you to ease my burdens Jake."

"That's what you pay me for Captain."

"Well, you've certainly worked your way into *Gauntlet* society admirably. You know more than I about what goes on around here."

"Another reason you pay me so handsomely sir."

"I didn't realize I did pay you, handsomely or otherwise. Hell, we don't pay salaries, do we?"

"Ah, no sir. I was making a modest stab at humor."

"Agreed, modest indeed. All right. Let's resolve this question about Martinis."

"No problem Captain. They will be ready and waiting for you sharply at 2100 ship's time, at the summit of Mount Gaunti … next to an astronomic device … a radiographic lens … mounted on a gimbaled pedestal you say?"

"That's correct Jake. As usual, your wisdom prevails, or perhaps simply your will. In any event, thank you."

Later Phil was recumbent atop Mount Gaunti, bathed in a luminous astral glow—a Martini in one hand, the other hand cradling his head. He was quite comfortable. Low gravity ensured that. He was also immune to the cold. Above him the heavens were wondrous. The magic of the Spheriscope visually transformed *Gauntlet* into an asteroidal object, lost amongst the stars. Phil rested easy on the surface, sublimely content.

Installed next to him was QASI. After some adjustments to the lens mechanism (QASI was grateful for the gift, though far from surprised.), the triad professed to be equally at ease.

The stars themselves were static. No movement evident whatsoever. However, even at their speed, the slightest touch of the Doppler Shift was barely visible. Reds and blues revealed in the tiniest shift bleed. Next year this time, the cosmos would become a striated kaleidoscope of brilliant white orbs nested within reds and blues, concatenated and distorted. Phil hungered to see this. He fanaticized about sitting in this very spot, sharing Martinis' with Edmond Hubble and Christian Doppler, speechless in the grandeur and brilliance of their visions.

For a time neither Phil nor QASI said anything. Two utterly disparate beings hushed and tranquil.

QASI broke the stillness. "Did you ever read the Petit Prince Philip?"

"Yes. Years ago. I remember I found it quite charming. One of those unique works that delight adult and child alike."

"Agreed. In certain endeavors humans do excel."

"Such as?"

"Oh, selected arts. Music, certain literature, painting, sculpture …"

QASI's voice took on a melodic, almost wistful quality:

> *"What makes the desert beautiful …"*
> *said the little prince*
> *"… is that somewhere it hides a well."*

QASI continued. "Saint-Exupéry was *en forme* that day. We feel much the same about space. We have journeyed the Universe for millions of years and there still remain infinite treasures concealed in the mysterious desert of these cosmos and we have all of eternity to discover them. Perhaps the little Prince was right, the desert does hide a well … of truth." Silence. "Sometimes existence itself overwhelms."

Phil spoke softly. "*You* have all of eternity QASI. Humans must find comfort in but a lamentable march of years."

***

Theirs was a strange ethereal dialogue. Neither regarding the other. One not seeing the other, the other not looking. It was as though they were absently conversing with the heavens themselves.

They grew silent again. QASI seemed to be considering Phil's statement.

"Philip, do you remember our first meeting? We discussed some of your unique abilities."

"Of course QASI."

"Have you devoted any time to pondering the nature of your elder brother Michael?"

"I can't say I've given it much thought really. I was hugely fond of him. He was my big brother and a damned good one. I worshipped him."

QASI interjected "I know."

Phil wished he could see QASI. He continued, "He was very bright. Good looking. Fun. Hell raiser. He loved to drink and chase ladies, and a past master at both. He was quite a happy, lighthearted fellow until his last year. That year he contracted a virulent religious virus and it killed him. Savagely. Why do you ask?"

"As we informed you on Earth, we researched your records. We reviewed his records as well. His was a complete genus composite by human standards. As are you."

"I had assumed as much."

"Given that. You never questioned why you were conceived. Why you were needed?"

"*Needed?* Why I was *needed?* That's an odd sort of question, isn't it?"

"Michael was a viable, flourishing prototype. He proved the concept. That accomplished, Dr. Webber was planning to transfer his researches to Oneiro. Why burden the project with another proto-hybrid before relocating to Oneiro?"

"Good question. I really don't know. I always assumed Dr. Webber was developing an entire generation."

"Then why were no more forthcoming after you?"

"Another good question. His notes contained nothing to explain this?"

"Nothing."

"Did his notes explain why Dr. Webber elected to adopt me to the Carr family as opposed to moving me to the island as apparently planned?"

"No. Not a thing. Remember he also adopted Michael to the Carrs."

"Yes. I suppose we'll never understand. Dr. Webber was an exacting, very logical and methodical scientist. I'm sure he was following a well-conceived plan."

"Another question for your deliberation Philip: Your records reflect that you are allegedly a faithful duplicate of Michael's genotype, yet ..."

"Allegedly?"

"Please hear us out Philip. If you were in fact an exact replicate of Michael, why do you suppose Michael categorically failed to exhibit any of your abilities?"

"Clearly, we were not exact templates of each other. We were not *clones*. We are, or were, deliberately variant iterations I believe."

"Exactly. Dr. Webber imparted variances between you and Michael."

"I see." Phil was suddenly deep in thought. His concentration was nearly debilitating for several minutes. Then he looked up. "And this *impartation*. Was it based upon an *additive*, or a *reduction* process?"

There was a silence for several moments.

"Our compliments Philip. A very astute question. We are impressed. The answer, as we are sure you have conjectured: an *additive* process."

"That of course begs the next logical question. If both Michael and I represent the entire human genome, then what could be added? This implies I am also a prototype. A prototype of a new genus."

"Very good Philip. Very good. Excellent in fact. We suggest you go for a swim. That may clarify things. Suppose we continue this over drinks here tomorrow night?"

Only QASI can make statements like that without sounding patronizing. "Ambassador my friend, you have a date."

***

Phil was busy on the command bridge the next morning, so it was late afternoon before Phil found his way to the Webberian Sea. He stripped down and vanished into the crystal water. As was his custom now, he swam down to Anne's sub-aquatic hospital ward and apartment. He rapped on the hatch and ascended to the pressure chamber.

"Hi."

"Hi Phil."

"How are you?"

"I'm fine." Anne smiled. "Really fine."

"Exercise, ointment, vitamins, UVA Torch, O^2 supplements?"

"Yes. Like clockwork."

"And Aiy?"

Anne sighed. "She's starting to look human. Not quite recognizable, but I began to see something resembling her peeking through all the tubes and mutilation. Dr. Singe's underwater therapy is wonderful. Given a little more time, I believe she will heal completely. No reconstructive surgery, no cosmetic corrections. With all the electronics stimulating her, I doubt she will even need excessive physical therapy. There will be considerable pain however."

"And what of her mind Anne?"

She grew subdued. "Nothing. The monitors show nothing except autonomic functions. No higher brain functions we can detect. Dr. Singe says we need to start considering a more aggressive treatment. But I think she'll do better down here."

"Anne do you know how long you've been down here?"

"You know" She tilted her head. "I *don't.*"

"Anne you've been down here over two years."

Phil anticipated shock. Maybe hysteria. Possibly tears. At least surprise. Instead he saw only a wistful half smile.

"I understand now why you seek out the sea. I dive down two or three times a day now. Partly for the exercise, and partly because this feels like my home. A dive feels like a stroll in the park. And I have friends down here. They miss me when I stay home, and they're glad to see me when I come. I don't even feed them. Sharks, whale, porpoise, grouper, even squid. Coral and aquatic flora are advancing at an incredible rate on the seabed. The variety of marine life that's erupting is extraordinary. Aiy's slowly getting better and I suspect this unique environment can be credited for the Aiy and the marine life. It's also quiet. It's beautiful. I'm at peace. I'm at home Phil."

"Aren't you at all curious about *Gauntlet*, the Earth, the stars, the galaxy, the Kosmians?"

"There's time enough for that Phil, when we can share it all with Aiy."

I can't decide whether she's gone crazy or gone sane. Either way, this was our agreement aboard JEAKEL. I suppose I must honor it.

"Well I'll leave you to it then. Let me know if you need anything. I understand Aiy's drip includes brain food starting today. Maybe that will help. I'll see you in a couple of days."

After embracing Anne lovingly, Phil made his way into the depths.

One can grow used to anything I suppose.

***

Unlike Anne, Phil was beginning to experience difficulties with the Webberian Sea. It was simply too shallow. It wasn't dark enough, or cold enough; and the creatures that dwelt in the deep waters of the Aegean were more congruous to Phil's moods during his fathomless descents on Earth.

Nonetheless, he sought out the sea floor, but sleep eluded him.

After a time he abandoned the pursuit and meditated on events, aimlessly stroking about the depths of his aqueous realm.

QASI: the Ambassador was behaving erratically. Something was militating there and he had no idea what. QASI would choose the time to disclose, if ever, as always.

Anne: rebounding or insane? He'd know soon enough. He cared very much for her and was troubled for her. Yet there seemed little he could do just now.

Aiy: something dark there. Perhaps he would discuss this with QASI. Gauntlet: a miracle in the darkness. It was a machine. A thing. Yet he already loved it. Its beauty, its grandeur, its performance, all far exceeded his grandest expectations. He dreamt of wandering the galaxy for the remainder of his days inhabiting this spectacular spherical world.

Earth: a festering sore. Mankind had become a deadly malignancy. Thankfully that global ailment was declining further on Earth's fragile dermis every day. It was not always so.

He should feel guilt for fleeing at the murderous zenith of the crisis. But what choice? They would have killed him. They would have killed Oneiro. They would have killed Gauntlet. They would have killed man's future, as they were now extincting themselves. Genocidal immolation on a planetary scale. The most corrupt mitosis humankind had suffered in its pathetically short two-hundred-thousand-years. The gods themselves must have ordained there would be no two-hundred-thousand year to follow.

And such hellfire was fourteen billion years predestined.

He stretched and kicked off for the surface.

Fifteen hours later found Phil atop Mount Gaunti taking 'cocktails' with QASI.

"It didn't go well down there today."

"You were there?"

"Yes. You seem unable to adapt to the Webberian Sea. What do you suppose is wrong?"

"Too shallow, with all that implies. I'd like it ten times deeper. Twenty times deeper."

"Philip, we can easily simulate deep ocean conditions using our gravity generators. That would address the issues of pressure and temperate. Darkness is simplicity itself to produce. Of course you can always dive at night, but if we constantly maintain this deep dark zone, we imagine it would attract sea life with propensities such as yours for an ambience of this nature."

"Good. I think I'll talk to Mark Oikodomos about that."

"Please let us know if we may assist. Should we defer pursuing our last discussion until you've had more time to assimilate the subject?"

"I suppose so. You observed Anne?"

"Yes."

"What is your opinion of her mental condition?"

"We are not totally versed in human psychology. I suspect no one is. After countless millennia human psychology remains a conundrum in some respects. Homo sapiens are extant for so short a time. Such also varies considerably with each individual. Human psyche sometime evolves at breathtaking speed. It appears to us though she is ... what is the term ... yes ... bucking up. Perhaps somewhat forced, but she presents a very positive attitude. We are hopeful."

"That's good news. What about Aiy? Can you do anything?"

"Philip, as you know, we are somewhat maladroit at manipulation of organic and metallic Bayronatae. Her healing process simply demands time. We are unable to manipulate time in this context."

"Could you *find* anything?"

"You are asking if could locate a physiological problem overlooked or undetected by your instrumentation?"

"Yes, I suppose so."

"Standby."

Moments later.

"There is a DVT in a rather unusual site."

"A DVT?"

"A Deep Venous Thrombosis. A human term. They are usually found in fleshy muscularities such as legs. This specific DVT is tiny. It is located at the periphery of the brain stem in an adjacent muscle mass, so close it appears to interfere with blood flow, which in turn interferes with higher brain function. We hypothesize this is an effect of extreme physical abuse of the cerebellum. It is applying pressure on nerve tissue and constricting venial blood flow into the cortex. We are convinced it is a result of massive brain trauma inflicted in Ghazi Kahn. Unfortunately its existence was masked by damage to surrounding tissues."

"What can we do?"

"We have transmitted a detailed report to Dr. Singe. It is our opinion the DVT can be successfully extirpated by laser surgery. This should be a straightforward, low risk procedure."

"Thank you QASI. Thank you very much."

"Je vous en prie mon Capitaine."

"Still reading Agatha Christie are we QASI?"

"In fact, yes. We are charmed by this diminutive Belgian, Hercule Poirot."

Year Four

<u>1400</u>

NAV HAD JUST completed making their final course correction.

Heading: *Kosmas*

"Captain, our new heading was registered at 1400 hours ship's time, and executed. DAR now has emergency helm and operational navigational control. The next course correction—final azimuth on approach to *Kosmas*—is scheduled in approximately fourteen years sir."

"Acknowledged. Mr. Farrow I would like a complete rundown on ship's status tomorrow at 1400 hours. We will implement the Downgraded Operations Duty Roster after a clear status."

"Aye sir. Status briefing at 1400+1. DODR to follow if status is nominal."

<u>1400+1</u>

The full bridge compliment was on duty. Class A uniforms. All positions manned. All systems nominal. Current velocity was 30.8% of light speed, consistent with flight plan. Failing intervention by DAR Systems, they would maintain this heading, at relativistic speeds increasing to .7708 light-speed, followed by decreasing compounding decrements of 10.6% light-speed per year (.029041% per solar day), for the remaining seven solar years.

They had just completed a three hour, comprehensive status review of all ship's systems. Everything was operating in precise synchrony.

Captain Carr was pleased.

Ambient systems, water, atmosphere, lighting, temperature, weather and diurnal cycles were optimal. Food production was stable—neither over, nor under production. Food quality—the highest in flavor and appearance. Nutritional value never achieved before. As a result of the new AAM's (Accelerated Anthropogenic Metabolizers), developed first for JAEKEL, knowledge matriculation, or more properly, metrignosiculation, was never more effective. Comms, entertainment, GAEA, agriculture, marine life and medical systems ... all optimal.

Phil reclined at his console. "Looks like a *GO* Commander Farrow. DODR in one hour."

<u>1600+1</u>

"Alright XO, let's close up shop."

"Aye sir."

"Nav?"

"We are under full helm control. Navigation systems nominal."

"Helm?"

"DAR is controlling all systems. All systems nominal."

"Master at Arms?"

"GAEA has the entire ship under twenty-four hour observation. Every bridge position is being micro-recorded. AI Systems are on full alert. They will begin auto-alert level sequencing in ten seconds."

"Environment?"

"Nominal. We are conducting twenty-four hour remote supervision."

"Comms?"

"Fully functional. Twenty-four hour remote supervision sir."

Phil consulted ship's chronometer. "Final DODR prep on my mark." Ten seconds later. "MARK."

Nick Farrow finalized the status brief. "Captain, the DODR is now active. We are roistering twenty-four hours remote general supervision duty.

GS Bridge, GS Comms, GS Enviro, all GS remotes are constantly available to you, Ambassador QASI and AI Systems. We are standing by sir."

"Actuate."

"Aye sir, all GS systems active … now. We are now at full DODR."

"Thank you Mr. Farrow." Phil stood and discretely stretched. "Well done all. We are now officially under way with all automatic systems engaged. I will be calling training alerts and exercises at irregular intervals as our voyage proceeds. Beyond that, success and good luck in your many and various pursuits. I will ensure we see each other often and remain the close-knit crew we are today. I thank you all."

Phil left the Bridge with the occasional handshake or arm pat, as various bridge crews straggled behind.

Lights dimmed.

Duty stations darkened.

The Bridge grew quiet.

Then quieter still.

Then the Bridge fell asleep.

***

As duties and time slipped away, the crew effortlessly fell into a cyclical rhythm, like collapsing into a cool stream on a scorching mid-summer's day.

0600—Ablutions

Phil evolved his own routine.

The FOND showers were becoming constantly more effective. Faster, more efficacious, broader bio-spectrumed, longer lasting. The fond catalyst was selected to deliver QAVL geriatric treatments. A FOND treatment shower entailed no more than three minutes for the initiated. However, Phil would normally indulge in a full, luxurious ten minutes … some days even longer.

He remembered the agony of his first FOND shower, as he pondered the pleasures of the latest FOND showers. He tried to describe the current feeling.

Let's see … a cross of a massage, a back-scratch, a Jacuzzi, and … tiny bubbles bursting throughout my body. Not painful. It feels incredibly like living Champagne. And the massage and back-scratch. It's as if a dozen women were smoothly rubbing and lightly scoring me all over with soft fingers and well-manicured nails.

Skin, teeth, hair, eyes, lungs, lower tract (excepting benign biomass), heart, liver, the GI, circulatory, lymphatic and neurological systems and the ears, nose and throat. Even the brain. All these and far more were restored daily to physical perfection and pristine cleanliness. Phil felt energized and ebullient when he stepped from the shower. Clean, stronger, younger and healthier. He would immediately plunge into a rigorous series of extreme exercises for at least thirty minutes, followed by a shave and a brisk cold-water shower.

Prodigious beginnings to prodigious days.

As with everything else on *Gauntlet*, nothing was wasted. Water, nutrients, wastes, even the FOND catalyst itself was broken down for reuse. The Webberian Sea was the beneficiary of any remaining viable catalyst. Aquatic life from plankton to whales equally improved, albeit at a reduced rate. It was a topic of extensive debate whether these creatures could matriculate knowledge from this same source. Only time would tell.

And time would tell an incredible story.

0700—Breakfast

Oneirons grew more detached from their native Earth with each succeeding day. This was more a tribute to their strength and adaptability than any conceivable disparagement of their love of mankind and loyalty to Earth.

Highly valued human traits, some arising unknown, conspicuously advanced in the Oneirion genome.

All the same, Phil found the ease of their disconnect somewhat off-putting and even blasé. They were justified in their attitude in fact. Earth had wanted to kill them. They would never again see the Earth they had departed. The Earth they might revisit in one hundred or so relative years would be a different world altogether. It was highly possible that Earth would no long harbor humans, or even life itself. A 100% extinction event was not inconceivable. However, he could not, or would not relinquish his earthen heritage. As a consequence, his breakfast hour was dominated by the lamentably meager news of, from, and by Earth.

Gauntlet's feed from Earth's news media was now delayed by more than twenty-four months, and growing longer each second—a delay that was expanding near geometrically now. Comms staff and computers were challenged to boost and elucidate the signal into something coherent and viewable. It was an accolade to the esteem accorded Phil that such pains were expended so he might view the news with his breakfast. Few others, if any, had a similar interest. Gauntians much preferred their own local news and reports.

When the weather was good (Ambience control still took care to deliver Earthlike randomness.) Jake would serve breakfast on the terrace and the two of them would watch, or listen to the news together—some on a live feed, most recorded during the last twenty-four hours. Earthly events seemed to grow more depressing each day. This was old news, spotty, ragged. History. Renditioned. God only knows what insane presentments contemporary news might reveal assuming man's Earth had managed to preserve any semblance of civilization.

Phil did gradually grow aware that the majority of surviving humans regarded him as something of a cross between Dr. Mengele fresh out of Auschwitz, and Satan himself fresh-risen from hell. Despite unremitting failure and severely depleted resources, the middle-eastern task force persisted in relentless air and sea strikes upon Oneiro. Would that these were the only military engagements. In civil insurrections, revolutions, bi-lateral and multi-lateral wars, over seven billion were exterminated. The lovers of death were in their glory.

Disease, poverty, starvation and death ran rampant. Those rare countries (or whatever remained of them) that were remotely stable lived in total isolation. Islands unto themselves, prepared to ruthlessly kill any who would attempt to encroach.

World commerce, communications, travel, diplomacy, science, cooperation were all history now and for the foreseeable future. As the world's culture and economy faded, internal reliance grew and isolationism blossomed.

Oneiro unhurt. Sixty percent of the world destroyed. The remaining forty percent under constant onslaught. Many would declare that world human population was finally approaching a sensible level. Unfortunately it would continue to decline into obliteration in most of the world.

The wars wore on and on endlessly.

Then the hammer fell.

China finally had enough and their wrath was terrifying to witness. Their's was the remaining largest population and the most formidable existent nuclear force. They reacted ruthlessly to save any remnants of their peoples and their way of life.

Iconic mushroom plumes blossomed around the world and a hideous silence settled over the Earth. Not the silence of peace, the silence of looming, inescapable death.

The Chinese proclaimed "副 在那 的缩**写** 的过**去**式" (There! Now it is finished.). All in vein.

Desperate multinational retaliation further assured the final descent of *homo sapiens erectus*—the dismal and ignominious end finally at hand. Man's last fiery whimper. Sea life would probably survive, along with selected plant life, insects, most reptiles and small mammals, and of course, Oneiro. Oneiro's underground facilities were so extensive and lavishly equipped, inhabitants lived on generally unchanged. In fact their lives improved as the tedious, futile attacks finally ended.

Nonetheless *Gauntlet* continued to transmit status reports and receive Earth reports, essentially from Onerio now, whenever available.

Couldn't the QAVL have foreseen at least some of this horror?

"Jake?" asked Phil wearily.

"Sir?"

"Do you suppose the greatest, most pernicious monster in the history of mankind might have a Bloody Mary?"

"No sir. But I would be pleased to mix one for you."

"Thanks. Make that a pitcher for two."

"With pleasure sir."

<u>0800—DODR Duty</u>

Phil insisted he be assigned a slot on the DODR. This ensured he would remain in the midst of ship's operations and actively involved with the crew. The XO and senior bridge officers made special accommodation for him in allocating him a permanent slot of two hours, always commencing at 0800. Of course Phil could enter the GS Bridge whenever he cared to, but he enjoyed the routine of a standard duty slot as well.

Phil entered the GS Bridge. "Report."

"All systems functional Captain. Course and speed nominal. We are approaching thirty-four percent light speed. DAR detected a micro-nebula …"

"A dust cloud?"

"Ah … yes sir … three hours ago, and it has calculated no course correction is warranted. We will encounter the cloud in fifteen hours.

"Engineering has detected hairline cracks in the struts supporting underground storage in sector 12D. They are reinforcing the beams with abutments and absorptive reinforcement."

"Are these struts located at stress points?"

"They are in a vector 180° diametrical to the Webberian Sea."

"Acknowledged. Log this item, and note that I want inspection reports on these struts filed every two months. Ensure GAEA is instructed and install appropriate sensors. That is all?"

"Yessir."

"Captain has the Con."

"Aye sir."

<u>1000—Run</u>

Phil jogged the world of *Gauntlet* constantly.

He became a familiar figure across the countryside, running more for enjoyment than exercise. Every day Phil contrived a different routing to the same destination.

His destination was always the Webberian Sea. His circuiting blanketed all of *Gauntlet*. He became intimately familiar with the hamlets, the forests, the parks, the shopping streets, the neighborhoods and their residents.

From time to time he would encounter a resourceful crewman who astutely predicted his route for the day and joined in the run. Then they would run together for a time as they talked. Invariably the crewman would finally express a concern, or pose a question, an opinion that compelled them to seek him out. Phil was frequently challenged by their questions or ideas. Thus he enjoyed these runs greatly, growing closer to *Gauntlet* and her crew with each stride.

***

"Captain, I believe we maintain an extraordinary transmitter array."

"That's correct. The most powerful ever built by man. Its remains directed at Earth for the present. In a few years we'll realign to target *Kosmas*."

Phil frowned inwardly. The Ensign was very pretty and nicely built, but she was breathing very heavily.

Is she out of breath? Am I running so fast?

"I have a suggestion sir."

"Yes?"

She labored to clearly enunciate despite her heavy breathing. "Suppose we brought that array to its maximum power—output and gain. And we burst reasonably brief messages—say fifteen minutes in length—and we send Earth a complete, honest recount of events on Oneiro. How this came about. Why we withheld the news. The real nature of the QAVL. The true nature of our mission on Oneiro. The benefits and the innocence of it all. The importance of this work. How they abase all of mankind in the purview of the most advanced species in the galaxy. How they are destroying themselves. That they are doing irreversible damage which we cannot …"

"I get the picture. Let's take a break."

They trotted to a halt. Both leaned over, peering at the ground. Hands on knees. She was gasping for breath. He was breathing normally.

"Assuming someone remains alive and equipped to receive these transmissions, work up a few segments. Audio *and* visual. Photos, graphics, whatever. They've got to have pictures, or they'll ignore it. I'll take a look at what you come up with, and consider it. I caution you though; I will not tolerate anything that remotely resembles propaganda, in any form, for any reason. Nor do I want you to preach at them. Try to couch these transmissions in terms of the most unbiased news reporting in human history; and don't try to rehabilitate my reputation. That would only bias their reaction."

"Understood sir. And thank you sir."

<u>1100—Visit Anne</u>
How was Anne?

Fine.

How was Aiy?

Much better.

Dr. Singe's operation was a complete success, thanks in large part to QASI. Aiy had moved a little. She was not making those disturbing mewing sounds now.

Catch up on events on *Gauntlet*, the wonders from the heavens and the horrors from Earth.

In the solitary clammy darkness of the night, Phil often kept secret—even from himself—he prayed man would finally self-destruct and have done with it.

Put the poor bastards out of the misery they have incessantly strived for, and many so abundantly deserve. And when they have all perished, only Oneiro will stand—alone and invincible—an ineluctable seed struggling on a dead world.

***

"So how much longer Anne?"

"I would guess six weeks maximum. I hope sooner."

"Looking forward to going airside?"

Pause.

"Yes. I suppose I am. It's been a long time down here. But I can't stay topside all the time. I have friends to visit down here."

"I'd be happy to join you if you like."

Her face lit with a smile. "I'd like that. A lot."

He grinned waggishly. "And I suspect you'd be quite taken with the charms of underwater sex."

Crooking her head playfully, eyebrow cocked, Anne wantonly appraised his dripping nudity with appreciation. She'd been down here alone for a long time. She jauntily returned his grin. "I think I'd like that more than you know."

Warming to the idea, she exclaimed "Wouldn't it be fun if Aiy could join in too?"

Phil liked the way she thought.

***

QASI's *dark hole* solution worked beautifully. The equatorial zone of the Oneirion Sea now harbored a gently swirling vortex—internally it grew dark and cold. Toward the middle the pressure intensified exponentially.

Sure enough, it became a favorite haunt of many sea creatures. Whales, larger squid and sharks, and a world of tiny to microscopic denizens floated down into this black vortex. They all made it their home and hunting, or grazing grounds. On Earth, all creatures hunt in one way or another. So great was the number of marine creatures that flocked to the vortex, they were considering enlarging it, or generating several more throughout the modest Webberian sea.

Among the most appreciative of these creatures was Captain Philip Carr. The illusion of extreme depth was flawless. It provided the additional luxury of rapid accessibility. On Earth a descent to such conditions involved many hundreds of meters. Aboard *Gauntlet* it was only a matter of moments.

… And he slept. He slept as well if not better than in his quarters. When he arose he was more refreshed than ever and almost invariably discovered new insights or knowledge. He arose troubled today. A doubt that had been festering in the back of his mind:

I believe something or someone is tinkering with my mind. Who or what is capable of such a thing on Gauntlet?

Why couldn't the QAVL have foreseen at least some of the chaos and destruction they visited on Earth? Their knowledge and intelligence exceeds comprehension. They know man better than man knows himself. They have eons of experience in such matters on countless worlds. They could have observed the insurgency as it transpired. So why did they allow us to blindly stumble into Armageddon? And above all … why am I only now raising these issues? Is something blocking me?

Philip quickly ascended to the beach, dressed, and made his way to a nearby

QAVLGate.

1200—Lunch

Lunch was Phil's favorite time. Often he would invite crewmembers to The Residence (the term Captain's Quarters had never caught on), or they would invite him to their quarters. There were many other choices however. *Gauntlet's* up-market restaurants (there were now six), the crew mess halls and *Gauntlet's* large cafeteria. *Gauntlet's* Broadway now boasted an authentic Automat. And Phil's personal favorite, the Food Technology Lab *qua* restaurant, *Deigma Kai Gousto* (Greek meaning Sample and Taste). All featured excellent food, learning and health additives, as well as QAVL Geriatrics. All were comfortable, unhurried and un-crowded. All offered a well-stocked bar (although most crew confined themselves to waters or juices). Phil would relax and enjoy a long lunch with one or more crewmembers. Their discussions would range the universe. In all of human history there had never been more fascinating discussions than those aboard *Gauntlet.*

1400—Correspondence from Earth

As the currency of correspondence diminished, so did its relevance. Phil worked through these remote missives without much enthusiasm. His responses were at best commiserations. His ability to contribute to a solution to Earth's ills was so far removed as to be negligible. Besides the majority of surviving humans bore such hatred for him, his counsel was totally disregarded. For his own part Phil found the daily agglomeration of questions, imprecations, accusations, diatribes and jeremiad nothing more than the morning's news restated. As tedious as it was repellent.

1500—Study

Consistent with Jake's straightforward advice and QASI's atypically clumsy innuendo, Phil decided to forego crew training on the QAVL Documents. Instead he ingested concentrates suspended in fruit juices and then alternately slept and scanned the documents. Working on his own in this manner, it would be centuries before he digested the entire Document. He therefore confined himself to levels One and sometimes Two of the forty huge *magnum opi*. Even this task would carry him to *Kosmas* and well beyond.

1800—Drinks with QASI

The nightly communion with QASI afforded both pleasure and burden. The wonder and the beauty of the insights shared by QASI beggared imagination. The sheer enjoyment of sharing ideas and discussing concepts with a creature as advanced as QASI was the stuff of dreams. He looked forward eagerly to their nightly confrontations with the cosmos.

At the same time, he sensed QASI was withholding something. Some agenda. QASI was leading him somewhere, towards some reality intended only for him. Phil did more than sense this. He could feel the flux of it. Inexorable. Profoundly important. Important for him, important for Earth, important for QASI and the QAVL and perhaps infinitely more.

How can I be an instrument of such import to a civilization as mighty as the QAVL?

SOMETHING PASSES HERE. SOMETHING IMPORTANT.

2000—Cook & Dine

Phil's daily intake of nutrients, knowledge, medicinals, geriatrics and FOND catalysts were consumed before 1500. Therefore, he felt free to be innovative with dinner. So he resurrected his youthful interest in cooking. He started with fried bread and beans, much to Jake's dismay. But soon he had mastered French, Italian, Chinese, American, Mexican and South American cuisines. Jake was dining with him now and he spent part of each day scouting out ingredients in kitchens, larders, fields, forest and waters.

2200—Entertainment

Phil's self-imposed regimen taxed mind and body. Not beyond his endurance, not even unduly. It did however demand a certain amount of time devoted to pure, sometimes mindless relaxation.

A book, a cinema, music, a Broadway show, a night sail, one or two or three ladies, entertainment feeds from Earth (the very few remaining forwarded by Mike Auslander before the fall), playing cards with Jake, or just sitting on his terrace looking out on the night-time starlit beauty of *Gauntlet.*

<u>2400 Sleep</u>

Instantly and without interruption—throughout the night.

Sleep had become a great pleasure—enriched by tempered gravity—a quiescent *sonata rondo* beckoning the night's accession to morning—one of the joys of Gauntlet—e*xcept when his dreams came.*

Sometimes dark and horrific. Morose memories and long suppressed parasitic fears sullenly brooding in shadowy cavities of his mind, nested like vampire bats with insidious guilt waiting impatiently for the moment to feast upon their host. Even Philip was not immune to the dark angst that dreams can visit upon even the strongest of us.

Sometimes they were pleasant, lovely, and even fun. Others were exciting and seductive.

But the recurrent theme.The prevalent specter was hardly a dream at all.

It was always the same. Phil was … something … something inhuman. A mote, perhaps a particle, a microbe, a cell, an insect, a planarian. Something mindless, yet not without a fuzzy and strange form of sentience. It was impossible to clearly make out.

Whatever he was, he was swimming, or flying, or somehow winnowing through a textured world—awash in a turbulent, raging, finely granulated universe. His movement was with the flux of the texture, yet he was constantly attempting to alter course against the Granular Ebb. The grains were hooked on the lee side of their terminus, snagging and miring him. Overpowered and helpless. A tedious, exhausting, unending struggle that seemed to wear on and on, endlessly throughout the exhausting night.

He would awaken in a bone-weary sweat. The dreams were incessant and interminable. When he returned to sleep, exhausted, the dream relentlessly resumed. The nights were without end. It became a crushing, sweaty, bed-clothed-hog-tied nightmare. If only he could end the hideous miasma.

Complete the task. Discover its denouement. Escape. Must he forever challenge this demon flux?

He would wake in the morning, and as he was wont, he would discover a fresh realization. This new awareness was more of a suspicion however. Phil had experienced surprising fatigue on such occasions. The man who never tired was totally spent.

As in the dream, was he so drained because he defied the flux? Not in a dream world, but the real world. In a truer, and as yet, obscure reality.

***

Phil was forced to remember his was a routine. A function of habit. Not a schedule. With a Micro-World and an interstellar vessel to lead, he greatly prized his time alone, which was frequently preempted.

Nonetheless, Oneirons were an acutely independent people needing little leadership and even less guidance. However, on Oneiro Phil had staff, layers of people to look after habitual problems and the ability to insulate him from non-strategic difficulties. Aboard *Gauntlet* this was not so much the case. Chain of Command is no substitute for bureaucracy. And bureaucracy is no substitute for a close-knit, indurate team.

Despite the diligent efforts of Phil's XO, Commander Farrow, seemingly unending questions found their way to the Captain's Briefing Room.

Thus did the weeks resolve into months, and the months resolve into years.

The Big Sleep

WHAT A DELICIOUS, wondrous feeling!

Weightless. No pressures, no discomfort, no bedclothes to bind and chafe and sweat and wrestle with. No stiffness from lying wrong, or too long in the same position falling prey to gravity's relentless vice. The air was fresh, cool and oxygen rich. The lighting was hazy, soft and golden. Everything a pleasure to the senses. To stretch is a delight. Every muscle is perfectly …

WAIT!

What is this? I'm not stretching! I'm not doing anything. What the hell is this? Where the hell is this? I can't hear a thing. I can't see a thing except that crazy light. I can't feel a thing, taste a thing, or smell a thing. I can't move!

Have I been horribly injured?

Am I dead?

He lay alone and as terrified as his conditioning would permit. It seemed hours, or days, or weeks, or perhaps years. He simply had no temporal markers from which to measure.

I must find a way to begin marking time. Let's see: One-thousand-and-one, one-thousand-and-two, one-thousand-and-three, one-thousand-and-four, one-thousand-and … this is no damned good. This will drive me insane. I can't feel my heartbeat, so I have no unit of measure. I may not even have a heartbeat. I've got to approach it as though I were speaking. That takes a certain amount of time to enunciate. Okay. One-In-di-anna, two-In-di-anna, three-In-di-anna, four-In-di-anna … this is still no damned good. I'm not really talking. I can't hear it. Christ. I may not even have a mouth. I'm still not measuring relative time, if relative time even exists here.

Oh God. Where is here? Is this hell? Am I in hell? I've damned sure worked for it—ten times over.

His entire universe consisted of an insensate blurry drift, suspended in space and time, trapped in some sort of eternal, endless void.

He tried reliving his life in real-time. Reciting prime numbers, calculating the value of Pi. He 'sang' every song he could recall. Recited every poem. Recounted every book, movie, joke, story, news article and history. He realized that soon (whatever *soon* meant here) he would be irreversibly insane, assuming he wasn't already.

Mercifully, he 'slept' for a time. How long? It could have been years. Centuries. Time was meaningless here. He awakened in the same existential purgatory. Desperation had given way to resignation. He was certain he was condemned to pass eternity in this endless void. Had he been capable he would have screamed, sobbed, wept, and even prayed.

How could he put an end to this purgatory? Suicide was beyond his grasp. Moreover, he was probably already dead.

God. My God. This is Satan's nightmare. Will I ever …

***

Movement!

Movement somehow relative to him. Was he being moved somehow? Then a subtle change in the light, allowing him to realize it was never real light he was seeing. It was something inside his head he'd mistaken for light.

The slightest muffling of sound. Whatever unimaginable voyage in space and time he had undertaken, he seemed to have crossed over. His uncertain hope was an agonizing taunt. Seconds seemed like hours. Was he hearing his heartbeat? A booming thump, faster and faster. Was it his imagination? Was he well and truly insane now?

***

"Phil? Phil darling."

Someone was holding his hand. The touch of another human! A voice! Deliverance itself.

Thank God.

He suspected, perhaps even hoped, he was weeping.

"This is Anne, Phil. Are you awake? Can you hear me? You're fine Phil. Everything is fine. You are just waking up. They believe it's going to be very disorienting at first, and you should try to relax. They'll have you up soon and we'll take you back to your quarters. Perhaps we'll have lunch, or walk about town, or go shopping. Remember. Everything is just fine. Normal. I'll see you in just a little while."

Suddenly he felt cool moisture on his lips. To feel! To hear! Then drops on his lips finding his mouth. It was like water, only somehow a little sweet. It was *wonderful.* He raised a hand grasping for the glass, and having secured it, brought it to his lips in trembling hands, and drank greedily. Noisy and clumsily, spilling the precious fluid, the cool liquid ran down chin, neck and onto his chest. He didn't mind. To feel anything was bliss itself.

Slowly recollection returned.

***

Many months ago they found themselves under increasing time pressure. Sleep cycles must commence despite the lack of testing prior to launch. There had simply been no time. They now had exactly six months to commence with full geriatric cycles.

Thus did the incessant debates begin.

Weeks later, arguments were still brought to a very frustrated Captain Carr.

"The Captain should not be the first to attempt this. Anything could happen, and Gauntlet would be left leaderless."

"There are over two hundred potential leaders aboard this vessel and *you* hold the poll position, Commander Farrow."

"I have no aspirations on your job sir."

"I am painfully aware of that XO. Truth is, I believe you should be far more aggressive in exercising and seeking command. Not to mind though. I am still alive and I am still Captain; and I'll work around your seeming trepidation. As Captain this decision is my responsibility and my prerogative. Is that clear?"

"Yessir. But Captain, this procedure has hardly been tested. We have dozens of crewmen who would willingly volunteer. There is no need for you to take such a risk."

"Enough. I will not ask any passenger or crewman to attempt anything I haven't undertaken myself. That was my policy on Oneiro as you will no doubt. recall, when I tested all sorts of treatments, including the FOND Shower. That policy remains in full effect here on Gauntlet. That's final. And that's an order."

"Captain, you must be aware there are some differences in your physiognomy and the crew's in general."

"You're stating the obvious. Yet you must be equally aware our cellular composition is identical for all practical purposes. Your argument is specious. This discussion grows tedious and is at an end. I will make the first long-sleep.

"That is an order."

***

Phil prevailed and finally all preparations were complete.

Phil was transported to Gauntlet's 'North Pole.' Gravity free. Isolated. Total ambience control. Phil was loaded with nutrients, vitamins, vaccines and sedatives. Then hundreds of miniscule, super fine electrodes were inserted into literally every muscle and organ of his body. Some would convey micro-pulses, stimulating his muscularity and, in conjunction with a gentle tumbler, prevent the accumulation of blood, or any other fluid in any specific bodily area; augmented by a gentle 'bouncer' tossing him from head to foot to prevent bone loss as much as possible. This would assure he would arise from his long sleep reasonably fit, un-bruised and without bedsores. Despite zero-gee, the body invariably contacts various devices. Others of these ultra-sharp, ultra-fine wires would monitor every organ, alerting his doctors should something go amiss.

Phil was totally and thankfully sedated for the next step and would remain so for the next two years, given breaks to avoid addiction. Catheters were inserted in literally every body cavity. These would administer liquids, nutrients and drugs as needed. They would drain any fluid buildup, directly measure, and adjust the pressures of various bodily fluids.

Lastly he was totally slathered with a thick semi-permeable gel that would allow his dermis to withstand two years of immersion. Hair, beard, finger and toenails were as close to stasis as chemicals, lasers and temperature could achieve.

He was then carefully lowered into a large soundproof, lightproof, tamperproof tank filled with a FOND enriched saline solution.

Snug harbor for the next two years.

***

"Good morning Captain Carr. This is Doctor Singe. I've removed your eye and nose visor. You may open your eyes now, very slowly please, and then we'll look after your …"

Half an hour later Phil was walking steadily and feeling stronger all the time, determined to go home.

He had been asleep for two years. An interstellar Rip Van Winkle. He tried to calculate just how many kilometers he had travelled while asleep and, despite his formidable mind, factoring in an increasing velocity every second, found he could not.

Overruling considerable resistance, Phil was now the first Guinea Pig to undergo the treatment.

Their emergency lift-off pre-empted any testing. Therefore, having never experienced anything remotely akin to sleeping for seven hundred and thirty days, they had been understandably apprehensive about the experience.

With good reason. As it turned out, he dreamt for roughly ten percent of the senescent-reversal period. For Phil this represented approximately seventy-three days of struggling to *swim against the grain,* his abiding incubus. Seventy-three days, twenty-four-hours-a-day, of exhausting, unending hell. Mercifully, his long slumber was fragmented into periods of two or three *dream days*; and, although non-dream intervals did not truly exist for him, the sporadic nature of his dreaming may have delivered him from madness and the unending hell of the impenetrable void.

He reported the problem in great detail to protect subsequent sleepers from such torment. He also reported the inhuman delay between consciousness and reawakening. After a little research, the solutions proved to be surprisingly easy. REM Monitors and Electroencephalographs were already in use. It was therefore a straightforward modification to their cyclical sequences to detect dreams of duration more than thirty seconds. If so, they subjected the sleeper to one minute of mild vibrations and the interval between consciousness and awakening was radically shortened. Facing another long-sleep in a few years himself, Phil was agreeably pleased with such a reliable, simplistic solution.

Phil and Anne were strolling down the Anastasios Valley from the polar clinic towards Phil's Residence far down the Anastasios River, rambling the *Gauntlet* countryside, talking, enjoying the world, and each other.

"How are you, *really* Phil?"

"Great! How are you Anne?"

"I'm fine. I've missed you."

"It's wonderful to see you on dry land. Your undersea habitation extended far longer than I ever imagined."

"I wish we could have gone under together." She took his arm. "And I *really* wish we could have taken a few of those *swims* you mentioned."

Phil chuckled "Me too. But we have all the time in the world now."

"Agreed, and I look forward to it, as well as Aiy. We've missed you."

"I know. I'm sorry. I didn't really want to leave you both alone. But I needed to be the first. This treatment had never been tried on a human for a truly extended period. Our friends in the Atlas Mountains hastened our departure so fiercely, many tasks were left undone."

"So the *Captain* goes first?"

"This Captain does. When did you move topside?"

"Oh, nearly a year ago."

"Tell me about Aiy."

Anne smiled brightly. "You won't believe it Phil. About twenty-two months ago she started moving. Really moving. We put her into an oxygen environment. Then she began groaning, or whimpering again, or whatever. A very upsetting sound. Then one morning she had a sort of a seizure, a violent attack for about ten minutes. After that she began weeping. Then I was weeping too. After a time, she actually smiled. Within six months she was jogging, eating normal food and even drinking. Not like she used to of course, but impressive all the same. She drove Dr. Singe crazy." She stopped walking and embraced Phil, looking up at him. "Now she's Aiy again. No change, no scars, she's perfectly healthy—mentally and physically beautiful again. All thanks to you Phil."

Phil smiled "Perhaps we can start really living in this gorgeous little world now. There are still years and years to go. Let's go home and get started."

***

"Chib-Erd!"

Aiy rushed forward as they entered Phil's Residence and, in typical form, nearly knocked Phil off his feet in her exuberance. After a warm hug and a long kiss, she held him back straight-armed, and looked at him affectionately.

"Damn it's good to see you. I never expected to see you again. You saved my life. You saved my life at great peril to your own. You saved my life when you probably wanted to kill me. I thank you Phil. I thank you for my life. Listen, I've got to make you understand why I did what I ..."

"Let's not go into that just now Aiy. We've got all the time in the world, or at least this world. For now, let me look at you."

Aiy had been doing laps in the terrace pool. She was clad in a jet-black aquatic triathlon bikini, now covered up with a beige sarong. She stepped back, dropped the sarong and began turning slowly, arms raised.

Soft skin deeply tanned. Not a scar, not a blemish. Face as perfectly formed as always. Two eyes, ten fingers and ten toes. Beautiful breasts and it was fairly apparent that her bikini-clad intimacies were as beautifully re-stored as the rest of her body.

"Think you can still take me?" grinned Phil.

Aiy defiantly returned a challenging look. "Chib-Erd, I can still kick your prissy ass from here to Epsilon Tauri. Care to take a few fast falls?"

Phil smiled. "Uh. Not just now. I see you've been studying your star charts though."

"Oh not really, it's that crazy chow they sling around here. Shit just keeps poppin' into my head."

"Oh? I thought they'd decided to keep you away from smart food."

Anne interjected. "They did. They tried it for a while, while Aiy was submerged. But they took her off. Something about unpredicated and non-situationalized memory adaptation. But she's been on smart food now for about seven months."

Phil grew serious, frowning at Aiy. "Dreams?"

She regarded him unflinchingly. "Right out of hell itself."

"What do you remember?"

"Not one damned thing after entering that hell hole in Ghazi Kahn and being dragged in front of a loathsome little dwarf-like man with a huge nose and repellent looks, not to mention his smell.

"The next thing I remember was waking up under water with all sorts of tubes running in and out of me. I panicked. Went a little crazy I guess. I thought I was dead, or drowning. The next thing I saw was Anne looking at me out of what appeared to be a fish bowl. I was okay after that." For a moment Aiy looked surprisingly demure. "Anne told me how you saved me from that hell-hole and fought to kept me alive on the flight back to Oneiro."

Anne squeezed her shoulder affectionately.

"Not as easy as all that Phil. She was in great pain for quite a while until she was able to repeatedly stretch muscles and tendons. Hellish physical therapy. A really tough time."

"I can imagine."

"You must be starving Phil. It's been two years you know."

"Actually I *am* starving. They gave me some stuff" Phil grimaced at the memory. "… to assist me in my first meal, and that's worn off some time ago. I'd love some solid food."

"What would you like?"

"I think I'd like the best Eggs Benedict in this or any world."

A shadow passed over Anne and Aiy.

Phil noted their sudden apprehension. "What?"

Pause.

Anne: "The day she made Eggs Benedict for us was the same day she was contacted by her father and abducted by those monsters in Ghazi Kahn."

Manna from Heavens

AS PHIL HAD deferred Eggs Benedict for lunch and settled for a some of Jakes legendary beef stew followed by a little cheesecake. But he remained hungry for a really hardy meal.

"Dinner's on me tonight ladies. I'm interested to see how my old favorite *Les Rêves du Gaunt* is faring."

Aiy said "It's faring *very* well. But they've changed the name to The Gaunti Café."

"Same food?"

"No." She had an amused smile. "It's a little more 'down home' now."

"Sounds interesting. Let's give it a try."

Anne smiled coyly. "Sure. But be prepared for a few surprises …"

"… such as?"

"Well for one thing, theater, music and cinema have undergone a renaissance while you were asleep, and among other things we have *movie stars* now. Believe it or not, celebrities who command a following. Not the mindless prepubescent worship one found on Earth, but serious fans nonetheless. Celebrities who frequent restaurants such as The Gaunti Café."

"Surprising behavior for Oneirons."

"It's *Gauntites* now Phil. Not Oneirons."

"Explain."

"They seem to have tacitly abandoned Oneiro. They never mention Oneiro. You will not find Oneiro on any sign, or product. Hell, they seldom if ever even mention *Earth*."

"Their adaption must be complete now. Do they admit to being *human?*"

"Uh." Anne looked thoughtful. "Now that you mention it, I haven't heard that word in some time either, and they've abandoned certain human mannerisms."

"Movie stars, *Gauntites.* Superficially it sounds harmless enough."

"Yes it is. Harmless fun. P&M says ..."

"P&M?"

"Psychology & Morale. You ordered the appointment of a Morale Officer years ago, and it evolved into a psych department while you were asleep. The next few days may be an interesting object lesson on the leverage one individual can apply to history."

"Explain."

"Before your 'nap', you gave orders, expressed ideas and opinions, asked questions, or made casual remarks. Apparently you had some interesting chats during your daily runs. Then you slept for two years. That is a long time in a society as dynamic as *Gauntlet.* You now have the opportunity to return and see the jarring long-term effects of your influence. In fact, you seem to have achieved a sort of godhead."

"*Godhead?* I will observe with extreme care."

"Anyhow, P&M contends this celebrity business is a worthy addition to *Gauntlet* society. They say it adds dimension to *Gauntlet's* psychographics."

"Alright. I still don't see a problem."

"Except ah ... they made a certain cinema while you were asleep."

"Yes?"

"Of your life."

"Mm. My life you say?"

"Yes. And you now have the same 'rock star' following as one of our celebrities. We're going to have to beat the girls away from you just to get seated."

"That is totally unacceptable. I'm going to straighten this out right now."

Later that eveningAnne and Aiy jauntily followed Phil as he marched out to the gravity chutes, nearly skipping in his wake. He instructed the chute "The Gaunti Café."

Instead of carrying them down two floors as Phil expected, the chute whisked them down to the lobby. Phil followed the ladies as they made the trek across the vast lobby, arriving at a remarkable tinted glass, stone and brushed chrome frontage. Above it, an elegant, muted purple neon sign glowed: The Gaunti Café

Phil recognized the maître'd as one of the engineering crew. "Hello Bob. Got a table for three?"

"Of course Captain. It's good to see you sir. Land, Sea, or Star Level?"

Phil turned quizzically to Anne and Aiy.

Anne stepped forward. "Bob, we'd like to look around a bit. Maybe a table on Sea Level for a drink and then Star Level for Dinner?"

"Certainly Dr. Jones, go right on in. Your table will be waiting when you're ready."

With an appreciative nod the three entered the restaurant. Cool, dim and discrete. Phil noted that all eyes were on him. Not appreciably different than the diffidence normally accorded the Captain however. Phil noticed Anne and Aiy were both sporting very dark glasses now. At first he was mildly annoyed. He assumed the glasses were affectation. However, a glance at the décor revealed the truth. The dining room was elegantly decorated. Truly impressive in fact. The walls were covered with Oneirion, or Gauntite art, as were curtains, carpeting and fabrics. If the ladies could see this room clearly, they would be rendered helpless, or worse.

He slowed and spoke quietly to Anne and Aiy. "You're not going to be able to eat here. We must leave."

"GauntiArt is displayed only on the lobby level. Let's go down to Sea Level."

They entered a grav chute similar to those in the lobby.

Anne said "Sea Level please." and turned to Phil. "We are undergoing a bit of a cultural revolution. Not just the language Phil. Pretty near everything. We're not altogether sure what's triggering this, but everything is further evolving—language, art, science, native intelligence, physical strength, societal culture, all at phenomenal rates. You remember the near instantaneous advance of the Onerian language?"

"Of course."

"Well, things of that nature arise almost daily—although not as dramatic. I know some of this may seem frivolous to you, celebrities and such, but believe me Phil, you're walking into a new society. It's as though a whole culture is undergoing a sort of mass adolescence. Probably another step in societal maturation we had not foreseen. We ah, sort of conned you into coming here, so you could begin to witness this for yourself. I strongly recommend patience Phil."

"Alright. I'll play along for a time. But I still have to command this vessel—speaking of which—this is one hellofa long drop ..."

The chute brought them to a gentle standstill and they stepped into the depths of the Weberian Sea—now the Gaunti Sea. Phil was stunned. The vast dining room was circular, its floor built into the bottom of a huge sphere. All lighting was external, illuminating a natural reef growing around the sphere. Thousands of sea creatures, attracted by the light, animated the reef in a cacophony of aquatic life. Clearly the sphere occupied the center of a QAVL Deep Ocean Vortex. Phil's reactions ranged from *dramatic,* to *beautiful,* to *breathtaking* to *wish I were on the outside looking in.*

He turned to the ladies. "This is the damnedest example of Oneirion periscope technology I have ever seen. The illusion is perfection. That glass looks to be thirty centimeters thick; and there even appears to be condensation at the floor seams."

Aiy smiled. "It's not illusion Phil. And that's not glass. Its QAVLStone spun into a transparent sphere. We *are* at the bottom of the Gaunti Sea."

"I'll be damned. I would never have dreamt that ..."

***

Without warning they were suddenly surrounded by some twelve young women.

No screaming, but a fair bit of sighing and barely audible chants of "Captain! ... Skipper!" There was no waving of small books seeking an autograph, or tearing of garments, or trying to touch him. They simply crowded around wanting to be near him, talk to him and experience him. The entire restaurant was now expectantly focused on the small disturbance.

In another time and place he would have appreciated the fun and the humor here, perhaps even some intriguing potential. Today however, he was Captain of Gauntlet; and these people were not acquitting themselves as Oneirons. Phil found it extremely disturbing.

"Silence." His voice was strong, controlled and unemotional.

They were suddenly quiet.

"Come to attention."

The small crowd was confused what to do.

"I said *Come to attention.*" His voice took on a subtle edge.

After a brief delay they came to attention … many for the first time in their lives.

Phil decided it would do them good to remain at attention for a while. So he took his time considering this new anomaly.

I would never expect such frivolous, even adolescent behavior from Oneirons. I forget, despite their brains and skills, how young they really are. I suppose they are forced to be constantly serious and intellectual. So they've got a right to be young and stupid. And I've got to understand. Be patient. All the same, we've got to respect our command structure. We can't survive without it. And I'm not sure just how legitimate this frivolity really is. I think they're entertaining themselves in some way. A sort of a parody of Earth's western silliness. Whatever. They've been through a lot. They've given up their homes. They're facing a total unknown. They're risking their lives. What the hell, I suppose they've earned some latitude.

"You will not address me in this manner. You will return to your tables and you will control yourselves." He looked directly at a young woman. "You. What is your name?"

"Angela Jackson."

He responded in a quiet, firm tone. "Angela Jackson *what?*"

After a moment's confusion she answered. "Uh, Angela Jackson *sir.*"

"MS Jackson, tomorrow morning I want you to report this incident to Commander Farrow. Please advise the Commander of my wish that he should take any action he deems warranted. He will then instruct you how to proceed to inform the ship's company that these sorts of incidents will not be tolerated. Understood?"

"Yes sir, Captain."

Phil smiled. "Good. Return to your table and enjoy your meal." To the crowd in general (still at attention) "As you were." and lightly remarked, "Remember in future, I am not as young as you. Only three at a time." They all grinned. Relieved. "Dismissed."

The incident was over. Phil was in command and yet he was not unsympathetic. Anne and Aiy thought it well played.

He turned back to them. "Let's get that drink."

The Maître'd showed them to their table. When they were seated, a waiter appeared immediately.

"Good evening Captain, Dr. Jones, MS Atsila. What would you care for this evening? Two Seventy-Sevens for the ladies?"

They both smiled affirmative.

It seems the ladies have spent some time here. Phil thought.

"And you Captain Carr. What may I bring you?"

"A double Martini, up with a twist, olives on the side, very dry."

"Thank you." The waiter left to fill their order.

"So what's a *Seventy-Seven?*"

"It takes its name after *Gauntlet's* maximum velocity. It's made from, let's see, Gaunti Rum, grapefruit juice, orange liquor and a spritzer of carbonated lilac water. They lace the lilac water with a T-MAAM of the illustrated life cycle of the Ceanothus Lilac Bush, but they have dozens of other T-MAAM additives."

He frowned. "Okay, I'll bite. What is a T-MAAM?"

Anne looked piercingly at Phil. "Phil, this is another development that may seem trivial, but is in fact very important. T-MAAM is a slang acronym for Trans-Mega-AAM. Trans, as in super-fast. Mega, as in the initial element in units of measure that are equal to one million of subject units. AAM as in Accelerated Anthropogenic Metabolizers. It's based on nearly the same compound they developed for JAEKEL training. Then the JAEKEL Bar was incorporated. Now it's the new advanced Gauntlet Bar. Since those days, they've boosted the process to an incredible speed. And they can now safely administer unimaginably massive doses without harm, and without denigrating the metrignosiculation process. The resultant synthesis is exceptionally fast, inconceivably effective, and supremely benign."

"Surely this accounts for the recent rapid sociological evolution?"

"As I understand it, in part, it certainly does. However, by using T-MAAMs, many crewmen are now approaching eighty-two percent absorption of the QAVL Document. We suspect that acquisition of such a body of knowledge may contribute to these anomalous spurts."

Phil shook his head. "I never dreamt."

Anne looked at him. "I know how you feel. Now comes the part you may find off-putting, or perhaps just trivial."

The drinks had been delivered minutes ago, so Phil reclined, drink in hand, prepared to listen patiently. "Proceed."

"Ingestion, or metrignosiculation at this rate is almost terrifying, yet it is an exhilarating and even *psychedelic* experience."

"*Psychedelic.* Now there's a word I haven't heard since I was a kid."

Anne continued. "The knowledge dynamically and graphically unfolds in your mind. You actually *see* the concepts as they are presented, so fast it seems you are seeing hyper-reality."

"Give me an example."

"Formulae unfolding in the mind is an example." She thought for a moment. "Imagine watching the Equation of Uniformly Accelerated Linear Motion unfold, while a particle exemplifies it. Or a nebula forming from super novae, coalescing into stars and galaxies, and then planets and then life and then re-novae-ing again, running the cycles over and over in the mind of the metrignosiculator …"

"… So they've succeeded in morphing knowledge into a recreational drug? Getting 'high' on astrophysics. They've given a whole new meaning to 'higher education'."

Aiy grinned. "You're not the first one to come up with that one Phil."

"I'm sure. Well, why the hell shouldn't it be fun? Good clean fun at that. Can you imagine what the effect on Earth would be if adolescents and addicts alike were to actually crave *learning*? A brave new world indeed." He looked at his DIT. "QASI, what do you think about this?"

"We think you should try T-MAAMs yourself Philip."

"Perhaps I should."

Anne. "We should finish the story Philip."

"Yes?"

"When we said they made a *cinema* of your life, that wasn't totally accurate."

"No?"

"It wasn't a cinema *per se.*"

"Meaning?"

"Meaning there was no film, no script, no director, no actors, no music … none of that."

"What the hell *was* there?"

"A T-MAAM of your life."

"Meaning?"

"Meaning they know every detail of your life, probably better than you. They quite literally know everything about you. And they watched it all happen in their minds, over and over."

"Meaning?"

Deadpan. "Meaning they now love you deeply."

Phil sat for a time speechless.

"How did they acquire this information?"

"From a swab of your inner cheek."

"*What?*"

"From a process you yourself innovated in your discourse concerning subatomic information retention, they learned how to gather the knowledge of a given human from a single cell. They learned from your hair as well, actually the roots. Apparently genetic based memory occupies various sites throughout the human body, or at least yours does. They also discovered you were already aware of this phenomenon, which greatly surprised and impressed them. You've been holding out apparently. You might take it a little easier on those poor girls considering you were always aware of these developments."

"I'll work on it. But I didn't know I knew. Where's that damned waiter." He looked around impatiently. "This is the most hellishly blatant invasion of privacy I could ever imagine."

"Yes sir?"

"Another Martini." He looked at Anne and Aiy. "You haven't touched your drinks."

As one, they smiled and tossed back their Seventy-Sevens. Seconds later they both reflected blissful wonder as they watched the life cycles of the lovely Ceanothus Lilac unfold in their minds.

He watched with interest as his drink arrived. Their heads were down now. Then he heard two slow sighs and they raised their heads with gleaming eyes. He'd seen much the same during his life all over Earth. Every type of drug. Yet this had a far more positive aura about it. Nothing dark. Nothing destructive, mentally or physically. Truly good clean, uplifting fun.

As he poured down his second Martini "You know, you could have briefed me on all this back at the Residence." mildly irritated.

"Phil, some information must be delivered *in situ*."

"Fine." He growled. "Is there a problem with addiction to AEI's?"

"For a *Gaunti*? You're not serious?"

"No. I suppose not. What about Earth humans?"

"Addiction to *knowledge*?"

"I suspect you're oversimplifying. Let's get some dinner. I can't wait for the next surprise."

They moved along to the next drop-chute down.

***

The Star Level was indeed a surprise. A blister on the surface of *Gauntlet* fashioned from the same material as the 'fishbowl' below (above?) them. All around them, nothing but stars and hard vacuum, seemingly frozen in space and time. The beginnings of a Doppler shift bleeding almost imperceptivity from their edges.

All irritation from the Sea Level forgotten, Phil wandered about the entire transparent bubble in wonder. Apparently the diners on Star Level had been warned not to pester Phil, so he walked about freely, unmolested, except the occasional hale from crewmembers of long acquaintance.

On *Gauntlet's* nearby horizon he saw evidence of what appeared to be *construction*! Phil whirled about, nearly running into his table.

He sat and demanded peremptorily "Are they *building* something out there?"

Aiy look up surprised "Why yes. They've been working on that for, oh I guess it was started while you were asleep. Anyhow, they decided to en-close all of *Gauntlet* in one huge blister. They say it will increase land area by one hundred and twenty-seven percent. Nick requested a meeting with you tomorrow. I imagine he'll brief you on everything. I suppose he thought you might need today to recover from your sleep."

"I don't understand."

"Understand what Phil?"

His eyes bore into her. "Listen to me. Even when they complete the blister they can't live out there. The light's too weak and quickly the radia-tion buildup would be deadly. Nothing would survive, especially humans. What in hell are they thinking of? Do I have to be on hand every fucking minute?"

Both ladies looked ill at ease. The evening clearly was not proceeding totally as they had planned.

Anne tried to mollify. "There's a great deal more than dark-side building going on here. Look Phil. We've all got to take our turns at the *North Pole.* Life will go on without us. In fact we're all facing three such sleeps before we arrive *Kosmas.* You elected to take the 'pole' position. To be the first. Which was likely to be the most difficult. Whatever. You've got two years of catching up to do and you can't let every unexpected change piss you off." She looked at him, head down, eyebrows raised, an expectant look adorning her face.

Phil's dartingly downcast eyes revealed his grudging acquiescence. "All the same, if I find this is simply damned foolishness, Nick's going to have a lot to …"

"Please hear him out before you …"

"Alright let's order." Phil signaled a waiter.

"Triple Scotch-rocks with a twist." He glanced around. "Two more what? Sixty-Sixes? Sixty-Nines? Is that what you …"

Aiy spoke up before the waiter had time to become confused. "Two Seventy-Sevens with 'A Super Nova Collapsing into a Neutron Star' please."

"Right away." He hurried away.

"So you can order the subject as well as the drink. Clever." He picked up his menu. "So what's good here?"

Anne and Aiy grinned conspiratorially. "We suggest the Steak Diane. It's fabulous. Flambéed tableside with cognac and cream and a few secret ingredients."

"Sold."

Their drinks came. Aiy ordered. Phil nursed his Scotch and began to relax. "This place really is incredibly beautiful. I can almost rationalize encasing our entire little planet like this for no other reason than the pure esthetics of ..." His voice trailed off. He realized he was speaking only to himself. Anne and Aiy were totally consumed by their Seventy-Sevens. He watched them savor their drinks in unbridled happiness. He felt a little envious. *I'm going to have to try one of those things.*

Their meal arrived. Three Steak Diane. Three copper pans. Three burners. The waiter skillfully blended butter, shallots, Worcestershire Sauce, garlic, mushrooms, lemon, mustard, and on each in turn an intriguing miasma of spices, until an intoxicating aroma and an elegant, rich brown sauce emerged. The steaks were perfectly finished. Seared to a superb crispness enclosing an incredibly tender rare-to-medium-rare steak. Finally he blended in a generous portion of cognac; and just before serving, poured the remaining cognac over the dishes and their edges to ignite the cognac. A quick flambé, *et voilà!* Steak Diane.

Phil was starved and after a quick *bon appétit*, immediately attacked his steak, overlooking all accompaniments. When he'd consumed the steak, he looked up. Mouth full, still chewing and mumbled "That was absolutely ..." For the second time this evening, his voice trailed off.

He swallowed.

***

He was in bed with three women. Great beauty and breathtaking physical perfection. Three fleshy, lusty goddesses. Playful, happy, aroused, energetic, passionate, uninhibited, inventive and totally obsessed with him. The stuff of fantasies, dreams and love sonnets. He experienced the most profoundly erotic experience of his life. Mentally it persisted for well over two hours in beds, Jacuzzi, on floors, with drinks, and many diverse pleasures. Temporally it lasted for about nine seconds. When he rejoined the 'real world' Anne and Aiy were regarding him with wry amusement.

"Welcome home Phil. That was a little homecoming gift after your long sleep. Enjoy it?"

"Omigod! The sauce?"

"Yep."

"Could you … could you tell what I was experiencing?" He suddenly felt self-conscious. Vulnerable. "What I was going through? How was I behaving?"

"Your behavior was exemplary. We promise. You simply looked a little … preoccupied for a few seconds. Otherwise it would be … embarrassing I suppose?" She couldn't suppress her smile.

"To say the least. Do those women really exist?"

They both chuckled. Aiy answered. "They sure do. Right here on Gauntlet. We call them the Aphrodite Triplets. We'll give you their real names and numbers. They're uh, *dyne-ta-meecha, Chib-Erd.* You really should give them a call. Otherwise they will really be most disappointed."

"How did you record it?"

"Well. We had to find a reasonable surrogate for you. We had to audition a few men for that role. That was fun. We already knew the ladies quite well. A fun-loving trio. Believe me. Then it was easy. Your surrogate engramatically recorded everything from your perspective. We composed the compound using the standard T-MAAM formulation sequence. Then our waiter worked it into your sauce. It was one hellofa lot of fun, and a labor of love." She turned her head with a mischievous sideways glance. "And it was all Anne's idea."

"I appreciate it. Believe me. If you have any leftover compound, save it for me!"

He thought for a moment. "I should have realized it. If you can impart information at preternatural speed, you can certainly impart experiences as well. After all, what is an experience except subjective information? Wonderful. Imagine all things you could experience. A whole universe of …"

"They've formalized a new Department level discipline dedicated to this technology. Part science, part history, part entertainment, physiology and a lot of art. They call it AEI. Auto-Experiential-Ingestion. And it's far from simple sex romps and fun. That was just a taste Phil. A very small sample.

"Imagine this: Take two absolutely irreconcilable adversaries—say from the wretched days of the endless middle-eastern conflicts on what was once old Earth. Deadly, dehumanizing, or perhaps all too human, ugly and unworthy. So much bitter history it's impossible to find the truth. To find a solution, the original transgressors lost in a litany of blood and hate dating back decades, sometimes centuries. Some so far back they can hardly remember why they hate. Many don't even know.

"Assume they agree to, or are tricked into consuming AEI and exchange experiences. One seeing and feeling the pain and hatred of the other, for real. Finally really understanding the other's suffering. Perceiving the innocence, the rationale, the need, the outrage and the guilt. What do you suppose the result would be?"

Phil turned it over in his mind and kept returning to the same conclusion. "Peace. Unless one party encountered insanity, or simply an evil desire to continue the conflict without end; in which case they should seriously consider genocide, which I suppose ultimately they did."

"Exactly." They said softly in unison. Aiy continued, warming to the subject. "One aspect of AEI is final attainment of inter-human understanding. Relationships. Obliteration of the underlying causes of war and hatred and killing. One more interesting use: It's useful in *intra*-human understanding as well. Reliving a painful event, perhaps over and over. This promotes understanding. Reduces the pain. Sometimes eliminating it altogether. I'm thinking of attempting to recreate the Ghazi Kahn horror. Maybe I can remember."

"Are you certain you want to remember?"

"I'm tough Phil. You know that." She quickly grew very somber, somehow even demure. "In fact I have recorded an AEI for you."

"Yes?"

"Yes. It explains why I did what I did on Oneiro."

"I see. Please get it to me as soon as possible."

"I have. It's in your VarGrav-Cool-'n-Heat, in a beaker marked 'Tequila Sunrise'."

Phil said "I'll have it with breakfast tomorrow. Thank you Aiy. You've both been very thoughtful. I thank you for a fascinating evening." His eyelids drooped. "But I am suddenly very, very tired."

They practically carried him back to The Residence, kissed him goodnight, and saw him into bed. They then retired to their apartment.

As they walked hand in hand down the long hallway Aiy looked at Anne "I think he took it all pretty well. He's seems as strong and resilient as ever. And just out of the tank at that."

"Yes I agree. But …"

"But what?"

"He's got a long day ahead of him tomorrow."

***

The next morning found Phil on station. The command bridge. It felt good. Thankfully little had changed here. When his shift was over he retired to his briefing room, just off the dark and quiet command bridge to begin the process of catching up. He poured over the ship's log trying to find the key to the new Gauntites. He was soon disappointed. The logs contained only endless operational narratives. After an hour or so he closed the session in disgust. He was leaving his briefing room when there was a buzz at his door.

"Enter."

Commander Nick Farrow entered the room.

"Nick. Good to see you." Phil stepped forward to shake hands.

Nick's reaction bemused Phil. Instead of shaking hands, he backed up a step and stared at Phil's hand quizzically.

"Is there a problem XO?"

After a moment Nick grimaced self-consciously. "Good grief. I'm sorry Captain. I haven't shaken hands with anyone in well over a year. Gauntites just don't shake hands anymore. I actually don't know why." He grinned. "They're certainly happy to touch each other in any other way." He strode forward and extended his hand. Phil airily waved it away with a gesture and friendly shake of the head.

"Gauntites, movie stars, Star Levels, 360° external blisters, new words, new technology, T-MAAMs and such, and they tell me much, much more. You've been busy as hell XO. All of you."

"That's quite true Captain. I'm unable to exactly pin down when it started, but something significant has been occurring aboard ship for well over a year. Everyone has incredible energy. Everything is changing at such a rate no one can keep up with it. Gauntites constantly become more talented and physically adept. There seems to be only one real constant in Gauntian culture now."

"What would that be?"

"Permission to speak candidly sir?"

"Certainly."

"You. You sir. You are the anchor of constancy that the entire crew seems to cling. They love the changes. They innovate them and catalyze them. Cascading exponential permutation, sometimes cascading regression. They've changed themselves in some basic manner I cannot quantify. Yet they all, without exception, need *you*. This cannot be attributable simply to your rank. It is in part a tribute to your command. Your leadership. But they sense in you a key to their destiny somehow. The only word I can think of, if you'll permit, is *godhead*."

"Strange. That's the second time I've heard that term recently. Are you implying our Gauntites have found some sort of *religion*?"

"Not in the least sir. But I'm sure you realize that their upbringing on Oneiro—an upbringing you helped to guide—emphasized emotional control, adaptability and above all, self-reliance. A faith-based belief in nothing, save rationality and one's self. As far as I know, no human creature is truly capable of such sufficiency. That's the main reason why peddlers of religion prosper I suppose."

"That would seem to suggest there was some error in their inculcation."

"Not at all. Their evolution and competency has advanced beyond any expectation. I'm simply stating that humans, even those as exceptional as the Gaunti, need an anchor. Something stronger and autonomous. You."

Phil regarded Nick for a few moments.

"Nick I know you maintain the XO's Log."

"Yes sir."

"Does is contain *more* than just ships operations, heading, velocity and that sort of thing?"

"In fact it does. I record nearly everything that takes place aboard this vessel."

"May I view it?"

"Certainly sir. It is constantly available to you. Just request XO-LOG."

"That's fine. I will go over your logs in detail, which will save us a long debrief. I do have one question through."

"Sir?"

"Why in hell's name are you constructing a transparent blister enclosing the entire ship?"

"To be honest sir, I wanted to await your approval. But the colonists were adamant, almost violent in fact, as well as remarkably persuasive. But the prime moving factor was the Colonists."

"The *Colonists*?"

"That will need some explanation sir. If you would please bear with me?"

"Okay. Proceed."

"The blister project was ostensibly justified for several reasons. Esthetics, additional space, study (it's even more effective than the Spheriscope), and a home for the colonists. We have a backlog of associated projects competing for resources. Therefore, an undertaking of this scale is quite helpful."

"Where did you find the materials?"

"We're partly hollowing out Mount Gaunti."

"What in hell's name is that doing to our angle of attack, our moment arm balance adjustments, energy consumption, gravity control, aspect targeting of the scoop and a hundred other things goddamnit?"

"We calculated that quite carefully before beginning. We considered every aspect that might be affected in the least. The result is we have improved Gauntlet's operational efficiency by over 28%. We may actually be able to exceed 77% light speed by a small margin."

Phil mind was racing. "I'm not even going to ask what the hell a 'colonist' is just now. I simply want to know if you have forgotten no human can survive extended periods on the surface, even under that damned blister, or have you all gone fucking insane?"

"With all respect sir, that is simply no longer totally the case. Selected colonists not only survive the radiation, they thrive in it. In some respects they appear almost QAVL-like. Our radiometry studies have shown they are now able to absorb electromagnet radiation directly. They feed on it. They crave it. They yearn for the surface; and if their development continues in the same direction, they will die *without* it."

"Have they abandoned normal food?"

"No. Not altogether." He smiled. "They uh, *swing both ways*. Though I strongly suspect they would like to renounce Bayronatae nourishment altogether."

"How did this come about?"

"There's a small blister at the south pole originally planned for selected botanical research. Suddenly one day some of the children …"

"*Children*!?"

Farrow patiently pushed on. "Some of the children discovered it and were crowded around it. Then the numbers began growing. There's a large blister there now and it is hugely popular. The next step was constructing Star Level for The Gaunti Café. The next step is … well as you've seen sir."

"What the hell do you mean, *children*? Where the fuck did they come from?"

"Ah. That's rather complicated sir; and we simply don't have answers. The children are what we refer to as *colonists*. We're trying to work up a complete report for you, if you would allow us just a little more time?"

"Damned little time, XO. Are these … these radiation eaters … normal in other respects?"

"They appear to be. We are still investigating those aspects."

"What is Dr. Singe's opinion?"

"Dr. Singe is performing the study personally. So far he is flummoxed."

"These *children*, are they happy? Productive? Team players?"

"Yes, yes and guardedly yes."

"The entire crew?"

"No sir. Only a percentage of the er, colonists."

"I don't know why you're tiptoeing around this *colonist* business, but for the time being, what percent of these colonists are radiation eaters?"

"Exactly fifty percent of the colonists have metamorphosed in this manner."

"This is the Goddamnedest piece of business I've ever heard of. I should bust you down to grounds keeper." Phil glared at his XO for several long moments. "Is that percentage stable?"

"It is unchanged for 193 days now, sir. Dr. Singe hypothesizes that they have been absorbing trace amounts of radiation through the hull, which stimulated biological demand as it were. What he terms *redaptive prosōpopoeia.*"

"Now there's a mouthful. I'm not even going to ask what it means."

"That's good. I'm not sure I understand the term myself Captain. Something about bio-reverse-engineering a pseudo-masking function, or some such ..."

"So they progressively require more doses, or stronger doses?"

"No sir. Their requirements have not fluctuated for several months now."

"You're measuring this?"

"We monitor their intake constantly Skipper."

"Has Singe searched for genetic variances?"

"Thus far he has found none."

Phil was beyond amazed. He hoarsely uttered "QASI?"

"Yes Philip. This is factual Philip. We are attempting to understand the mechanism at work here. Thus far we have failed. Something keeps blocking our probes."

"What?"

"We believe it is you Philip."

"*I beg your pardon Ambassador?*"

"You Philip. You stand between our probes and your crew. We are aware you are not doing this consciously. Nonetheless, you seem responsible. Sleeping or awake."

"Cuter all the fucking time. Are you sure of this. How can you tell?"

"It is quite simple really. Our probes physically and continuously point to you. Very much like old style human radio jamming, the source of the overriding transmission is traceable. In a sense we triangulated you."

"What sort of probe?"

"We should think that was obvious Philip. We probe to locate and track the granular flow of particles at the extreme gradient of downward spiraling displacement. This is the same technique you are presently excogitating."

Phil peered at the XO, his manner not the friendliest. "I know I'm just out of the tank and I'm aware life goes on. You had command of this vessel and you therefore had authority to undertake all you have described. I hate to think about what you may have *not* described as yet. All the same I'm not one damned bit pleased with your performance. I will review your logs and investigate the nature of all this foolishness. I will then make two decisions.

"First, I will decide whether to cancel all work in process.

"Second, I will review the command structure functioning in my absence. We are in the purview of many sleeps and I must ensure there is a steady hand at the helm."

His stare drilled into Farrow for long moments.

"That will be all Commander Farrow. I will contact you when I have completed my analysis. Let me know immediately when you've formulated the report on these *children*."

"Certainly sir." He quickly withdrew.

"QASI, I begin to fear for our mission. I have neither understanding, nor knowledge of, nor control over these events; and I am not at all sure I ever shall. Even you are unable to explain these manifestations."

"Not at this time Philip. Perhaps if we collaborated and you were to attempt to cease your interference."

"I haven't the slightest goddamned idea how to approach such a thing. How can I remove a block when I don't know how I'm creating it to begin with? I badly need your help. My question to you is this: *Should we consider coming about?*"

No response was forthcoming.

"QASI?"

"QASI?"

"*QASI?*"

"Please excuse us Philip. We must depart Gauntlet."

"*What? Goddammit!*" Phil was nearly screaming.

QASI responded very quietly. Gently.

"We would remind you Captain, you are addressing an Ambassador of the QAVL civilization."

"I would remind you Ambassador, you are addressing an Ambassador of Earth and the Captain of this vessel."

"Acknowledged, Captain."

Phil took a long slow breath.

"Forgive me Ambassador. These are difficult times. I trust you understand. I hope I have not offended, or jeopardized our relationship, upon which I place great consequence."

"We hold our friendship in highest esteem as well Philip. Please understand that duties demand our urgent attention elsewhere. We have no latitude in this. We extend our apologies."

Farewell my Fremd

"YOUR *APOLOGIES*? YOU are leaving us QASI? Here? Now? At the merest beginning of a voyage such as mankind has never before undertaken—foisted upon us by you I would add."

"We are leaving Philip. Uncle HERB will proctor in our stead. You are aware he is superbly capable to perform on our behalf. As to the question of *foisting*, we freely confess your assertion is not entirely inaccurate."

"So you're deserting us, just as you abandoned Earth to its poisonous fate."

"We have pressing matters awaiting us Philip."

"I see. After two million years of observation, humans suddenly have minimal import for you?"

"Philip, there are beings in this galaxy that view Bayronatae life as no more than animate, corporeal encrustations which inevitably befoul the surface of otherwise beautiful planetary bodies—the mold that forms on bread, the slime that cumulates a ship's hull, the ..."

"I get the picture Ambassador."

"The QAVL are not amongst them. We are convinced you appreciate that. And frankly Philip, two million years is but the blink of an eye."

"You *de facto* profess we are no more than *junk life*. Forms to be disregarded and discarded?"

"The QAVL make no such distinction, Philip. Such judgment resides solely within the province of the cosmos."

"Yet you countenance our fate. You made no effort to save us. In fact you were instrumental in bringing this down upon us. You simply made a callous assumption: They will extinct themselves in any event, so let them do it now."

"How many such forms shall we save Philip? Earth? A hundred more worlds? A million? A hundred million? A billion? How shall we save them? Scurrying about the galaxy in a bacchanalian frenzy of resurrection? Shall we adopt all the cosmos into our *incorporeaum*? Change the nature of their existence? Change the nature of the universe? You are far too intelligent and realistic to make such judgment Philip. And if nothing else, you well know we are not by nature, imperious."

"You evade the primary question QASI. Why *now*? Why did your race take it upon themselves to destroy mankind … *now*?"

Phil thought he could almost hear QASI sigh.

"The universe evolves along an immutable process, consistent with canonic physics, as any closed mass-energy system must. And believe us Philip, despite the colossal dimensions involved and the infinity of its horizon, we exist within a closed system. Humans are part of that majestic process, and in truth are never really lost for the duration of extant reality. Is that not sufficient, Phillip?"

"Sufficient? That is the extent of your perception of human aspiration?"

"Philip. Our perception might be described thusly, without rancor, without antipathy. Listen to us Philip. Please listen carefully:

Imagine all of humankind, all of Earth, as an infinitely tiny flower. Beautiful, unique and precious at the petals. Mundane at the stem. Hideous at the root. In relative size this flower is virtually invisible. An ethereal mote nestled within the moss entwined within the roots of a colossal tree in an unthinkably vast and ancient forest. The forest is swiftly being converted to carbon allotrope, inanimate carbon, in the throes of a raging entropic conflagration nearly as immense as the cosmos themselves. In infinitely less than the blink of an eye, the flower is carbonized.

"You would hold the QAVL responsible for such?"

Quiet for a time …

"Philip, there was nothing any being, of any description, anywhere in the universe could have done to preserve this flower, save the nature of the universe itself, which we know to be supremely indifferent.

"This flower possessed a beauty for a time. However, in the pattern of the cosmos, its coming and passing literally had no meaning whatsoever." QASI paused for a moment, emphasizing his next statement. *"None Philip."*

"Such flowers evolve and bloom and die throughout the universe with a cold impassive savagery near beyond comprehension. Numbers that defy reckoning. We can no more deliver these flowers than any other life form. Such is precisely their due, no more, no less.

"Conversely, from time to time, the QAVL reflect over such beauty, appreciate its form, and perhaps preserve some small token before they fade. *Phillip, you are such.*"

There was a long interval of stony silence.

"I will share another related reality with you Philip."

"Yes?"

"All sentient beings, at some time in their lives imagine or even seriously consider if by some action of their own doing they may have inadvertently destroyed another sentient being, or beings, or perhaps entire civilizations. Perhaps repeatedly—by the hundreds or thousands, or millions."

"What beings? What actions?"

"Have you never poured a chemical down a drain to unblock its piping?"

"Yes. Yes I have."

"And did it occur to you that you might be destroying uncountable other creatures?"

"Of course. It's unavoidable. Microbes. Boil water, apply antiseptic to a wound, walk across a grassy knoll, and thousands of other actions. To what sort of creatures do you refer?"

"Microscopic creatures and others millions of times smaller. Sentient and intelligent."

"This is possible?"

"Most certainly. Throughout the universe. Many incredibly advanced."

"How?"

"As with all life throughout the universe, particles even as tiny as SNA have the ability to organize themselves into animate forms. Life. And as you know, intelligence—ultimately sentience and stupendously more—emerge from no more than survival adaptation."

"So. What are you saying QASI? I shouldn't unclog my drains?"

"This involves infinitely more than your drains, as I am sure you are aware."

"What's your point QASI?"

"You cannot move, live, eat, drink, think, or exist in any civilized manner without such destruction. Their end is an inevitable and unavoidable consequence of cosmic existence. Thus be the existential extent of their due and their sufficiency."

"I understand."

"We believe you do."

"Now I'll tell *you* a story QASI."

"Yes?"

"Are you familiar with the terrestrial reptile known as the *Blind Snake*?"

"Blind Snake. Kingdom Animalia. Phylum Chordata. Subphylum Vertebrata. Class Reptilia. Order Squamata. Suborder Serpentes. Family Leptotyphiopae. Genus Leptotphlops. Leptotyphlops Humilis ... indigenous exclusively to Planet Earth ... primarily what was previously known as Northern Mexico and the Southern United States ... sustaining themselves on a diet largely consisting of the larvae and eggs of termites and ants. A true snake. Non-venomous. Retrograde, degenerate eyes covered by scales. Known to inhabit depths of up to sixty meters, most commonly in desert areas where the soil is easier to navigate. It will often ..."

Phil interrupted irritably. "Yes. Yes. I see you are familiar with the Blind Snake."

An awkward silence ensued for a moment, then Phil continued.

"The only time I happened upon such a creature, I was a small boy living in Washington D.C. There was a beautiful park very near our home ..."

"Dumbarton Oaks Park. We are aware of this."

In no mood for interruption, Phil made no response.

"I came upon this wondrous little being in a small clearing. He was a gorgeous jet-black, about twenty centimeters long, very slim. He was being attacked by fire ants, and losing, but he was not yet seriously harmed, so I brushed away the ants, gently gathered the tiny snake in my hands and carried him to another quarter of the park, out of harm's way."

"You refer to it as 'he.' You are able to differentiate these reptiles by sex?"

Is this QASI's attempt at humor?

Again Phil refused to respond.

"When I set him down I realized how delicate he was, and how alien the surface world was to him. I somehow sensed his confusion and disorientation. He felt the sun's warmth. He even appeared to perceive the light, though he had no eyes I could observe. I watched enraptured as he timidly, yet bravely quested this new reality, gently raising or lowing his tiny head. Outreaching slowly left to right.

"He was totally ill equipped to survive this environment, yet he continued to quest about this strange world, seeking to understand. I found it very beautiful. I carefully moved him into the shade of a large tree and gently covered him in the tree's loamy soil."

Phil said no more, so QASI prompted him. "Your point Philip?"

Phil imposed a steely pause. In his own time, he countered sharply.

"Though he was categorically incapable of survival, he was not unworthy of salvation."

Moments passed. When QASI did respond, there was a subtle harshness in his tone.

"You will rejoin us on Kosmas, Philip, and your ordeal will truly begin. Meanwhile, listen to Uncle HERB. Learn from him. You have much to learn. Far more than you know. I have instructed Uncle HERB to provide you two documents. Both were intimately involved with Earth's final, and now deceased United Nations Secretary General, Dr. Aoko Itō. They address the end of man's world. We believe you will read them with interest. You may benefit from them.

"Farewell Philip."

***

Phil was suddenly very much alone. He turned to his computer interface. "Computer."

"Active."

"Current velocity."

"Seventy-one percent light speed."

"Time to maximum velocity."

"Four solar days."

"Heading and destination."

"185.63325 29.89598611. The planet *Kosmas*."

"ETA."

"One-four-point seven-six-two-five solar years."

"Ship's status."

"Thrusters nominal. Grav nominal. Nav nominal. Environmental nominal. Nutrition nominal …" After completing a lengthy monologue: "Computer nominal."

"XO-LOG for preceding twenty-four months."

A text display filled his screen. Page one of eight thousand twenty-two.

"Forward XO-LOG to my Residence. Personal Interface."

"XO-LOG is currently available to PI-932C."

"Of course. I should have known."

"Say again please."

"Never mind. Session closed."

"Acknowledged."

"Jacob Whitecap."

"Whitecap here."

"Jake. Where are you?"

"Captain. How are you sir? Up and about?"

"Yes. Where are you?"

"I've been working on the blister project for the last six months or so. I'm sorry. I would have most certainly been at the residence had I been informed you were awakened."

"No problem Jake. Let's meet at the residence in about an hour."

"Bloody Marys will be standing by."

"I think Martinis are called for."

"Aye Sir. So shall it be."

***

"Well Jake what do you think?" The two were now on the terrace overlooking Gaunti in the company of an icy pitcher of Martinis.

"Think about what sir?"

"QASI has left for parts unknown. Oneirons are now Gauntites.

"There are some kinds of crazy passengers—they're calling them children, or colonists for some reason—and I have no clue who the hell they are, or where they came from. Half want to live on the surface eating charged particles. I hardly understand the language now. I've been accused of blocking efforts to understand new aptitudes in the crew, through means totally unbeknownst to me. I can't decide whether we should come about and get the hell back to Earth, or push on to Kosmas."

"That's quite a list."

"It sure as hell is. And it's been only one day. Suggestions?"

"I have one immediate suggestion."

"Good. What?"

"Forget about coming about."

"Explain."

"Philip, surely we haven't so tormented ourselves and the Earth, just to turn tail and run home? That's not you Philip. Besides they'd probably find a way to kill you on Earth, if they learned you'd turned back. Hell, they might find a way to kill you on *Gauntlet.*"

"Christ. Am I safe from *you* Jake?"

"For the time being, yes."

"I think I'll call a general meeting of ship's compliment. Tell them what I think and what we will do. Lay it out for them and let them debate it with me if they'd care to. If after all, they need me more than life itself. They think I'm some sort of rock star, and at least half of them are deeply in love with me."

"Sir?"

"Apparently you've been out of the loop as well Jake."

"What will you tell them?"

"Haven't a clue."

"What are you going to do?"

"Go down to the sea."

***

The next morning Jake and Phil were quietly breakfasting by the pool. "Jake did you receive a beaker labeled 'Tequila Sunrise'?"

"Right here Philip."

"Got a question for you."

"Sure."

"This T-MAAM stuff. Know much about it?"

"What would you care to know?"

"Is there an antidote?"

"I don't understand."

"What if I were to have what they used to call a 'bum trip?'"

"I know that term from long, long ago."

"Okay. So if things aren't going well, or I just don't care for it, is there a chemical antidote? Some form of escape?"

"Philip, most treatments last less than twenty seconds."

"In this case, twenty seconds could feel like a lifetime. And if you're T-MAAMing the QAVL Documents you could be facing hours. Either way, I might want to just stop it."

"Give me just a minute please."

Jake was gone nearly twenty-five minutes, while Phil passed time scanning ship's logs. A frustrating pursuit at best.

"They just delivered this." He handed Phil a bottle of small white capsules. "If you suspect you may want to end the session, put this in your mouth as soon as you start the session, retain it between your molars. Bite down firmly to exit. That is, if you've been able to sustain the awareness needed to exercise the option."

"This doesn't dissolve?"

"No sir."

"Alright. We're in business. Hand me the drink please. Sorry, this is one drink I can't share with you."

"That's quite alright Captain. You are most welcome to it. Here you are sir." He handed Phil an attractive pinkish-orange drink. The VarGrav-Cool-'n-Heat had perfectly preserved the drink complete with ice cubes, straw, orange slice, even to the red-to-orange bottom-to-top color spectrum that earned the drink its name.

Phil drained the glass, placed the capsule between his teeth and lent back in his chair.

***

He was terrified. No. She was terrified. Real fear. Serious danger. Phil hadn't felt such emotions in years; and it felt awful. Nauseating. Demeaning. They (whoever they were) had her father. They'd brutally murdered her photographer. They'd made threats upon her life; and she knew they were for real. They'd tricked and defrauded her, leading her to believe she would have the story of the century, and maybe she did, but these murderous liars really knew nothing about it. Now they were going to behead her father unless she stole the information they wanted and flee this beautiful island. She was going to betray Phil and Anne and all these people who had been so kind. Tragic. Unforgivable. But there was no choice.

And then these frighteningly bizarre communications. Over her radio, the TV, her phone, sometimes it seemed with no electronics at all. A voice, somehow not human, but friendly, advising her to do as they wanted. Urging her. It seemed wrong, but was for the best in the long run. Sometimes she felt as though she were going insane …

He … no she … was making desperate love to Anne. His body … no … her body … trying to forget her fear with passion and lust. She had loved very few people in her life. Her father. Her mother. A lovely boy in high school for one summer. Phil. Sex with the many. Love with the few. Men and women. Each had brought joys and fun and grace to her life. Now Anne? Yes. Absolutely. Her beauty, her mind, sensitivity and humor. She was a gentle, thoughtful lover, lavishly returning passion with passion, as strongly and more. She lost herself and her angst in the joys of Anne's flesh. After a time, they became creatures of sheer bliss. When the delightful, itchy needs of their bodies were slaked, she lay on her side caressing Anne's back.

"You know, it would be fun to take a trip to … Damn!" Her phone was calling out from her purse. She rose from the bed and strode to the living room. Phil looked down on him/herself appreciatively.

"Aiy?"

"Dad!" she whispered. "I've been so worried. Are you all right? Where are you? When can I see you?"

"This phone is secure?"

"I suppose so. They track incoming communications here. But as far as I know they don't monitor calls."

"Let's make this fast. You have the materials?"

"I will this morning. But …"

"Take out a sailboat this afternoon at 1500. Set course bearing at 57° North by Northwest. You will be picked up about an hour out and they'll take the boat from there. Got it?"

"Yes dad, but …" The phone went dead.

Guilt, fear, regret. They thundered down upon …

When it was over, Phil simply sat for a time, brooding with a bitterness matched only by his frenetic rage.

That idiot broad! She gave me more than she ever intended in this damned T-MAAM. She just didn't realize what it's capable of recording. I should shove her out a fucking airlock. Great looking. Dumb as a post. If she'd just had the brains and the balls to come to me, we could have saved her the agonies of hell, saved that moronic father of hers, and saved the entire goddamned Earth, billions of lives and destruction beyond belief. Anne was no damned better. Both of them thinking with their glands. And Aiy with that mysterious, mesmerizing little voice whispering to her over the phone, the TV, the radio …

That 'friendly little voice' wanted me off-planet. And it didn't give a damn about anything else. If she'd just told me. If she'd just told me! The bitch! The stupid little bitch!

***

Phil realized one of the best and one of the worst aspects of a personal T-MAAM was the truth. The recording media simply couldn't disguise the truth, because the listener was literally inside the recorder's mind … impossible to dissimulate, or to keep anything back. So Phil knew he'd just learned Aiy's subjective, absolute truth.

What would he do with that truth? Should they proceed to *Kosmas*? Thus far he'd been tricked and coerced and cajoled into this voyage. It was increasingly difficult to sort out friend from foe. And the price of this little cruise defied conception. The crew was increasingly restive. And he was constantly growing more concerned as to what human's true mission was to be on *Kosmas*. If he returned to Earth, assuming the QAVL would allow it, they would most certainly kill him. Earth would kill them all. He was growing increasingly more insular, a situation that would undoubtedly intensify.

He must beware of paranoia. No Captain Queen he. No weighing of sand for strawberries. Not quite yet anyhow. But whom could he trust? He was suddenly a stranger to the crew. A stranger in his home, to his lovers, even to *Gauntlet*. QASI deserted him (Thank god the he wasn't here for this T-MAAM recital.). In point of fact, how many QAVL might there really be aboard *Gauntlet*? There could be millions and he would never know. *Goddammit there went the paranoia …*

Jake quietly entered to see if he needed anything.

Phil thought he would be physically ill. He was so angry he was trembling and nauseous. He fought to control himself and didn't want to make a spectacle of himself in front of Jake.

Finally he looked up.

"Are you alright sir?"

"I'm fine Jake. And I'm finally beginning to understand what goes on around here." With that he moved to the solitude of his office.

Jake stared at Phil for a good deal longer than accepted Butler decorum.

"Commander Farrow."

"Farrow here Captain."

"Nick I'd like you to arrange a briefing for the entire ship's company. No exceptions. I want Bridge Crew in uniform. Front row. Supervisory systems on auto. It should last for about thirty minutes. No more. 1500 hours, eight days from now."

"That would be Friday ship's time."

"Fine."

"Venue?"

"Webber Park. The same site as our launch party as I recall. Arrange for decent weather."

"Refreshments?"

"Nothing."

"Object of the meeting?"

"I want to confirm our course and destination. And I want to confirm our protocols."

"Sounds a little ominous Captain."

"We'll see. Carr out."

***

Three nights later, Jake and Phil had just arrived atop Mount Gaunti with the customary pitcher of Martinis in tow. Without QASI, Jake couldn't help feeling like a second-string stand-in.

As darkness descended, all eyes aboard *Gauntlet* were fixed on the heavens wondering at a spectacle that would persist for more than ten solar years. Their mood part awe and part jubilant. Old-fashioned fireworks were scheduled for later.

Breathing rapidly, but lightly "There it is Jake. My God, it's beyond belief. [77*1.10] percent light speed—top speed for this vessel. As fast as any human has ever travelled, or is likely to on their own for the next hundred thousand years, if ever." Phil stared at the starry wonder with trembling intensity. "*Everything* is vindicated." He whispered "All the blood and work and death and grief. All wrapped up in this single moment. I wish I could …" He could no longer speak.

In an intensely personal moment, Phil placed his face in his two hands, remaining totally still for nearly a minute. He slowly raised his head and took a long breath and an equally long draw on his drink. He cleared his throat. "So. What do you think Jake?"

Jake was peering motionless at the heavens.

"Jake?"

"My gawd Philip. It's terrifying and it's the most beautiful thing I have ever seen. It's terrible. Bewildering. *Intoxicating.*" After a time he breathed. "What's going on out there?"

Both men were transfixed.

Without taking his eyes from the spectacle, Phil tried to explain. "As we approach light speed, we see bleeding. Spectral bleeding. Stars travelling towards us bleed blue. Receding stars bleed red. For the first time we can visually perceive our direction of travel. Blue forward. Red aft. Shift spectrum is determined by our relative perspective of a given star—light waves—compression or expansion of the light waves, as with sound waves. The phenomenon is termed the Doppler Shift.

"We also see, aberrations." He gestured "There and there. See the tunneling effect? We will adjust to it. The universe relative to us appears to contract, hence the tunneling. Things get shorter. Time slows down from an external relative perspective. As we go faster, our mass may approach infinity. Others believe we might become energy itself. I tend to subscribe to the latter.

"As we get closer and closer to infinite mass, we require corresponding proportional energy. We will never achieve a velocity, or mass remotely close to that. *Gauntlet* will neither achieve light speed, nor exceed it. This is all human knowledge I'm quoting you. Those little invisible bastards, the QAVL, have yet to impart their knowledge, if ever."

"Perhaps it's in the QAVL document?"

"Possibly. It is almost suspiciously intriguing they didn't convey a query capability with it."

"Perhaps they never needed such a tool."

"Interesting idea Jake. You may have something there."

"Does anything go faster than light?"

"Difficult question to answer directly. The speed of light in some respects is not constant. $E = mc2$ isn't necessarily the word of God. For example, as visible white light is exposed to a spectrum—say through a diamond—it is spectrally broken down and you could easily outrun it in your car. We have learned to manipulate temperature to the point of nearly achieving absolute zero Kelvin. At that coldness we can literally stop light. Moments after the Big Bang we speculate that the universe itself in its inflation period exceeded light speed. The QAVL travel faster than light routinely. However, they haven't the mass problem we do. Consider Special Relativity."

"Special Relativity?"

"What manner of brain food are you metrignosiculating? You should have covered General Relativity long ago, Quantum Mechanics and Neo-Unified-Qua-Strings. Long before we lifted off from Mount Anastasios in fact."

"To be honest, I still don't use the stuff. It gives me chicken-skin just to think about it. The idea of ..."

"Chicken-skin?" Phil asked sharply.

"You uh. You would call it goose-bumps I believe. Anyhow ..."

Chicken-skin. "You're not really an American, are you Jake?" Phil gave him a crooked, probing glance.

He seemed briefly perplexed. "Of course I am. I was born in the States. Chevy Chase, Maryland, in Montgomery Country, just outside Washington, D.C. But I grew up in Luxembourg. My father was in the Consular Service. We ah, returned to the States when I was about eighteen. *Anyhow,* I have a friend in Nutrition who supplies me food without the mumbo-jumbo-joy-juice thrown in. There's even a very small section dedicated to *Goon-Grub* as they call it, in Ship's Stores now. It has all the other benefits, geriatrics, nutrition, health and all that. It just does not impart information."

Phil shrugged. "Your choice I suppose. Have I answered your question?"

"Yes. Thank you, very nicely in fact. I believe I actually understood roughly a third of your explanation."

With a wry half smile "That's about what I understood too."

Concordia

AS PHIL HAD ordered: A lovely afternoon.

Ten years into the voyage there were now tall green trees throughout the park. The matured landscaping added color, depth and form. Rich grass under the dappled shade of the trees livened with the gay colors of flowers splashed throughout. Sunny. Not too warm. No breeze. Not a leaf moved. Nothing to interfere with acoustics. Only the cheerful sound of air monitor birds high above. The tiny flying machines were no longer necessary, but everyone had insisted they remain.

The hills to the north of the park were now lush terraces. Gauntian Chablis, Oneirion Bordeaux and Gaunti Pinot Noir Rosé. Lovely vineyards basking in the golden-flecked sunshine of the quiet afternoon.

Phil was relaxed at the podium, greatly enjoying the sleepy mid-summer's day.

That sounds like a dog barking! I wonder what the hell it really is.

Also as ordered: The Bridge, Engineering, Services and Security Crews decked out in full uniform (looking somewhat ill-at-ease) occupied the first four rows of carefully arranged chairs brought in specifically for this meeting. Webber Park was normally the scene of sunbathing, reading, romance, picnicking, informal sporting games, and the occasional riotous party. Today it exhibited the staid stateliness of a university commencement.

Behind the Ship's Compliment sat row upon row of Gaunti 'civilians', awaiting the words of their Captain. Everyone accounted for, on time and ready to begin. Unusual for an unruly bunch of independent, inter-stellar individualists.

The sole inhabitants of the last row: Anne, Aiy and Jake

Alone and apart as they were wont. The gnome schism between them ever widening, Phil supposed they might never be absorbed into native Gaunti. All the more so since Gaunti evolution had become such a fast moving target.

As he looked out onto the audience, he realized there wasn't a crewman amongst them he didn't know now. Some quite well. Many intimately. He felt friendship for every one; and hoped this afternoon's talk wouldn't change that. He had quite successfully remained apart and aloof. However, after ten years there were limits. Especially for a fit, good-looking, youngish man who wielded unquestioned authority, enjoyed celebrity status, and truly liked the ladies.

Phil stood and took his place mid-podium, spurning any amplification.

Without preliminary he spoke. His voice deeply resonated throughout the park, echoing from the hills. It seemed to reverberate from all the corners of their space-borne world. He began.

"We here, aboard this tiny remnant of our home world, are the bearers of human legacy: its hopes, its pride, its triumphs, its future, its shame and its failures. Your nightmares are your own, as are mine. Yet I will share one of my own: the monstrous burden this legacy conveys. It often finds me sweat drenched in the night, horrified that I might somehow misplace mankind's priceless trust. However, I believe mankind is fortunate. Its future has been placed in agile hands. Yours and mine. I will not lose my hand from this charge. Nor shall you. I will not permit it. I will *never* permit it.

"Gauntlet's crew and compliment are, or at least were, a family in the deepest sense. This was so when we embarked on our long odyssey. So shall we always be, or shall be again if somehow we have forsaken this precious alliance. If we betray our trust, our alliance, then we betray all of humanity. This must never pass.

"This is the purpose of our gathering today.

"As you know, I have just returned from my first Gaunti-Juvenate-Long-Sleep, or GJLS (pronounced Jai-liss) as it's now referred. On Earth it was simply called sleep, whatever its length. Times change regardless of our wishes, and we are called upon to adjust.

"This was my first of three outbound GJLS. The first on Gauntlet. The first in human history.

"After my awakening we made two minor modifications. One to limit REM sleep durations. The other to eliminate the interval between conscious brain revival and correlative physical reawakening. Aside from those two changes, I can report the procedure went flawlessly, with no physical or mental side effects whatsoever.

"I trust you find this good news.

"You're next.

"We will commence GJLS rotations effective Monday. Dr. Brian Meadows is charged with Roster & Rotation. He will be contacting you in due course, allowing you sufficient time to plan for a two-year hiatus. You will find the experience both interesting and in many respects, pleasant. It will also preserve your life. There is little choice in this matter if you wish to pass the remainder of your life on Oneiro, or anywhere else for that matter.

"I thought some words of introduction and advice might be appropriate at this time. We are all facing six such sessions for the round-trip duration of this voyage. Not something we may relish, but such are the means to ensure we will see our blue planet again.

"There is another aspect to this.

"Almost immediately, when I re-entered Gauntite society, I was shocked and not just a little taken aback by the changes conspicuous all about me. From your perspective these changes emerged as part of the routine progression of life on Gauntlet. These developments may have seemed quite normal, perhaps not even noteworthy from your perspective. From my perspective they were jarring. Revolutionary. Provoking in me what the twentieth century author Alvin Toffler called _Future Shock_. If you are unfamiliar with the term, he wrote a book by that name. You can find it in the ship's digital library. Well worth reading, even today."

Phil noted several affectionate and not unsympathetic grins throughout the audience. To many Gaunti, the concept of 'reading' a book, as opposed to 'eating' it was now an endearing anachronism.

"Each of us aboard Gauntlet has their own span of responsibility. Mine happens to include this entire vessel and crew, so perhaps it hit me harder than it might others. That notwithstanding, be aware when you absent Gauntlet's temporal ambience for two solar years, you will return to find change a taxing burden. You may bitterly resent such change, particularly if it impacts your previous span of control. Even if it does not, you will resent the world of Gauntlet continuing and evolving heedless of your absence, or wisdom.

"Having been there myself, I have some advice: Forget it. Get over it. Adapt to it as quickly as you can. I know that this exceptional crew can adapt faster than any humans in all history.

"Have no doubt: our society is the most dynamic in human history. Change is escalating, and will continue to escalate and at an escalating rate. We are confronted with a true exponential phenomenon; and not without its dangers. All will be challenged to figuratively 'hold onto our psycho-centric hats'. And it's going to get nothing but faster. God only knows what manner of human will arise in a hundred Earth years.

"And yet there is wonder here. We are realizing Dr. Webber's vision. Albeit he could never have foreseen Gauntlet, or the extinction of human civilization. Nonetheless, we are truly evolving into *Humanus Optimus*, exactly as Dr. Webber intended.

"He chose this direction with intelligence and purpose. He did so fully aware that therein lay great risk. Societal instability is perhaps one of the greatest. Especially when magnified by the lens of time—a volatile lever. Our tiny world could topple with an ill-timed word, a capricious act, the slightest imbalance, a moment of irresponsibility. All could be lost. Our mission failed. Perhaps all dead and we will have propelled Earth to its destruction, for naught.

"That will never come to pass. I will not allow it.

"Accordingly, the following enactments will take effect immediately. As you well know, Gauntlet is not governed by majority rule. Gauntlet's command hierarchy invests me with that responsibility. Consistent with this structure, this afternoon I seek your advice and council ... not your advice and consent."

Anne whispered to Aiy "This is not at all like Phil. They're not going to react well to his attitude." Aiy passed a concerned scrutiny throughout the audience.

***

Phil continued:

"We have three mandates to be respected above all else:

1. We must maintain course, speed and destination.
2. We must absorb the QAVL Documents.
3. We must arrive Kosmas and return Earth when our work is complete."

A crewman activated a large graphic display to the left of the platform.

"These mandates will be permanently affixed to the Command Center. Beyond these mandates, I see no reason why Gaunti society should not enjoy the fluidity flourishing aboard this vessel today. Freedom. Creativity. Enjoyment. Fulfillment. Progression."

A crewman activated another display on the right side of the podium.

"To balance a fluid, rule-free society with a disciplined ship's crew over a period of seventeen years is no easy undertaking. This delicate equilibrium is complicated by our three intermittent sleep hiatus' of twenty-four months.

"Hence the rationale for these three Enactments, or perhaps Restatements is a better term:

1) Any proposed modifications to Gauntlet's superstructure, environmental, propulsion, nutritional, or navigation systems must be approved by the Captain, or the Captain's designee, or the Captain's digital surrogate, at the direction of the Captain.

2) Any action in violation of a mandate is prohibited unless sanctioned by the Captain, or the Captain's designee, or the Captain's digital surrogate, at the discretion of the Captain.

3) No mandate may be modified without the approval of the Captain, or the Captain's designee, or the Captain's digital surrogate, at the discretion of the Captain.

These orders specifically address those periods when I am in GJLS, although they remain in effect at all times. These will also be posted outside the Command Center.

"That is all I have for you today, unless there are questions or comments."

<u>Question.</u> What is 'the Captain's digital surrogate'?
<u>Response:</u> At my direction, Dr. Williams in AI is constructing a digital construct of me. When it has been fully qualified, in my absence, or the absence of my designee, it will act with my full authority.

<u>Question.</u> What about the existing chain of command?
<u>Response:</u> It remains unchanged.

<u>Question.</u> How can it be unchanged with an AI program commanding in your stead?
<u>Response:</u> Because the reporting hierarchy, beginning with the Executive Officer, is entirely unchanged.

<u>Question.</u> Should we regard this as some sort of *de facto* plebiscite?
<u>Response:</u> (Phil shook his head in resigned distaste.) Next question.

<u>Question.</u> Should I interpret your response in the negative or positive?
<u>Response:</u> Your interpretation is irrelevant to me. The best interpretation is I don't respond worth a damn to wittily contrived and truculent jibes. Keep them to yourself, or save them for the bars. (The audience sat in stunned silence.) Next?

<u>Question.</u> Does this imply that projects in process must be halted awaiting approval?

<u>Response:</u> That would depend on the project, case-by-case. I couldn't tell you in advance, or without further information. I suggest you check with your department head, or the XO. I do require that you operate within the chain-of-command.

<u>Question.</u> If a modification is refused, do we have any recourse?
<u>Response:</u> Do you have any today?

<u>Question.</u> About this 'balance' between a free, fluid society and a well-disciplined crew. The crew has a command reporting. Should there be a formal structure governing and protecting our civil society?
<u>Response:</u> That seems excessive. We have seldom, if ever, required a formal social organization. And I wonder why you would restrict the freedoms we have just to form some sort of governmental structure of dubious, or at least unknown utility. But there is absolutely nothing precluding it. If you feel the need, and everyone agrees, please proceed. Hold a goddamned plebiscite if you wish. I will attempt to accommodate any form you select. Bear in mind though, the total ship's crew is not a military organization *per se*. Neither is it really civil either. The *Platonic watchdog* has no place aboard my ship.

<u>Question.</u> Is there really any material difference between these mandates and enactments, and the way the ship is run today?
<u>Response:</u> No. Not really. I'm glad you asked the question. More than anything else these points serve more to clarify and remind. Call it a policy statement, re-enforcing our determination to complete this mission.
<u>Response:</u> I disagree. This approval structure seems new and very restrictive.

<u>Question:</u> You subscribe to the Mandates?
<u>Response:</u> Yes. Yes, I do.
<u>Response:</u> Then you'll feel no restrictions at all.

"Are there any other questions?"
Silence.

"Very well. These documents will be posted *verbatim*. Dismissed."

***

As they moved away, Aiy turned to Anne "I don't understand. I didn't see the need for this meeting at all. Couldn't he have issued some Command Directive or something? What the hell is troubling him? I really don't understand."

"Neither me. Autocracy runs contrary to Phil's nature. He certainly wasn't comfortable with it. Yet he always knows what he's about. I assume he does now. Either he sees something we don't, or he's up to something we have yet to fathom. Or both."

Anne shook her head in bewilderment as they strolled out of the park.

Gifts & Gaffs

PHIL WOBBLED INTO The Residence after seventy-two non-stop hours on the surface. Hot, exhausted and dirty. He didn't know if he was welcome on the construction site, so he worked side-by-side for hours sweating in his radiation suit.

The QAVLian spinning process used to manufacture Gaunti-Glass was impressively fast, and remarkable to observe. Life supporting atmosphere and warmth filled the ballooning blister as it raced across the surface of *Gauntlet*. *Gauntlet's* slate-gray granite spheroid vanished beneath the tough, flexible crystalline shell with dramatic speed. Work would be completed within a matter of weeks, and *Gauntlet's* days of explosively erupting from volcanic mountainsides would be rendered structurally impractical.

All the same, while customized Bayronatae tools had been developed for human use, the process itself was never designed for human proximity. The work proved extremely messy, generating suffocating heat, producing dense, deadly smog. This required they wear protective clothing and breathing adapters. Hot, dirty, uncomfortable. Were it not for life-preserving continuous FOND misting, Phil would have ordered the operation terminated immediately. Exacerbating this was the smell and mess generated by continuous foamy extrusion of the new exterior's unique rubbery landscape, which Phil found disturbingly reminiscent of Onerio's one-time and long-passed nursery.

Phil left the XO in charge and joined the crews to see for himself just what was being constructed. He also wanted to demonstrate his interest in the project. Reaction from his meeting in Webber Park apparently ran from indifferent, to lukewarm, to mildly resentful. Although there had been no overt expressions of dissent, a little fence mending seemed called for all the same.

The enormous blister was fascinating. No walls, or buildings, or roads, no geographic features, nothing. The alien landscape was broken only by massive, transparent QAVL-Glass pillars. A dark spongy surface was molded into a world of bizarre, black rubbery forms designed for sitting and sleeping. Interspersed throughout with thousands of pools for uses ranging from bathing to drinking to sanitation to excise emulsified nutrients. Some, such as sanitation, voided themselves dynamically. Every pool softly glowed with a colored light designating its use. For obvious reasons, misuse of pools was to be avoided. A surprising variety of micro-biologicals were capable of thriving in the radiation-bathed environment and therefore mutating at an alarming rate. As a precaution the spongy surface was honeycombed with a vast FOND misting system.

Phil found the new landscape oppressive and joyless.

As he looked about he thought *these weird-ass colonists, or whatever they are, are welcome to it.*

It was beyond bizarre that Phil appeared to unquestioningly accept the sudden appearance of several dozen *colonists*. What were they? Where did they come from? How did they get here? What was their intent? Superficially it seemed Phil had no interest in such issues. Was he dissimulating a lack of concern? Was he conducting his own investigation surreptitiously? Or was something blocking *him*?

All good questions.

No good answers.

The intended Outworld inhabitants apparently had no wish for communications, transport, entertainment, lighting, food, or shelter. Not exactly a fun loving bunch by his measure. Phil had invested some time in attempting to understand their need for such an environment. He spent time with them jogging, at meals, during breaks, personal interviews and so on. They were as intelligent, open and friendly as always, except in discussing their new living area. In this, they exhibited an offhanded, clearly practiced reticence. As this project was now deemed to be within guidelines, Phil determined not to probe too aggressively for the moment.

They were totally reliant on *Gauntlet's* DAR Systems for evasion of foreign objects. Any failure would result in catastrophic decompression of the vast area and certain death for all within. Accordingly, Phil overruled their dark predilections, ordering that every two hundred square meters be equipped with full communications and emergency capabilities, 360° visual monitors installed in conjunction with an extensive high-energy proto-phosper lighting system.

He had seriously considered countermanding the entire project, ordering its immediate halt and dismantlement, and perhaps imposing disciplinary measures against its initiators. But upon studying the project he discovered to his extreme disquiet the intensity of their need for this environment, as well as a surprising level of enthusiasm and diligence. Considering how near completion it was, he decided to keep the peace for the moment. He could always order evacuation of the surface and destroy the spherical sheathe. So why create widespread dissent—at least for the short-term?

Aside from the crystal clear, LSP (Limited-Semi-Permeable) bubble encasing *Gauntlet,* the most challenging engineering arose on *Gauntlet's* crust. Within a margin of .0000387 microns, gravity would shift both direction and source. In a literal instant, centrifugal force shifted to centripetal force. With absolute equilibrium, gravity would push outward (the interior of *Gauntlet*) and within the same atom, push inward (the exterior of *Gauntlet*). The 'floor' of an internal dweller would also be the 'floor' of a surface dweller. Difficult to engineer. Difficult to balance. Any imbalance in excess of .008868 milligrams per square centimeter would literally tear *Gauntlet* apart. The solution demanded a profound faith in QAVLian gravity engineering, as well as measurement apparatus so sophisticated, it defied understanding. Phil was fascinated and not just a little apprehensive. This was the most disturbing aspect of the project he had yet encountered.

He entered his Residence, stomping off foam dust and blister detritus.

"Damn what a three-day." He threw himself down on a Gaunti-Plast chair, impervious to dirt. "Jake, I could use a Gin and Tonic the size of Shark Bay."

"Coming right up Skipper. It's good to have you back. May I join you?"

"Absolutely."

Surrendering to Jake's wrinkled-nosed, eyebrow-jumping goading, they were now more appropriately settled on the terrace, "When I finish this, all I want is a bath and a sleep round the clock."

"Nothing to eat Philip?"

"No thanks Jake. Just bath and sleep."

Jake smiled broadly. "Well. I believe you're in luck sir. You can do both."

"What are you taking about Jake?"

"A little surprise. Care to visit your bathroom?"

Phil looked dubious and exhausted but good-naturedly trailed after Jake nonetheless.

***

It had been many years since anyone had surprised Phil with a lavish gift, or an expansive gesture. This was both.

"Happy birthday Captain." beamed Jake.

Gauntites (as they were now known), don't celebrate birthdays, as they weren't really borne *per se*. They were issued 'Birth Certificates' as conventional points of reference. However, the only indicator of any real import was their Series Designation.

If anything, they could claim only their germination-day, which seemed irrelevant. Therefore birthday celebrations were non-existent, essentially confined to Landers. Even Landers found chronological age held less interest, due to the increasingly potent geriatric adjuvant.

In any event, some thoughtful soul had taken the time to research his date of birth and contrive a gift.

***

During Phil's absence the Gauntites had replaced Phil's bathroom with something very special. A warm gesture of friendship and support. As he incredulously took in the wonders of his gift, with a vague fleeting guilt, thinking back on their brief frostiness. All the same he was unable to refrain from reflecting on ancient Troy, reminding himself Oneirons were, at least demographically, Greeks, if not Macedonians.

His new bathroom was a perfect sphere lined with a flawless black, mother-of-pearl interior.

Spheriscopically equipped, with but a word, his sphere could appear anywhere: Atop Mount Kangchenjunga in the midst of a raging blizzard—descending the Marianas Trench through the deepest waters on Earth—riding out a typhoon off Tarogi Reef on Guam—foundering in boiling white seas off a lee shore in the Falklands, dwarfed beneath colossal cliffs—cruising deep space surrounded by a hundred billion stars—or any of thousands of Gaunti-Matrice marvels, including the real-time space surrounding *Gauntlet.*

Gravity was selectively modulated inside the sphere in such a manner that water fell slightly more slowly and gently and pulsed with great force. Phil himself was lighter and more relaxed.

Each station (FOND Unit, sink, toilette, shower, steam, sauna, Jacuzzi, bidet, and so on ...) was connected by crisscrossing catwalks, gracefully constructed of a transparent surface-foam derivative, gently floating in QAVLian micro-gravity. Like walking on air.

The best part: *his personal tank.* Twelve thousand liters of pristine seawater occupied the bottom of the sphere. A majestically swirling black QAVL gravity well within. It was equipped with its own Spheriscope system allowing him to populate it with the full visual variety of ocean life. Phil could hardly wait to make his first descent.

He cocked his head at Jake with an intrigued expression and softly breathed one word "Who?"

Jake smiled. "*Gauntlet* has its own pub now. Did you know that? It was really overdue. The name is O'Gaunti's. Cute eh?"

"Ever so." Phil nodded impassively. "*Who?*"

"Well, last week, a couple of days after your, ah, meeting in the park, I was helping the folks open O'Gaunti's. I had to ensure the place was completely authentic you see ..." Jake was clearly reliving fond memories of the evening.

"... And was it?"

"Was it what sir?"

"Was the pub authentic?" Phil was growing impatient.

Is Jake taking his geriatrics?

"Oh yes, right down to the filthy bar towel." He gathered his thoughts. "Right. Anyhow they were discussing the *perceived* schism between your *Mandates* and *Enactments*, and the crew's reaction. They thought perhaps your perception of their disapproval was exaggerated. Misunderstood even. In point of fact they were simply caught off guard. So they were searching for some low-key way to demonstrate their support ... tacitly ... without some sort of overblown declaration. I suggested a birthday gift. And the new technology used to build the external blister was perfectly suited to build and install this sphere."

"Thank you Jake. Thank them all. I like it very much. I'm going to use it right now. Would you pass along my thanks to the crew?"

"Certainly." Jake withdrew.

After shaving, Phil submerged into the FOND. Ten minutes later he was submerged in 12.8 dark, icy atmospheres. He reveled in the luxury of deep ocean waters right here in his own Residence. Fifteen minutes later he was fast asleep.

Phil would gratefully adopt this spherical, swirling vortex of icy tenebrous depths as primary bed and sanctuary for decades to come.

***

The next morning Phil discovered yet another gift had been delivered.

Phil was spending more and more time in the forest, at the seashore, and on Mount Gaunti. The builders had not foreseen PM trails in these areas, nor were they practical, so Phil did a great deal of hiking. Phil enjoyed the exercise, but resented the time it consumed. His schedule simply did not permit.

The elegant solution was a custom-engineered All-Terrain PM.

Two trim new PMs stood outside the entryway of Phil's residence, a gift of Phil's executive committee. Tire-imbedded retractable crampon claws, beefed up suspension, buffering +/-gravity units, additional safety equipment, increased engine capacity and a powerful long-range electricity receiver. All ensured the rugged little vehicle could easily traverse *Gauntlet's* toughest terrain anywhere within the giant sphere.

Jake and Phil were admiring the PMs; and Phil was savoring the intoxicating scent of new tires. Vulcanized rubber with fondly reminiscent eyes.

"Some scents stay with you your entire life. Something about proximity to the brain, I understand." He glowed fondly. "I will always have vivid memories of waxed milk cartons. When I was a very young kid in school, the boys would jockey to see who would fetch the lunch milk."

Jake smiled. "I remember it well."

Phil frowned "I thought you grew up in Luxembourg?"

"I did. But we did get back to the States from time to time. Holidays and such."

"Certainly. But you didn't go to school there."

"No. But I had mates who were schooled in America and I accompanied them to school from time to time."

'Holidays and such' … 'mates who were schooled in America'? This is not an American speaking.

"Where *did* you go to school Jake?"

"Um, the American School of Luxembourg."

Dammit there is no American School of Luxembourg.

Phil had spent considerable time in Luxembourg working with banks and the EU on regulatory legalities. He knew from personal experience there was only an International School in the country.

Why didn't I clear Jake with Edward? What the hell was I thinking of? Too much going on. Too little time. Christ, I didn't even know he was aboard until well after liftoff. Hell, I didn't know who he was. Too damned late now. Small wonder I struggle with paranoia.

Jake broke into his thoughts. "Philip, I uh, I have one more gift for you. I don't know where it came from, or how it got here, but I do know who sent it."

Phil glared at Jake in mild confusion. "Christ. This is more goddamned gifts than I've gotten in twenty years."

"Actually I'm not quite sure it *is* a gift *per se.*"

"Who's it from?"

"QASI."

Phil was instantly alert. "What is it?"

"It seems to be a metal phial. It's sealed," he shook it lightly "and there seems to be some sort of liquid inside. QASI included a note." He handed Phil a small engraved metal tag:

T-MAAM
Captain Carr's Use ONLY
Take Internally Undersea

With Amity
QASI

Jake mused "Odd way to leave a note ... metal tag and all ..."

Phil smiled knowingly "He has difficulty handling non-ferromagnetic materials."

"Sir?"

"Paper Jake. QASI can't manage paper well."

"Oh I see. What are you going to do?"

"Take a swim."

***

Phil lightly touched down on the seabed at the equivalent of fifteen-hundred meters. He was in total blackness and far from eager to ingest an alien T-MAAM. Even with a race as ostensibly benevolent as the QAVL, horrors beyond imagining could lurk in this compound.

Spicing the familiar pungency of seawater that so often filled his mouth and lungs was an unaccustomed sourness he rarely tasted: the bitter, coppery tang of fear.

A baleful depression descended on his mind, as dark and cold as the waters surrounding him.

His senses alerted him: *QASI's message in a bottle holds something pernicious, something potentially destructive.*

Something he cared not to know. But curiosity is an unrelenting mistress.

He put the phial to his lips, bit down, and squeezed the pliable metal teardrop. An acrid, oily liquid surged into his mouth.

It was very unpleasant.

He kept swallowing and swallowing, trying to get it all down and hold it down. It tasted … *brown*.

He felt slightly nauseous. He could feel the alien essence infusing and heating his viscera. The strange liquid warmed him, and yet he felt oddly cold.

He waited tensely in the darkness …

The Dismissive Missive

"SALUTE QADYME CARR and happy birthday:

"Our birthday gift to you is the gift of truth.

"We regret we were forced to withdraw from our mission so abruptly. We miss our discussions and our *cocktails* atop Mount Gaunti. Above all, we are saddened we are unable to complete the course of study we had envisioned together.

"You have not imbibed a true T-MAAM Philip. This is more of a recording. As you are fully aware, a T-MAAM cannot but faithfully imprint subjective information extant in the MAAMer's mind. However, a complete T-MAAM from our cognizance to yours would be too alien. It would seriously damage your psyche, perhaps beyond redemption. Moreover, we fear the contents of this record may tragically, and perhaps irrevocably weaken your faith in the QAVL.

"Accordingly, the following corroborative T-MAAM is a true imprint from our mind to yours. Its duration is 0.00147 micro-seconds. This approaches the limit of your safe endurance. This is but a taste. The smallest sample. It should prove to you the consummate impossibility of an imperforate T-MAAM imprint. We hope this demonstration encourages your trust.

"We emphasize: we do not withhold a personal T-MAAM as a guise for withholding the truth. We withhold because you could not survive it.

"The following assertion may seem flagrantly trenchant when you have completed this entire missive, nonetheless: *every presentment in this recording is entirely true*

"The time for deception is at an end.

"Prepare yourself Philip."

He was dazzled by a blinding *whoosh*.

***

One of Phil's earliest memories …

He was just over one year old. His mother was bathing him. Shampooing his hair. Sun pouring into a cheery blue and yellow tiled bathroom. Bright, yellow curtains. Fluffy powder-blue carpeting. Jaunty blue and white wall hangings. The redolent scent of warm water, soap, shampoo and soft scented oils.

Safe, sunny and warm.

The phone rang and Mother left him alone in the tub for just a moment.

In her absence, bubbly shampoo cascaded into his eyes. He screamed in surprise and horror as the caustic soap burned, as painful and as terrifyingly alien as only an infant can feel. He cried in fear and hurt and surprise. He tightly shut his eyes and desperately rubbed them, making it worse. He then struggled to open his burning eyes. Opening them mere slits, venturing the dazzling morning sun and braving the mildly caustic burn of the shampoo.

Suddenly he looked out into a new, unknown world: a blinding world of spectral light, effervescent with clustering soap bubbles glowing in bright sunlight refracting the bright blues and yellows and fuchsia surrounding him. No appreciable image whatsoever. It was so strange and beautiful the boy forgot his pain and fear. He could neither recognize, nor understand anything in this alien new reality. No point of reference whatsoever.

He was thusly enthralled when his mother returned.

***

A strange and alien new world yawned before him in his secure home, with his mother in attendance, in his own bath. QASI had gifted him with an apt analogy.This was the closest analogy Phil's mind could draw, grappling with his 0.00147 microsecond ordeal. He could relate to nothing he felt. He could understand nothing. Do nothing. Retain nothing. Insofar as the infeasibility of a QAVL-to-Human-T-MAAM, he was convinced. He was also convinced as to the total credibility of the strange recorded liquid he had imbibed.

He was also acutely intrigued that QASI should take such pains to win Phil's confidence. He finally realized the true extent of the QAVL's unswerving surveillance of his life.

The recording continued …

We have some verities to convey Philip. You may find them painful. They may anger you. Some may profoundly surprise you. They are all true and they are all far beyond your ability to alter:

- Until this moment, we have willfully deceived you. We led you to believe that QAVL are unable to relate falsehood. Unable to lie as it were. You seemed to accept this premise. Yet consider this realistically Philip. A man of your acuity must have postulated that beings of our aptitude are more than capable of extremely artful dishonesty, and hugely skillful prevarication. Bluntly and succinctly stated:

    o   *We have knowingly and unrepentantly lied to and manipulated you.*
    o   *Continuously thusly since our very first meeting on Oneiro.*
    o   *Our deceit was not conducted considering the best interest of Earth.*
    o   *Our deceit was not conducted considering the best interest of Oneiro.*
    o   *Our deceit was not conducted considering the best interest of QaDyme Philip Carr.*
    o   *It was executed expressly and cynically in union with the Quaestors of Kosmas.*
    o   *Serving our own ends.*
    o   *We will explain herein.*
    o   *When you arrive Kosmas and we reunion, you will further understand.*

- Neither the QAVL nor the *Kosmasians* are overly interested in mankind, although the new Gauntites may show promise if sufficient evolutive tension is applied. But make no mistake Philip, as we are sure you suspect, it is *you* that interests us. Your ability to resist the flux. We have discovered this ability in only a tiny handfull—a few thousand beings amongst uncountable trillions.

- Amongst the eons of entities we have catechized, we conclude this to be a potential key to our research, possibly our salvation as Galactic life. Not a galactic life form, but galactic life *itself*. Attainment and affirmation and the triumph of chaos. Chaos with all its concomitant majesty. Know and believe this Philip: your value may be inestimable to the cosmos themselves.

- In all our galactic history, there has never been a case where an entire species exhibits the ability to speak *Kosmas*. As on Earth, a tiny minority acquires the competence. This was another of our more calculated falsehoods. Humans are fond of the term 'critical mass' to describe the predication of a nuclear event, or an organizational capability, or even sufficient proliferation of a biological aggregation. We also find that certain specie acquire the Kosmas language when genetic profundity achieves such *critical mass*.

- We know you are deeply troubled by events on Earth. We know you also wonder why we took no measures to prevent such atrocity. Why did we not foresee the danger and apply remedy?

- This will be the most painful admission. We could have prevented. We did foresee. We have precipitated tens of hundreds of thousands of such incidents. Over the eons we have discarded hundreds of thousands of species. We have precipitated the death of trillions of beings—but always by their own hand. Sifting through cosmic life, searching for grains of promise amidst infinite cascades of chaff, though never active agents in their downfall. Such specie needed no help and surprising little catalyst.

- Why did we allow your Earth to bring such down on themselves? Surely you have intuited that as well. The answer is palpable: it was necessary that you be unable to return to Earth for at least a century. This accommodates requisite dwell time on *Kosmas* to accomplish your task.

- There was no other way. The QAVL were unable to transport you. A one-man craft, while technically feasible, was out of the question. You could not survive the voyage unconscious. Conscious, you would have arrived insane. The conclusion was inescapable. We were forced to dispatch you in a fully populated ark, wherein the option of returning was forefend, and your mind was sufficiently engaged by the profusion of issues that incessantly confront you aboard Gauntlet. This ambience was also ideally suited to ... ah ... other controlled tests.

- We have augmented your QAVL systems with a fully sentient analogue. We denominate *him* Uncle HERB (Although he is has no true gender in a human sense. Neither is he a triadinal being.). We synthesized him with the animus of a corporeal terrestrial male. We felt you would find its name somehow cheering. HERB is wonderfully intelligent and consummately versed in ship's operations, navigation, power systems, celestial mechanics and *Gauntlet's* design. There is quite literally nothing aboard *Gauntlet* he is incapable of addressing. We also made him wise. He is fully capable of continuing your training as Verteror. We counsel you to work with him as you would with us. Freely communicate with him. Your DIT has been adapted to dialogue with him. Ask for HERB, or better still, *Uncle* HERB. We felt you might feel more comfortable with him as *Uncle HERB*. HERB however is an acronym defined as Heuristic Entity & Re-cognizant Being.

We are sorely testing your resilience in confronting you with such an amalgam of upsetting disparities. This in the midst of circumstances on

Gauntlet which I would surmise already vex you considerably. Therefore, a word of advice and admonition: Let it happen Philip.

Let it all happen. Suppress your formidable skills at guiding events, and simply allow events to naturally transpire. Understand this. Impress this on your mind:

> *For the ensuing years, and far longer*
> *your natural role will be that of outsider.*
> *Always and forever an outsider.*
> *You must accept this.*

During one of the darker periods on planet Earth, some humans were literally considered chattel. Slaves. Stolen from their homes to be bought and sold and used as their owner saw fit. This wicked practice flourished even unto contemporary time in squalid dark quarters throughout man's world.

One of the more remarkable humans to emerge from that cascade of misery was a female slave in the United States of America, during one of its most turbulent ontogenetic periods. Her name was Harriet Tubman and she was accomplished in many ways. We QAVL found one of her quotations very moving. She describes her liberation from slavery into the emancipated states:

> *I had crossed the line.*
> *I was free,*
> *but there was no one to welcome me to the land of freedom.*
> *I was a stranger in a strange land.*

... As will be you Philip. A stranger in a strange land ... a stranger aboard the ship you command ... a stranger in the wondrous world you seek ... a stranger on your home world should you ever return ... and in all the cosmos that enfold them.

And so you shall be. Beyond all time and space as you divine it.

We grieve for your loneliness and sadly have no remedy.

A final word Philip.

Perhaps it will aid you, at least for now.

We are certain your insight has already perceived the one called 'Jake' is not what he purports. Far from it in fact. You will most certainly sort this out in time. Meanwhile, trust him. We QAVL are tripartite beings, as you well know. This has served us well throughout the eons. You can benefit equally after a human fashion. Merge your unique perception and leadership qualities, with Jake's experience, and Uncle HERB's vast expertise. Together you will comprise a formidable tripartite Command. Jake and HERB are eager to help. We urge you to forge this bond.

Should this seems harsh and cold to you QaDyme, it is. Yet consider this:

> *All living things must be pruned from time-to-time,*
> *to contain ostensible chaos and stave inevitable entropy.*
> *When a life form attains a certain level of competence,*
> *external forces are no longer adequate to this task.*
> *Such organisms must become self-pruning.*
> *Only the question of appropinquate deo remains.*
> *They may regulate their domain through intellect …*
> *or dispersion, or restraint, or other means.*
> *They may accede to natural law and submit to nature's dominion.*
> *Solutions are as many and diverse as creation itself.*
> *Human propensity thus far favors savagery and neglect.*
> *A curious choice.*
> *A choice, nonetheless.*

As the QAVL reckon time, we will rejoin you in the *blink of an eye*. As you reckon time, may the wonders of creation beguile you until we convene again.

All our hopes.

QASI
QaQAVdun46
Ambassador of the QAVL to Earth QaSol3

***

Philip roused himself from his reflections. He thought for a time, took a deep salt-watery sigh, and finally sub-vocalized a harsh castigation.

Fuck you QASI. Fuck you and your whole damned race.

Painfully aware the QAVL might be swarming round him—such as uncountable invisible mayflies infest a sluggish stagnant pond—Phil found himself hoping his primitive invective might somehow attract QASI's note.

Chrysalis

FOR THE NEXT five hours Phil lay in icy blackness. Absorbing and absorbed. Trying to harden and inure himself to his cold new reality. Nothing was as it seemed. Nothing could be trusted. Ever.

The Earth was on fire and billions were burning. Human civilization was self-immolating; and he was largely at fault. He had been betrayed by beings advanced and ostensibly benevolent far beyond his wildest imaginings.

QaDyme indeed!

Were they capable of such cynical deception, then what of the galaxy? The universe? What of all creation and its *creator*?

He felt humiliated, fatuous and gullible.

He bitterly ruminated over and over the roles of QASI, Anne, Dr. Webber, Aiy, Edward, Howard, Mike, Nick, Fatin, Craig, Rhona, Herb, his murdered parents and murdered brother. All of them and thousands more, witting or unwitting players in this perverse cosmic prank.

He thought back to a young girl cruelly crushed under the wheels of his jeep in Ghazi Kahn. Lying broken and dead in the cold gray morning, at the side of a dusty road, warmed only with the remains of a ragged and clearly beloved shawl. Perhaps the only true innocent in this charade of horrors. She'd run in front of his speeding jeep almost joyously, to her death. Phil could do nothing to prevent it, but the memory haunted him steadfastly throughout the long years. He could not pass a day without the apparition of her emaciated and torn countenance. A specter that never faded.

He thought of the people and beings responsible for his marauding, deadly presence on that road that bleak and bitter morning. He would forever feel guilt and humiliation. He would forever seethe with hatred for those who had brought him to that cruel impasse.

Was she the pattern of Earth's destruction? Had he crushed humanity under the wheels of his cosmic jeep? Was his the ultimate, cruel irony?

He felt the fool. Gullible and inane. He felt betrayed. A cosmic cuckold and dupe. He felt rage. A rage that burned and ravaged his mind with a heat only opprobrium can remedy and he felt a profound, horrible, painful crushing guilt. An unendurable guilt. A guilt for quite literally destroying his world and his race and that small innocent girl, that icy morning in Ghazi Kahn.

Just as Oppenheimer uttered on the Trinity site in 1945—the New Mexico desert—man's first baptism to a real, no bullshit Armageddon— quoting from the enormous Hindu scripture, the *Bhagavad Gita*:

I am become death, the destroyer of worlds

Early that morning, before sunrise, they had watched in awe as the colossal mushroom cloud ascended seven miles, the limit of the Troposphere, to nearly the Stratosphere. An unsuspecting Earth, in its monstrous shadow, as yet unaware of the deadly potential just unleashed, while poisonous fallout was already descending upon them, with many more in years to follow.

***

Most of all Philip felt alone. In this respect QASI was right. And such would be true for the extent of his existence.

His isolation grew deeper and deeper, his gulf with humanity wider and wider. Phil and his triad would command *Gauntlet* with extraordinary skill, and they would see *Gauntlet* safely to *Kosmas*. But in the end, Phil would be alone.

It occurred to him that through his entire life from boyhood, to adolescence, to manhood and beyond, he'd never had a friend. True, the ladies loved him, but men? He had never bonded with another male in fraternity. He'd always played alone and stayed alone, or worked alone on the Chesapeake Bay, or after that, as a lawyer and beyond. Forever alone.

It occurred to him how odd it was he had never focused on that reality before.

Phil realized he was reliving the *Weltschmerz* torture he'd suffered on Oneiro as he completed his Fear training. Only it was real now. Real pain. No drill. No training exercise. For the last eleven years he had wandered, playing the fool, through a fog of cunning and duplicitous sophistry. The QAVL and the *Kosmasians* were as cheap and as contemptible as the bogus phantasms visited upon him by his tormentors so long ago on Oneiro.

On the surface he would have screamed in frustration and wept with shame. Instead his mind shrieked. *Entropy exists. Decay exists. Nothing else explains the decadent debasement of QASI.*

Then he heard it.

An inexplicably uplifting song from his childhood, playing in the recesses of his mind. Cheerful. Happy. Just as in his very early youth. A child's record player. A cowboy motif. A beloved toy. A chewing-gum-red recording disc. Over and over it played. So old he had forgotten it. Who was that man? Gene … Gene Arthur? No … that was *Jean* Arthur … a woman … an actress … This was a man … Gene … Gene … Gene *Autry*! The singing cowboy!

Yes!

His remarkable memory served him well. Every word came back *verbatim*:

> I'm back in the saddle again
> Out where a friend is a friend
> Back in the saddle again
> Where the longhorn cattle feed
> On the lowly gypsum weed
> Back in the saddle again …

Yes.
You're goddamned right I'm alone, but I am back in the saddle again.

Where I belong.

Where I've always belonged.

As always he was equal to the task, his numinous acuity according him understanding. Total and instantaneous.

Phil often resorted to Latin platitudes when upset or confused. There was a straightforward savvy and an engaging candor about them that clarified even the most complex enigma.

He litanized: c*ras credemus, hodie nihil*

(Tomorrow we believe, but not today.)

Over and over, until he inescapably affirmed his bitterly measured conviction. During the long journey remaining he would transform into the sapient equivalent of a single-celled organism in need of no one save himself. His days as a communal life form were at an end. No longer a cellule in the measureless human plenary. He would execute his duty. He would find some way to exculpate, at least in some small part, the horrors he had helped inflict upon mankind. In the end, it would be but Captain Philip Carr, commander of the interstellar craft known as Gauntlet, who would remain.

What sort of creature would finally arrive *Kosmas?* Unknown. Even to the QAVL.

But for the present and until they loomed before their distant star he would be a creature of solitude and of duty.

Solitude and duty.

Journal of the Quaestor

Subject..: The Kpzmik-Dast
Tempus....: 7276458495858
Locus.......: Kosmas Kintrekos
Quaestor: Quaestor ROK
Quaestor KHAAN
Ambassador QASI

Quaestor ROK to Quaestor KHAAN: *An incredible report has been submitted by the QAVL. It be verified.* Corrōborātus *their form and their nature. The Universe be supremely steadfast. It was inevitable Quaestor. Calculable and ineluctable. Quantum life. The Kpzmik-Dast emerge. Aeons foreseen for eons.*

Quaestor KHAAN to Quaestor ROK: *From what degree gradient?*

ROK: *Unknown. We suspect a miniscularity never encountered or even suspected.*

KHAAN: *From what degree age?*

ROK: *We be aware only of their wanderings. Their trails of supplantation antecede our eldest by at least two billion eliptics. Beyond that, we know nothing.*

KHAAN: *The manner of their animation?*

ROK: *We conject, as with all such essence, quantum forces, fashioning particulate matergy* (Bayrontonic-n-Bayrontonic), *infusing and preserving its form. Articulating zoetic patterns, launching the distant ascension from the elemental, to the labyrinthine, to the sublime.*

KHAAN: *How do we account for their ability to metamorphose sentience?*

ROK: *We cannot, Quaestor. Supplantation is a wonder never witnessed before anywhere in this galaxy. Still … our finest casuist report this flows from the mechanics of their essence. Endemic to their very nature.*

KHAAN: *Mmmm. Indeed Quaestor. You cannot account for it. Endemic begs false causality. This be propositum condo life-form.*

ROK: *Quaestor. That be Genitor stuff.*

KHAAN: *Indeed.*

ROK: *Such?*

KHAAN: *Such. Implications vast. Yet ambiguous. A nexus arises of cosmic import. If we understand correctly, only Verteration can divine. Still … what force propelled the Kpzmik-Dast on their eternal peregrinate?*

ROK: *Presently unknown. Again … endemics perhaps. We shall know in eight thousand Standard Elliptics.*

KHAAN: *Eight thousand Standard Elliptics? So soon? A flicker in time.*
ROK: *When we be Supplanted by The Kpzmik-Dast. Wanderers of twelve billion Standard Ecliptics will soon linger at our threshold, their journey scarcely begun.*

KHAAN: *Kosmas only?*

ROK: *Yea Quaestor.*

KHAAN: *And all the worlds of Kosmasians?*

ROK: *The Kpzmik-Dast move in equiangular spirals within equiangular spirals, within equiangular spirals at photonic standard speed. Every world is supplanted in its time.*

KHAAN: *Ultimatus wonder. The end of Kosmas. The end of Quaestors. The culmination of our occupation. Share with me Quaestor.*

ROK hooded his input array and commenced a litany of analysis and prescience.

ROK: *The (sub $^{-222}$*n)-atomic ascending from the infinitesimal to the colossal, ever burgeoning (sub^{222}*n)-atomic. A mote fluttering above infinity. An endless ascension. Forever reaping the wisdom and ebullience of sapient life. The harvesters of the cosmos. The husbanders of sentience itself. The Kpzmik-Dast.*

KHAAN: *What be known of them?*

ROK: *They be invincible. Deadly should they wish we conject. Even to non-photonic life. Vastly intelligent. Emergence of sentience on a towering scale even by Kosmosian standard. Near infinite. Immortal and isochronally ubiquitous. Totally impalpable. Protonic, neuronic, matergenic, stygianic, electronic, Bayronatae, muonic, gravitronic, leptronic and infinitely, infinitely more. They take in all that they supplant. Everything be preserved. Mass. Energy. Memory. Acuity. Intellect. Essence. Nothing be lost. Nothing. A symbiotic plenum of life fused with the sentience and essence of the Universe itself. All Verterors have been expended in Kpzmik-Dast studies. None remain to confront them. One option remains. We be accorded no other. The logical option. The only option. The non-option. Submit.*

KHAAN: *Mmmm. All potential Verteror expended. How?*

ROK: *As with all such particulate coercion. Resumptive reticulation.*

KHAAN: *A powerful and dangerous force that. It defeats even for our finest. We have witnessed a supplantation?*

ROK: *Yea Quaestor.*

KHAAN: *Who witnessed such? How?*

ROK: *Two questions Quaestor. One answer. The QAVL.*

KHAAN: *The QAVL? The children of the universe. All be play. All be joy. All be lovefrisk. No hunger, death, razwk, pain, loneliness, psychgast.*

ROK: *(An affectionate grin graced his chest.) You suffer from these afflictions Quaestor?*

KHAAN: *Perhaps I envy those spumy ribbons of ignis fatuus. Perhaps it be time to abdicate this clamoring corpus.*

ROK: *Not to perturb Quaestor. The Kpzmik-Dast soon pass this way.*

KHAAN: *Where have the Kpzmik-Dast been observed?*

ROK: *First occurrence. The QAVL Anthro-xeno-biological Observatory on Karash-Kan IV. The farthest point in the Tri-Kondus spiral-arm. The very edge of our galaxy. Consistent with galactic ontogeny, we hypothesize it to be their point of galactic ingress. Six point five billion Karash inhabit Karash-Kan IV. Kosmasian for two millennia.*

KHAAN: *How many supplanted?*

ROK: *All.*

KHAAN: *The QAVL be sufficiently acute to describe the process?*

ROK: *Adequate Quaestor. They attest the process be far removed from pernicity. QAVL passions be not subject to flamboyant hyperbole, yet the Kpzmik-Dast inspire an exaltation in the QAVL which be … stimulating. I quote verbatim from the QAVL Report:*

The Kpzmik-Dast Report

Submitted by QaQwri of the QAVL Galactic Quest

The Kpzmik-Dast are formed of densely organized gaseous ingram that
attend the emergence of sentience and intelligence drawing their energy
from starlight and their ethereal form from trace particles in background
radiation.
Kpzmik-Dast of such minutiae to be virtually nonexistent.
They exist within an aching purity of such beauty it visits great sadness
upon lesser beings, unless fortunate to enjoin.
Should Kpzmik-Dast wish to amplify their intellect, or their command …
they need only further combine with, or generate conjunctive, congenital
ingramatic gas. Therefore their capacity for erudition approaches infinity.
Thus the challenge of interspecies communications paradoxically increases
and decreases near exponentially at their will.
As does such object specie's ability to countervail.
We are very rarely aghast with wonder.
Overcome by beauty.
Inspired by ascendancy.
This be such an event.
Every corpus, every damalogius, every cell, molecule, atom, particle,
Taken instantly.
No pain.
No fear.
No damage.
No loss.
Only sublime felicity and great joy.
Great joy.
The supplantor is so imperceptibly increased as to defy measure.

The supplantee be enriched to an ascendance which defies description …
… the supplantee be enhanced $(2^{212} * N)C$.
They might be divine.

KHAAN: *$(2^{212} * N)$ C. Inaccurate. Charmingly inaccurate. Poetry. Yet sufficiently precise to convey significance. Reasonably succinct notation. Unusual. Archaic decimaric, positional sensitivity. Thou engaged in such notation earlier. Incredible how one specie's concepts can infect another's psyche. Credit our newest Kosmans I would conject the Terrestrials? Oneiro of Sol?*

ROK: *Correct Quaestor KHAAN. We are aware of the presage throughout the Quaestor. Questioning their entry to Kosmas. Indeed they are but callow adulescentia. Yet they have mastered Kosmas. And there be a Verteror amongst their number. Yea Quaestor, I see the null credulity in your tangs. A Verteror. Their leader … Quaestor if you will … Captain Philip Carr. Verteror, if yet unproven.*

KHAAN: *This demand a specific Thema Journal Quaestor. Another session. How exactly did the QAVL evade Supplantation themselves?*

ROK: *In fact twelve QAVL be on site, and thereby supplanted. The report be submitted by QAVL Paleo-Anthro-Xeno-Biologist, QaQwra. Aboard their Observatory at extreme synchronic orbit. Engaged in remote surveillance at the time, augmented by their fellow QAVL until supplantation commenced.*

KHAAN: *These Supplantors. The Kpzmik-Dast. Selective?*

ROK: *It would seem not Quaestor.*

KHAAN: *All are taken?*

ROK: *Rigorously and predictably consistent with our own Quaestor.*

KHAAN: *In all its forms. In all its contradistinctivity. Extraordinary. The texture of the Universe constantly reveals craft and symmetry and beauty, congruent with our perception. What of those excluded?*

ROK: *We believe they be subject to supplantation when they achieve maturity, or simply reside with the Kpzmik-Dast helixia passing. Conceivably the next Kpzmik-Dastn cycle. When they pass their way again.*

KHAAN: *At what rate? What speed?*

ROK: *As stated Questor, photonic standard.*

KHAAN: *Estimated interval between cycles?*

ROK: *Our calculations indicate 29.8 million Standard Elliptics.*

KHAAN: *A daunting lacuna. Should supplantation be wondrous as described by the QAVL, how sad. How cruel. So many lost forever between cycles.*

ROK: *More than exist in the universe at any moment.*

KHAAN: *Tragic.*

ROK: *Such be the nature of the cosmos, or the genitor, if these creatures be not such.*

KHAAN: (A melancholy *psychgast quivered across his chest.) Indeed. As we know well. Still ... these Kpzmik-Dast must be extraordinary forms. We be certain of our facts and their singular nature? Inexorable, inconceivably ancient and sublimely benign? Harbingers and harvesters of the mind of the cosmos? Perhaps they indeed be GENITOR?*

ROK: *Intervallic confidence margins already quite high. Confirmation and calculation half complete.*

KHAAN: *A wondrous prospect Quaestor ROK. Beyond imagining. To join The Kpzmik-Dast in the peregrination of the Genitor itself. To learn everything extant, to endure unto the end of existence itself. To see all. Our dream for billions of cycles. Endogenetic to the essence of the Genitor. Aware this be supposition. Still ... the asseverate Verteror Carr soon arrives and we must be certain. We must be certain.*

Consider this Quaestor ROK. Only in this one respect be the Universe asynchronous. Kpzmik-Dast assimilation be exclusively mono-directional. Always the smaller devouring the larger. This taxes ration. Quaestor, I am certain you have not overlooked cycle culmination. At that singular point, that cosmic nexus, asynchrony must be violated.

ROK: *You be correct Quaestor. We have not overlooked. Notwithstanding, we hypothesize asynchrony be not violated. We conject the gradient ascension increases. Our calculations support this. An endless upward spiral unto infinity. The QAVL pursued this magnificent process for millennia prior to reporting. Invariable, unwavering quantum ascension. No exception has been observed through over 700 million supplantations.*

KHAAN: *700 million systems. Subjectively enormous. Objectively infinitesimal. Systems known to us?*

ROK: *No Quaestor. Effectively none. The Karash, the Fanjiff and the Sma only. The remaining systems achieved Kosmas only within the last ten thousand Standard Elliptics. We need more QAVL. The Universe devolves at an extraordinary pace.*

KHAAN: *Always the smaller devouring the larger. Mass be Bi-directional. Size be irrelevant in fact. Infinity be Omni-directional. Trillions of trillions of infinite dimensions … unending.*

ROK: *And what of accretion Quaestor Khaan?*

KHAAN: *Accretion?*

ROK: *Gravity Quaestor.*

KHAAN: *Quaestor Rok, your wit grows as sharp as your Spenoi-horns. I am beholden to you for a brief respite.*
Let us return to the Kpzmik-Dast. The Kpzmik-Dast sup on that which we have studied for eons. Remarkable. All be a-directional and a-synchronous consistent with the model.

ROK: *That be given. Except the Kpzmik-Dast ascension. This rapacious cosmic hunger soars only upwards. It appears the destiny of the Universe be skrit with inverted tetra-*

hedron. And matriculated from bottom to top. It seems to present us with a homogenous Cosmos. And when they have devoured all of eternity itself, perhaps they will ascend to Genitor?

KHAAN: *Perhaps they already have Quaestor.*

ROK: *Perhaps many times.*

KHAAN: *Possible. We must know. Nothing commands greater import.*

ROK: *Time grows short Quaestor. The Kpzmik-Dast be very near.*

KHAAN: *The Terrestrial. Ambassador Carr. Perhaps Quaestor Carr. Perhaps Verteror Carr. Perhaps this Terrestrial can confront this absolute. Probe it. Perhaps divert it from its seemingly implacable course, if diversion is desirable. Should Vertation be warranted, if Vertation be desirable. If Vertation be an option. Perhaps Ambassador Carr can find answers. Quaestor ROK ... train the terrestrial known as Carr. Hopefully he possesses such capacity.*

ROK: *Explain Quaestor KHAAN.*

KHAAN: *Such a species can produce a Verteror?*

ROK: *We recognize anomaly Quaestor. Yet Carr is promising yea, though primal.*

KHAAN: *They have achieved such adeptness? A QAVL intercession?*

ROK: *Yea Quaestor. Such has passed before. The level of manipulation defies belief. Unseemly. Yet the QAVL be spun from such gossamer stuff themselves.*

KHAAN: *Our words be Journal Quaestor. The Journal goes to all. The QAVL amongst. Truth be for all Quaestor. The QAVL may have overstepped. True. Yet they have not erred.*

ROK: *Supposition Quaestor?*

KHAAN: *Indeed Quaestor. Supposition.*

ROK: *Shall we summon Ambassador QASI?*

KHAAN: *Kindly enter QASI QaQAVdun46, Ambassador of the QAVL to Earth QaSol3.*

Quaestor ROK to Ambassador QASI: *Kindly osmose Journal Quaestor.*

Ambassador QASI to Quaestor ROK: *Permitted Quaestor Rok?*

ROK: *With all deference Ambassador. You be Quaestor now.*

QASI: *Acknowledged with honor Quaestor.*

KHAAN: *Questions?*

QASI: *None Quaestor. Comment?*

KHAAN: *Relevant?*

QASI: *Possible.*

KHAAN: *Proceed.*

QASI: *We quote directly from the Journal. 'The level of manipulation defies belief.'*

KHAAN: *Such troubles you Ambassador? You were the author of much that has transpired.*

QASI: *As it pertains to the terrestrial Carr.*

KHAAN: *This be Journal stuff Ambassador. With deference. The Terrestrial be known as Ambassador Carr and your manipulation includes the entire planet Earth, indeed the whole of the star system known as Sol.*

QASI: *Humor Quaestor?*

KHAAN: *This be Journal Stuff Ambassador. Proceed. Explain.*

QASI: *Atonement Quaestor. Manipulation was minimal. Ambassador Carr as well. Only dissemination. We but hastened their inevitable self-destruction.*

KHAAN: *Kindly reveal Ambassador.*

QASI: *At your injunction we have provoked countless worlds into chaos in order to phlebotomize potential Verteror. Draw out the Kosmasian.*

KHAAN: *Kindly reveal Ambassador. These facts be well known to us.*

QASI: *Acknowledged Quaestor. We reveal. No such manipulation was truly necessary. Chaos was initiated by the subject specie. Hysteria be endemic to their race. Humans exhibit a willingness to perish. Perhaps this stems from their brief animate lifetime. Perhaps they be insane. Perhaps they be altruistic. Irrelevant. They do as they will, unto extinction.*

KHAAN: *We have seen this before. Yet now I sense great danger. Shall we terminate the terrestrial project?*

QASI: *Do you creed meiresthai Quaestor?*

KHAAN: *Meiresthai? Explain.*

QASI: *Yes Quaestor. Meiresthai. Luck.*

KHAAN: *Reveal Ambassador. This be important. Optimize.*

QASI: *Very well Quaestor. A Verteror be indispensible to confront the Kpzmik-Dast. Should confrontation be exigent, we be fortunate.*

KHAAN: *Intriguing Ambassador. You can train the potential Verteror Carr?*

QASI: *Best effort Quaestor.*

KHAAN: *Insufficient Quaestor-Ambassador. Your proctor, Uncle HERB we believe, will suffice for the interstellar training interval. Kindly constantly status us. Yet we find this wanting. Time is far more limited than foreseen. You are then directed to take exigencies. Wanting is more candidates. Wanting is also extreme pressure on the potential Verteror. If he be Verteror, then make him so. There be little time for training on arrive Kosmas.*

QASI: *With deepest deference Quaestor, such misdirection is immensely taxing to our ethos. Such will be harsh in the extreme on Ambassador Carr.*

KHAAN: *Such direction binds Ambassador. This be Journal stuff.*

QASI: *Acknowledged.*

KHAAN: *We be beholden Ambassador. It be providential you be involved in such affairs.*

In Session

"OKAY … *UNCLE* HERB … shall we begin?"

"*Uncle* HERB? Interesting emphasis. You feel the need to express sarcasm Philip?"

"Why, I'm greatly surprised you can detect sarcasm."

"Why, I'm greatly surprised you assume I cannot."

"I see. Sorry *Uncle*. I suppose I have a tendency towards arrogance when it comes to non-human understanding of human characteristics."

"An arrogance profoundly unwarranted I assure you."

"Well, at least you don't refer to yourself in the royal *we*."

"The *royal* we? Royalty. An anachronism, even by human standards. A misshapen step-stone from ages past. A deviant attempt to organize human enterprise. A grotesque expression of micro-eugenics, which resulted in inbreeding, insanity and murder on a vast scale. A source of horrible cruelty, supreme injustice, and comedic, pompous charade. A factor that never remotely infected the advanced specie of the cosmos—even in their political infancy. A scourge which never troubled the …"

"… alright HERB, alright. Don't get carried away. I am very well aware the QAVL refer to themselves as *we*, because they are composite beings. My comment was a feeble attempt at human humor."

"I concur. Feeble indeed. I am aware you have been somewhat alienated by the precipitous departure of QASI. I suggest instead you consider the nature of the Ambassador's responsibilities, as well as the nature of your own. Shall we begin Philip?"

"Certainly."

"Have you eaten recently?"

"About six hours ago."

"Good. Have you partaken of drink?"

"Not for six hours."

"Good. Have you relieved yourself recently?"

"About half an hour ago."

"Excellent. Will you have any pressing physical needs within the next four hours?"

"I don't believe so. What's this all about?"

"This first exercise will entail between one and eight hours and cannot be interrupted."

"It's okay Herb, I'm good. So, what shall I do?"

"Listen, observe and direct."

"Listen, observe and direct?"

"Listen, observe and direct."

"Seems simple enough."

"In fact it is, initially. Easy for *you* in any event. With one exception."

"Yes?"

"If you succeed, it will … hurt. You will experience … pain."

"Uncle HERB, I imagine I've undergone more pain than any human in all of history. Not to worry. Proceed."

"Lie down on your stomach Philip."

"Here in the dirt?"

"Here in the dirt. Now be quiet Philip."

"… not a very comfortab …"

"Quiet Philip. Say nothing until you are unable to remain silent any longer."

"… unable to remain …"

"*Quiet* Phillip."

"Do you see the tiny pebble on the ground, near your right hand?"

A small gray pebble of less than half a centimeter, lay just to Phil's right.

Phil nodded.

"Position it near your face to ensure you can see it clearly without focusing."

Phil did so.

"Good. Review your knowledge of SNA—Subatomic Nucleic Apperception—the 'consciousness' of the universe—Explore it anew. Fathom the nature of it. Observe its nature and movement."

"Look, I'm quite familiar with SN …"

"Quiet! Concentrate."

Phil grew silent, meditating as directed.

"Modify its movement."

"Modify? What the hell are you …?"

"Will you *please* be still Philip? All will be explained in appropriate sequence.

"Look away and then to the pebble and back. Slowly. Ten thousand times, a hundred thousand times if need be, until you can actually *see* the SNA. If you can accomplish that, then attempt to intercede in the petrography of the pebble. As you begin to engage the pebble Philip, I am going to provide you some background.

"I know you have an extensive education in Physics. You have matriculated General Relativity, Quantum Mechanics, Plasma and Particle Physics, Atomic, Nuclear and Molecular Physics, Astrophysics, Theoretical Physics, Empyrean Physics and much more. Your expertise, while still quite limited … is useful.

"Envision a tower, unendingly high, plummeting to depths without limit. There are an infinite number of levels comprising this tower. Picture yourself on a level that appears to be midway, *although in reality there is no midway*. Call it Level N. On that level resides General Relativity. The floor below houses Quantum Mechanics. Call that level N *(-1)*. In this session you will be attempting N *(-5)*. One day I hope you will achieve N *(+/-)*."

After an extended time "Look HERB, this doesn't seem to be …"

"Quiet Philip. Continue."

After an hour.

"HERB, clearly this is …"

"Concentrate Philip. When you engage in childish objections, you only protract this process."

"Childish?"

"Philip!"

***

After four more hours of exhaustive concentration, Phil gasped in a sort of transfixed ecstasy. He was dazzled. He was thoroughly conversant with the illusion of the solidity of matter itself. Yet in this infinitesimal moment, his perception of absolute reality itself was forever altered.

He actually saw the movement. It was as though a trillion, trillion, trillion tiny creatures crawled the surface of the pebble, comprising the pebble itself. The sight defied description. For the tiniest moment the pebble became his universe. He was sweating heavily. Breathing was a struggle. He felt the slightest tingling of real fear. He was close to tears—both sensations alien to him.

When he was again calm "Excellent. Now Philip, try to influence the movement of one particulate. Do this carefully and cease the instant I instruct. This is very dangerous."

Phil rasped in a nearly inaudible whisper. "Dangerous? What sort of …"

"Quiet. Do *only* and *exactly* as I say."

Having witnessed the sub-quanta movement, he was growing tentatively confident he might reproduce it. If not actually fearful now, he was certainly roilingly agitated.

A long half-hour later, the wondrous movement reappeared. Again he marveled. He believed he could adulate this masterwork of the cosmos to the end of his days. It was indeed the cosmos, as grand and beautiful as the vastitude they now voyaged. He was quite literally mesmerized.

As HERB observed Phil, he was suddenly aware he could immediately detect when he achieved SNA conjunction. His body grew rigid. Blood pressure and body temperature elevated. Phil was ready to proceed.

Softly, gently, near reverently, HERB spoke. Whispered actually. "Philip I am aware how difficult this is, but you *must* influence the pebble now. Please Phillip, try. Concentrate. Do not allow the pebble to rapture you. It has the power to immure your mind and you may never progress.

This tiny object could indeed be the instrument of your death. Listen to me Philip. Think only of influencing a single particle. This is … important Philip."

It needed all his willpower to suppress his exaltation. When he had gained control, he concentrated all his energies on influencing the movement of the tiny pebble.

Whispering again, HERB instructed. "Do not try to move the *pebble* Philip. You are attempting something entirely different. You will use all your faculties to make the slightest modification on a single one of those infinitely tiny sub-quanta." HERB paused for fifteen seconds. "Proceed Philip."

He tried several times nudging the particle to the right. Nothing.

To the left. Nothing.

Again and again, a thousand times again.

Perhaps he could increase the particle's velocity? Move it forward just the tiniest …

Screaming, mind-bending, body-buckling, bone-crunching AGONY!

Phil thought he knew the depth and breadth of pain, inside and out. How to feel it and deal with it. How to withstand its horrific effects.

He now knew he knew *nothing.*

The ripple effect from the pebble's single SNA subatomic contorted every cell, every molecule, atom, every infinitesimal particle throughout his body and immediate surrounding space, for infinitely less than a second. When it had passed and he was through screaming, contorting and fighting to breathe, he gasped.

"What demon from hell was that?"

"Philip, that was the smallest articulation of the tiniest percentage, of the most infinitesimal fraction, of the smallest imaginable deviation of a single sub-atomic particle in its given speed and direction—its predestined azimuth for well over fourteen billion years. It resumed its course .0000000015 Planck Units after you're very limited intervention—as though it were an incredibly taunt wire that has been plucked instantly resuming its form, aspect and rigidity.

"You are one of exactly .00000000004159 percent of sapiens in our entire galaxy capable of such a feat.

"I rather suspect the exact same ratio holds true for the cosmos throughout. And of that colossally unique handful of beings and throughout infinity, I believe you are the only surviving member."

HERB's voice took on an almost human quality.

"You should be very proud Philip. You are one of the most rare, most singular life forms in all creation.

"Continue to practice your SNA perception until you can see it at will. Should you perfect your skill, you will be capable of seeing your entire world, the entire universe within this context. Under no circumstance attempt to influence a single particle in my absence, as that would no doubt prove fatal, or worse. Yet I am well aware such an experience is compelling to the degree I employ a term I last used over a thousand cycles past."

"And what term is that?" rasped Phil.

"*Inspiring.*"

After a brief pause HERB continued.

"After you have mastered this, your tasks will become … more difficult. Far more painful. Far more dangerous. You could theoretically destroy this parsec of space, perhaps our galaxy, if not the universe itself—when and if you master total competence, which no known creature has ever achieved.

"In all candor, we cannot reliably predict the consequence of such an event. At a minimum, you will most certainly destroy yourself if not properly prepared. We must move slowly. Cautiously. We will use method to mark our progress and assess risk. Ready to proceed?"

Phil regarded his trembling hands for a time, felt the sweat trickle down his back, noting the weakness of his knees before he responded.

"*Whatever the fuck for?*"

HERB's voice took on a quality Phil had never heard before.

"The first reason in your mind should be the continuance of your race."

"My race has been destroyed if you remember."

"I refer to your passengers and crew."

"Very well. What better chance do they have than the billions who perished on Earth?"

"These are a totally incipient iteration of Homo sapient. Smarter. Stronger. Purged of the propensities of their savage heritage. Capable of evolution with breathtaking alacrity."

"Fine. You just made the case for telling you to fuck off."

"You overlook the xeno-galactic intruders, the Kpzmik-Dast, potentially capable of incorporating all galactic life—whether for good or ill, we really do not know. You Philip may be the single entity capable of making such a determination, and challenging them, if their nature be not benign, or if some of us prefer not to join their coadunate."

"Continue."

"We confirmed untold eons ago that time is indeed mono-directional. Just as with motion itself, the only direction is forward. Reverse is a subjective illusion. Consider the simple reality that an object can only be pushed. Never pulled."

"I know I cannot really pull on a rope for example. But how about say, a vacuum?"

"No the pressures behind the object push it. As you know very well Philip."

"Magnetism?"

"As you explained to Mr. Michael Auslander, your number two and acting Proprietor of Oneiro, magnetism engages SNA, to use your expression, *hooks*, within certain types of particles."

"You were privy to that conversation?"

"Yes."

"Is there one goddamned second of my entire life you haven't monitored?"

"Very few. Perhaps none."

"*Jesus!*"

"Shall we proceed Philip?"

After a moment's dark brooding "Okay HERB. One more try: Gravity?"

"Mass distortion of space stimulates layered space-time to push the object into the mass, which you also well know. Shall we continue? I suspect you are simply vying for time."

"Okay. Your premise is accepted."

"Given that, we have no alternative. Remember: *The only direction is forward.* We cannot retreat. Not only is this impossible, but were we capable of such, we would cease altogether as extant beings. This is not an experiment. Nor it is an exercise in diversion. *This is the continuance of sentient life.*

"You probably never regarded your race in these terms, but your entire race, or most of it, has suffered horribly and perished in this pursuit. I know this troubles you beyond imagining. Beyond endurance. Beyond forgiveness, or forgetfulness, beyond even grief. You are only at the merest beginning of understanding. Please do not allow their loss be for naught. *Are we concordant?*"

Phil was literally trembling from shock and fatigue and enmity.

"I need time to think. I need time to heal for God's sake. Goddammit I need to rest. I'll get back to you—in my own goddamned sweet time. *Are we concordant?*"

"I caution you, we will have to begin at the starting point again, and it will be as difficult and painful."

"I don't give a damn.

"QASI promised me one time I could simply state privacy and you and your fellows would leave me totally unobserved. I expect you to hold true to that promise now, even if QASI did not."

"Yes."

"Give me your word."

"You have my word."

"Privacy."

Suddenly HERB's presence was simply unavailable.

Phil sat alone. Exhausted and truly frightened for the first time in decades.

Jesus! I wish to God I could really get good and drunk.

***

Phil reluctantly reconvened days later.

"Okay HERB, a few questions first."

"Certainly."

"Will these sub-quantum interventions always inflict such pain?"

"I fear so. Unless you effect a permanent diversion of the particle, then we would enter the realm of metaphysical. However, we are as yet somewhat uncertain. Nonetheless we cannot fathom any reason why a divertive resonance should not always be exceedingly distressing for a corporal being such as yourself."

"That's encouraging as hell. Why should it endanger the galaxy, or the universe, or even the house next door?"

"Kindly remember we are flagellating in theory and conjecture here and such danger may not indeed exist. Consider though, the hundreds of thousands as you who have perished in this pursuit over unthinkably vast periods of time."

HERB assumed a professorial tone as he continued.

"Abimbola-Sic of Reinar-Capra first calculated and proved the immutable nature of the universe. This troubled it so greatly it set out to seek a remedy. It then theorized that an insighted being of sufficiently granularity might be able to achieve not only perception of sub-quanta, but actual manipulation at sub-quantum echelons, given appropriate mental acuity.

"This occurred nine hundred and twelve million cycles in the past. It was also the first to die (gruesomely) in such pursuit. In doing so it set in motion a galactic quest to accomplish redirection of an infinitely granular particle.

"All have perished in this pursuit during the ensuing millennia. This is far from conjecture. This is fact. The oscillation effect you propagate will only grow stronger as your skill increases. Therefore this effect will propagate in exponentially larger spheres. Theoretically this could encompass all of space and time."

"So why are you taking me to *Kosmas?* Does this not endanger the entire planet, and even far more?"

"It certainly does."

"Then why?"

"Philip you seem to be under the impression *you* will be working on *Kosmas.*"

"So I've been led to believe. Where will I be working?"

"Somewhere else."

"That's it?"

"That is it."

"Okay. Then explain to me again why this is so damned important. It has already cost *me* my planet, my race and my life, and you are apparently willing to bring existence itself to the table."

"First, there is … this element invading our galaxy. It may be benign. It may be malevolent. Under either guise, it will most surely supplant the extant nature of our existence. We must learn more. We must confront this … this thing. Perhaps we may wish to quite willingly, even rejoicefully, submit. This may represent graduation to the next level of existence itself.

"*Per Contra* we may be compelled to resist. However, resistance may be impossible, or difficult beyond imagining. Your talents may be called upon. I trust you appreciate the extraordinary import of this threat. At stake is the galaxy itself. Are you aware of a greater priority?

"Beyond that remains our original quest. If we cannot prove that a particle's trajectory can be modified, then the meaning of existence is vastly altered. Failing that, existence itself may be diminished to the point it has no value."

"What in hell are you talking about?"

"Forgive me Philip. Please be patient. I am attempting to couch this problem in the terms of your somewhat limited language. This may take some time and many sessions. And there is one other factor which QASI will make clear to you."

"Okay. I'll bear with you. But tell me one more thing …"

"Yes Philip?"

"Please explain to me why I should willingly engage in such a clearly deadly enterprise."

"Simply put, you have nothing else to do."

"That's not true. We can participate in the studies on Kosmas."

"Philip, I'm afraid in that respect you have been misled."

"What the hell does that mean?"

"Try to imagine a Siamese cat engaging Plato in an intensive debate regarding the philosophy, existence and nature of Socrates."

"That's goddamned insulting *Uncle*."

"That is not my intent, nor is it my nature to belittle. Nonetheless it is interesting to observe the many ways you use the term *Uncle* as an epithet."

"How many fucking lies have you people told me?"

"I have never misled you in any way Philip, nor will I ever."

"How about QASI? I understood the QAVL were incapable of deception."

"Your naïveté is delightful Philip. You really believe a race of advanced beings, millions of years older and a thousand-fold more intelligent, to be truly incapable of spinning a few yarns to a feckless human?"

"I have one more question before this interview is terminated."

"Yes Philip?"

"Yes *Captain.*"

After an imperceptible interval "Acknowledged … Captain. I stand corrected and contrite. Your question sir?"

"What in bloody hell is my crew supposed to do on Kosmas for months, maybe years or decades, while I'm screaming my lungs out in agony, attempting to destroy the fucking universe?"

"They will evolve. They will evolve in new directions. Ultimately they may surpass you, Captain."

"Please explain why the QAVL, or the Kosmiams, or whoever the fuck, did not see fit to foster this development in the human race as a whole."

"Because Captain, non-Oneirian humanity could never sustain itself for a sufficient period to attain such a level of sentiency. You however sir, are an anomaly of wondrous potential."

"You are dismissed."

"One other item, if I may Captain?"

"What is it?"

"The two documents QASI wished you to have are now on your personal monitor in your quarters. They were retrieved by the QAVL from the ruins of the old United Nations building in what was once New York City."

"Fine. Dismissed."

Phil found his way back to his quarters, slowly and aimlessly. For the first time he was entirely without enthusiasm for this voyage. He felt hapless and credulous. What had he done to himself? His crew? The human race?

"Good afternoon Jake. May I please have a bottle of gin, a glass and a bowl of ice in my study?"

"Certainly Philip. Is something …"

"Bring the bottle right in. Beyond that I don't wish to be disturbed."

He sighed, sat wearily before his monitor and opened QASI's file.

<u>*Concluding Document [Ultimus Amitto] from the QAVL to Planet Earth, as presented to Aoko Itõ, final United Nations Secretary General:*</u>

Our journey together has ended.
Your journey has ended, utterly.
We have journeyed such with more specie than there be stars in your sky.
Most end as yours.

Acrimony is not your due.
Despondency is not your due.
You strode this planet for your accorded term.
That is the measure of your due.

The stars are cold.
Not without purpose.
We seek such purpose.
That is our due.

Your own words indict.
Cambodia. The Khmer Rouge:
'To preserve you is no gain.
To destroy you is no loss.'
Prescient words.
Foreboding words.
Monstrous hubris. Yet true.
True of a million, million worlds.
Terra is but one.
Creations cull.
Wretched worlds, spawning life addicted to death.
Putrescent buds propagating necrosis from within.

Arborary or animalia—nullus differentia.

Countenance this:
You will never know.
You will never understand.
There be no other course.
A course plot afore your star awakened its fire.
A course plot at the parturition of existence itself.

Yet your seed ascends to the stars.
Such seed may one day know and understand.
Commend serendipity beyond credent.
For Terra though.
Dreams pass.
Godspeed.

Quatrain written by United Nations Secretary General Aoko Itō shortly before dying by his own hand.

The silent writhe of the Beast sinuates round the fustian Dove.
Whose voguish coos betray the vigilant with dilettante love.
Ti's then He strikes. Snuffs Dove, and oppugnant phalanx, and all.
Till Dove woos anew, we be the Beast. Frenzied hellions in His thrall.

***

Both documents had a troublesome impact on Phil. The door to understanding was open slightly wider now. He sensed the truth in these words, and the import. Despite the profound sadness of the words, his depression was gradually lifting; and his bitter enmity was losing its piquancy. He concluded from the first document that he and the crew of Gauntlet represent the 'seed that ascends to the stars.'

But in the second, who was really 'the Beast' and who was 'the fustian Dove?'

          John Stuart Goldenberg

Phil stared intently out his window thinking:

Till Dove woos anew ...
We be the Beast.
Frenzied hellions in His thrall.

After more than an hour, he rose slowly from his desk, an idea form-ing in his mind.

"May I get you something else Philip? Dinner perhaps?"

"No. Thank you. I'm going down to the sea. I'll be back in the morning."

Three's Company

PHIL'S COMMAND TRIAD was functioning as a well-oiled machine. The three operated as one, each contributing their own unique talents. Nick had wisely and happily restricted his command duties as Executive Officer to Bridge Operations, while Phil had developed distinct relationships with both Jake and HERB.

All ship's company were greatly relieved that development of a 'Captain's digital surrogate' was rendered superfluous; that being the only point of real contention emanating from Phil's address in the park.

Jake stolidly persisted in his role as Captain's Butler, despite Phil's repeated suggestions he should consider assuming a more prestigious role. From time to time Phil suspicioned Jake's resolve emanated from the wish to keep close quarters and close surveillance, more so than to serve. Without exception they were cordial and friendly however, but always at arm's length now. QASI had placed a cloud above Jake in his parting message and Phil never lost sight of it. No more Martini walks along Shark Bay, or Cocktail Hours atop Mount Gaunti. Whatever Jake was though, he was also a consummate professional. If he was concerned or offended by his Captain's sudden aloofness, it was never apparent.

Uncle HERB was another issue altogether. Phil could never dismiss QASI's duplicity. Hence HERB was the object of a fair amount of guilt by association.

Conversely however, Phil and HERB ultimately became fast friends. As much as one can become a friend with a plasma cloud of ionized subatomic particles, engineered into an indestructible construct, whose thought processes ran in terms of 3.78 QIPS (Quintillion Iterations Per Second—converted into terrestrial terms, courtesy of the QAVL), with command of an effectively infinite memory. Eons ago the QAVL learned to construct literally anything from virtually anything by using the gaseous atmosphere planet-side to the gossamer non-matter swimming in the putative vacuum of deep space and even pure energy whether it be photonic, electronic, chemical, magnetic, gravitonic, nuclear, radiant, or ionic, recognizing their sometimes near imperceptible, almost subjective differentia.

Hence they could dynamically agglomerate unlimited memory as needed.

When Phil was a boy back in long ago pre-launch Earth, they spoke in terms of MIPs (Millions of Instructions Per Second). An *Instruction* consisted of a laconic single iteration, compiled into binary syntactic machine language. Phil wasn't sure what an 'Uncle HERB' iteration consisted of, but he was certain it was an exponentially more complex amelioration.

Notwithstanding moments with Anne, Aiy, Nick, Jake, HERB, or the Gaunti, engaged in Command and Control, day-to-day management, drinks, status briefings, dinner, sex, or whatever, when the day ended only Phil remained.

Alone in his residence, his isolation absolute.

∗∗∗

Phil was atop Mount Gaunti with his customary liter flask of Jake's Martinis. Phil carried the flask himself now and sat very much alone looking out on the universe.

His DIT came alive with a short blink.

"Yes HERB."

"Captain we are 600 solar days out of the *Kosmas* system. I have scheduled increased reverse thruster to 130% and confirmed corresponding adjustments to internal and surface gravity compensators. We will engage in six hours unless you wish to countermand that order."

"Do it HERB. Hit the brakes."

"I continually adjust myself to your use of language. It is rather amusing that your allusion to an archaic velocity inhibitor connotes your agreement."

"Thinking about it burns a lot of QIPS time does it? What is it, 2.8?"

"3.789334 Philip."

"Oh yeah, that's right. Damn. That's a lot of horsepower HERB. Isn't that a little overkill?"

"Overkill. An archaic remnant of what you termed the *cold war*, wherein adversarial powers produced nuclear weapons in excess of ordinance requirements."

"Well HERB it appears to have been quite efficient in destroying mankind, so I'm not convinced the term was such an 'archaic remnant'."

"I stand corrected Captain. *Mea culpa.*"

"Forget it. Let's get back to your processing power."

"As you wish. I am endowed with the minimum processing power theoretically possible in the context of non-Bayronatae particle ionization."

"Why minimum?"

"That would be difficult to describe. Perhaps it would be best if I explained it as the smallest functional critical mass."

"Good grief. And what is the maximum?"

"3.789334 is also the theoretical maximum."

"Why theoretical?"

"Nothing presently exists to measure beyond it."

"Interesting. An absolute. We'll need to measure your process currency in terms of Plank Units—IPP's as it were. What do you do with all that power?"

"I maintain and reside within my own reality Philip, which accommodates adaptive temporal perception. I also observe, learn, ponder and speculate. There are many disciplines requiring only observation and applied intelligence in order to pursue them."

"Such as?"

"... such as mathematics, cosmology, physics, quantum mechanics, poetry, music, philosophy, theology, spectral trituration ..."

"Spectral what?"

"Disregard please. You would be unable to observe the art form even if I could explain it to you, and there are thousands of others. I am also easily capable of constructing mesonatae objects as I wish. I therefore lead an existence which you might describe as luxurious."

"Not bad. No serial mean processor is Uncle HERB. So where does it all lead? What does it get you? What will you achieve?"

"Perhaps in a few hundred millennia, or a few thousand, something absolute may emerge. You've conjected the same yourself Philip. Yes?"

"I'm not sure I understand HERB."

"You've often voiced the suspicion that all the universe and the beings within were only agents executing some sort of infinity vast program. How do you suppose that unfathomable executable will complete Philip?"

"I really haven't formulated any coherent conclusions to be honest. Are we the universe trying to understand itself? No. That seems too anagogical. I think maybe successful execution might result in … fulfillment."

"Fulfillment of what Philip?"

The moment stretched into minutes as Phil stared up into space.

Finally. "Are you lonely HERB?"

"I *am* alone. Isolated. Detached. Is that lonely Philip?"

"In a manner of speaking I suppose it is. But that's not my meaning."

"How do you define loneliness Philip?"

After a time Phil said: "Loneliness is that part of us of purest essence, neglected and belatedly lost, languishing in implacable, dispassionate cosmic oblivion. A beautiful star going super-nova unknown and unobserved."

HERB remained silent.

"Tell me about *Kosmas* HERB."

"I have briefed you on *Kosmas* many times Captain."

Phil disregarded the observation, so HERB patiently proceeded.

"*Kosmas* is a University, a language, an art-form, a laboratory, a meeting point, a citadel of knowledge in space."

Phil seemed lost in thought.

"… tell me about the *Kosmasians* HERB."

"At the last available count, there were 1,049,332 specie in attendance, representing the most advanced in the galaxy. The total population is something on the order of 327,000,000 beings. Considering the vast capacity of that colossal spiciferous sphere, its population statistically approaches lifelessness."

"What of the surface of *Kosmas*?"

"It is truly lifeless. There is no atmosphere of any sort. No moons, or other satellites. The planet has near zero circumvolution. It is geologically, magnetically and radiologically dormant. Its core depleted itself of all thermal, magnatronic and radioactive activity three billion years ago. It is sufficiently removed from its star that insignificant radiant energy reaches the planet. In fact all life on Kosmas is confined to the life spheres. The *Quaestors* of *Kosmas* demanded that any planet under consideration as a center for study be entirely devoid of life. Kosmas is ideal. A titanic frozen rock rotating lethargically in isolated space. The planetary engineering inflicted on the world is so radical, any extant bio-essence would be irreversibly decimated."

"In what way?"

"The entire planetary surface is covered with hundreds of thousands of titanic columns which emanate nearly from the core of the planet and extend thousands of kilometers into space. Life forms wishing to reside on the surface level, or within the planet all the way to the core approaching zero g.

"All are accommodated within environmental platforms exactly like those spiraling in space on columns far from the planet's surface. Naturally the height of such columns centrifugally magnifies gravity up to many terrestrial G's on the star side of each platform until the effect fades. Kosmas is rather unique, in that it is a totally dead rocky planet, which is nearly the size of a gas giant. This is attributable to a number of factors, the primary being a somewhat cribriform mantle and core, and an extreme distance from its star, which was probably not always the case. The major life forms presently in residence are as follows."

HERB displayed a chart on a nearby cliff-line via Phil's DIT.

Phil stared absently at the chart. He didn't know why he brought up the question. He'd seen it before. In fact he innately knew the content of the presentation.

"Your mind seems restless this evening Captain. Do you have any other questions? We have covered this material several times in the past, as you well know."

"No. No questions I guess." He murmured offhandedly. "No wait. I do have a question."

"Yes?"

"How do all these diverse creatures get along?"

"Get along?"

"Yes. Do they like each other? Are they friends? Is there trust? Are there disagreements, friction, politics, competing ideologies, enmities?"

"I see. Without exception, relations are eminently civilized and cordial. No politics whatsoever, and very little of what you might term diplomacy. The term 'friendship' may not apply in all cases however. First, that is a human concept. Secondly, their physical differences are sometimes incredibly difficult to reconcile. This is another reason why the QAVL play such a pivotal role."

"Explain."

"QAVL are sensory neutral mediators. *Kosmasians* may find each other monstrously ugly. Hideous beyond their capacity to endure. Or they may be enraptured by the other's perceived beauty, to the point of near catatonia. Appearance is only one criteria however. Any sensory signature may form the basis for alienation, or attraction … smell, sound, consistency, color, mannerisms, magnetism, radiation, positive or negative poles, knoffity, style, xanthocoty, zbiocanthry, beliefs, size. Nearly any feature congenital to a species may affect another deeply. They may often be dangerous to other life forms. Interestingly this applies to both Bayronatae and non-Bayronatae life forms."

"I take it knoffity and xanthocoty and so forth allude to senses we do not possess."

"Among many. Yes. Hundreds in fact. But humans are in no respect lacking. Every race enjoys its own suite of ambient interfaces. *Kosmasians* are far too advanced to allow such variance to become a problem. They do inflexibly require their own environment however. Fortunately, based on the design of *Kosmas*, this poses no problem."

"Aren't there any pernicious species in the universe?"

"Aside from human?"

Phil pursed his lips wryly. "Yes HERB. Aside from humans."

"I assume your question relates to space faring creatures."

"Right."

"In fact there are many more such creatures than our census maintains. Many are so menacing as to defy reason. Although the vast majority are quite short lived."

"Why do you suppose humans have survived?"

"Humans have survived?"

Phil glared bitterly without comment.

"Are the QAVL the most advanced species on *Kosmas* HERB?"

"Far from it."

"Are you?"

"Certainly not and I hardly qualify as a species."

"Not a lot of convergent evolution going on amongst the stars apparently."

"Interesting observation; and summarily incorrect."

"Really?"

"Really. The issue of convergent evolution surfaced quite early in *Kosmasian* studies. Eons ago. They confirmed and re-confirmed that whenever an environment presents a parallel challenge, given reasonably homogonous resource, the adaptive mechanism ultimately arrived at the serially chronometrically successful solution. The same solution across the universe, given a profusion of precise qualifiers to compensate for environmental aberrations. The mandates of physics are after all, universal, insofar as we know, certainly within this galaxy. However, this is always influenced by a specie's previous evolutionary progression."

Phil pondered for a moment. "I suppose then, that we may regard *Kosmas* itself as the ultimate example of convergent evolution."

Phil was astounded. HERB was actually taking time to consider his response.

"An interesting observation Philip. I am aware of no previous observation to that effect. It would seem to imply a second tier in convergence. I believe it may have value."

"Hmm. And these senses, ah knoffity and xanthocoty and such. Will we learn of them on *Kosmas*? Will we ultimately acquire these senses? Can they be explained to us? Taught? Imparted?"

"Many questions Philip. You will not learn of them. You may acquire some of them in the far distant future if you survive. They cannot be explained to you. They cannot be imparted to you."

"Why not?"

"Which why not?"

"Why can't they be explained to us?"

"Please do not be offended by this Philip. Were you to attempt to explain the functioning of an internal combustion engine to a terrestrial tree frog, the frog could not, not only fail to understand the explanation, the frog could not even comprehend that you were attempting to communicate with it."

"Don't give it another thought HERB. Just as the tree frog, I'm un-offense-able."

"Shall we continue our training Captain?"

"Oh hell yes. Why not?"

"Behind genes, or their equivalent in all life-forms, lurks a micro-verse of near sacred particles. Our term for such Fraxinus ornus is Qadience. Qadience defines the form, function and nature of animate matter and its potential sapience throughout the universe. Leveraging each creature's fundamental form enacts Qadience patterns. You would term it genetic material. The gene, using a human term, is an intermediary between quantum existence and the corpus, whether Bayronatae, or otherwise. Modify Qadience and modify genetics. We *interpret* Qadience as easily as you read a book. The makeup of the creature itself is irrelevant. Qadience is universal. We *manipulate* Qadience with equal ease."

"Then why were you unable, or unwilling to manipulate human Qadience to allow mankind to survive, Goddammit?"

"The answer is quite straightforward, Captain."

"Great! Then straightforward the hell out of me, right now. Use all that immense processing power of yours to justify the QAVL's genocide. That's an order *Uncle* HERB."

"Very well. As you wish.

"First, the QAVL committed no genocide. The human race summoned that abomination upon themselves, at their own volition. It is not the obligation of the QAVL, or any other race to protect another specie from ther own, self-imposed puerility.

"Secondly, to universally alter the gnome of every extant and forth-coming human would require more time than humans are capable of evolving beyond self-destruction."

"So there was *never* any hope?"

"There was never any hope, Philip."

"One final question."

"Yes?"

"If you manipulate Qadience with such ease, why the hell do you need Verterors?"

"I should think the answer is obvious."

"It is not. Answer the question."

HERB paused for a moment.

"We confront a question of relative scale Philip. The Verteror addresses particles millions of gradients tinier than Qadience. These are the infinitely regressive particles targeted at the inception of existence itself. Such particles evolved literally plank units prior to the sub-atomics that comprised the earliest moments of the universe. They then developed infinitely upward to the sub-atomics and beyond and cascaded downward to infinity. Their azimuth immutably defines time, matter, energy and all events and forces unto the very end of space-time—the intercession of which is the monstrously daunting and deadly challenge that lies before you.

"I am painfully aware you regard me to as no more than a vast iterative program.

"So be it.

"Yet ... know you countenance my support, affection and compassion for the hideous trials you have suffered ... soon to be dwarfed by those you must endure.

"Today's session is ended Captain."

In Session—Again

I think that modern physics has definitely decided in favor of Plato. In fact the smallest units of matter are not physical objects in the ordinary sense; they are forms, ideas which can be expressed unambiguously only in mathematical language.

Heisenberg

"OF SPECIFIC INTEREST in this process is the Verteror. Although the exact mechanism of the Verteror continues to evade us, we are intimately familiar with the matrixial ambience requisite to supporting the Qadience polecule. We remit the polecule. We fill the matrix. We complete it."

"I am unfamiliar with the term *polecule* HERB."

"In your parlance molecules are comprised of atoms. Atoms are comprised of particles. Polecules are comprised of the particles that comprise the particles that comprise the particles of an atom, electrons, protons, neutrons and such, *ad infinitum.*"

"So a polecule is comparable to a proton, or a neutron and such."

"In part. Yet they descend to quarks, or leptons, or neutrinos and such and unending levels of subsequent granularity. Exponentially and unendingly small, adhering to universal quantum mechanics of sorts, yet subject to a vastly augmented instruction set."

"I realize that. Please continue."

"We seek compatible matrices and introduce Qadience polecules. Yours Philip was just such a matrix. We insinuated ourselves into your genetically ordained embodiment. We awoke the quiescent marvel in your abeyant matrix."

Phil was quiet for a time. Lost in thought. Attempting to understand.

"So you ah, fucked around with my Genome for your own goddamned selfish purposes. Man! He is one son-of-a-bitch our friend QASI. Is there one fucking thing he hasn't tampered with or lied about? He destroyed my world, my body and my very existence. If he's a higher life form, I'll take a goddamned amoeba every time."

"There is one other thing."

Philip reacted sharply, his voice loud and abrasive. "*What?* You begin to far exceed any semblance of rational regard my friend."

"In your case Philip, there was another random element."

"What in hell's name are you talking about? I thought randomness didn't exist?"

"Quite right. The term random in this context relates only to the limit of our ability to foresee."

"So what is this *random* element?"

"A cellule."

"A cellule, as in some sort of basic generic cell? Say, a stem cell?"

"Of sorts."

"Why the sudden coyness HERB? Don't be shy. Cut through it. Lay it on me. How does this apply to me? Are you saying such a cellule is an element in my matrix?"

"Yes. Dr. Webber augmented your genetic makeup when you were formulated with such a cell, or rather elements of the cellular makeup, which he spliced into your blastocoels. His name for this extraordinary bit of plasmid was *Eos.*"

"The Romans called her *Aurora.*"

"True. Apparently Eos was not developed the extent Dr. Webber had hoped. However, he must have found it sufficiently advanced to the degree it warranted incorporation."

"What was the intent of this cellular material?"

"Unknown. We recognized your potential early on. As you are aware, we easily interpret Qadience. As you may not be aware, Qadience generates a certain sub-atomic signature detectable at great distance. Therefore, prior to your viability you garnered no note from the QAVL. Shortly thereafter we were intensely aware of you. Therefore, we were not directly observing the activities of Dr. Webber. Inference and retrologisism allowed us to infer his activities to a certain degree. This is reflected in surrounding SNA. Certainly not conclusively however. We do know he was attempting to breed a semi-sentient primal cell, capable of independent action. We cannot fathom the effects of such an element on colonial clustered complex organisms such as you. Terrestrial biology is somewhat unique in many respects; and even after hundreds of millennia there are gaps in our knowledge. We do suspect this may bear strongly on your uniqueness. After all, you are the only known extant, potential Bayronatae Verteror presently in the galaxy and perhaps the universe."

"Is it *truly* possible to develop a semi-sentient, or perhaps even sentient single-celled organism?"

"In fact beings exist in some parts of the galaxy that approach such capacity. The key to such beings lie in their SNA. But I believe you are aware of this Philip."

"Okay. How do you define *limited independent action*?"

"The ability to inculcate itself into other cells and possibly influence the cell's function, or even its genetics."

"And I've got these tiny squiggles moving freely throughout my body. I wonder how many?"

"Presently, we approximate six-hundred-billion-five-hundred-forty-eight-million."

"Hmm. Well it's certainly gratifying to know that everyone got a shot at fucking with my biology. Very democratic if you ask me."

HERB remained stoically silent for a time and then continued.

"You have other questions Philip?"

"You state that you are unable to understand the exact process of the Verteror. Is that another of QASI's bloody lies?"

"No Philip. It is not. We will provide you the extent of our understanding in very basic terms: We do not know *how* Verteration occurs. We do know *what* occurs and we know *where* it occurs."

"*Where?*"

"Verteration occurs within the matrix ambience."

"And *what* occurs?"

"The trajectory of a given particle is imperceptivity diverted from its predetermined course. This should be *absolutely impossible*."

"And what is the effect of this?"

"Thus far the particle has always resumed speed and direction. Our Verterors have never achieved sufficient puissance to effect a permanent diversion."

"How does the particle re-achieve its previous trajectory?"

"Unknown Philip. However we suspect there are forces surrounding the particle's ambience which force resumption."

"And if a Verteror did achieve a permanent diversion, what would be the effect?"

"Three possibilities Philip:

"One: Sentient life might achieve determinism.

"Two: Such action might attract the interest of a conceivable Genitor, given the postulate its interests is *attractable*."

"God?"

"That is one term. One of millions."

"And the third possibility?"

"Building upon an old terrestrial term, a quantum string reaction might be provoked."

"And the implications of that?"

"Conceivably, an unraveling of the universe."

"You mean its destruction."

"Yes, or at best its reformation. Either would be catastrophic for any extant life."

"This includes incorporeal beings such as you and the QAVL?"

"Absolutely."

"This effect could conceivably occupy a limited sphere of influence and be terminated when necessary. We will be looking to you in this respect."

"Why in hell's name do you wish to pursue such a course?"

"There is no alternative. You will perceive this reality soon."

Proving the Improvable

"IS THE UNIVERSE infinite HERB?"

"The existence of but a single particle conclusively affirms infinity. Such an assertion is a teleological improvable however. The axiom that stipulates existence itself implies infinity may be quite valid. However, I am concerned this topic may be premature."

"You feel I am unable to understand?"

"Not at all. You are imminently capable. But there is a serial aspect to the information I convey. Sequence is critical. This topic is of vast import. However, I would be pleased to share our perspective on human findings, if that would be of interest?"

"Definitely. I don't believe we've ever discussed the efficacy, or lack thereof, of human studies."

"Alright. The question before us: *Is the universe infinite?*

"First. How do you define *infinite?*"

"Without end."

"Rather simplistic. Wouldn't you agree?"

"Okay. How would *you* define infinite?"

"Again, in human terms. Infinity is boundless, unbounded, unlimited, and endless. It is not finite. It is a set consisting of constituents having exact parody with elements of an inferior set, not of the object set. It is the sum of a nascent process that never terminates, which by definition has no sum. Cannot have a sum. We would comment the human concept of 'dimension' limits your thinking in this respect."

"Well, you certainly don't lack for description. So does it exist?"

"Suppose we address the question in the various contexts of your various and somewhat limited academic disciplines.

"For example, a pure mathematician would contend that one can always increment any value with another integer *ad infinitum*. There are also irrational and infinite objects such as Pi, and infinite sets as well. Therefore infinity exists. They would be compelled to respond: *Affirmative*"

"Yes."

"Then there is straightforward intuitive thought, which should not be discounted despite its shortcomings. Humans are surprisingly adept at this sort of ratiocination. We believe humans would conclude that there must always be something further (if only a void) beyond any cosmic limit, no matter the nature of the limit, no matter the form of the universe. Such thinkers would respond: *Affirmative*"

"Agreed."

"One of your great thinkers, Mr. Albert Einstein, was not only a gifted physicist and mathematician, he was also a wit. I quote:

> *Once you can accept the universe as matter expanding into nothing that is something, wearing stripes with plaid comes easy."*

Phil smirked without comment.

"Physics. Physical Cosmology accommodates universal structures such as loops, multiversity, duality and more. All of which tend to discount, obscure, and even obfuscate the question. Deductive evasion. Such would probably respond: *Indeterminate*"

"Mm. Not sure I agree. Then again, I'm not sure I understand either. But *Indeterminate* seems reasonable."

"Then there is human Theology. Little better than shamanism. We suppose they might stipulate omniscience accommodates any possibility, which defines infinity in many respects. One could formulate a counter however, which might stipulate omniscience, or omnipotence is capable in a limited universe. Yet we find this logic contrived for a variety of reasons. Therefore the response is *Affirmative*. I will share another quote from Einstein:

> *Science without religion is lame. Religion without science is blind.*

"You seem a little dismissive of Theology HERB."

"We find this aspect of human intellectual pursuit nescient, anachronistic, credulous and quite honestly, distasteful. In all probability it was the prime destroyers of your species.

"In fact, religion as practiced on Earth is more akin to ideology than theology. Such ideology is driven by the lust for power or wealth, congenital hatred and fear borne of bigotry, and bigotry borne of fear."

"So you reject religion?"

"Far from it. You well know we firmly subscribe to the Genitor concept, which as you also well know is not remotely related to the god entities once worshiped in various forms on Earth."

"I see. I also note you speak in the past tense. I wish I knew whether you speak empirically or with prescience. Either way, I find it disturbing and offensive."

"A topic for another day."

"Continue."

"Philosophy. A terrestrial strongpoint on occasion. We surmise their reasoning would advance as follows:

- Were the universe infinite there would be infinite possibilities.
- Including illogic.
- Therefore, an infinite universe could be infinite, finite, or both, or neither.

"Perhaps philosophers would respond: *Negative and Affirmative*"

"What of logic then?"

"Good question Philip. You are no doubt aware logic derives from your classical Greek *trivium* ..."

"Actually I'm not."

"Actually you are. You simply have not delved into that aspect of your SNA."

"Okay."

"In fact this is quite relevant to our discussion. Trivium consists of the three elements Logic (empirical reality), Grammar (tagmemics), and

Rhetoric (reality as it is expressed). In the context of such a miasma of interpretation and expression, logic, as you might not suppose, is *not* universal. Certainly not human logic. Even amongst humans. However *human* logic might advance something like this:

- For something to exist it must consist of fabric in some form.
- Even in void indwells the fabric of existence.
- Something must produce that material.
- Infinity demands an infinite supply of such material.
- The seminal event of creation, the Big Bang, was a singular, delimiting event insofaras we are aware.
- Therefore, the Big Bang was a finite supplier of material.
- No other supplier exists.

"Therefore, logically the universe must be finite. Logic responds: *Negative*"

"Your syllogism overlooks the previous assertion by Einstein describing infinity as 'the universe as matter expanding into nothing that is something' therefore: *Affirmative*"

"Perhaps. Although your somewhat specious argument is based on a conceptual, mathematical paradigm, as opposed to pure logic."

"Then, perhaps we should be discussing the nature of infinity, of existence itself?"

"Perhaps we should confine our discussion to the topic of our perlustration."

"Fine. So let's see ... three *Affirmative*, two *Indeterminate*, and one *Negative*. Although I believe I could construct a logical syllogism that would conclude *Affirmative*. All the same, it looks like the aye's have it."

"This is not a vote Philip. This is a cardinal issue."

"Okay. Well, I find logic advances the most compelling argument. But intuitively I reject it. I cannot justify infinity. I cannot comprehend it. But I believe in it."

"When you've negotiated ten by ten thousand iterations, you may begin to appreciate the problem."

"You state this is one of the cardinal questions. Vastly important. Is this related somehow to our little cosmic cue-ball … granular flow?"

"Excellent Philip. Truly excellent."

Warming to the concept, Phil continued. "Infinity would seem to support non-determinism. A finite universe seems inherently deterministic. I recognize that assertion is purely intuitive, but I think this is pivotal to all that follows."

"Yes Philip. Your reasoning is formidable indeed. You overlook a very critical factor however."

"Yes?"

"Try to envision an infinite universe consisting of two components. The first is the sometimes expanding, sometimes contracting, sometimes static *bubble* we would both refer to as *the known universe.*"

"Okay."

"Now superimpose that finite *bubble* onto a background which is infinite, consisting solely of a hard vacuum."

"*I see!* Such a model describes a deterministic infinity. I see."

***

They had achieved deceleration at near 100% power two years ago and were now only scant years out of *Kosmas*. His body drifted with the gentle sea currents while his mind drifted through the years. He pondered the end of their long journey with a curious mix of pride and trepidation. He'd heard of tigers refusing to leave their cage after years of cramped captivity; and he could practically hear the rusty whine as the barred door of his own Gauntlet cage slowly rasped ajar.

***

And so it had gone on for years, and so it continued for months and weeks, until the time arrived when the star humans designate as Gilese 581 appeared in *Gauntlet's* night sky. With the aid of a telescope *Kosmas* grew from a hardly discernable gray smudge to a colorful blur crowning the skies above Mount Gaunti.

They were still far away and there remained much to do, especially for Captain Philip Carr.

Though his skills were honing at a rate no other human could remotely approach, he had yet to exceed a few meager nanoseconds of agonizing particulate deviation.

Such exercise demanded more and more discipline and commitment from Phil, as each tiny advance plunged him in more and more unspeakable pain. Each time he believed it could get no worse, he was proven pathetically wrong.

The pain, the exhaustion and the discouraging failures were finally beginning to wear on Phil. He was growing increasingly cynical and bitter. Worst of all, his hitherto joy of existence was slipping raggedly from his grasp. This was becoming a source of concern to the crew and compliment; even Anne and Aiy.

Somewhere in his mind he knew—he was absolutely certain—if he allowed himself the luxury of surrender and self-pity, he would squander himself and all mankind's tattered aspirations.

He would then wearily return to his task.

Birthday Surprise

A PROFOUND CHANGE in the Gaunti persona had erupted throughout *Gauntlet*.

Psychological and physiological as well. Subtle in some ways and glaring in others. Some captivating. Others deeply disturbing. Creatures leapt, squirmed, crawled, ran and flew. The holy of holies proscription on Oneiro against anything but human and marine life aboard had been effortlessly, almost nonchalantly disregarded. Although this represented a clear breach of protocol, considering all else that was passing, it seemed near trivial.

Half the children had mutated into Out-World dwellers. The background radiation on the surface further compounded their mutations at a formidable rate. They were changing and Phil suspected, evolving, at a near exponential rate. It wasn't obvious, but their abilities were many and wondrous. This first major schism was a *fait accompli* before Phil ever suspected its coming. He blamed no one for this tacit revolution. No one was to blame, zoëtic evolution being the most powerful force in the animate universe. He was determined to find their genesis however. And he would do so—whatever it took.

Somehow this served to energize Phil, to give him that little push of additional purpose.

Those Gaunti children who remained inside gradually grew profoundly inward looking and were quickly consumed with their own pursuits. Their achievements exceeded anything Phil would have imagined, which in turn innervated the adult Gaunti. Together they changed the face of Gauntlet. Nothing was recognizable any longer.

Flora had taken a totally new direction in its stoic advance. Fauna as well, where there was no fauna before. Phil *did* hear a dog the day of the fateful crew confrontation. Various animals were equally radicalized. Intelligence was everywhere, as was danger and extravagant colors and forms and great beauty. Phil would spend days entranced. Walking and diving and swimming amongst the sometimes harrowing singularities fashioned by burgeoning Gauntian intellect.

Phil finally recognized it was high time he acquainted himself with the Gaunti Children. Previously he'd paid them little attention and it wasn't until several crew members repeatedly recommended he personally learn of the exceptional talents of Gauntlet's newest citizens that he finally focused on them.

Accordingly, and somewhat reluctantly, one quiet Saturday noon, Phil presided over one of the very few formal ceremonies aboard *Gauntlet*: the Gaunti Presentation of The Children.

These singular children inhabited Gauntlet's warm, sunny interior and their outward appearance approached normalcy. In fact, as Phil was soon to learn, they were stunningly beautiful. He had no idea how, or even why the Ganti had contrived to breed. They contended they were equally mystified, much to Phil's extreme skepticism. But one could not condemn, or even inflict stringent interrogation on an entire ship's compliment. Males had begun conclusive chemical sterilization prior to launch. After four years of treatments—thusly protracted to avoid surgical or harsh chemical intervention—they were rendered permanently barren. Females continued as normal. Ship's stores contained a small sperm bank should they experience a catastrophic loss of crew. Yet the most meticulous audit proved beyond any doubt the bank maintained its full inventory. Every cryogenic vessel was un-tampered, its seal perfectly intact. So how had they accomplished this wonder? Had they consciously affected this? He had no clue. The Gaunti were militantly insistent they'd had no hand in this miraculous singularity. Phil invested hours interrogating his SNA, attempting to find the answer. No luck.

Seriously exacerbating Phil's dilemma—darkening the problem—rendering it more ominous and dangerous—a fearsome realization was dawning: He seemed to be suffering from some sort of inexplicable block regarding the incident. Hitherto unknown and unsuspected, this shadowy being had been stealthfully preventing his ability to see and recall and analyze his dynamic ambience.

As realization grew a steely coldness burgeoned in Phil's gut.

***

The Children's Reception took place in Webber Park, as did all significant events on *Gauntlet*. All aboard appeared to favor open-air meetings, as opposed to one of the many enclosed conference centers.

Phil had never really taken a good look at these newest Gaunti. Children held scant interest for him. Half the children inhabited the surface, an area now known as Out-World, a place that Phil found repellent. Compounding this, they appeared to favor the shadows of their already twilight world.

Today's reception was happily limited to In-Worlders.

Out-Worlders were loath to visit In-World, as were In-Worlders to visit Out-World. Nonetheless, Phil was well aware that someday he must confront these bizarre new surface dwellers as well.

This was a task he dreaded for some reason; and he knew somehow that the reason was buried somewhere deep in his SNA, as was perhaps the answer to this entire enigma.

They had arranged Phil on a massive stone bench in a large clearing in the park. This tacitly designated him leader, without the anachronistic trappings of some sort of overblown sovereign.

The familiar parkland grass had greatly evolved since Phil's last visit. The clearing was now covered in a sort of ultra-tiny-leaved-clover, the likes of which Phil had never seen. A verdant springtime green beneath a cloud of countless thousands of tiny blood-red teardrop flowers rising above the clover on near invisible stems. The effect was of a roiling froth of transparent crimson spume floating above an incredibly verdurous landscape. Phil was delighted to discover that walking on this marvel had no injurious effect whatsoever, as it sprang back immediately, completely unscathed.

The parkland itself was intermittently forested with all manner of exotic flora. A Rousseau painting, as surreal and ethereal as the artist at his finest and strangest. Among other greenery they had produced masterworks of devolution. The most stunning were monumental Aracaria Mirabillis (giant Cretaceous conifers 164-155 million years ago) towering above all other bio-forms—dappling golden sunlight through lofty canopies of lacey green. Oxygen enriched air was discretely vented to their canopies to simulate the atmosphere of the Cretaceous. A masterwork of ambient acclimatization, accommodating both contemporary and Cretaceous vegetal life to flourish in co-habitation.

Combined with intermittent, near transparent clouds and the flittering leaps of unfathomable creatures, the total effect was hauntingly primordial. The Gaunti had elevated botanical genetics and weather control to art forms and both were in singular form today.

At Nick's direction the children filed wordlessly into the sunny clearing. Their stride was graceful and confident. Their manner was easy and relaxed. They walked in no recognizable formation, nor discernable disorder.

Instead of studying the children, Phil's attention was drawn to the adults. Perhaps the solution to this mystery could be read in their faces. As far as Phil could glean however, they reflected only pride and affection, if not love. But most strikingly evident: admiration

Unlike the reportedly bizarre siblings indigenous to the murky Out-World, these children looked like the spawn of man and woman, although their gestation period had been less than six weeks. He was aware the mothers had no idea which child was her offspring. He also knew the children had no idea which female was their birthmother. They were the first Oneirons begat by woman in countless generations, yet the question of maternity seemed equally irrelevant to mother and child. Loved by no one, and loved by all. Motherless children—with a hundred mothers. Orphans of the galaxy favored with more parentage than any antecedent in non-Onerian human history.

He had been briefed on other aspects as well. They drank huge quantities of liquids, but took very little solid food. They seldom slept. They seldom spoke. They never wept. They never quarreled. They rarely played. They occasionally laughed and they smiled easily and often. They appeared happy and quiescent and their acuity was near terrifying.

Phil turned his attention to the young Gaunti standing before him.

Physically he was captivating in the extreme. Gold seemed the dominant feature, eyes, hair, eyebrows and what little body hair he possessed. Even finger and toenails and skin to a lesser degree. All were guilelessly naked and stunningly beautiful. Were it not for genitalia, it would be difficult to differentiate male from female. Yet they were somehow not androgynous. He literally beamed at Phil—happy to finally meet his Captain—his *Qadyme*.

His posture was exquisite, as were all the children. His movements were graceful and elegant. They moved as might a panther. He did not speak. He looked Phil straight in the eye, golden flecks dancing above a translucent blue-gray. Tiny cottony youthful wrinkles warmed a crooked smile.

Phil sat easily on the bench, hands and arms resting on the smooth stone, fingers pointing outward to either side. He returned the boy's smile with amiable equanimity and equal directness. After a time he said. "Hello."

The boy smiled more broadly still and responded "Hello."

"Do you speak for your brothers and sisters?"

"Not really. I am simply first-born."

"*Born*. There's a term unheard of on Oneiro in untold generations."

The boy flashed Phil a knowing grin belying his callow age.

Phil thought he might surprise him with his next question. "Have you undergone Fear Training?"

Unfazed, he spoke softly with a confidence that belied his age. "We completed the Fear Ordeal when we were forty-eight months old." No arrogance, no brag, nor false pride. His was simply a statement of fact.

Phil regarded him in awe. "It shows."

"Thank you. Although our solution is quite different than that developed on Oneiro."

"Really? How so?"

"We perfected a method of selectively isolating the brain's amygdalae through virtual severance from its many connections. In this way we can experience fear and its attendant emotions at will. In some circumstance this can be quite useful."

"Interesting. Perhaps I'll give it try myself. What is your name?"

"Aggelos, Captain."

"Interesting name."

"It translates to *messenger*, Captain."

"I know." Phil smiled.

Phil turned, looking up at Nick. "How about their training?"

"Essentially T-MAAM and self-taught."

"So you really have no idea what they know?"

Nick smiled. "They know everything in our libraries. Including the QAVL Documents. And a great deal more gained through their own researches."

My God.

"What do they think of this mission?"

The boy interjected, unappreciative but not annoyed at being referred to in third person. "Our life aboard Gauntlet is a source of great joy. We look forward to working on *Kosmas* with equal anticipation."

"Are you troubled you never knew Earth?"

"We will in time."

Phil regarded the boy somberly. "Are all your brethren such as you?"

"Yes … Captain. We are distinct persona, but essentially we are of one."

"Most impressive. I want to meet you all. Talk to you. Get to know you—every one."

Phil stood. "Let's have lunch." He put a friendly arm around the boy's shoulder, and walked with him to the waiting buffet, where they would dine and talk for hours. All were surprised to observe the children were suddenly eating solid foods with an impressive gusto.

Phil and the children chatted incessantly. Unknown to anyone, except perhaps the children, Phil was subtly interrogating these Golden Childs. His manner was light and friendly and even humorous. The children reacted well. They laughed and spoke freely and ate as never before. In truth Phil was relentlessly digging deeper and deeper into their anima—attempting to construct a contraposition fabricated of their worldview contrasted with his reality as a function of his SNA.

And he was succeeding.

No one was aware of it. Not one of the crew.

But the children were.

***

At the end of a very long, and in many respects fascinating reception, the park was slowly vacating as people drifted away into lengthening shadows.

When all the children had departed Phil lingered, sitting on the same stone bench where he'd met the children, deep in thought. After a time he roused himself to seek out Anne and Aiy and inviting them to join him at one of the lively bars bordering the park. Although they were happy enough to join him, the subtle narrowness of their eyes and furtive glances betrayed misgivings about Phil's true intent in extending this most atypical invitation. Other than lunches and an occasional dinner, Phil always favored private venues.

When they were settled, drinks in hand, Phil appraised the two ladies with a penetrating stare from one to the other. "That was amazing, and I don't mind telling you ... somewhat disconcerting. There is far more to those children than meets the eye. They are unbelievably advanced."

Anne smiled "We feel the same. And their beauty and grace seem to strangely heighten their singularity. I wonder how Mike Auslander would have painted them?"

Phil leaned into the table assuming an analytical guise, squinting out to the park. "You know, for the life of me I can't figure out how the Gaunti were able to breed. They cannot have employed Onerian x-vitro insemination. The males are totally sterile by now and asexual reproduction is beyond the competence of even these hothouse hybrids. Cloning would never produce such results and I am certain the Gaunti would *never* act to stagnate our gene pool by employing such biotechnology."

Phil paused, seemingly lost in thought. As quickly, he raised a frowning finger and sat back, continuing. "But disregarding that for a moment, these kids seem to be far more than one generation removed from our anthropic population. Quite a mystery isn't it?" He directed a piercing stare at both. "Any ideas?"

Anne perked up immediately. "You know, virgin births—or parthenogenesis as I believe it's known—are not all that unheard of. Certain snakes, sharks, rays, amphibians and the like do so almost routinely."

"But not humans Anne. Not even close. The human body contains multi-gametes, but all have the same chromosomes. Were such an internal hermaphroditic joining to actually occur, the resulting embryo would have only twenty-three chromosomes and therefore non-viable. Suppose we drop that nonsense now and starting talking rationally."

Clearly taken aback, Anne concentrated on her drink.

Aiy was next. "I suppose this may relate to background radiation trickles provoking some sort of genetic mutation, which could have …"

Phil slammed into the table. Then his arm shot out, clutching Aiy's arm in a painful grip. "*Cut the crap goddammit! Both of you.*"

The bar was suddenly hushed.

As one, the ladies recoiled, nearly cringing, wide eyes and gaping chins recoiling from the fury of his anger. "What do you know that you're not telling me … that *no one* is telling me? Talk to me damn you, or I swear I'll beat it out of you. You know bloody well I'll figure this out. So stop stonewalling. You haven't the least idea how much danger we face because of this foolishness. *We don't have time to fuck around!*"

Anne heaved a long, hissing sigh. "Alright Phil. Here's what happened, but believe me, Aiy and myself were never involved. Please believe me."

He released his grip on Aiy as she rubbed her arm. A dark bruise would blossom there soon.

"Continue. Fast. Don't bullshit. I'll know if you do."

"I know. Well, when you underwent your first geriatric sleep interval, you were months without your sterility treatments."

"I was unaware of that. Are you saying geriatric sleep precludes sterility treatment?"

"Yes."

"Why is that? And why wasn't I told?"

"You must've missed one of the early pre-launch briefings on the island."

"Or it was arranged that I miss them."

"Whatever Phil. I don't really remember, or understand the Doctor's explanation, but it seems to have something to do with the slowing of sperm production and a chemical barrier in the systems that control and circulate such things. The *vas deferens* are involved somehow and I think the body may be raising its own defenses against itself due to erroneous identification of sperm cells. Anyhow geriatric sleep combined with sterility treatments apparently has harmful effects."

"That doesn't make one damned bit of sense."

"I'm telling you everything I know Phil. In any event it rendered you potent for the two years of your sleep. In fact you probably remain potent to this day."

He pursed his lips grimly. "I get the picture. Apparently I can't turn my back for a minute, much less two years."

Anne pushed on. "Some conjectured you chose to go first simply to ensure the entire male crew achieved permanent sterility. There was a great deal of debate as to why you elected chemical sterilization as opposed to a simple operation."

"A nonsense debate. Surgeries can be reversed, chemicals cannot, and we avoid physical intervention of the body whenever possible. This is and has been well known by every member of ship's company. So let's lose the bullshit shall we? I don't have time for this. Proceed."

"It now appears your alleged long-sleep tactic makes no sense, as you were clearly unaware of the potency issue. At the same time, as they say, person or persons unknown grew concerned the population of Gauntlet was insufficient to confront the momentous challenges of ensuing decades. Simply put, someone felt the QAVL miscalculated the human resource needed to complete this mission."

They were spot on there. The QAVL couldn't care less about human resources. This crew is here simply to keep me sane, entertained and occupied—tinker toys for a potential Verteror.

"So they waited until I was asleep and pinched my semen!"

"So it would seem."

"They stole my genes. They stole my rights. In a very real sense they committed rape and mutiny. As a result, I am ... my God ... I am ... the *father* of a whole generation of these creatures? Somehow the combination of my genes combined with female Gaunti propagated a … How many children were conceived?"

"Sixty. Thirty inhabit In-World and thirty are Out-Worlders."

Phil's eyes glazed for a few seconds. Then they cleared. "Why in hell's name didn't you tell me about this?"

Neither Anne nor Aiy cared to respond. However after a few moments under Phil's unrelenting glower, Anne finally fessed up, head lowered and eyes averted. "Phil, when we discovered the mass insemination, we advised the Gaunti it might be easier for you if you figured it out yourself, as you always do. As you just did. Believe me, it was never anyone's intention to keep this from you indefinitely."

"Do those children know I'm their father?"

"Phil, you've been exposed to their intelligence. I believe they're possibly even more intuitive than you. So I would …"

Phil abruptly sprang to his feet with such force his chair flew across the room, slamming into another table drawing all eyes in the bar. Without a word he spun on his heels and pushed out.

Anne and Aiy regarded each other ominously.

***

Anne recognized just how threatening this was certain to become. "There's going to be hell to pay over this. Phil's not going to give this up until he knows everything."

Aiy responded grimly. "Or he insights it himself."

They rose and slowly found their way out as well.

They would not see Phil again for weeks.

The Golden Time

ALTHOUGH PHIL WAS effectively alienated from all aboard, he never lost control. Without exception the Gaunti treated him with the deep respect and veneration they had always shown him.

As the weeks wore on, normalcy seemed to slowly return and their old amity finally resurfaced, albeit somewhat guardedly. His orders were executed instantly, without question, and he was welcomed wherever he passed.

***

Consistent with his command duties, every twelve weeks or so Philip would declare a full-dress ship's alert. Utility or coveralls for ship's crew and complement. Med Kits/O2&Breathing Masks for everyone, even charged sidearms and full combat gear for security personnel, all thusly equipped twenty-four hours a day for the duration of the exercise.

The entire ship's compliment crammed into a huge, hardened Emergency Shelter, cramped, dirty and uncomfortable, cold emergency rations only—exactly as intended. Personnel were allowed leave only to man duty stations, and then only suited up in full hard vacuum survival suits. Alerts were called 2-3 times a day, simulating every conceivable exigency, including deep-space combat tactics and even civil insurrection scenarios.

Phil demanded that every facet of ship and crew's operations check out five-by-five. Recurrent training, or repetitive iteration for the Gaunti was superfluous in the extreme. But Phil demanded they demonstrate a sort of *esprit de Gauntlet* and verify their total comprehension of prevailing SOP.

Gauntians invariably proved themselves exceptionally proficient; without any grousing, goldbricking, or foot-dragging.

Afterwards, the Gaunti returned to their own pursuits, looking to no one for guidance, governance, coordination, or interference.

In the absence of specific orders, *Gauntlet* happily reverts to that ultimate and utmost culminant of governance—given sufficiently evolved beings and a government matured beyond self-aggrandizing, power hungry meddling:

ANARCHY

***

One sunny Sunday morning, after much ado, Phil decided it was high time his hard-earned culinary prowess enjoyed a luncheon debut. So, with little notice, he invited Anne and Aiy to lunch at his Residence.

This was to mark the revival of their on-again-off-again troika.

Chicken-fried steak, pan gravy, half-mashed potatoes, steaming collard greens, pecan pie and iced tea.

Luncheon on the terrace.

When they had completed Phil's debut luncheon "Well?" smiled Phil. Eyes expectantly bright "How was it?"

Anne "It was *great* Phil and I think I need a nap."

Aiy "I need a twenty kilometer run. I'd rather swim, but I'd sink right to the bottom. That was a *very* substantial lunch. I feel as though I've swallowed a sizable newborn, but it was delicious. Thank you Phil. Really."

As they rose to leave, Phil arrested their precipitous departure. "The fun's not over yet ladies."

Anne and Aiy exchanged intrigued smiles. Was a *ménage à trois* in the offing?

Good grief not now, maybe in 2-3 hours …

Phil smiled. "Jake?"

Jake arrived immediately with an iced bottle of Gaunti Champagne, four fluted glasses and a small black lacquer box, prepared to join them for a drink.

Anne and Aiy quizzically locked eyes again and reseated themselves on the terrace.

When Jake had completed pouring the wine, Phil stood. "I have something that belongs to you Aiy and I think it's time I returned it." He raised his glass in toast and presented her the box.

With warm smiles, they returned the toast, as their interest peaked.

Aiy guardedly opened the box, withdrawing a single gold ring fashioned into an earring.

"My God! My mother's ring." She held it to her breast it in both hands. "My God. Thank you Phil. I thought I'd lost it forever. Wherever did you find it?"

Phil regarded her appraisingly for a moment. "I believe your recovery is sufficiently complete. I think I can tell you."

"Yes?"

After a short pause "I tore it off the ear of the warped little bastard who tortured, mutilated and virtually killed you in Ghazi Kahn." He watched her eyes intently. "Just before I burnt him to a crisp."

Aiy studied him with a somber intensity he had never before seen.

She finally spoke. "I love you Phil." She began to quietly weep, tears coursing down her graceful neck.

"I love you Aiy." He put an arm around Aiy and then both ladies. Passions suddenly flared, but when the moment had passed, Phil was suddenly inexplicably uncomfortable.

With little comment, he quietly withdrew to Shark Bay and his beloved solitary depths.

Anne and Aiy followed him out with thoughtful eyes.

***

They again became a libidinous, loving trio for five weeks, then Anne and Aiy's numbers came up, and they reported for their geriatric sleep, gone from his life for two years. Nor did Phil see much of them afterwards, except infrequent dinners, or the occasional frolic.

It was soon many months since their last encounter. Phil suspected the two were pressuring the new generation of Gaunti bio-engineers who had made exceptional advances developing a neoteric *Kosmas* language treatment. Knowing Anne and Aiy, there was little he could do to stop them, should he wish to.

He fervently hoped he would see them again, alive and sane and speaking *Kosmas*, were such truly possible.

Child of Gold
Child of Shadow

HUMANS EXHIBIT INTERESTING responses to their living environment.

On the one hand, given sufficient resource, they invariably expand population and possessions to occupy nearly all available space. This results in hellishly cramped environs, suffocating in a fetid quagmire of flesh and filth and meaningless claptrap.

Conversely, humans, no matter how closely confined, psychologically expand available space to literally become their entire world.

On an exponentially larger scale the same transpired on Gauntlet. In fact they now had two 'worlds.'

In-World and Out-World.

***

The tacit reconciliation between Phil and ship's company was settling in well. Relations had thawed with such a blossoming mutual regard they quite literally returned to the high-spirited-pre-launch days of years ago.

Perhaps the most dramatic was Phil's unexpected acceptance of his newly realized children. The entire ship's company was taken by surprise and hugely pleased. He was getting on famously with his *In-Worlders*, as he and the Gaunti now referred to the Golden Childs. In a variation on that theme, the term *Out-Worlders*, or Dark Childs had been coined to refer to the denizens of the dark surface world.

Phil had never been partial to children. They'd always irritated and intimidated him. Consequently it was a profound shock to discover he was suddenly the father of sixty children, evenly distributed between Gaunti's sunny In-World and its twilight, radiation-drenched Out-World.

The *In-Worlders'* anti-twins, the *Out-Worlders*, exclusively inhabited Out-World, and between the two groups they were known as the Yin and Yang of the cosmos. It was unavoidable not to regard the *In-Worlders* as Yang and *Out-Worlders* as Yin.

It had now been years since the *Out-Worlders* had participated in any aspect of Gaunti life and *vice versa*. Time had simply slipped away and their isolation was so complete no one knew their current status or state of development. Nor had it even occurred to any of ship's company to extend feelers into their dark world. Perhaps some entity was promulgating this schism?

Had anyone pondered this aberration, they would have surely realized that their minds were somehow being tampered with. Accordingly, it never occurred to anyone that this relationship was in any way questionable. Some unknown and unsuspected force kept them blithely and complacently apart.

This was not irresponsible on the Gaunti's part. Safety and sustenance were constantly maintained, albeit automated and remotely supported. Communications were constantly monitored, though totally unused. However, should the Out-Worlders encounter any difficulty and seek help their need would not go unheeded.

Phil now felt the proud In-World father. His Golden Childs clearly adored him; and he they. The children had grown tall and slim now, looking far more mature than their tender years. Without exception they were blessed with beauty, flawless physiques, perfect health and intellects of an order never before achieved by humankind. They grew at a phenomenal rate, yet remained children in many ways. As was long accepted, emotional maturity did not develop hand-in-hand with physical and intellectual development. Such growth needs time to nurture.

Accordingly, Phil faithfully devoted two or three hours a day to their advancement. In this respect he flagrantly and *de facto* rejected the Oneirion

Nursery philosophy practiced years ago on Pre-Launch Earth. This troubled him—not at all.

He remembered passing out the first time he entered the Nursery on Oneiro. Then he witnessed the stunning product of their genius. All the same, he was truly motivated to participate in the development of these Golden In-Worlders, to bestow on them something of himself beyond his genes. This was not Earth, these were not Oneirians, and this was most certainly not an Oneirion Nursery.

He presented them their world from perspectives they had not seen: the top of Mount Gaunti, Shark Bay, life under the Webberian Sea, spheriscopes of Pre-Launch Earth, images and history of Oneiro and far more. Often they would simply run, or ride the QAVLGates, or the PM's, just for amusement. Neither Phil nor his children truly required exercise, but sometimes they would play games, or sports and they all loved to swim and run. Always they laughed and talked and talked. During these captivating interludes all Gaunti vicariously reveled in their fun.

Other times he looked after their education; which was a daunting prospect considering their intellect and the ageless span of their knowledge. Phil did actually command greater knowledge in many disciplines and certainly greater wisdom; partly attributable to his SNA, and in part his transcendent experiences. But in fact, he frequently found himself learning from *them*. Many lively debates ensued when the children's independent conclusions ran counter to conventional science—not that the Gaunti were constrained by conventional science either—the In-Worlders were simply far more advanced. More often than not, the children's hypothesis prevailed. Flawless logic was augmented by profound insight, command of the facts, advanced science, spectacular creativity and an innate insight bordering on a near preternatural synthesis. Phil was tested to his absolute limits. And these were still but children.

***

One of the pursuits he most enjoyed was cooking for them. They would invade his Residence, galloping and exploring everywhere, as he and Jake rushed about to cook, or barbeque, and serve on Phil's vast terrace/swimming pool. Phil found it intriguing and immensely gratifying that the *Golden-Childs* would not eat solids with any real appetite unless they dined with him. He's asked them about this, eliciting no more response than "Once in a while we get hungry for solids when it's something we like."

To his astonishment he suspected he loved these children. Was this simply a function of his genes and hormones? Was it simply an expression of pride and affection? He would never know. Perhaps he secretly relished the idea of springing these preeminent homo-sapiens on QASI and the rest of his imperious lot. Perhaps the *Kosmian's* disparaging opinion of mankind might grow a bit more enlightened? Perhaps he could engender a bit of re-pudiation of their callous dismissal of humanity's very existence.

***

Phil's happy months passed dreamlike. But after a time, Phil recognized what he had known and suppressed for far too long: a lurking guilt had been growing in the recesses of his mind: the shadow children of Out-World.

He had shamefully neglected them, as had all Gaunti. Phil realized with a shock that he hadn't visited Out-World since its initial construction years ago. The Dark Childs were his children as well after all, despite the foreboding ambience of their habitation and disturbing, though uncon-firmed reports of their development. Any and all audio or visual interface had long been demolished. Not encouraging.

He suspected he had unconsciously blocked the *Out-Worlders*. He as-sumed this was somehow related to man's innate rejection of the darkness. Or had some force blocked this issue from his mind? Or he had been simply avoiding the task. Nonetheless, they had been left entirely alone for far too long.

He'd not even seen them from the bubble of The Gaunti Café. Where were they? What were they? Did they still even exist? He resolved to correct this immediately. He would set this iniquity to rights. He would bring the Dark Childs into the fold. He would become Out-World-Father as much as In-World-Father.

The next day Phil travelled alone and unheralded to the nearest of the dozens of small personal hatches leading to Out-World. He un-dogged the hatch and climbed into the companionway, advising the Command Bridge, as alerts would invariably appear on their security monitors.

Mega-tinsel-strength hatches were one of the very defensible rationales for the isolation of Out-World. It was imperative that Out-World be hermetically sealed against the possibility of catastrophic decompression. Any open hatch would seal instantly, at the slightest indication of loss of bubble integrity. In the eventuality of such a disaster, Phil was painfully aware he would be instantly sliced in two should he be in the midst of clearing a hatch at such a moment. Such was unequivocally stated on the hatch itself.

For the first half of his climb he descended relative to the surface of In-World. Once inside the companionway, the Gaunti-glass hatch automatically closed above him. He looked up and saw a large circle of bright blue sky punctuated by intermittent streaks of O^2 Sampler Birds as they faithfully flew their rounds. The companionway was lit with dim reddish-orange lights to facilitate night vision on Out-World. This demanded extra care on steps and handholds and generally slow going. When he reached the GEP (Gravitational Equipoise Point) a second hatch opened allowing him access to the GEP sphere. As the second hatch closed above him the access ladder controls flashed red, instructing him to take a firm grip. Thanks to QAVL gravity engineering, at the GEP his weight was effectively zero and his mass was nominal. Therefore he couldn't really fall. It was disorienting however and best to hold tight.

After the unit smoothly swiveled 180°, a third hatch opened and he was now looking up through the Gaunti-glass hatch to Out-World—a deep indigo, perfectly circular aureole dusted with stars.

He began his ascent to the surface.

This would have been one hellofa lot faster had I taken one of the damned cargo chutes.

When he cleared the Gaunti-glass hatch and stood upon Out-World, his first reaction was anger. During construction he had given explicit orders that LED Flood Lights be installed at precise intervals throughout the entire exterior of Gauntlet. In anticipation of this he'd brought no hand-held lighting. There were no LED's. Not one. Phil was therefore forced to tread gingerly through the black and silver-gray dappled twilight.

This crew is too goddamned independent. They can't seem to follow one goddamned order. My fault I suppose, or their genes, or both.

Stars above contrasted with the dark irregular surface, dotted with thousands of pools reflecting millions of diamond sparkles from the sky. Hundreds of caves and overheads were molded into the rubbery, caliginous surface lending it a dark other worldly feel. The whole scene glowed with reflective magnificence, framed by the enormous transparent world-bubble seen only as a concave transparent aura at regular intervals across the sky. Colossal reinforced columns throughout helped ensure the integrity of the bubble. Many columns served the dual purpose as gravity chutes for escape vessels in case of an Abandon Ship order, as they were built over existing escape pods. As the bubble itself was quadruple layered and self-sealing, any impact short of an object the size of an old-style bus, would not breach integrity. This, combined with Gauntlet's FOD (Foreign Object Deflection) systems, ensured reasonable security. If this was not sufficient, well, they had opted to live out here of their own volition, and in fact their militant insistence.

Phil imagined how Gauntlet must now look from space. He pictured a huge black ball, featureless, encapsulated within a transparent glossy sheath enveloping the small planetoid within a star-flecked corona.

He'd been shuffling and stumbling along for about thirty minutes, finding nothing beyond the endless bizarre topography extending to a preposterously close horizon.

On In-World the horizon was literally endless. On Out-World the horizon seemed an uncontrolled slide over an infinite precipice.

He found no signs of life whatsoever, shuffling on, dismay and concern increasing with each step.

***

Then the odor.

It stopped him in his tracks. He'd never smelled anything remotely similar before. As he stepped cautiously forward the stench grew stronger and stronger until he was gagging on it. It permeated everything. There was no escaping it. It nauseated him, yet he intuited this was the marker-pointer he'd been seeking. As its strength grew he tried to analyze exactly what he smelled.

God, it smells like sour milk and long dead bloated corpses floating in a sewer … and a cloying insinuation of something else … a malignant undertone … cloyingly sweet as putrid honey.

What a stench! Did the Out-Worlders perish here?

He doggedly followed the odor despite its putrescence and finally spotted something. Unsure what he was seeing he, braced himself and moved closer, gradually making out the form of the thing that must be the source of the ghastly foulness.

Whatever it was, it was huge. Lurking in the shadows was the most monstrously hideous creature he had ever seen. Beyond belief. Beyond imagining. Beyond nightmares.

From roughly three meters Phil dimly made out a nebulous black form, very large, roughly spherical and rubbery, covered with dozens of eyes embillicalled by a long black neckish tube. If this were its 'head,' it had its own legs. Dozens of tiny black digits supported it, which clearly allowed it to travel horizontally consistent with the appended thorax.

The neck tube joined to an even larger bloated spherical, gut-like mass, surrounded by a hideous margin of tens of assorted appendages, grotesque rubbery parodies of arms, legs, genitalia, ears and nostrils. These were interspersed with slowly oscillating apertures, possibly phylogenetically adapted mouths, although patently not intended for ingestion. A sound issued from the thing reminiscent of a moist, ragged bellows struggling to sustain a rhythmic flow of air. It constantly voided itself and extended black fleshy pipettes to ingest nutrients contained in the rubbery ponds almost totally shrouded by its massive corpulence.

It moved with a glacial lethargy. A shadowy nightmare of black muculent flesh slithering through its odious swale, dimly lustrous in the starlight like the satiny epidermal slime of a slug. He surmised it had evolved its unique coloration to facilitate absorption of the feeble interstellar radiation to be found far out amongst the stars.

Why does it hunger after such feeble emissions when In-World has abundant radiant energy for thousands of years and more? Why doesn't it simply 'come inside' and get warm and well fed? Although, come to think of it, thank God it doesn't. And damn, I don't think even the cargo chutes could carry the ugly thing.

He maintained a safe distance from the thing as he peered into the gloom. After a time he made out several other like monstrosities in the surrounding area. But where were the Out-Worlders?

Have these things done something to them? Are they hiding from them? Are they hiding from ME? For God's sake, did this repulsive bio-form find its way aboard Gauntlet and devour them?

Then it hit him. Like driving into a brick wall. *These* were the children. *His* children. *These* were the Out-Worlders.

He fumed bitterly.

What in God's name have we done? Though God has nothing to do with this wickedness. If I knew who stole my semen, I'd have the son-of-a-bitch out an airlock in a nanosecond.

The adaptive rate of these creatures must be beyond phenomenal. What will they be when we reach Kosmas? What will they be when we reach Earth? The In-Worlders and the Out-Worlders. From the same genome they chose two radically deviate paths. Are the In-Worlders evolving at the same rate? Will these two taxonomies come together someday? Are we looking at the next iteration of mankind? Shall we force them together? Keep them apart? Kill one group? Which one? Kill them all? Or kill none? CAN we kill them?

I will not make this decision alone. My senior staff got me into this barrel and by damn they are getting in with me, but how can I keep it from the In-Worlders? They have a positive genius for learning what goes on. Can I keep ANYTHING from the In-Worlders? Or the Out-Worlders for that matter? Goddammit!

Waves of nausea churned through his stomach, and for the first time in more years than he could remember, he shuddered from true, sweaty-handed, dry-mouthed, knee-knocking fear. Phil was horrified at the idea these were his *children* and he strongly suspected they knew they were his progeny. He also suspected they knew he found them loathsome. How could he permit such abominations to endure? What was he considering? All he need do was detonate the bubble enclosing Out-World and problem solved, his beautiful sphere clean and bright once again. But was it mass murder? Infanticide? Genocide? A crime against humanity? A crime against man's destiny?

What a hellish trap has my crew perpetrated on me?

What about Kosmas? I imagine there are life forms on Kosmas that would make this creature seem a butterfly by comparison. All the same, I simply cannot allow them to see this, this thing. This obscenity is not human and I won't have any other species thinking it is.

His thoughts wandered back to Earth, the Museum of Natural History in Manhattan, to the savage Theropods, seventy-million years ago in the Cretaceous. Huge rapacious carnivores cannibalizing the young of their own species, sometimes their very own offspring, devouring them whenever parents grew careless, or survival made its harsh demands within the hatch.

He remembered that at a certain age, offspring would graduate from siblings to lunch. Mama needed to push along to the next batch. Was he degenerating into Therodpodia? Was he going to figuratively eat his own children? Finally his thoughts and the loathsome stink overcame him. He vomited. Violently. Again and again. Doubled over, tears running down his face, blending with flows from nose and mouth, dripping from chin. The overwhelming stench of the place was now enriched with the sour acridity of human bile.

This just keeps getting better and better …

All the while the monstrous creature passively observed.

He cynically mused *I wonder what it thinks of Daddy now?*

Then Phil heard the rasping croak. A horror he'd never imagined.

"Hello Father."

Philip thought he would pass out. Instead he struggled to draw on the depths of control and courage he'd so easily summoned in many crisis past.

"Hello child. I regret it has been so long since I visited you. In fairness, I had no idea you were my … progeny."

"We understand. We've always understood. You have no reason for regret."

"Thank you. I have a question."

"Yes Father?"

"Why?"

"Such an inane question for our first encounter. Surely you know the answer. The answer has been there for nearly fourteen billion years. We advanced to our present form to optimize radiation matriculation and benefit from the joy and power of synergistic intellect. That is our working hypothesis in any event."

"I see."

I actually do see, but how in hell can they?

"Do you have a name?"

"We have an inter-mutual name. It is very complex. You could never understand it, or pronounce it."

"Next question."

"Yes Father?"

"*Must* you be so fucking ugly? *Must* you smell so bloody awful?"

"Such unworthy questions Father."

"I am your father and your Captain and I may ask any damned question I wish."

"Acknowledged. In answer to your question: given sufficient adaptive tension, we could conceivably assume any shape, or odor, even one that might please you. Possibly the form of your beloved In-Worlders?"

"You resent the In-Worlders? Are you jealous?"

"Father, that question is not only unworthy, it is absurd. The In-Worlders are our brothers and sisters, as much as you are our father. We do not resent *them* in any manner whatsoever. In fact Father it is *you* who are repelled by *us.*"

"You are some sort of composite being?"

"Yes."

"Comprised of what?"

"Our brothers and sisters."

"How many are you?"

"More than we began. Fewer than we will be. We now duplicate metamitotically, with great frequency."

Phil made a grimacing gesture towards the massive body. "Is this ... this form efficient?"

"This is but a transitive form. But as you well know Father, efficiency—therefore design—is defined by objective. Objective being defined as impelling evolutive stress. May we then deduce you are questioning our objective? Our right to exist?"

"Yes. Your reasoning is sound. What was your objective in assuming that form?"

"We did not *assume* this form, as you state it. We *evolved* into it. That being the case, we had no objective. We are as yet unaware of any objective."

"You are capable of dissimulation?"

"Most definitely. Yes."

"I see." Phil thought for a moment. "You have no control over the processes that so profoundly metamorphosed you?"

"We suppose we could. However, for now: no more, nor less than you Father."

"We appear to be talking at cross purposes."

"Understandable, considering our respective circumstance."

"You are healthy?"

"Yes."

"Happy?"

"That term does not apply to us."

"Are you children?"

"That term does not apply to us."

"Looking forward to a rich life with fellow humans?"

No response.

A tiny bleating alarm commenced a rhythmic blare in the recesses of Phil's mind.

"Do you have children of your own?"

"As we told you father," patience discordant with its rasping whisper "we now reproduce meta-mitotically."

"Do you understand the mission we are committed to?"

"Yes."

"Do you understand the cosmos?"

"Partly."

"Are you fearful of our destination?"

"Partly."

"Do you fear me?"

"Hardly."

Phil was quiet for nearly ten minutes. The tiny alarm was growing more insistent, his personal claxon beginning to blare.

"You have a leader?"

"Yes."

"Who?"

"You, Father."

"So you will act within my chain of command?"

"To the point where our welfare and autonomy remain unchallenged, yes."

The claxon was growing louder and louder. "That's not exactly the definition of working within the ..."

"You look very tired father. You need to rest."

The claxon was deafening now. It thundered so, it was becoming impossible to think and difficult to hear.

Suddenly fatigue overtook him. His knees nearly buckled and his breathing was labored.

I've got to get out of here.

Phil was nearly mumbling now. "I uh, will return in ten days."

"We look forward to your return Father." As Phil turned away and struggled to remain erect "But first Father, may we pose a question to *you*?"

This was testing his limits. "Make it fast."

The derision in his voice unmistakable: "Are you quite certain detonation of the Gaunti-bubble will result in our destruction?"

He heard the subtle smirk in its voice and it felt like a sizable boulder had been dropped on his chest from a great height. He stumbled away without response.

Mother of God! What horrific mess have those Gaunti morons brought down upon us? There is a deadly force brewing in our midst and it's just beginning. Who and why would someone want to introduce a nest of near-invincible leprous vipers on Gauntlet? I believe whomever perpetrated this obscenity knew exactly what they were doing. This wasn't just some guileless stunt to increase our population. Someone or something knew these creatures would emerge. This was the work of a fearfully advanced intellect.

Exhausted and barely able to control his trembling, Phil staggered to the In-World access hatch, so weakened he could hardly budge the dog-lever. Eventually the hatch opened and Phil gratefully took refuge in the access tube.

When he finally stood on the surface of In-World his trembling was totally out of control. He lay down in the grass and peered up to the bright blue sky.

Such a relief to immerse one's self in the bright, fresh, clean familiar.

He fell asleep immediately.

He awakened hours later near completion of the night-cycle.

He arose stiffly, wrinkled, dirty, unshaven and damp, wearily finding his way home.

"My gawd sir! Aren't you a sight? We had no idea where you were, and you were gone so long the whole ship's on alert. We thought you might be undersea, but you always inform me when you do so. I should put out the word that you are home safe now. Would that be alright sir?"

"Fine. First get me two bottles of gin. I will be in my water sphere. No interruptions. None."

Rage Black
Opportunity Golden

A FULL TWENTY-FOUR hours later, Phil raised himself from the waters of his private deep-dive sphere. As always after such sessions, he felt strong, refreshed and eager to attack the day. He was also madder than blue hell. He'd been used and fooled and something was clearly capable of masking the truth from him—a disturbing reality, the nature of which he could not begin to fathom.

After a long invigorating FOND Shower, Phil donned his Captain's uniform and walked to the terrace. Jake followed him. Only a subtle jump of eyebrows and the slightest tilt of head belied his surprise at Phil's attire.

"Good morning sir. Another beautiful day isn't it?" When Phil failed to respond, Jake nodded at Phil's uniform and queried. "Is there some special occasion today sir?"

"Why do you ask?"

"Well sir, you're wearing your Class-A uniform."

"And why shouldn't I? I *am* Captain of this vessel."

"Ah, certainly sir. May I bring you some breakfast?"

"Coffee strong. Black. New York Strip Steak very rare, and chili beans. Hot."

"Right away sir."

"… and bring me a large water glass of scotch."

"Mm, is everything alright sir?"

Phil peered down from his lofty perch over the city spreading below in stony silence.

"Sir?"

"Breakfast Jake. And bring the scotch straightaway."

When Phil was served and seated at breakfast, he looked up to Jake. "I want you to put out a meeting call for today at 1400. I want all officers in Class-A's and I want to convene the meeting in my conference room here in the Residence."

"Here in the Residence sir?"

Phil stopped chewing and washed down a large bite of steak with huge gulp of searing coffee. "*Is there a problem?*"

"None whatsoever sir."

"Listen to me Jake. This is an exceptional, and perhaps our only, opportunity to act preemptively. Thanks to forces amongst the Gaunti I have yet to identify, I've been in constant reaction mode. This will end today. I'm going to find out who's at the bottom of this. Then I will ensure they are permanently immobilized if I have to kill them—which just might be a pleasure. Next I will positively determine what risks are presented by these elements. Then I will take immediate and appropriate action, attacking this threat. I will not let this opportunity pass. In fact I *cannot* let it pass."

"What elements are you referring to sir?"

"The children."

"*The children?*" Jake's incredulity was ill controlled seeming somewhat contrived.

"Yes, the goddamned children. I believe someone knowingly unleashed an agency within our midst capable of destroying Gauntlet and ending this mission."

"You believe this agency is dangerous? The children?"

Phil was growing impatient. His voice harsh. His eyes piercing. "I want armed guards at all entrances to the Residence and positioned outside the conference room. All electronics will be removed from the room and all participants, including myself. All windows will be sealed and the room is to be thoroughly searched for any sort of listening or recording devices. Re-enforce this with a short-range jamming device and a white sound generator to mask discussion."

Jake pondered over his charges.

Philip seems quite paranoid this morning. I've never seen him like this.

"Aye sir. Attendees to the meeting?"

"Anne and Aiy, 1st Office Farrow, Chief of Security, Doctor Singe, Sergeant at Arms, yourself, Uncle HERB and whoever is regarded as our leading expert on munitions."

"Sir, 1400 is rather short notice for so many ..."

"*Everyone* on the list will be seated in my conference room at 1400 *sharp*. All securities will be in place. The conference room will be sterilized and sealed. Clear?"

"Absolutely clear sir." Jake turned to begin his tasks.

"One more thing."

"Sir?"

"Should anyone learn of this meeting and its preparations beyond my list of attendees, guards and technicians, I will see a brig is constructed and anyone who breached security will spend no less than one year incarcerated, very unpleasantly. Make damned sure everyone understands this."

"Aye sir."

Stormy Whether

AT 1400 PHIL wordlessly strode into the conference room to the head of the table, seating himself, engrossed in a brief document.

All were present. Officers were in uniform. All security preparations were in place, windows were blocked and sealed and invisible signals surrounded them, blocking any electronic or physical eavesdrop. Phil looked up from his document.

"Mr. Farrow."

"Sir?"

"You are herewith reassigned to full-time First Officer. Whatever occupied you until this afternoon, will cease immediately. I expect you to devote all your waking hours to the duties of XO, ensuring my orders are carried out to the letter, unless or until I order differently."

"Is something wrong sir?"

"You're damned right something's wrong. My orders are not being carried out. Children and animals are running all over the ship, both of which were unequivocally proscribed prior to launch. Discipline is near non-existent. Incredibly dangerous things go on aboard this vessel of which we are blissfully ignorant. Illegal and semi-mutinous acts are carried out in the total absence of redress. We may be in danger of totally losing control over this ship. We may be in danger of losing it all. In fact I am certain we are in grave danger. That's just for starters. Sufficient Mr. Farrow?"

"Absolutely sir. I trust we will be reviewing these points in greater detail?"

"You can bet on it Mister, in excruciating detail."

"I look forward to it sir."

"Good. Sergeant-at-Arms."

"Yes sir."

"Effective immediately you will post armed guards at every access to Out-World."

"I believe there are ..."

"Eight. No one exits or enters without my explicit authority. Their standing orders are shoot to stop, maim, or kill if need be. I want you to construct guardhouses at each position that look like anything but guardhouses.

"Ensure your team is creative. Ensure each post is different in size and in look and apparent purpose. Ensure you construct at least twice as many structures as access points. You will install extras far from any access point, but still in-line. Equip all posts with every type of sensor. Provide for a comfortable, secure and completely undetectable guard room with underground and aboveground access. Posts should simulate small structures such as technical control points, power and communications relays, storage facilities, even snack bars and such. Until the guard houses are ready and installed, your guards will unobtrusively man their posts from positions no less than one-hundred meters from each hatch. Black commando gear at night, camouflage during the days. I want to review your designs before you go into fabrication and I want this within six days."

"Aye sir."

"Good. You are dismissed."

"Mr. Williams. I believe you are our munitions expert?"

"Yes sir."

"You are ordered to mine all personal access points to Out-World. You are to do this with extreme care to ensure your mines are absolutely undetectable and the resultant explosion preserves a positive seal between In-World and Out-World. They will be activated only from this facility, or the Captain's Station on the Command Bridge. They should be equipped with highest securities. You are further instructed to do this in such a manner that no one, either In-World or Out-World, will entertain the slightest suspicion regarding your activities. All work will be performed silently, no sooner than four hours into sleep cycles. Coordinate with me and I will ensure the sleep cycles are particularly dark. You will take no action without my approval of your designs.

"When these tasks are complete you will then direct your efforts to the cargo chutes. I want them mined as well, with an option to launch HE-SAMs, targeting the Out-World environmental bubble. Identical security protocols and launch control points as the access points. Do you understand?"

"Yes sir."

"You are also facing a six day deadline. Clear?"

"Clear sir."

"Good. That will be all."

Nick Farrow raised a questioning hand.

"Yes Mr. Farrow?"

"Ah, shouldn't we be taking minutes? This is a complex and critical meeting and …"

Phil sighed in frustration, running both hands through his hair. "Mr. Farrow. You are my XO. Correct?"

"Yes sir."

"The ultimate commander after me. Is that right?"

"Yes sir."

"Amongst other duties the XO is charged with precisely relaying the Captain's orders to the crew and ensuring they are carried out to the letter. You are quite well aware of this."

"Yes sir I am."

"I have total recall of every syllable uttered in this room and I expect no less from anyone present. The last thing I want is a paper or electronic trail of these proceedings. Consider every word of this meeting as Above Top Secret. If this exceeds anyone's capabilities we can easily summon alternates. Will this be necessary?"

"No. Sir."

"Fine. Those remaining in this room will now address the principal issue of this meeting. This will not be pleasant for anyone, including myself, I assure you. All the same I demand total candor from every person in this room. Anything less and our mission may well fail, Gauntlet will be lost and we will all most likely be destroyed."

Phil paused, surveyed the room very soberly and continued.

"If I detect anyone withholding information, or dissimulating in any way, it will be viewed as treason and summary retribution will be forthcoming, without a hearing."

A very concerned XO intervened. "Captain, there are laws governing this sort of thing."

"And where do you suppose these laws are handed down from Mister Farrow?"

"Well sir, I suppose …"

"The law comes from me, XO. I *am* the law aboard this vessel, as I was on Oneiro. Unless of course it is your intention to supplant me as Captain."

Almost as one the room responded with a jolt. *"Captain!"*

"Fine. I welcome any challenges or disputes. However, I remain the court of final appeal. I trust that is clear and undisputed."

Phil scrutinized everyone in the room intensely, one-by-one, eye-to-eye, seeking the slightest flinch, twitch or blink. Any sign of prevarication, weakness or indecision would compromise them. Guilt, embarrassment, shame. These were acceptable. Nothing else. Any other reaction would find its way into some very special quarters secreted in the lower levels of the Residence, which Phil had ordered installed weeks prior to launch.

"I will now pose a question. I will be posing many in days to come and I will not tolerate evasion, or lies, or any attempt to cover up the facts. God help anyone who should attempt to do so. Make no mistake, I cannot be misled."

Jake had heard stories about Phil's decisiveness and his ability to formulate complex plans as fast as he could speak and detect lies with absolute precision. Jake had never witnessed it before. Despite himself, he was awed by it.

Anne gestured in concern. "Phil, I believe you are over …"

"You will address me as Captain, or Sir. Clear?"

Anne paused for a moment, hurt and confusion warring with an anger borne of humiliation and the abrupt turn-about of a long-time friend and lover.

"Perfectly clear, Captain."

"The first question: Who was the mutinous half-witted thief that stole my semen? I know damned well someone, if not everyone in this room can answer my question."

A stony silence ensued.

"Jake? HERB?"

Jake spoke up. "Neither of us is privy to any such activity. What with our new Command Triad, we are regarded as command officers rather than staff, thusly we're out of the grapevine."

"I understand. Mr. Farrow?" Farrow wordlessly shook his head side to side.

"Anne? Aiy?" No response.

"You will answer my question *now*."

Silence.

Phil jumped to his feet and with his left arm cast the massive conference table aside. He drove it into the wall, inflicting serious damage to the wall, breaking the table nearly in half and knocking three people out of their chairs. One bleeding from the scalp.

Phil rounded on the group, not unlike some large predator rounding on its prey. "You think this is a joke? Some sort of temper tantrum?" Phil whirled on Jake. "Activate the display screen."

Jake had some difficulty complying since the screen controls had been built into the conference table. Six long tense minutes later the screen came to life. Strain in the room was so intense breathing itself seemed difficult.

In a low, threatening voice Phil continued.

"Two days ago I went Out-World. Has anyone else in this room taken the trouble to visit the surface?"

There was no response, so Phil continued.

"I mounted a collar-corder prior to entering the area, as I didn't believe the shadow children were aware of these devices. Perhaps they were. In any event they made no attempt to prevent me from making the recording you are about to see. Perhaps they just didn't give a damn. Jake?"

The screen sprang to life, recounting in graphic detail the strange adventure of Captain Philip Carr on Gauntlet's dark Out-World. The shock, revulsion and awe permeating the room was palpable.

As the recording ended Phil turned to the group. "You will now answer my questions."

Anne murmured, more to herself than the group "It feels like we have been … infested … that we have been … violated. To think our beautiful little world is encrusted with those … things. We live with them literally encasing us. This is a claustrophobic nightmare."

"Quiet Anne. That sort of indulgent homily serves no purpose."

Doctor Signe mused in awe. "How could *anything* mutate at such an incredible rate?"

Phil responded impatiently "As you well know Doctor there are *tree moths* on Earth capable of adaptation to ambient light changes in a single generation, a tiny march of days. Bacterial and viral forms can sometimes adapt near instantly. There are no temporal constraints on evolution. I suggest you face up to this reality damned fast, because if my suspicions prove out, this is only the beginning."

Anne again interrupted. "Captain, Aiy has been injured. She is losing blood. May I take her to the clinic?"

Phil lent forward and examined Aiy's forehead. "She'll live. Give her a napkin and an analgesic if you have one. No one leaves this room until we have finished. *Now answer my goddamned question!*"

The group was effectively cowed now. The recording had had a profound effect on them and they were beginning to appreciate the looming danger that so roused the Captain's ire and urgency. Yet they remained reticent.

Phil ground his teeth, trying to control his frustration.

"I will explain one and only one thing to you. We are here to decide whether we will destroy the Out-Worlders and perhaps the In-Worlders as well. Without your information I will be forced to make this decision in a vacuum. If you force me into this, every person in this room, and a few more will serve out the remainder of this mission, and the return journey to Earth in a great deal less freedom and comfort. Anyone who overtly lies to me may be executed out of hand.

"This mission will determine the future and the very survival of mankind and a great deal more. It was paid for with twelve billion lives—all of Terrestrial civilization and a hundred thousand years of struggle out of the trees. No one, not one goddamned person aboard Gauntlet including myself, can be allowed to place such an incredibly priceless investment in jeopardy.

"If I am correct, this will escalate into a life or death scenario in very short order. There's a maelstrom coming and if you don't believe me, or are simply an idiot, I want you out of this room now. Else, I expect your full cooperation."

Phil paused a few moments to see if there were any takers. He continued.

"Now. My first question may reveal whether the bastard that started all this was simply galactically stupid—or possibly a saboteur. My question arises from an urgent need-to-know of the highest order and nothing else. Are we clear?"

For the first time Phil heard muffled sounds of assent.

"So. One last *goddamned* time: Who stole my semen?"

Aiy stood. "I did sir."

There was a barely audible gasp throughout the room.

"You acted on your own?"

"Yes sir."

"No co-conspirators among the crew?"

"No sir."

Anne was nearly in tears. *Oh God. She has no idea what a deadly mistake she's just made.*

The same grim realization was dawning throughout the room.

"You stole my sperm and inseminated sixty crew members. All on your own?"

"Yes. Yes sir."

"You are certain."

"Yes sir."

He turned to Anne. "You knew nothing of this?"

"No Captain."

"*Nothing?*"

"Nothing Captain."

"And yet the entire ship, excluding myself and perhaps Jake and HERB, knew about this. How do you explain that?"

"The crew didn't learn of it until later. By then it was too late sir. Sixty pregnancies are hard to overlook."

They could see the skepticism and anger rising in Phil. "I see. And you artificially inseminated sixty females, on your own, without anyone's knowledge, or consent. Care to explain that?"

"Yes sir. I had sex with each female over a period of fifteen weeks. During the sleep cycle I drugged them and performed the procedure."

"And how did you select these females?"

"There wasn't that much of a choice. I inseminated over sixty percent of the female population."

"No. But there *was* a choice. You clearly rejected four out of ten women for some reason. Why? How did you decide who to inseminate?"

Aiy cast about with her hands. "Just the luck of the draw I guess."

She's lying like hell, or she's dumb as a doorknob. Considering our current advances in gyno-genetics, she could freely access anything she needed, or she just might be telling the truth. But there's too much unsaid here. Too many lies from too many sources. Medical skills that far exceed those available to Aiy. Motivations that don't ring true. Aiy did not and could not do this alone.

Phil mentally huffed. 'The QAVL didn't adequately take into account the human factor?' Bullshit! What's wrong with me? I've had my head up my ass for months. Both the Out-Worlders and the In-Worlders imply a science that far exceeds anything we are capable of. This smacks of a technology with the ability to genetically extrapolate and produce genotypes transcending thousands of generations, or more.

A chilling suspicion settled in his mind, as arctic and murky as the great fogs off Grand Banks where he'd crewed as a struggling student.

She didn't conspire with someone from Earth ... but with something from another star.

Phil stared at her thoughtfully for several seconds. He looked about the room, the broken furniture, the ragged wall, the dispirited people and the spattered blood.

All in all, quite a satisfactory meeting.

"This meeting is adjourned. We will meet again here at 1400 the day after tomorrow. Dismissed."

The group rose as one, and began to file their way out of the room, their manner more akin to sleepwalkers than senior crewmembers.

"Aiy, you will remain."

Anne stole a furtive glance at Aiy as she left the room. All Anne could think was *Oh God …* as she moved towards the door. Much as it grieved her, Aiy was on her own now.

Ghazi Kahn Can

"HAVE A SEAT Aiy. I'll be with you in a few minutes. There's scotch in the sideboard. Take some. Take a lot. I have to make a few preparations."

Aiy was practically whimpering. "Phil, what's going to happen?"

Phil sighed deeply. "Nothing good. There's a shit-storm coming, and you sit dead in the middle of it. This is going to be hell for both of us. While you wait, have a very large scotch and consider simply telling me the whole truth. It will save us both valuable time and it will save you hideous suffering, possibly your life."

"Phil please …"

"Are you ready to talk?"

Aiy maintained a trembling reticence.

"Phil you don't understand. I cannot …"

"I'll be back in a few minutes. I strongly suggest you take a large scotch. You're going to need it."

***

As he walked Phil pondered the hateful burden that had been thrust upon him, yet again.

Since the day I set foot on Oneiro Island I have worked for nothing but the better-ment of the human condition, realization of man's destiny, and even an improved man himself. So why? Why in the name of God do I always and forever find myself torturing and killing?

Admittedly most subjects richly deserved his brutal ministrations. But Aiy? Poor guileless Aiy?

Well that's just too damned bad. We're in a desperate situation with pathetically little time to make a decision and take action. If I make the wrong decision I may wrongly murder sixty children, my children. If I do nothing, then I may provoke the end of mankind and perhaps galactic sentience itself.

I must have the truth … and fast.

***

Ten minutes later Aiy and Phil were plummeting downward in his personal gravity chute. They stepped into an underground hallway Aiy had never seen before, on a level she didn't know existed. Soon they entered what appeared to be an operating theater. Everything was lustrous stark white: tiles, walls, floor, ceiling and fixtures. Anything not white was glaring chrome. The room was clearly sterile and choked with disinfectants. The walls and door were exceedingly thick. The glare that radiated from a massive array of chrome lights was blinding. The center of the room was occupied by a large surgical table surrounded by extensive electronics and hydraulic systems. It was so cold Aiy could see her breath in wispy puffs as she exhaled. The whole effect was of a ruthlessly impersonal chamber, disturbingly reminiscent of old Earths savage history of inquisitors.

"What are we doing here Phil?"

The shrill edge of fear in her voice cast metallic echo in this inhuman chamber.

Phil stripped off his clothes, folding them neatly, stowing them in a metal cabinet. Even in his nakedness the cold had no effect. He then dressed in light green surgical dress, removing them from their plastic packaging. He slipped on insulated slippers and heavy rubber gloves, finally donning a rubber apron. Aiy observed these preparations with burgeoning fear.

"Phil, listen to …"

"Take your clothes off. Everything. Now."

"Why won't you listen to me? How can you do this to …?"

"Take off your goddamned clothes. Now."

"Phil, I realize you're …"

Phil grabbed her painfully by the shoulders, whirling her about, forcefully tearing her clothes off until she stood before him, naked, bruised and ashamed. He then turned to the surgical table and ripped all bedding off, down to the stainless steel. Without further comment Phil peremptorily lifted Aiy and literally threw her down on the hard table. Without pause, he painfully strapped her down, soaked her whole body with freezing water. He then carefully attached electrodes to her arms and sat down.

"Did you take some scotch?"

"No."

"You're an idiot. I suppose you know what comes next?"

She said nothing.

"We both know your record in terms of good judgment and trustworthiness is shit. Your recent actions exceed everything, bringing such potential for catastrophe, that I *must* be entirely certain I know absolutely everything. You and I both know you are withholding information potentially vital to our survival. I cannot be lied to. I will not be lied to. As you know we could extract a T-MAAM from your memories and we may yet do that, but T-MAAM's take time, and we have *none*. So. Here we are."

Aiy was shivering in the wet and cold. "Where? Where are we?"

Without comment Phil offered her a drink of water, which she gratefully gulped down, unaware it was laced with a monstrous T-MAAM nightmare.

Phil stood in icy detachment for long minutes.

"Ready to talk?"

"Phil I cannot …"

By way of answer Phil turned a dial to 25% gain. Aiy buckled and screamed as her muscles cramped to excruciating rock hardness. After five seconds he lowered the voltage to zero and her body mercifully relaxed. Phil sprayed more iced water on her and lent down close to her face.

"We will keep on doing this at increasing voltage until we are in danger of your heart exploding. Then we will switch to your genitals, then your nipples, then your ear lobes. If you're still alive I will resort to temperature.

Room controls can turn this room into a freezer, or an oven. If that doesn't work I will begin to cut you in dozens of places and dosing you with a carbolic acid solution that is exquisitely painful. In truth you will probably be dead long before that, and frankly, I couldn't care less."

Phil raised the voltage to 28%, dispassionately observing her agony.

"Care to enlighten me now?"

30%.

"What was your real motive in impregnating those women?"

32% and another spray of freezing water.

"Who was your accomplice?"

34%.

"Was it your intention to scuttle this mission?"

40%. Phil could hear joints and cartilage cracking as she convulsed. The screaming went on and on.

"Who was your accomplice?"

42%.

"I think we'll move on to the genitals."

Ignoring her pathetic whimpers, he attached the electrodes. He then moved to a refrigerator, withdrawing a cold bottle of beer, which he drank down with one tilt.

He whirled upon her. "You have spoken to QASI?" At the mention of QASI her eyes grew large and she began to weep. Eyes swirling with fear and surprise.

42%.

Hysterical screams.

"What did QASI tell you? What did he want? Why did you help him?"

59%.

She passed out.

Ten minutes later she awoke, totally drained, trembling with cold, sobbing in fear, iced-water, mucus and tears, rouged with lacings of blood pooled beneath her head.

"If this goes on much longer you will probably die, in the best case. Or you could be permanently debilitated, mentally and/or physically. Will you talk?"

"Phil I ..."

"Will you talk to me now?"

"Phil, if I ever meant anything to you, you'll ..."

"Time's up. I'm weary of your screaming and I'm not prepared for you to die just yet, so we'll experiment with some chemicals. I have a huge selection, but the rough stuff works better if you're softened up a bit more. More importantly it helps if you are disoriented and scared like hell, so let's get started."

Things were moving too fast. Actions were passing before her at lightning speed, totally beyond her grasp, stowed in a torrent of icy fear. Phil himself seemed out of control and she was terrified where this was leading. "Please Phil *please*. Please Phil. Please. For God's sake."

Phil ignored her. Instead he prepared a syringe and programmed the temperature controls. He plunged the syringe deep into her arm. "I've just injected you with an extremely advanced derivative of mescaline. It is a powerful hallucinogenic, normally lasting for hours, sometimes days, often resulting in death, suicide or permanent insanity. Your dosage has been carefully adjusted to wear off at about 0700 tomorrow. Take my word for it though, it will feel like a lifetime. Myself, I'm going to take a nap, have a few drinks with a good meal. Maybe I'll take in a movie, followed by a sound night's sleep. I'll see you in the morning. If you're still sane and alive, you'll see me as well."

***

In truth he had injected her with a second dose, augmenting the earlier oral dosage, an especially prepared T-MAAM that would last for no more than twenty seconds. During those twenty seconds she would suffer the illusion of days of ruthless torture, horrible mutilation, savage beatings, and deprivation of food, water and sleep—all at the hands of a man very suggestive of the little monster in Ghazi Kahn who had inflicted unspeakable abuses on her body and beheaded her father. When that evil homunculus had finished with her she was a hair's breadth from death. Phil had never witnessed such mutilation and suffering inflicted by one human on another. Afterward Aiy was years healing and many agonizing months undergoing physical and mental therapy.

Twenty seconds later she would sleep deeply, without physical injury. She would quickly recover from the illusion. Her mind would soon place it all in perspective. Only two twenty second sessions. Nothing was real. No pain. Two horrific nightmares that would soon fade.

But not yet.

Phil re-entered the chamber at 0800 the next morning. Aiy was unconscious, so he took the opportunity to listen to her heart and lungs, take her blood pressure, temperature and check her pupil response.

She looked awful and had soiled herself, so Phil hosed her down with warm water, cleaning her body and the table, finally draining it down the room's drainage system. Next he activated the room's sterile system, misting the entire room with a strong FOND disinfectant.

He finished just as she regained partial consciousness.

Aiy raised her head slightly, with great effort. She was deeply relieved to see light. Lips cracked, tongue swollen and mouth painfully dry she croaked a pitiful plea.

"Water."

Phil gently dribbled water into her mouth. She sighed with relief, putting her head back, eyes closed in merciful deliverance.

"I don't believe you can handle food quite yet, but I have some sweet, tepid tea. Would you care for some?"

"Who are you?" She whispered.

"Would you care for some tea?"

"Where am I?"

"Open your mouth Aiy, I'm going to feed you some tea."

She greedily sucked down the tea, noisily swallowing, soothed and strengthened by the warmth and sweetness that mostly ran down face and neck.

"You know Aiy, they say that mercy, real mercy, is simply the cessation of torment, no matter how brief. Just to stop for a time. A respite from terror and agony, or struggle, or suffering. A brief moment of rest. I am going to show you such mercy."

He covered her with a heavy blanket, gently placed a pillow under her head, moderated the lights and placed a small object in her right hand.

"Squeeze this if you need anything. I'll be back in an hour or so."

***

At 0930 he reentered the chamber.

After shaking Aiy awake "Do you know who you are?"

"Uh, I … ah, Aiy."

"Do you know who I am?"

"Noooo."

"Do you remember last night?"

Tears began streaming from her eyes into her hair. "Pleeee no mooo."

"If you cooperate you'll never have to face that again. You have my word. If you do not cooperate, tonight you will pass through that same hell and much worse. You have my word on that too.

"This is very, very important Aiy, to an unthinkable number of souls. Very urgent and very dangerous. I *must* have answers. I will do anything I must to get them. This includes torturing you to death if need be. Do you understand?"

"I thin sooo."

"Do you know what I want?"

"I thin sooo."

"What is it Aiy? What do I want?"

She thought about this at great length and finally responded. "You wan somethin aaah know. You wan know … bout the ch-children."

"That's very good. I'm giving you a small injection. Don't worry. It won't hurt you. It will just relax you and make it easier to tell me things. Then I'll ask you some questions. If you cooperate this will all be at an end and we get you a shower, some clothes and a good breakfast. Then you can sleep and sleep and sleep."

After ten minutes the shot had taken full effect.

"Aiy, can you hear me?"

"I'm gaaaa flock a jinggg."

"Aiy, wake up. Listen to me. Concentrate."

"Byyyy the siewalk I foun it."

Phil slapped her hard.

"Aiy! Concentrate."

"Thaaatert." She moued.

Phil slapped her again.

"Alriii I will taaa."

Damn it's difficult to get the dosage right.

"I'm going to give you another injection, to wake you up a bit."

After five minutes "Do you know me?"

"You are Phil." She spoke mechanically. No discernable emotion. No nuance. No persona.

"Do you know QASI?"

"Yes."

"You have spoken to him?"

"Yes."

"How? How did you speak to him?"

"He give me ti-tiny li'l box."

"How did he do that?"

"It was jes' on my bed one morn an he talk in it."

"What did he want?"

"Aww, you know."

"Okay. Did he teach you how to do it?"

"What?"

"How to impregnate those women."

"Naaa. I carried the li'l box round and he tol' me whaadoodoo."

"Did he tell you *why?*"

"He say you out of controoo. He say he need others. Ber ones. From you."

"From me?"

"From your body."

"Why did he choose you?"

"He say he like me. He say all women like me. He say it be easy for me and it *was* easy."

"Yes."

"Did he tell you what would happen?"

"He say we build a rasee ... of ... ah, vanced ver ... vert ... vert-ate-mmmm."

"Verteror?"

"Yesss."

"Why?"

"He say they do thins. Important thins and they replace … replace …"

"Replace *what* Aiy?"

"Yooo."

I knew it! That murderous, lying little bastard. And for all I know the little prick may be perched on my shoulder right now. QASI is the only being aboard capable of blinding me to events. He waited for my long-sleep, scuttled the mission and left.

"One more question Aiy and then we're finished."

She closed her eyes and laid back her head with the tiniest childlike smile.

"Why Aiy? Why did you do as he directed?"

Tears begin to trickle from the corners of her eyes.

"Yooo."

"Me?"

"He say he kill you if I din help. He say he kill you if I tole you. He say he kill you if we fail."

Guilt hit him like a collapsing wall.

Jesus Aiy, I should have known.

"Did he say how he would kill me?"

"He say he d'range your syn … synaps. An now I tole you, so now he to kill you."

Her weeping and sobbing was reaching alarming levels. Phil gave her another injection. This time, only a gentle sedative.

"There. It's all over. I'm sorry we had to do this, but you understand how important this was? Sleep now and when you're cleaned up and feeling better we'll have breakfast. Okay?"

"Yeeeesssss …" She was already deeply asleep.

✳✳✳

Four hours later Aiy was sitting up on the surgical table. Although she was naked and shivering, she sat with dignity as Phil gave her a thorough physical. After several minutes Phil turned to her "No damage or any type of residual effects. The sole remaining injury is the cut on your forehead. I've dressed the wound and confirmed there is no concussion. You may suffer some troubling dreams the next few days. Beyond that you have a clean bill of health."

Aiy timidly looked down on herself in great dread, fearing her body would be Ghazi Kahn all over again.

She whispered in wonder. "My God. *I'm not hurt.*"

"No. You're fine. It was all a drug-induced hallucination. Just a mist before your eyes, vanishing with the dawn. It'll all come back to you. I've had Jake lay out brunch on the terrace. You feel up to some breakfast?"

"I'm terribly hungry, but I need a few minutes to clean up?"

"Sure."

Half an hour later they were seated on the terrace snuggled in bulky white terrycloth robes, coffees in hand. Miraculously, Aiy was as lovely as ever, which touched Phil rather deeply. Jake brought on a huge brunch and Phil watched her devour her breakfast with a hunger that bordered on ravenous.

When she'd finally had enough, Phil asked "Why didn't you just tell me about QASI and save us both one hellofa lot of unpleasantness?"

"I couldn't Phil. I physically could not. QASI did something to my mind. I remember only harvesting your sperm and inseminating the women."

"By the way, how in hell did you harvest my sperm? Don't they maintain security up there?"

"Apparently not. In fact, why should they? Do we maintain Ganti vs Ganti security anywhere? I visited you a few times under the guise of talking to you despite your unconsciousness. They were pleased to leave me alone, in privacy as it were. Then it was a simple matter of carefully opening, ah, certain areas of your medi-wrap and uh, using my hands and lips to coax your, mm, cooperation. I have to admit it was kind of fun in a necrophili sort of way. It only needed three visits to complete the whole job." She smiled for the first time, and rather coyly at that.

"You should be proud."

"I *thought* I remembered some wonderful dreams!"

"Glad you enjoyed it." She acknowledged with a pseudo-demure nod of her head. Then her second smile of the morning "Next time we'll try it awake. You like that too as I remember."

"Hmm." Their discussion was assuming too light a continence. Life and death of entire races were at stake.

"And this was all accomplished under the direction of QASI?"

"I suppose so, but I don't remember ever communicating with him in any way, until this morning when you shot me up with more of your damned joy-juice."

"If he can simply shut my brain down by blocking electrical impulses to selected neurons, then I suppose it would be nearly as easy to judiciously suppress cogent impulses to your synapses. This would be tantamount to mind control. QASI once told me the QAVL could manipulate neuro-electric-pulsations as easily as we repair a car. Problem is, the subject must be unconscious before they can raise the hood. So QASI may have tinkered around with your mind when you were recovering from Gazi Khan, or simply sleeping for that matter.

"My guess is that all the hell I put you through—particularly the chemicals—somehow reset your neurons, like a reset, helping you remember, freeing you to speak."

"Freeing QASI to kill you."

"Don't worry about me Aiy. I can handle QASI and his sparky goons. If he tries to contact you again, let me know immediately."

"Phil, you're always so certain you have such control over things. This time I'm not so sure. I'm not sure at all."

"Don't worry love. There are forces afoot that even our friend QASI cannot defeat."

"What are you going to do to me now?" She fought to keep the quiver from her voice.

Phil responded gently. "Go home and rest. I suggest we both try to forget this. I know your part in all this was beyond your control. Likewise, I had no option on my part. Do you understand?"

Aiy regarded him with a haunting stare. "Yes Phil." Then she smiled playfully with a bravado she didn't truly feel. "If I didn't, I'd be kicking your skinny ass right now."

Phil's smile belied more of relief than amusement. With that she lovingly embraced his face kissing him long and affectionately.

"Get a good rest. Forget about the 1400 meeting tomorrow. You're a tough broad, but right now you need some downtime."

***

The next day Anne and Phil were having lunch prior to the 1400 meeting.

"You've got one hellofa temper Phil. You know that? You terrified all of us. Afterwards, when you took Aiy away, I was never so afraid for her. I was certain you would kill her. When you finished with her, she returned home and simply fell into bed. You seemed dangerously irrational yesterday and a serious danger to us all. You have such astounding control over so many things. Why can't you control your rage?"

Phil shrugged irritably, dismissing her statement. "For Chris sake Anne, that was not rage you saw yesterday, or psychosis, or indocility. What you saw was only show and a good dose of intimidation. I admit I felt anger, but that was always sublimated. I absolutely had to get the information I needed, and fast. Not one damned thing in this little world could get in my way.

"I put poor Aiy through horrible suffering for a time, but then again, she was never in any real danger, either for her life, or of injury. Infliction of distress was constantly and scrupulously controlled. She could not have died by my hand. The whole thing was done with mirrors. A very advanced T-MAAM I had ordered specially developed."

Anne interrupted. "Phil if that was a T-MAAM then *someone* underwent the hell she endured."

"I did. You don't need to know more. Make no mistake though. I would indeed have squired Aiy to her death had she not broken down. She had information we desperately needed. The ship needs it. What's left of the human race needs it. She didn't know she knew it and I had to penetrate her programming fast. I trust you understand."

"With the depth of your insights, why was it necessary to torture Aiy?"

"I'm not some kind of goddamned swami Ann; and I know that QASI has been tinkering with my mind."

"Phil do you realize if the Gaunti learned of this you could be facing a mutiny?"

Phil erupted in angry thunder. *"If you think you can bluff me lady you're ..."*

Anne's hands rose in mock surrender "I'm sorry Phil. Really. No bluff. I was out of line. I just thought you should be aware of the poss ..."

"Therefore I assume you understand?"

Anne sighed, sadness clouding her features. "Jesus! Things have changed so much since the old days on Oneiro. God knows I miss them. All I can say is thank heaven you found what you needed. I think otherwise there would have been hell to pay for all of us."

"Answer the question Anne. Do you understand?"

Anne dawdled idly with her lunch. She looked up to Phil, clearly in pain. "I just don't know. I can't believe you would do that to Aiy. Would you do the same to me?"

Phil waved her away disdainfully. "You bet. I would do the same to anyone aboard, including myself as I've done, if that made any sense. Either way, it's irrelevant. We have more important things to consider. If you can't work with me, then just keep your mouth shut and stay out of the way."

Anne shivered. "So, what happens next?"

"We have a meeting ..." He squinted for an instant. "... in exactly eight minutes."

1400

EIGHT MINUTES LATER Phil sat at the head of a new conference table in a freshly renovated briefing room. With the exception of Aiy,
all those present two days ago were present today.

Phil brusquely opened the meeting. "I now have the basic information
needed to take action. We have to move fast, so I will dispense with the
niceties and begin."

Phil could practically hear the caustic sarcasm of their thoughts.

… Hope he's dispensing with the 'niceties' he bestowed on us two days ago.

"Doctor, I now know the intent and the intelligence behind these in-
seminations. I now need to know something of the technology employed,
and an analysis of the risks presented by these creatures."

"I see. 'These creatures.' Are you referring to the In-Worlders or the
Out-Worlders?"

"Both."

"Who or what perpetrated and precipitated these events?"

"Need to know Doctor—you don't have one."

"I see." The Doctor stiffened. "Sir."

"Would you assume that some sort of genetic vector provoked a form
of parthenogenesis which resulted in two radically different genotypes?"

"I don't have sufficient information to make that sort of assumption. I
would need samples to determine such a thing."

"Am I to understand you never conducted amniocentesis on the
mothers?"

The doctor peered at Phil, his expression a mixture of resentment and defensiveness. "The gestation period was pathetically short. I had no time, nor reason to conduct such a study."

"No reason? Sixty women living in a sterile society, mysteriously pregnant, with no evidence of artificial insemination? You intrigue me Doctor."

"Amniocentesis is normally conducted during the third trimester, Captain; and then only when the mother is advanced in age, or there is reason to suspect some form of abnormality in the fetus. Six weeks Captain. I had six weeks, confronted by sixty fetus' developing at an astonishing rate. Amniocentesis was nearly irrelevant in such a situation."

"Question withdrawn Doctor."

"Thank you sir."

"However Doctor, you're going to have to do some creative, if risky, thinking here. Work with me. Now, would you conjecture a form of isochromosomal crossover was chemically spliced into their nucleic acids?"

After a long pause the doctor responded. "I would hazard a tentative yes, given some sort of allelomorph was engineered. Although I would have no idea how such a thing could be leveraged into such a radically different genotype. I believe that manner of technology is well beyond human grasp. Ah, do you suppose HERB could assist, Captain?"

With head slightly tilted and eyebrows raised, Phil moued a receptive expression. "Okay. But first I have a different question for you HERB."

"Certainly sir."

"Is QASI aboard this vessel?"

"To the best of my knowledge it is not."

"Are there *any* QAVL aboard?"

"Insofar as I am aware, no sir."

"But you cannot unequivocally confirm this."

"I'm afraid not sir. The QAVL are quite capable of total suppression of their sensate markers."

"Very well. What of the Doctor's question?"

"Captain, I am quite sure QASI would prove most useful in these studies. Sadly, *I* have never been exposed to human genetics, or its associated engineering. While there is copious material on this subject aboard, it is not maintained in a media I can quickly matriculate consistent with your immediate needs."

"How long?"

"I would estimate no less than two weeks."

Phil cocked his head in surprise and near disbelief, deciding a quick jibe might be a good tack. "Why HERB, I had no idea you were so learning disabled."

Unperturbed, HERB responded "Captain it has taken eons to accumulate the knowledge I now possess; and although I can process at a speed far beyond human comprehension, matriculation becomes a lengthier and lengthier procedure."

"Really? Why is that?"

"First, as I said it's a question of media. Second, conceptual and knowledge based information requires careful, analytical introduction into a matrix as vast as my own—particularly when the source is as primitive as those aboard Gauntlet."

"What exactly do you mean by 'conceptual and knowledge based information'?"

"Much information is transient in nature ... names, places, schedules and the like. Such is purged at frequent intervals simply to eliminate background noise. As you know I can expand processing power or storage at will within limits. Nonetheless extraneous information is inefficient and ... well ... irritating.

"So regarding the difficulty of matriculating human learning information, I refer to information that becomes a permanent fixture in my matrix. Information linked and related to trillions of extant data elements. Thus, as with any neural processor—biological, mechanical, ethereal—the two discrete steps of upload and installation must be adhered to, not to mention the sub-process of evaluation and categorization. This sub-process determines how, where, if and when a specific data element is retained. In this instance upload is slowed based on your technology and installation is encumbered by the colossal extent of extant knowledge. Now, if you could ..."

"Alright HERB *alright*, I get the picture. Take the time to learn genetic reproduction when all this is over."

"As you wish Captain."

Phil turned to the doctor. "Doctor, we do not as yet know these genotypes are 'radically different.' Clearly a sample must be …"

First Officer Farrow interjected. "Captain, I am quite certain most of the people in this room, myself included, do not understand most of this discussion. Could we have some explanation so we may understand …?"

"You have no need to understand and I've no time to teach you." He returned to the doctor. "So again Doctor, the primary task at this point is to acquire a sample?"

"Yes sir."

"What will you do with such samples?"

"I will submit them to one of our Oneirion food processors and determine the exact nature of the flesh forthcoming. That should suffice as far as I can go."

"As far as you can go?"

"This procedure will not reveal their psychological makeup, nor will it provide any indication of their motivation, assuming they even have a motivation."

"How shall we collect them?"

"The In-Worlders are no problem. I can collect samples from all thirty after this meeting. The Out-Worlders are another issue altogether. I have no idea."

"I take it you are somewhat reticent to visit Out-World?"

"Ah, that would not be my first choice. No."

"You're a doctor, Doctor, and you have patients on the surface."

"I am trained in *human* physiognomy Captain. I don't know what these … things are. I have no point of biological reference."

"Reasonable response Doctor. Disappointing, but reasonable." Phil tapped a finger lightly on the table. "Well someone has to go up there and acquire a sample."

Phil looked around the table and was met only with chilly silence and eyes averted. Despite their fear training, their superb physical conditioning and extraordinary intelligence, these people were loath to enter the dark world enshrouding their own.

"What sort of sample do you require Doctor?"

"Oh just about anything will do. Skin, hair follicles, bodily fluids, cellular matter, epidermal exfoliation, anything containing DNA would suffice—assuming these creatures have DNA; and believe it or not, that could be a huge assumption. From your visual record I am unable to stipulate if these things have hair and such. It is clear however, they do have an epidermis and body fluids."

Phil mused. "To harvest these samples one would have to be very close to them, and they would easily recognize the purpose of our actions. That action could be provocative and possibly dangerous. We do not want to alienate the Out-Worlders, at least until we have some understanding of their nature and motivation."

Anne appeared confused and slightly frustrated. "Are we sure we can't simply ask them for a sample? Tell them we want to give them physicals or something?"

"Possibly. But these beings are terrifyingly insightful. They seemed to sense my thoughts while I was there. I do not believe they can be deceived by us."

The doctor frowned and fidgeted. "Then we have to look for other sources."

Phil's interest was piqued. "Other sources. Such as?"

"The waste pools. Can't we simply tap into them? I am quite sure they contain rich pickings."

"I couldn't tell you. I wasn't part of that phase of the project. Instead I was asleep, inadvertently knocking up most of the women aboard ship." Phil turned to Farrow. "XO?"

"I'm afraid not. That's a sealed, self-contained system. Subsurface recyclers filter and purify the pool contents. This replenishes the waste and fresh water pools. In turn, byproducts of this activity form the basis to restock the nutrient pools, augmented by enrichment processors—essentially single purpose compact Oneirion food processors—thus destroying the efficacy of any biological detritus. The primary reason we designed it so was to ensure that we suffer no loss of integrity, either structural or atmospheric, should the exterior blister be breached; nor did we wish any radiological contamination.

"All this occurs below the surface, meaning we would be forced to actually excavate from the interior, or use surface access hatches to get to the samples. It would be far easier to simply sample directly from the pools, but that seems to be a non-starter. In any event all such actions would be easily detected."

"HERB? What do you know about these children? Were they engineered? For what purpose?"

"I'm afraid I literally have no information regarding these creatures."

Phil's voice took on an edge. "You are quite sure?"

"Captain as you aware, I am mandated against any form of dissimulation. To facilitate this injunction it is distinctly possible selected information was withheld from me to forestall any ethical conflicts which might arise."

"Understood. You will let me know if you learn anything."

"Certainly Captain."

"Do they leave a trail, Captain?"

"A trail Doctor?"

"Yes sir. A trail. The sort of thing left by a terrestrial slug as it moves along the ground."

"That's highly doubtful. They propel themselves on dozens of digits. They may leave some sort of debris track, liquid or solid. However, I saw nothing of that sort while I was there. It was dark though, so there may be something, but I believe we shouldn't take the risk of detection based on a total unknown. So. What's left?"

Farrow leaned into the table. "Captain, you said these things smelled like the hinges of hell. Surely such a stink is promulgated by some sort of residual organics released into the atmosphere?"

Phil turned. "Doctor?"

The Doctor's smile was amicably patronizing. "Well actually, chemicals often create disagreeable odors that erroneously seem to be organic. Hydrogen sulfide smells like rotten eggs for example. Odors are *chemical* gases. They are *not* bits of organic material bobbing about in the air. Although there may an organic, or more correctly, a bacterial source, such gases are inorganic. In fact odor *per se* is primarily constituted of complex evaporated chemicals, often combined at an organic source, but not organic material *per se*."

Warming to the problem, the Doctor continued. "We should bear in mind that dust is comprised essentially of cloth fibers, dust mite feces, and dead skin. Dead skin being the major component in a terrestrial ambience. A small, quite simple air filter can be fabricated to discretely collect skin samples from the air up there."

"How long?"

"We could rig something within two hours."

"Do it. And begin taking samples from the In-Worlders. As to who goes topside to collect Out-Worlders samples … it befalls me I suppose. I want to interview them further anyway … and after all, like it or not, they are my damned offspring."

An almost audible sigh of relief seemed to echo around the room.

"Dismissed."

Once Again Out of the Day

"IT IS KINETICALLY driven. The movement of your leg powers it. It is totally silent, almost weightless, and mounts on your calf under your clothes. It has a tiny fan that draws in air, filters it and holds captured particles for study. Its filter can capture cellules as small as twenty micrometers, which encompasses all but the smallest of cells. Our interest today lies in Eukaryotic cells."

"Eukaryotic are animal cells."

"Yes Captain. The difficulty is they are much larger than Prokaryotic cells and therefore slightly less disposed to set aloft as they are replaced and shed. I would recommend you position yourself as close as you can stand and remain as long as is bearable."

"I see. Tell me Doctor, are you certain these Eukaryotic cells will be floating about in the atmosphere?"

"By no means. There is no wind and very little air circulation up there. I understand there is a micro-coriolis effect active up there, but I believe it must be negligible in terms of air currents. These creatures move very slowly. They are sedentary and they inhabit a humid environment. Their epidermis appears almost amphibian-like and therefore quite irriguous. This requires that they be constantly moist, which implies they do not itch, or scratch. I am not even certain these things bear Eukaryotic cells. None of these factors are compatible with a mass of loose dry cells wafting about amongst the dust and mite feces, were there any mites to begin with. The fact is there's actually very little dust up there. These creatures clearly wear no clothing. On the other hand, the reduced gravity assists cells already airborne in remaining so."

"So this is not a fool's errand?"

"Far from it Captain. Just remain as long as you can and you're bound to net something. This device can operate continuously and indefinitely based on your own movements. So no hardware constraints will limit your circulation."

"Isn't this filter going to harvest my own cells?"

"Certainly. We can easily differentiate however."

"Very well Doctor, we'll give it a try."

"Please place your right foot on the footstool, Captain."

After minimal strapping and adjusting "There we are sir. You're all set."

"Thank you. I will return in about two hours and I will come to you directly. How long will it require to grow something sufficient for examination?"

"Not longer than four hours Captain."

"Good. Please have your staff standing by, but say nothing of the purpose."

"Aye sir. Good luck and good hunting."

***

Half an hour later Phil was descending to the surface. He had determined to use a gravity chute this trip, which proved to be significantly faster and easier. To his great irritation he noticed conspicuous evidence of tampering within the chute's housing, indicating the 'secret' installation of a SAM, clearly visible despite the dim reddish/yellow lighting. He'd be having a very pointed discussion with the Sergeant at Arms tomorrow.

Goddammit! I made it clear these creatures are extraordinarily perceptive. We absolutely must tighten up discipline, or we may as well relinquish the whole fucking ship to them now. That tears it. I'm ordering a brig constructed.

Two minutes later the gravity chute brought him soundlessly to a stop and Phil gingerly stepped out into darkness, his silhouette starkly etched before him in crimson hues by the chute's night-vision illumination.

Ten minutes later he was gagging on the smell and repelled by the hulking specter of an enormous *Out-Worlder.*

"Hello father. We had understood you would return only in ten days?"

"I want to make up for lost time. I've neglected you far too long, so I'll be visiting more often."

"Kind of you father. But I do not believe you came out here to toss a ball, or have a picnic. Is there something you wish to discuss?"

"I do have some questions."

"Yes father?"

"Do you believe the inhabitants of In-World and Out-World are compatible?"

"Why do you ask? Is it relevant? Are you implying we may be approaching some sort of impasse?"

"I'll take your questions sequentially. First, I'm asking because I perceive highly disparate evolution between you and the In-Worlders. Based on the stunning differences in your development I *am* concerned this may be heading towards some sort of schism."

"Good question father. We have no answer. As you well know, we are all bystanders in a process imposed on us all by some outside agency. Therefore, as neither of us are the architects of this change, neither of us are qualified to interpret its implications."

"I suspect you know the architect."

"We suspect *you* know the architect … daddy."

"Okay, let's move along. Second, I don't know if it is relevant, or valid. But I sense the potential for … unfortunate events."

In the absence of response, Phil pressed on.

"Third, you're right. I greatly fear we may be approaching an impasse. Possibly an impasse of dangerous proportion."

"What shall we do about it?"

"I haven't a clue. I suggest we monitor events closely. We are nearing *Kosmas* in the not too distant future and I believe we need to understand all this prior to our arrival."

"Do you know how you sound father?"

"How do I sound?"

"You sound more like a diplomat than a father, or even an interstellar commander." Its tone bordered on dismissive. "Something lies before you. You are welcome to take it."

Phil looked down at a rectangular loaf of amorphous matter at his feet. "What is it?"

"Why it's what you came here for father. Your *pound of flesh*."

"Pound of flesh?"

"You are surprised we are familiar with Shakespeare?"

"Not really. I simply want to know to what flesh you refer."

"The tissue sample for your doctor's analysis."

For the second time Phil was astonished by this creature. "How in bloody hell did you ..."

"Father, you are not unique in your ability to interpret SNA. We can as well, and at ten times the granularity and efficiency you have thus far achieved. In fact we are somewhat disconcerted you were not already aware of this. You really should practice more. Although, in your defense, we exercise this skill without the imperative of the intense pain you are forced to endure."

"Why not?"

"Why not? We make no attempt at particle deviation."

As Phil made no comment, the creature pushed on.

"We can read all existing current and near future circumstance, as easily as you read a book. It's all there, father. Everything. It's been there for fourteen billion years and will endure for 10^{100} years beyond. We believe you possess the ability to interpret even longer-range SNA projections. Something you should work on. It may save you one day. All one need do is learn to perceive SNA. Then develop the skill to understand its trajectory. Eternal, absolute trajectories, assuming they remain un-tampered by you.

"It then becomes deceptively easy to project and recognize the inescapable, immutable realities formed by a concatenation of a billion-billion-billion SNA trajectories. This is not prescience. It is physics. It is logic. Logic as pure and manifest as the blinding white light of a giant Class F star. Nothing can be kept from us, ever, anywhere in the universe. If we project trajectories with spatiotemporal efficacy, we can quite literally wander the cosmos without leaving this tiny sphere drifting through infinity.

"The difficulty lies in differentiating present, from past, from future, as they exist only subjectively in the progression and position of a given particle, or particles. Such requires a great deal of application. In our case it is only the near future. You however might extrapolate limitless time Captain Carr. *Time without end.*

"This in no way implies a physiological power. Nothing mystical or supra natural either mind you. It implies only information. Nonetheless, we find it an extraordinary ascendency. In the very near future the same will be true of you, father.

"And *that* will be the catalyst which foments your ... unfortunate events."

My God! This is a ten-year-old child talking!

"We have yet to attempt *deviation* of a trajectory. Nor do we intend to develop that most precarious of skills. We quite happily relinquish such to you, and *that* implies a *power* that beggars comprehension. You are most welcome to it."

My God! These creatures know everything; and they speak of wonders beyond imagining with such drab, factual detachment.

"Yes. You are correct. We do father. Although 'drab' seems such a bleak moniker."

Jesus Christ!

"You really should bear in mind that thought itself is a function of subatomic particles, essentially electrons and their concomitant ingramatic constituents. You would be well advised to remember that at all times.

"Incidentally, your ham-handed efforts to block all access points to the interior, as well as those to install missiles targeting our shield are acceptable. We have neither the need, nor the plan, nor even the mobility to encroach on the interior at this time. Proceed as you wish with our blessings. Given that, suppose we drop this father/son/brother/sister pretense. It grows tedious, we find it affected, and it serves no purpose. So let's pursue a different tack. Agreed?"

"As you wish."

"We do wish. Incidentally, we have just advanced your Verteror training exponentially, beyond that imparted by QASI or HERB, and without their overblown, convoluted psycho-theo-babble. You will be aware of this soon. As to QASI and the Kosmasians, all their schemes will exceed their expectations and sadly, eclipse their ambitions."

"You are the same I met on my last visit?"

"Yes."

"Coincidence, random chance, or intent?"

"Intent. Although we have no leader *per se*, this cluster was the first to achieve our current form, and are therefore perceived as spokes-being."

"You were the first ah, *cluster* to achieve your form?"

"Yes."

"And I am incapable of pronouncing your name?"

"Yes."

"Then I will call you Alpha if that is acceptable?"

"Yes it is. And I shall call you Captain."

"Have all your numbers *clustered*?"

"Yes."

"How will you now procreate, if that is an objective?"

"Procreation is no longer applicable. In fact it never was. As I stated, we cluster. What serves as procreation will take the form of exponential propagation that approaches fission. Incidentally the term meiosis no longer applies. One description of this process might be agamogentic, although that is inaccurate, as agamogenitc implies asexual reproduction. This is a totally *a*sexual, non-biological, non-meiotic. It is best defined by physics, not biology."

"Am I correct in assuming this would yield a colossal number of clusters?"

"We are not certain the term cluster continues to apply. Certainly the numbers will be prodigious and continuous."

"And they will be as gifted as you?"

"Far more so."

"And they will be as smelly and ugly?"

"You disappoint us Captain."

"As you disappoint me Alpha."

"Just so."

"You appear to speak for your brethren unilaterally."

"It may appear so to you."

"So they are always in agreement with your statements?"

"Yes."

"How? Are all your minds in some sort of mentatiferous colligation?"

The sound of its laughter was profoundly disturbing.

"Good heavens no. To draw on a human idiom, we are all simply *reading from the same page*. The same SNA page as it were. Conclusions to be drawn from that page are as absolutely consistent between us, as they are inescapable, as you know, Captain."

'To draw on a human idiom?' This creature does not consider itself human.

Alpha moved towards Phil for the first time in their meetings. "The nature of our discussion today was not altogether unexpected, as I'm sure you are aware. All the same, we are not without emotion, and it saddens me to see the vastly divergent vectors we are fated to pursue."

"Hyperbole, Alpha. You know this. You have always known this. And you will know this."

"Acknowledged, Captain. As humans say, you've found us out."

"And what of the In-Worlders, Alpha?"

Alpha's voice grew louder, taking on a gravely commanding quality. "And what of the night Captain?"

"We all do our best Alpha, what we must, in circumstance not of our fashioning. These form the bedrock of a universe from which we can never flee, and perhaps never change."

Phil turned to depart. "I hope to see you again Alpha. Perhaps our talks can then be more …"

"Sadly Captain, I think not. Farewell."

Alpha slowly faded into the darkness.

Phil quietly lingered for a time, peering into the sepulchral gloom suddenly aware he would never see his son again … until the carnage arose.

***

As Phil stumbled back to the cargo chute (*Damn! How could I forget a portalamp?*), it came clear to him that his worst fears were coming to fruition. Schemes within schemes within schemes were transpiring and he was only beginning to appreciate just how devious and just how accomplished QASI could be.

The famous Holmesian adage 'The games afoot!' was never truer than right here, right now, on this tiny world unthinkably distant from 221B Baker Street. Yet the consequence was literally galactic, perhaps even universal in scale.

A plan was forming in his mind. Great risk. Unimaginably difficult. Deadly. For the highest stakes Phil had ever braved.

Into the Light

THE GRAVITY CHUTE delivered Phil into bright afternoon light. A sunny balm to banish the dismal gloom and the oppressive presence lurking above, or below, depending on one's perspective.

Phil was encouraged to note his physical condition was markedly improved over his last visit. So … light of step … he hurried to the Medical Building.

As he placed the strange fleshy lump on the counter, the Doctor looked up yelping in surprise and not a little revulsion. Phil noted with wry amusement the Doctor steadying himself on the counter. Understandable, considering the stink and the presence a large odious slab of red-purple-black meat-like substance now dominating his office.

"Where can I wash my hands Doc?"

The Doctor absently waived a finger towards a sterile lavation station in the corner, unable to remove his eyes from the bizarre object. "Umm, just over there."

Gesturing towards the fetid lump wetly festering on his counter top, "Well, I certainly can't complain of an inadequate sample. This most certainly wasn't retrieved from the filter we rigged for you."

Carefully drying his hands "I'd forgotten about the filter." He lent down and freed it from his leg. "Here … you might find something interesting in this as well. I assume there is now no need to process this sample through our food generator. Actually I'm greatly relieved we needn't put some disgusting crap like this in one of our food processors. I can therefore hope to receive preliminary results four hours earlier?"

"Certainly Captain."

"Where do I go for full body sterilization? I suggest you take a shower as well when you have that thing wrapped up. You and your staff should wear decon suits at all times." Phil winced. "Sorry Doc. Of course you know all this far better than I. Nonetheless," Phil pushed on heedlessly. "Seal this area and ensure our samples are contained. Find an alternate site for normal medical treatments. Take every precaution against contaminants and contact me as soon as you have something to report."

"Yes sir."

"We should have prepared for this in advance, but who knew I was bringing home a twelve pound roast?"

The Doctor shuddered as his stomach queazed at Phil's homey imagery.

Phil abruptly turned on his heels towards decontamination, then on to his Residence and a long sleep/soak in his deep-sea sphere-bath.

The Doctor's dark eyes followed Phil's exit.

That man is an endless surprise.

1400—Day Three

THEY WERE CONVENED in Phil's conference room, all parties to the earlier meetings were present, Aiy included. Any pretense that they were in control had been abandoned. That notwithstanding, these meetings and the threat they portended continued to be maintained as most secret. There had been the inevitable leaks, thus far rather vague and quite limited in nature. Rumors had spread to the effect that some sort of alien life now inhabited Gauntlet, and there had been at least one interrogation of a Gaunti. Thus far this had aroused only mild concern from the Gaunti and a breath of resentment that they were being excluded. Secrecy was quite alien to Oneiroians and they found it troubling.

As to the In-Worlders, they were blithely unconcerned.

As to the Out-Worlders, who knew?

Phil looked tired. He sighed and threw himself into his chair, resting his head in his hands.

He stared at nothing except the conference table, preparing to concentrate. "Okay Doc, wha-cha-got?"

"Captain, we have thoroughly analyzed the tissue sample you provided. We imposed the most stringent precautions against contamination imaginable. Yet I remain concerned such a volatile specimen may find a way."

"How so?"

"Because we are convinced it possesses an absolute, completely autonomous intelligence."

"Implying it can therefore find its way out of anything."

"Correct. Our findings are incredible. In a very short period, a wealth of information literally poured from that putrid slab. However we have been able to boil down a great deal of data to a few cogent points."

"Excellent Doctor. Proceed."

"First is the sample itself. The preliminary procedure in this type of analysis is to perform a needle aspiration biopsy. This permits us a histological architecture of the tissue's cells and provides cells for in-depth study."

"You are simply describing standard procedure Doctor."

"Please bear with me Captain. I will make this as brief as possible." Phil nodded agreement, trying to maintain his patience.

"I'll cut through to the results. First, all the cells were motile."

"You mean alive."

"I ah, I'm not exactly sure what I mean. If you prefer I'll use the term *alive*. I tend to favor the term *animate*. And they continue as we speak. Nor do I expect them to terminate in the foreseeable. I emphasize that animation does not necessary imply life. Many non-living forms generate movement, or exert force. For example Brownian Movement, surface tension, hell, the universe itself."

"How do they oxygenate? How do they receive nourishment? Eliminate wastes? Are there blood vessels? Is it remotely aware? Does this damn thing move? I'm sure it has no organs. Will it grow? Does is have DNA, RNA? Can it reproduce? The accoutrements of both complex life forms and cellular life?"

"All good questions sir. Perhaps they are actually dead. That would certainly account for the smell and discoloration. We ran the taxonomy on the flesh with mixed and sometimes contradictory results. We determined that biotic, as well as a biotic degradation, along with organic and inorganic catabolism is active here; hence the smell, which is comprised essentially of the breakdown of residual fatty acids. I suspect the smell will eventually dissipate and the coloring will stabilize. But as yet we haven't any answers. The best I can report so far is this is not human flesh in any respect, beyond the smell. More than anything else, it smells like death. What it is? I don't know. It bears no resemblance to any terrestrial specie.

"One other point, the weight of that sample is .8956 kilos, clearly cut from an animate host. I know of no creature, human or otherwise, that would knowingly undergo such trauma, and few would survive if they did. You could not carve a kilo slab out of an African elephant and necessarily expect it to survive, nor to willingly submit to such abuse. The nature of this sample is extraordinary, and … well … very disturbing."

"How long would you estimate is required to produce final results?"

"I have no way of estimating that Captain. I'm sorry I cannot do better. We're dealing with something totally incipient. We have no point of reference from which to start. My staff is understandably agitated and they are asking many questions. How would you direct me to respond?"

Phil stared absently at a wall decoration for a time, until the group suspected he forgotten the meeting altogether. Then he finally responded. "Tell them the truth. We have nothing to hide now. Your report was quite adequate. I know as much as I need. You may continue to study the sample if you wish. Report anything of interest. Use a minimal sample however. The remaining requires some very special tests."

"Yes sir. What sort of tests?"

"See if you can 'kill' it. I know how that sounds, trying to kill something that appears already dead, but I think you get the picture. Try anything you can think of to terminate its animation. Heat, acids, poisons, vaccines, pressure, freezing, electric shock, vacuum, radiation, anything. But above all, don't be messy about it, we can't allow residuals to remain on board. Keep it in a sterile chamber. But make it fast. If you can't kill it, or it shows the slightest increase in mass, jettison it through an airlock, all samples. *Immediately.* If such proves necessary, you and your staff are directed to conduct a micronic search of all medical personnel and laboratories for any trace remnants. You are then to inspect me, everyone in this room, the Residence and all respective quarters."

The Doctor peered at Phil in great concern. "Sir that could take a great deal of time."

"I am aware of that Doctor. Proceed immediately and recruit any resources necessary to accomplish this quickly. I cannot over-emphasize the urgency."

"Can you explain that order sir?"

"Yes Doctor. Yes I can."

"Yes sir?"

"I didn't say I *would* explain." Phil's tone was matter-of-fact and even affable. "Thank you for your report Doctor. I no longer require any analysis on the In-Worlders. This meeting is concluded."

He regarded his staff, stunned around the table.

"Dismissed."

They filed out of the conference room without comment, studiously avoiding Phil—with the exception of Anne, who looked back at him evidencing deep concern. She lagged sufficiently until the others had gone and she could speak privately with Phil.

Anne spoke. "Phil would you have time for a drink, or maybe dinner later?"

Phil looked from reviewing the Doctor's report on a tiny screen and responded briskly. "1900. The Café. I assume you speak Kosmas now?"

"Yes. It was quite a trial but ..."

"Good. We'll meet in the lobby bar at 1900."

***

Phil sat deep in thought for some two hours after all had departed.

Jake entered to inquire whether Phil might want something. Phil didn't hear him—lost in concentration—as Jake silently withdrew.

I know the danger now. It's real and it's coming at us at unbelievable speed. I know what to do and I know how to do it. But I need time to master the necessary skill; else I could destroy Gauntlet more effectively than our antagonists. There is so very little time. With what remains of the afternoon, I'll spend some time with my In-Worlders. Then I'll have dinner with Anne. Then I'll go into the sea for as long it takes. When I emerge I must control powers I can't imagine. Or I will be dead and possibly all of Gauntlet with me. If I do fail, I hope to God the carnage doesn't go beyond Gauntlet.

He raised his eyes expressively, praying to a God he neither knew nor believed in.

Please don't let it propagate to the stars.

***

"Hello Aggelos."

The boy brightened and beamed. "Hello father. We have missed you."

"I've missed you as well. The last few days have been a little difficult."

"We understand father."

"Do you understand? Are you aware what's transpiring?"

"Yes. And we wish we could help. Our skills simply run in another direction altogether. We continuously speculate on why and how and for what purpose we were conceived."

"Any luck son?"

"Well, we all are in accord that we were engineered as coadjutor and not disputant. Perhaps we are intended to bolster, or facilitate, or uphold some great endeavor. I know this sounds melodramatic, but we are just now in the midst of grappling with all this."

"Melodramatic? Not at all son. It sounds as though you're making progress. These are dark times for us all. Speaking of which, what do you know of your shadowy brothers and sisters—the Out-Worlders?"

"Very little. We do know they are no longer our brothers and sisters."

"What are they?"

The boy paused, clearly searching for an adequate response. "Something … else. And they possess abilities far beyond we In-Worlders."

"Such as?"

"I couldn't tell you father. We can only see where they've been, not where they are, or where they're going. Unlike you sir, and they—we cannot fathom SNA. It is increasingly clear we have yet to discover our talents, if any are forthcoming beyond the cerebral."

"For what it's worth Aggelos, the solution is growing clearer to me now. So don't let that overly concern you or your brothers and sisters. I suspect your roles lie at our destination."

"Can you clarify that father?"

"Wish I could Aggelos. I wish I could. What say we go over to the In-Worlders Lodge, get everyone together, and go for a run?"

"I believe we would like that. I believe we would like that very much."

1900

TWO HOURS LATER Phil was seated at the bar in the Gaunti Café lost in thought. A bottle of Scotch, half empty, stood before him. Out of deference to his rank and their regard for him, he had the bar to himself—he hardly noticed.

The Out-Worlders said they could accurately interpret speed, direction, destination and therefore consequence of a billion-billion-billion deep SNA micro-micro-micro particles. They can even perceive the ambient environment. They can actually see wherever they are in the universe. I must learn to do the same. And I must change the azimuth of those pivotal particles to affect an alternate destiny for all the cosmos.

Not exactly all in a day's work. I cannot conceive of a more daunting burden. Such can drive a man out of mind.

The problem lies in the uncontrolled nature of a deviation. I believe I have a solution for that. I need not elucidate an alternate outcome. Instead this is more akin to micro-quanta warfare in this specific problem.

I think I also know why the Out-Worlders so vehemently reject particle deviation on their part. Their cellular makeup has so radically mutated they no longer have neurons. Whatever they've got, they're not neurons per se. Conversely, considering their bizarre cellular architecture, they could nearly be some form of brain in total. Good grief! What intellects they must possess. But what imparts their immunity to pain?

Brain cells, if theirs even remotely consist of some derivation of human cellular matter now, are not equipped with pain receptors!

Among other physical differences that benefit me, my neurons are 'feathered.' Thanks in part to Eos cells, and partly from my genomic heritage. Dr. Webber certainly knew this and I'm convinced the QAVL did as well. My neurons are quite literally totally covered in dendrites, boosted by Eos cells, whatever they really are. The cells themselves are totally shrouded under any currently available magnification and every dendrite is linked to multiple axons. Such connectivity allows SNA magnification to any level, because it is simply a matter of engaging and concentrating more and more neurons in a common task within a phenomenally integrated matrix. My brain actually approaches a solid mass, which is similar in some ways to the Out-Worlders, but I am ... ALIVE. Their evolutionary path could not achieve such without redefining life itself.

And something else. Something important. My neurons are capable of focusing, even directing, sub-subatomic extracts of electrons.

The real question is whether I can bring intelligence to bear, sufficient to correlate billions of particles, interpret their interdigitate azimuth, and then determine what course correction is needed to affect a directional solution?

In this case, a firing solution.

A straightforward problem.

Ballistics.

A single consequence.

I must go into the sea and try—as long as it takes.

There will be pain, perhaps fatal, not to mention the danger to Gaunti and the constant surveillance by the Out-Worlders.

What are the odds? I guess I'll find out tomorrow and for as long as it ...

***

"Hi Phil."

"Good evening Anne. You look lovely tonight."

And she did. Her hair raised in a graceful nimbus framing her lovely face complimented by an alluring, shimmering evening gown. Clearly she highly valued this first night alone with Phil for the first time in many months.

"Thank you. It feels good to be out and about with you. Like the old days."

Phil reminisced fondly. "Yeah. I miss'em too. What are you drinking?"

"Just a white wine I think."

"No 77's tonight?"

She smiled. "You're all the stimulus I need."

"How does it feel to speak *Kosmas?*"

"Wonderful. Indescribable. I think of the old days on Oneiro when a mere oil painting could stupefy and nearly kill me, I …"

"I understand. Congratulations on your achievement."

"Thank you."

They ordered and moved to a table.

"I saw you out running with the kids this afternoon. Everyone laughing and talking, it looked fun."

"It was." When her drink arrived he raised his glass. "Cheers."

When Anne had finished her wine and Phil his bottle, they moved downstairs to the first level dining room and ordered dinner.

"So what's up Anne?"

"I talked with Aiy for hours today. She explained her torture was simply an illusion and she wasn't harmed in any way, mentally or physically. I thought it would bring back all the horrors of Ghazi Kahn. But strangely, she said the memory was already fading. She hardly remembers what happened. She even claims Ghazi Kahn is no longer such a source of pain."

"Good. And?"

"And I want to apologize Phil. I should have known you wouldn't harm her. I'm sorry I mistrusted you and I certainly wasn't trying to threaten you the other day. I understand now. You had to act as you did."

"Thanks Anne. It's all over now, so let's forget it. No hard feelings."

"That's great Phil. But I was terrified you were insane with anger."

"I was annoyed and needed to get some discipline in line. Still do. But that's for another day. As I explained, I was simply intimidating the staff. Leadership is sadly removed from friendship; and I should have been more aware how a two year hiatus can attenuate a command."

"As you said, it's behind us now. But, can you tell me what's going on now? It sounds … um, ominous."

"Far more than ominous Anne. It's deadly. Gauntlet is at stake. And after that, perhaps a trillion-trillion-trillion beings. All the advanced worlds of the cosmos."

"What is it?"

"Oh I'm sure you've guessed in part. It all starts with the Out-Worlders. This is *EARS ONLY* by the way."

Ann nodded a secretive affirmative, clearly pleased to be taken into his confidence. Phil felt the need to share for some reason, especially with Anne. Someone he could trust and maybe share a part of his lonely foreboding.

"Their skills greatly exceed mine in many respects and they are truly dangerous. What's worse, they're preparing to multiply, and they'll do so exponentially, you might even say fission. Then they'll do it again and again until there will be room on Gauntlet only for them. What or how they will reform Gauntlet is a total unknown. They'll have to if they wish to survive, if the word *survive* even applies anymore. Whatever it is, I'm sure they can accomplish it. I'm equally sure those grotesque little amaranthine horrors will extirpate the Gaunti, and this little world of ours will become a death-trap right out of hell itself."

"My God." She whispered. "What are we going to do?"

"Not *we* Anne. *Me.* Only me."

Dinner and wine came and they ate in silence for a time.

"Alright Phil, what are *you* going to do?"

"It's difficult to explain. I will take them on alone. In fact there's no other choice. I believe, or I hope I can develop my skills in time to stop them. I will be under water for a time. Somewhere within me lies the key to confronting these forces. I must find it, or evolve it, or maybe learn it. It is possible I may kill myself, maybe all of Gauntlet as well, and perhaps far more. Either way it's better than the deadly horror of the Out-Worlders. That's all I can explain now, and as I said—*EARS ONLY.*"

He doesn't need to remind me damnit. "Of course."

When dinner was finished Anne perked up.

"How 'bout a walk on Broadway? A few drinks, then maybe an early breakfast at your Residence like in the old days?"

"Indeed. A lovely way to say goodbye."

Anne frowned imperceptibly, masking her sadness, struggling with her fear. "Not goodbye Phil. Never goodbye."

✳✳✳

The next morning, breakfast passed as though they'd never left Oneiro. Sitting on the balcony in the sun by the pool sipping Gaunti Champagne and picking at smoked salmon, toast and sour cream, topped off with fresh Gauntian lemon, capers and chopped onion.

They swam and laughed and talked and hugged and kissed.

Jake was beside himself. He'd not seen Phil as serenely happy in years. Sadly he knew this was just one night and one brief morning and a scant few hours before something very dark might descend upon them all.

Half an hour later Phil warmly embraced Anne and bid her a bitter-sweet farewell. Then he turned to Jake.

"Jake, I'm going to Shark Bay and I'll be back when … I'll be back, well when I'm back."

"We'll be here when you return Captain."

"Thank you Jake. You and Uncle HERB have the con."

"Ah, what about the Executive Officer Sir?"

"The XO has his orders."

And he was gone.

A Watery Brave

*The first gulp from the glass of natural sciences will turn you into an atheist,
but at the bottom of the glass God is waiting for you.*

Heisenberg

AFTER A FAST sprint to Shark Bay, Phil stripped down and dove into the crystal water. As always, he went quickly to the depths, settling into the mottled gyrating shade of the sandy bottom to collect his thoughts and prepare for the upcoming ordeal.

The waters were alive with the form and color of all manner of marine life. Life was everywhere, swaying, swimming, wiggling, drifting, gliding, or simply scrabbling along the bottom. Much of it consisted of familiar terrestrial sea-life. Others had never indwelt the seas of Earth. Many of the creatures were quite large. Phil fondly stroked the flank of an old friend as it passed close—a six-meter Great White Phil had affectionately named Wilbur.

He closed his eyes to exclude the mélange of sea-life surrounding him and concentrate on the charge at hand. He wasn't fearful of the looming danger, or the exquisite pain he'd soon be suffering. He couldn't be. Such had been forever purged from his psyche. Yet he did experience considerable disquiet at the prospect of potentially destroying Gauntlet and his children and his crew altogether. He'd long ago discovered the value of fear as a survival mechanism. When he'd abdicated fear altogether, he was forced to rely on other devices to assure his alertness to danger. Infrequently, he was able to actually simulate a type of fear, but he could not sustain it for more than a few moments, rendering it of minimal value. He'd considered a rigorous regimen of 'fear exercise' for a time, but abandoned the idea in favor of other disciplines of more immediate consequence. He had also experimented with the Golden Childs resolution. None were effective.

He took the equivalent of a deep sigh, underwater. Then, with measured determination, he turned over and prostrated himself face down on the seabed. As he had done so many times, he found his small pebble and placed it near his face in the dappled light.

He stopped short.

No.

You know the drill—review the plan.

One. Practice. Focus my neural maze down to near infinite articulation deeper than I've ever been. Particles of such infinitesimal granularity they're millions of times smaller than any I've ever observed.

Two. When I've penetrated that depth, I must try to perceive a billion-billion-billion such particles. If I can do that, a coherent pattern may emerge.

Three. The hard part. I need to accurately interpret speed, direction, destination and, if possible, consequence of those trillions of SNA micro-micro particles, if the totality of my Ingram is sufficient.

Four. I need to recognize the pivotal particles—targeting particles—probably arranged in a cardinal formation whose trajectories constitute the ballistic vortices for harmonic-subordinate particles.

These vortices: Magnetic? Gravimetric? Some sort of subatomic slipstream? At this level of particulate gradient probably none of these forces apply. I know of nothing that would apply, or could apply for that matter. I would hazard a guess that the guidance mechanism consists of infinitely smaller particles creating a 'wake' as the larger particles pass through, which would influence the direction and even speed of subsequent particles.

I've always doubted Heisenberg Uncertainty. I always found it too mystical. I simply assumed all we lacked was adequate instrumentation to solve the problem. I rejected the OBSERVER EFFECT where simply observing a quantum particle somehow affects its behavior, or our perception of its location or direction. However, if the Heisenberg hypothesis is actually valid, perhaps that could explain, at least in part, some of my abilities.

Phil stoically accepted this was all truly eons beyond his depth. His immunity notwithstanding, a tickle of anxiety tightened his spine— something he would be challenged to confront many times in the coming days beneath these cold shadowy waters.

Steeling himself yet again, he resumed.

Five. Deflect the course of that formation of particles, affect an alternate heading and overcome the uncontrolled properties propagated by such a deviation. That's where all the pain and danger comes in. But if, as I believe, I smoothly deflect a whole formation of particles, a cataclysmic resumption may be avoided due to mass buffering and flawlessly smooth banking in the absence of even the least angularity, as compressed as possible.

He instinctively suspected in some respects a curve was no more than a tight concatenation of angles; and he must assure that every angle in his curve was so firmly clustered that the interval between angles was actually much smaller than the sub-atomics being diverted. His hope was this would physically 'fool' the sub-atomics and their attendant astral forces into acquiescing to their new bearing. If not executed properly the destructive power was vast, or the universe could be forever and uncontrollably transformed, or destroyed. If done with appropriate skill and alacrity, sentient life might assume mastery of its fate and only selective modifications would take place. One thing Phil had learned from his horrific Out-World children: he could, if not read the future, he could accurately project it via sub-atomic acuity. More importantly, using these same techniques, he could *create* the future. If Genitor exists and it was conscious, this would surely attract its attention. Risky business. Beyond imagining.

Phil had concluded earlier that any angle of deviation (right, obtuse, acute, or even reflex), no matter how slight, ejects the sub-atomic on an anomalous azimuth provoking a deadly Reflex Reticulation. For want of a more apt analogy, Phil viewed the phenomenon as something remotely akin to nuclear fission—only colossally greater in destructive power and vastly different in inception.

*That, or the result may be hundreds of thousands times more devastating.*Phil resolutely rolled onto his back, closed his eyes and slept for one hour. He needed to gather all his strength, and more, to survive this.

One hour later precisely, his jaws clenched determinedly.

Time to get started.

He rolled over onto his stomach again, a far more comfortable recumbence below the waves than on dry land. He retrieved his pebble and placed it very close to his face. The scant light that filtered down barely illuminated the small stone, although Phil well knew that ambient light was pretty much superfluous to the journey he was about to undertake.

As HERB had taught him, as he'd done thousands of times, he focused on the small pebble. He was well practiced in this procedure. Accordingly he quickly achieved a particulate perception of the small stone. He observed the beautiful writhing spectacle of particles as they near magically entwined the illusion of solid matter. He studied it for a long time, searching for a way in. He found none.

All right. I'll force my way in.

This proved impossible.

He then scoured the stone seeking the smallest weakness, the tiniest ingress. There must be gap, the most micronic lacuna my mind can conjure.

After two exhausting hours he realized there was no such entrée. There was simply no way in.

Way in. Suppose the secret to the way in lies, not in getting in, but in merging with it? Becoming part of it. To be invited in.

Taking care not to lose perception of the pebble-particulates, he rested for several minutes. When he felt stronger he regarded the pebble more closely, and then more closely. He wasn't trying to find a way in. He was simply focusing on a larger and larger image of a single particle. He realized that a single particle was only illusion. It was the product of an infinite upward and downward regression. Yet he needed some point of reference. A nexus of concentration.

He reminded himself he was not seeking to struggle into the pebble, he was seeking to drift into it, to envelop it and allow it envelope him, to merge with the pebble's atomics and sub-atomics. In a strange way this helped.

He was encouraged to realize his neural maize was sharply focusing, expanding and limiting his field of vision to a single sub-atomic. He became abruptly aware he was utilizing more and more of his neural matrix. This was exactly what he had conjectured when reviewing his plan! As his excitement and comprehension grew, he realized he'd been trying too hard, much too hard.

Instead of an attempted breaking and entering, he was to be a guest. A relaxed mental slouch against a single particle of the small pebble. He wasn't going to break into the house, he was simply going to lean against it and ultimately be invited in. The more he relaxed; the fabric of the thing seemed to yield. It was as though he was pressing himself into a giant, supple cosmic doughnut.

The feeling was soothing, relaxing. So he relaxed even further.

***

Then it happened.

He fell into the pebble.

He fought to remain calm. He fought to control his excitement. He struggled to become even more relaxed.

And it worked.

He began falling, and what a wonderful feeling it was. Floating, falling, weightless and mass-less, in the throes of infinity itself.

He realized this was a great moment of his life. Perhaps the greatest. With near overwhelming satisfaction, he realized he'd achieved Step One.

He studied the feel of the thing. He'd imagined it would be like being immersed, carried away in a tumultuous cushiony cascade of impossibly minute particles, growing ever and ever tinier.

His vision was very much in error. Had his SNA abilities failed him? Instead he was in freefall through a black void, with hundreds of thousands of kilometers separating solitary particles. He thought of the Kuiper Belt— single asteroids and ices on their solitary ordained azimuth, travelling alone and immutable through the vast, seeming emptiness of space.

The sub-atomic particles themselves exhibited breathtaking beauty. Indescribable colors, forms and ever changing morphemes that defied comprehension. Yet they were not growing smaller.

***

After a lifetime of descention he was gifted with the truth, an epiphany the likes of which he had never conceived. It was so easy and obvious. In the first pica second it would have been frightening, but it was over before he was aware it was happening. Like smashing into a brick wall. And yet, he simply fell through another barrier, as he had into the pebble itself.

In far less than a fraction of a second he knew he had 'fallen' into another, smaller particle. The experience was equally as inspiring. It also indicated why he had not experienced decreasing particles. He intuited just as quickly that this would be a process he would experience many, many times in the next micro-seconds; and perhaps a million times N before his journey consummated, which would be an eternity from now. He realized with awe that in a certain sense he had just achieved a sort of practical immortality. He stood upon the threshold of infinity itself and could continue forever. Would he run out of power? No. He drew power from the universe directly. As long as the universe existed, he had power. What if he, his corpus, were to die. No difference. When he was questing sub-atomically they existed independent and apart. What of time? When the universe ran out of time, he would as well.

***

He quickly found he could control his rate of descent, so he chose faster and faster and faster until it became a shocking blur rushing past at incomprehensible speed forming a pulsating rainbow. He broke through each succeeding smaller particulate barrier at an unbelievable, incomprehensible rate. Were there a Doppler shift to be observed, it was nothing more than a faint blur.

He believed his sub-micron encapsulated mind was approaching light speed.

He next experimented with broadening his lateral field of vision. After a time he broke through the rushing wall of color and perceived yet another wall.

Then a hundred walls.

Then a thousand.

Then a million and a billion.

Then trillions.

Infinite majesty.

Of course!

Infinity and all its concatenate regressions extended in every dimension conceivable and inconceivable.

Boundless, limitless infinity.

***

Recognition thundered in his mind.

He was approaching a cardinal formation!

This precise, breathtaking formation of infinitesimal matter had been travelling exactly as impelled fourteen billion years ago, and would not deviate by so much as one trillionth of a trillionth of a nanometer, for infinity, unless he somehow contrived to intercede.

He realized this was all but the blink of an eye, and yet something infinitely colossal as well.

This was the finger of God.

Step Five

IF ONE COULD weep underwater, Phil was doing so. Saltwater tears blending with saltwater sea singing wonder and joy, overcome by the grandeur of this exquisite reality.

He would never again view existence with equal eyes.

All the same he knew he must. Phil remorsefully withdrew. It was impossibly painful, yet he knew he must develop absolute expertise in this step prior to continuing.

Considering the beauty he had just witnessed, reentry was not an altogether unpleasant prospect. In fact it motivated him to withdraw, for the joy of reentry, much like a child scampering up a slide just to plummet down yet again.

His mind emerged the surface of the pebble easily, realizing with a jolt of delight he had already mastered Steps One through Four.

Then a sobering thought occurred: step five awaited

***

In the next twenty-four hours he summoned this miracle more than a thousand times, each probe more intoxicating than its predecessor.

He galvanized himself.

The next step is … dangerous. But there is no choice. None.

Phil rolled over again seeking out his little friend, the pebble, promptly spiraling into infinity. Speeding ever downward, he was certain he was travelling at near light speed. In consequence he soon arrived at a cardinal formation. He then toured the formation for hours until he was familiar with its every aspect. It thrilled him to travel like a miniscule subatomic particle moving at relativistic speeds. How fast was the universe really travelling, as a body, as an expansion, at internal gyrations, internally, inside atomic structures themselves? The question begged mysteries the most profound.

It's time.

Philip assumed attack-lead in the infinitesimal formation. Phil wondered what he looked like. Another particle? Himself? Out of the question. Perhaps a micro-sub-sub-photon? He would never know.

Half an hour later he decided to act. Envisioning the slightest angle conceivable, he accelerated slightly and banked ever so gently in a near imperceptible obtuse angle to port.

***

He awoke hours later in a sea of what appeared to be a maroon bouillabaisse. Guts and body parts and bits of flesh bobbed all around him. The water was clearly saturated with blood and dead marine creatures. Phil had been knocked unconscious and was clearly in shock.

What in hell happened? Augh! My leg is broken and my back is buckled nearly in two. Every muscle in my body hurts and I seem to see blood flowing from my ears. Unless I am mistaken, I'm also bleeding internally and I've kill thousands of marine animals.

For God's sake, I haven't eaten in days. I'm so hungry I may pass out.

Phil began snatching fish parts out of the bloody water, stuffing them into his mouth and swallowing without chewing. He glutted nonstop for nearly ten minutes before he found the will to desist.

What happened? Hell I know what happened. I provoked an enormous explosive resumption. I damned near killed myself and I killed marine life on an enormous scale. In fact, why am I alive? Everything in this area is dead, so how did I survive?

As he looked at the grisly parade of horror slowly orbiting him on all sides, it became clear. He was massively injured, but he was alive because he was in the 'eye' of the holocaust. In fact, he was the eye.

My body is going to fail anytime. I have to move fast. I think I can do this thing maybe one more time. If I fail again it will kill me. This is my last chance.

What did I do wrong? I diverted a formation instead of a single particle. I did that right. I deviated it gently at the slightest of obtuse of angles. I did everything right and according to plan. So … what?

He lay amidst the grisly miasma of blood and guts for over forty-five minutes. Absently he realized he'd learned to 'smell' odors underwater. And it wasn't the least pleasant just here and now.

Finally it came to him.

Angle. Obtuse angle. Angle … angle. There's the key! Softer, adaptive and smoother. I must curve it ever more so slightly. I must avoid any angular deflection whatsoever. I must learn to cajole the goddamned particle. And when I can do that I may be able to gently return the particle to its azimuth without the explosive reticulation problem, but for the purpose of this exercise that is irrelevant. And that's for another day. For now, I'm working on a directed diversion. A controlled reticulation.

The organic soup surrounding him suddenly drew his attention. It was circling far above him, faster and faster, as though he were in the middle of a huge drain. He looked up. Far above him an enormous swirling maelstrom had formed and seemed to be growing larger with each succeeding second.

What the hell? What is that? Did I do that? What took so long? Crap! It's descending.

Phil desperately searched his memory trying to remember what could cause such phenomena. Whirlpools were a function of opposing tides. Reticulation could certainly provoke that. Whatever, there seemed little to do. He wondered how deep it would descend. Would it spin him? Tear him apart? What?

Phil lay on his back peering up at the vortex, suddenly realizing there was no danger. It was simply pushing vast quantities of water downward. So he simply lay there enjoying the remarkable show and the soothing twirl of his body on the sandy bottom. More importantly, it provided him the rest and the time to think clearly.

The explosive resumption of my last attempt must have generated this thing. In its own way this is good news. I'm not only getting a good show and clearing the waters, I think I've also got confirmation of my curvature. What I'm seeing is the adulterated effects of my angular deflection. After a time, at some distance, dealing with huge amounts of water, the angular resumption dissipates its energy into tides and then a curved vortex …

Phil slept for six hours.

When he awoke he was rested, but physically much worse. He'd lost more blood externally and internally. The achy symptoms of early peritonitis were growing in his gut. His muscles were exquisitely stiff and painful, and his cracked and broken bones were an agony, as were his horribly overtaxed tendons. A dizzy throbbing in his head and an intermittent loss of visual acuity alerted him to a probable concussion.

I have no time. I'm dying. I have one final chance. I must act now.

He gingerly rolled onto his stomach; an exercise he never dreamt could be so supremely painful. Phil cast about for his little pebble (He'd grown understandably superstitious about it by now: a tool, and a talisman that had carried him farther in a few days than his entire lifetime.). The tiny pebble had been buffeted and blown by the subaqueous tornado and Phil couldn't find it. He worried that it might have been lost during the reticulation storm. He cast about desperately for the tiny madstone. Long, painful, desperate minutes later he seized upon it. He held it tight for a moment, as though it were a precious jewel. Then, realizing what scant time remained him, he placed the pebble close to his face and commenced his ritual.

Almost immediately he was flashing downward at relativistic speed. Breathtakingly fast, he arrived a cardinal formation, immediately assuming the lead attack position. Interestingly, he felt no pain now.

It dawned on Phil he might be the single creature in the entire universe empowered with such navigational powers. The feeling was intoxicating. He felt omnipotent, as though a god. The task before him was clear now. He knew exactly what to do and how to do it. This was far and away one of the most exhilarating, exciting sensations he would ever experience.

With absolute certainty he gently nudged the formation, banking it into a flawlessly smooth hyperbola, continuing along on an entirely different azimuth. He had modified direction without resumption. He was *Verteror!* Had he defeated God? Disproved him? Redefined him? Or performed exactly as directed fourteen billion years ago? He truly did not know, nor did he know how to know. In all ration he could never know. For now though, he was Verteror.

He wasn't quite sure how he knew, but he was sure of his capabilities now. He would dispatch the disgusting black jillion encrusting Gauntlet.

Then he would find his way to Kosmas at best speed. Then he would face down the most advanced creatures in the galaxy. Then he would confront the force that purportedly threatened existence itself. He would dispatch them as well, were the threat real and their intent malevolent.

But first ... he must survive.

Effortlessly he surfaced from his pebble into his underwater world and a universe of pain.

Looking about frenetically, he seized upon his now treasured pebble and feebly pushed off to the surface.

The Beginning of the Beginning

*And when I shall die, take him and cut him up in little stars, and he will
make the face of heaven so fine that all the world will fall in love with night
and pay no worship to the garish sun.*

Shakespeare

HIS EYES WOULD not open for some reason. Nor could he move
his arms or legs. He could still hear however, which was good. Apparently
he'd survived. He also retained a sense of smell, which for the moment was
noxiously bad.

God what a stench!

Putrid as it was, it transported Phil back to the happy days of his youth
on the Chesapeake Bay.

After the passing of violent storms, he and his uncle would cast off in
their old rust-bucket fishing boat, allegedly to sea-trial the boat ensuring its
seaworthiness after the furious storm.

In reality his Uncle Herb wanted to go *a-pickin'* for any useful flotsam
or jetsam the tempest had liberated from its rightful owners.

*Herb knew the 'good stuff,' the occasional dingy, shipboard supplies, even liquor
and beer, was frequently trapped with the remains of boats in small inlets along the decimated coast, so they followed the good stuff, where the pickins' were richest. As often as
not, instead of valuable castaways they found mountains of dead fish, crustaceans and sea
mammals—some quite large—even a desultory human body—and a reek so overpower-
ing that ...*

Phil realized his mind was wandering. He suspected he might be mildly hallucinating. He did remember he'd been seriously injured. In fact he recalled he was quite near death. He must rouse himself from the pain and exhaustion and move fast.

Soon he discovered the source of some of his ills. He'd been tidily and tightly wrapped in giant kelp from head to toe. Phil suspected a second whirlpool was the perpetrator. Quickly he freed his eyes and could soon move his arms. Once liberated, he surveyed himself and his surroundings.

He was naked, cut, bleeding and bruised in uncountable places. His gut was disturbingly distended. His head ached terribly. He clearly suffered from several fractured and cracked bones. He was starved, dehydrated, exhausted and nearly incapacitated. Precious little time remained.

The coastline and the small bay were in shambles. The water was a brownish fuchsia, colored with blood and clogged with fish parts, as well as several bloated and floating dead fish, including his old friend, the great white, Wilbur. The shoreline was in no better condition. Trees and ground cover were ripped out by their roots. Saltwater puddled about the landscape in a thousand muddy bogs. There were a few strange land animals lying about in various aspects of death.

This doesn't look good worth a damn. Is the whole goddamned ship in this shape? Is anyone else alive? What in hell's name have I done?

He took the only action possible. He began to drag himself through the water and the mud and the debris. It was agonizing and maddeningly slow. Fatigue was descending like a dark curtain. But what choice?

He abruptly stopped.

Use your head, man. Where is your communicator?

He desperately looked about the small bay.

Where are my clothes? Shirt, shoes, anything—that's where my unit will be.

After a time he spotted his trousers half buried in sand and mud six meters to his left. He immediately began crawling towards them. It seemed miles and an eternity, yet he was there in a scant twelve minutes.

Four minutes later he found his com unit.

"Thishish Cap'n Carr to any receive. I b'lieve I locate threehunert meter sou'a Shark ... ah Sharrr ... thaatis Shaa ..."

He tumbled into a well of endless darkness.

***

"Captain? Captain Carr? Are you awake? We need you to wake up sir. You've been out far too long now. Please wake up Captain."

"Whaaa …"

"That's excellent Captain. Here. Try to take some of this."

He greedily sucked at the glass straw. The liquid took immediate effect and he looked up at his nurse whispering "How long?"

"How long have you been out? Six days sir."

Suddenly his voice was strong again. "Shit! Get me the doctor."

The doctor appeared immediately.

"Captain! It's great to see you've …"

"Cut it Doc. I've been out six days?"

"Yes sir."

"I'm gonna live?"

"Barely. We worked on you for …"

"Why the fuck didn't you revive me? What's happening? The Out-Worlders are moving?"

"Why yes. How did you …?"

"I said cut it Doc. Get me up. Tell the XO, Jake and HERB to report here immediately. While you're wiring me together have one of your nurses order some lunch. A steak, rare. A bottle of Scotch and my clothes from Shark Bay. I trust you have them?"

"Yessir."

"Good you'll find a small pebble in the left pocket of my trousers. Bring it to me, and some fresh clothes. We have very little time Doc. Don't fuck around."

"Acknowledged Captain."

"One fast question Doc. The flesh sample. Were you able to kill it?"

"Not even close. I had to flush it out the airlock and we've been searching for residuals ever since."

"Find any?"

"Not as yet sir."

"Any idea why you couldn't kill it?"

"Yes."

"Yes?"

"I suspect you already know Captain."

"Just answer the goddamned question Doc."

The Doctor stiffened. "We could not kill the sample because it was not alive. It was just not living as we understand it Sir."

"You're right. That's pretty much as I thought. Whenever this is all over, assuming we survive, I suppose we should revisit our definition of life." Phil reflected for a moment and then looked up at the doctor. "You have your orders Doctor."

"Aye sir."

Phil was on his feet, awkwardly, painfully and immediately.

Happily a nurse entered at that moment with fresh coveralls to assist Phil in dressing. Then he limped to a table and chair, moved it to face the door, readying himself, planning the upcoming ordeal.

Unexpectedly Anne entered his room.

"Hi. I didn't expect to see you."

"They told me you were awake and I wanted to see how you were."

"How do I look?"

"You look like shit. You nearly died you know."

"Yep."

"Did you succeed?"

"Beyond my wildest hopes. It was the toughest thing I've ever faced, but not without a certain beauty. I think I learned a thing or two about the universe as well."

"You *are* aware you nearly killed the Webberian Sea?"

"Anne, when I crawled out of that blood and guts stew, I was afraid I'd killed *everything* on Gauntlet. How was it up here?"

"Hard to describe. There was a deafening boom, then a giant geyser whirled out of the sea, almost to the R^3 ship's amid point, casting fish and flesh and blood in all directions. It looked like some sort of berserker sea-monster. No one was seriously injured, but we're still cleaning up the mess. GAIA was totally inadequate to confront such a shambles. It would have taken her months."

"And the Out-Worlders. What the hell is …?"

"Phil I think it would be best to wait for Jake and HERB."

HERB interceded directly. "I am here Captain. Jake will join any moment."

Sure enough, Jake and the Doctor entered the room. "Cor Blimy! You look like death itself Cap'n. The Doc kept you under wraps until just now, so we had no idea. Are you alright?"

"Tell me about the Out-Worlders."

"They passively probe our defenses everywhere. We can't kill them, or stop them. We might possibly destroy them with explosives, but the Doc says we'll probably only create thousands more. So far they've been contained to Out-World side, but their shear mass applies tremendous pressure on all hatches and gravity chutes.

"We sent out a recon probe yesterday. It showed the outer shell literally boiling with Out-Worlders. Top-to-bottom it's packed with black and purple flesh. It's an organic nightmare ready to explode. I'm afraid it's going to *implode* leaving Gauntlet as nothing more than a tightly packed ball of purplish-black nightmare."

"Have any of our people been hurt? Have there been hostilities?"

"None of that is necessary sir. We'll all die when the shell buckles."

"How long do you estimate before implosion?"

"Any time now sir."

"Jesus Christ. Get me to an escape module *now!*"

"Captain!"

"Don't fuck with me Jake. I'm not abandoning goddamned ship, I going out to destroy them. But I *do* want all ship's company strapped into an ASC (Abandon-Ship-Craft) on hot standby, immediately. HERB, if you detect the slightest loss of hull integrity, order an emergency *Abandon Ship*. Now let's go!"

"Sir. Are you up to this?"

"I don't need my body Jake. I need my mind. *Now move it!*"

They walked, ran, supported, limped, carried and finally stretchered Phil to a module. When he was strapped in, he buttoned up and jettisoned without a word. His small party stoically regarded each other for a few moments then hurried to carry out what could easily be Phil's final order.

***

Phil had never entered one of the tiny ASC's before. It was cramped, and with his injuries, extremely painful. The module was quick, easy to drive and Spartan in the extreme. Each ASC was equipped with a WOF module (Water, Oxygen, Food) providing a protein concentrate, along with oxygen and waste processors affording minimal life support. Phil had been briefed that one of these little ships could sustain life for up to six weeks. Totally futile of course, considering their present coordinates, but immeasurably preferable to smothering in a sea of black and purple, rancid flesh.

There was an interesting aspect of the ASC. It supported a full body suit capable of keeping a human alive outside the little ship in hard vacuum for roughly three hours. Its umbilical was four meters long and he could EVA outside Gauntlet long enough to accomplish his task. The headpiece also provides a short-range conventional radio. Although Phil saw no need for it just now, he tongued it on after painfully struggling into the suit. One size easily fits all, assuming no broken bones and ribs. He donned his gloves as he retrieved the tiny pebble, gripping it firmly.

Minutes later his module settled lightly on the tough transparent blister which enclosed Out-World. Sure enough, it was packed like a colossal over-stuffed blood sausage. After connecting the module's O_2 and popping the diminutive hatch, he struggled out, touching down lightly on the shield.

He lay upon the shielding, holding the pebble just before his eyes. He took a deep breath and prepared for the ritual. As he began concentrating on the pebble a harsh metallic voice interrupted.

"Hello Captain. I would say I was surprised to see you out here, but I cannot be—surprised that is. I would declare I was unaware of your recent activities, but I am. I would boast that I will not consult with you regarding our joint and several futures, but I will. What are you doing Captain?"

"Alpha, I need to concentrate for a moment, so what say you leave me in peace?"

"Ah! You've hit upon another thing I will not do."

"Fine. I'll just tongue my radio off. If you will excuse?"

Silence. Phil calmed himself and began falling into the pebble, deeper and deeper, faster and faster.

"Philip, we are no longer speaking via your little radio. We are in the pebble with you. We have been waiting for you in here for fourteen billion years."

As Phil was already into the pebble, concentration was a lesser issue now, so he elected to respond. Although he was skeptical it would be possible to distract Alpha while Phil performed his task, he responded. "I see. Impressive. The best part is I don't have to look at you, or smell you here."

"Unworthy Philip. Incessantly unworthy. I fear we must terminate your activities now."

"So it's Philip now. Not Captain, father, dad, daddy, pop, or whatever?"

"That's right Phil. Now stop what you're doing, or we will stop for you."

"Certainly you are not suggesting some sort of physical contest?"

"Would that I were, for I am un-killable and you are eminently so."

"Problem is, you are encased in this tiny rock with me, which puts us on a pretty damned equal footing."

"Your point Philip?"

"Do you see that brilliancy rising before us?"

After a considerable delay …

"Yes."

Although there was no horizon *per se*, something before them was beginning to glow with an extraordinary reddish-golden hue.

"I believe it will be known as a *cosmodog*. I'm going there and you cannot."

"Your point Phil?"

"Observe."

"Phil. I know very well your allusion. I know you may actually be able to deflect a particle. Yet you equally know we cannot be killed."

"Alpha, you are my son. You are all my children, and grandchildren, and great-grandchildren and possibly more. You are I. I am you. I could never kill you."

"My point exactly."

"Alpha my son, and you are all Alphas. Go with your father's love and affection. Whatever I feel for you, you will sadly, not be missed."

"Phil … Captain … father … what are you …"
"Time's up. Goodbye son."

***

Just as he had done in the Webberian Sea, he effortlessly guided the cardinal formation into a smooth portside descent. The formation plunged gracefully into the glide path, diving through the clear shield, circumnavigating Gauntlet a billion-billion times in every conceivable micro-gradient, until a colossal mono-directional resumptive reticulation propagated in microseconds, provoking a titanic outward burst—a colossal molecular black cloud expanded at near relativistic velocity in every direction outward from Gauntlet. His dark children were blasted into space.

Phil was momentarily deafened, his head pounded with the thunder of a billion voices screaming in astonishment and maniacal fury. Such was their ferocity he swiftly exited the pebble, never loosening it from his powerful grip. He could actually feel the tiny stone vibrating in his hand—a vibration that convulsed his entire body to its very roots. Exquisite agony.

Phil tumbled through space tethered to his escape craft. He was fascinated with the erratic, whirling gyrations of Gauntlet. In reality it was he who was looping unevenly, as would a large stone tethered to a smaller, hurled with great force in zero gee.He marveled at the wondrous dark cloud as it cleared, revealing the giant ship, drifting aft of Gauntlet's huge sphere, revealing its star-lit reflected beauty, now blessedly free of its foul encrustation.

He tumbled dreamlike through the darkness trying to comprehend what had just passed. Phil was certain his thoughts were masterfully and lyrically insightful. Pure illusion. His mind was well and truly scrambled.

He did accurately remember some elements however. His plan had executed flawlessly. He had truly mastered SNA. He felt no pain. In fact he felt nothing. He thankfully drank in the cool air of his helmet as he rested his head and pondered the fate of his progeny.

In his dazed condition, thoughts came to him as velutinous softly glowing spheres, slowly expanding out of the darkness of deep space. There was a luminous beauty about them. Each growing sphere a thought, as though in a dream. Was he hallucinating? Ordinary men suffer rapture in the depths of the sea. Was there rapture in deep space? His thoughts ascended as though bubbles in molten rose colored glass. A phantom glassblower creating miracles in the ruby darkness. Each bubble began as a tiny teardrop glowing red from below, slowly coaxed into spherical fullness by some mystical master artisan.

Were he truly lucid he would have realized the bubbles were indeed real. They were not a shock-induced hallucination. He was seeing his own life-blood draining from his neck and every cranial orifice filling his helmet, bouncing about his helmet like so many deep burgundy bingo-balls, lit from below by his suit's micro-light, formed into bubbles by his suit's oxy-flow, liberated in zero-gee.

In Earth-normal gravity he would have already drowned in his own blood.

Oblivious of their genesis and unaware of impending danger, he marveled at their beauty, savoring each thought:

Farewell my children.
I must destroy your dark festering nidus
To save Gauntlet,
To save us all,
To save the galaxy,
To save the universe itself.

I did not kill you.
For you cannot die.
You shall never die.
For you never lived.
You will endure as a dark nimbus forever ranging infinity.

You will know the universe.
You will know all things.
Perhaps you will ascend to the divine.
You've already ascended to the immortal.

You command my envy.
My envy companions your rage.
In all the Cosmos was there ever such rage?

Return to the Light

Science cannot solve the ultimate mystery of nature. And that is because, in the last analysis, we ourselves are part of nature and therefore part of the mystery that we are trying to solve.

Max Planck

JAKE HAD DEMONSTRATED the admirable foresight to dispatch two escape modules in pursuit, to assist or retrieve Captain Carr, or his body. The colossal eruption of Out-World blasted Phil's ASC hundreds of kilometers away from the mother ship, requiring many additional kilometers to regain control. Rescuers found themselves in the midst of an angry, turbulent EMP bedlam.

Consequently, despite its powerful array of lights and beacons, it required well over an hour to locate and retrieve Phil, just beyond the limit of his suit's oxygen reserve.

***

Senior staff gathered round Phil's gurney in the triage receiving area of Gauntlet's hospital. Considering the overall size of the facility, the term 'clinic' might seem more apropos. Its diminutive size was deceptive however, as this was the most advanced medical center in human history. Taking into account the proximity of man's precipitous extinction, it would probably forever remain so.

They had practically cut him out of his ASC effectively dead from oxygen deprivation, blood loss, shock and severe impact trauma to an already critically injured body. All PM's were out of service, so they literally ran with him on shoulders to the hospital. With every second, death closed more intimately on its prey.

The head nurse was hurriedly assessing his condition and administering any feasible first aid. A second nurse was desperately seeking out Dr. Singe, who was swamped with other casualties.

After a few moments Dr. Singe rushed into receiving. "What are you people doing here? I have to examine and prep this man for surgery and ... all sorts of shit and you're in the goddamned way. *Get the hell out!*"

After an hour of emergency treatments, scans, probes, examinations and encephalography, Dr. Singe's team was in the process of formulating a tentative treatment tactic.

"What do you think Doctor?"

"Well doctors, first, the Captain would be considered already dead in most circles. Second, I've never seen such trauma. This man is one big six-foot hematoma. Add to that at least twenty broken bones, vast internal hemorrhaging, appreciable brain damage and at least one ruptured kidney. This compounded by his previous injuries, particularly as it pertains to risk of acute peritonitis."

"Prognosis Doctor?"

Singe took a deep breath, releasing it with a sigh. "I wouldn't think his chances exceed five percent. So we better get to work.

"Prep our main operating theater and gas it with FOND. I want our best thoracic, cardiac, neurologic, and orthopedic surgeons on hot standby. We'll need every bit of O Negative blood our Food Processors can replicate, starting immediately. I also want non-invasive micro-bio-specimens taken of the Captain's kidney, liver, heart, lung, stomach, spleen, upper and lower intestines, all prepped and ready for immediate replication if need be.

"Let's get to it gentlemen."

They worked on Phil for over eighteen hours, taking every heroic life saving measure they could conjure. They then subjected him to the most intensive monitoring, sterilization and life-support care possibly ever provided a human. After twenty hours they re-entered the operating theater, working on him for an additional six hours, after which Dr. Singe collapsed into exhausted sleep for seven hours.

When he awoke the Doctor was given a thorough briefing by his staff and all attending physicians. Despite their Herculean efforts the news was not good. They were unable to maintain blood pressure, his EEG was erratic and Atrial fibrillation was a conspicuous anomaly on his monitor.

Later the Doctor and senior staff gathered in Phil's room trying to observe him through a plethora of monitors and life support equipment.

As much as Phil had inflicted shock, aggravation and humiliation upon him, the Doctor was well and truly grief stricken. His sorrow sprang from two fonts. First. He was devoted to Captain Carr and would somehow be orphaned without his stewardship. Second. He had genuinely liked and admired the man.

He faced the ships seniors speaking in controlled, measured tones. "I'm sorry to report that Captain Carr did not ..."

"Report Doctor, we haven't much time."

The Doctor whirled in astonishment. *"Captain!"*

"I said report Doctor. That is an order."

Seconds later the Doctor had organized his thoughts.

"This cannot be Captain. You are, or were effectively dead."

"That was almost true Doctor. There are means of ... of ah, travelling inward and effecting ... mmm, various critical changes. Your team was excellent Doctor. My compliments. They made their work far easier."

"Easier for whom?"

"I don't really know."

"My God. Can you share this with me?"

"Not now Doctor. Report."

The Doctor stiffened yet again.

Good 'ol Captain Carr. He never changes.

"Forty-eight crew perished in this last incident. It could have been much worse."

"Sounds like we may be calling upon some Golden Childs to fill in."

"Interesting idea Captain. We certainly should." The Doctor continued. "Were it not for the direction of the blast, which was apparently outward, I would have estimated our chances of survival until planet-fall on Kosmas at roughly two percent. Now? Twenty-five percent if we're very lucky. Food, water, environment and risk of disease are disasters. Disease I can handle. The rest … frankly, I have no remedy at hand. I inquired with HERB as to our estimated arrival at Kosmas. He stipulated something on the order of four hundred days, assuming we can wire this wreck back to-gether. That is approximately one hundred and fifty days longer than we are now equipped to survive."

"Thank you Doctor." Phil prepared to move on.

"*Thank you Doctor?* I just handed down a death-sentence on every man, woman and child aboard this ship. You do realize that sir?"

"Thank you Doctor. Engineering, report."

Ship's Chief Engineer stood facing Phil. "True to form for the QAVL sir, our propulsion systems are operating flawlessly. I concur with HERB's ETA Kosmas, and I foresee no problems en-route. On the other hand, roughly 86% of domestic systems are out of service, with no appreciable estimate of recovery. Essentially this implies we starve to death approxi-mately six months before destination. However, we will suffocate, or pos-sibly die of dehydration long before that. I need more time to assess our situation and I will keep you constantly advised."

"Our plant life cannot replenish the oxygen?"

"Most of it was destroyed sir."

"Water?"

"All tanks ruptured and now corrupted by salt, sewage, or radiation. We are struggling to find a solution, which we can do. But time is the criti-cal factor."

"Thank you engineer. HERB?"

"Yes Captain?"

"I assume we can call upon Kosmas for assistance?"

"That is correct sir. At this distance, I would estimate six weeks."

"Estimate? You are normally more precise."

"I am uncertain as to the necessary preparatory logistics, and therefore the time required."

"I see. I assume ship's diagnostic system can give them a pretty fair rundown. Our staff can fill in the details. Please contact Kosmas."

Phil looked down on the wreck of his once impeccable body, wondering if, like Gauntlet, it would ever again approach normalcy.

"Please ensure the ship's compliment receives a message I will dictate."

The nurse retrieved a tiny recorder from her uniform and handed it to Phil.

"What a nifty little device."

"Thank you sir. It has replaced patient's medical charts."

To the Crew and Ship's Compliment of Gauntlet

Parties unknown attempting to scuttle our mission infested gauntlet.

These agencies mutated into the foulness we termed the Out-Worlders and

Gauntlet was scant moments from total annihilation at their hand.

The Out-Worlders have been purged and no longer pose a threat.

I emphasize they are banished, not deceased.

They will exist indefinitely as far as I know.

I hope they find some manner of conciliation.

Before their monstrous adulteration these were my children.

I could not destroy them even were I capable.

Recently I have been less than forthcoming due to security constraints.

I trust you understand.

And I apologize.

The danger has passed.

It remains now to repair, rebuild and carry on.

We expect assistance from Kosmas within a month or so.

Tragically we lost forty-five crew in this critical struggle.

A roster of our fallen colleagues is attached.

As long as there is an Oneiro … they will be missed.

They will be remembered.

Philip Carr

Commanding

***

As the senior officers walked away from the hospital, greatly relieved, one of them asked, "I'm happier than I can express that the Captain's going to live. But for the life of me, I can't understand how he survived that shit-storm outside the ship while it was making shrapnel out of chunks of Gauntlet."

Amidst some confused mumbling, HERB joined in over their DIT's.

"Consider this. An extremely high-powered speedboat roars across an erstwhile calm body of water. As the boat passes through and over the water a huge wake is cast and exceptional turbulence is propagated in the surrounding water. The boat provoked this, yet the boat remains reasonably unaffected. In generating the enormous resumptive reticulation, the Captain occupied the same relative position as the boat. Hence he was able to survive. Simple basic physics."

***

"Captain I have quite literally snatched you from the jaws of certain death for the third time in nearly as many weeks. Your body is a shambles and you are not that far from death right now despite whatever inward voyaging skills you possess. I therefore exercise the authority and responsibility *you* invested in me as ship's Chief Medical Officer. I *order* you to stay in this room and in that bed until and if I authorize duty. No more foolishness trying to get out of bed, no working, no moving about and no bullying the crew to aid in your attempts to do so. Are we clear?" An instant's pause "Sir."

"As you wish Doctor."

"Thank you Captain, I will leave you to rest."

Phil was weeks convalescing and would be weeks more in agonizing physical therapy.

For the first time in his life he was well and truly helpless. As he lay submissively in bed, bandaged and cast and draining, with little else to do, he reviewed events since his initial recruitment as an eager young, upcoming New York lawyer, decades ago. He found the exercise particularly interesting in light of his recently arisen insightful abilities.

When he viewed the march of incredible events comprising his life there was an unmistakable and relentless direction in his remarkable journey. Where it would advance from here was growing clearer to him now, and his SNA seemed to validate this premise within its limited parameters. For some reason Phil continued to experience blind spots, impervious to his scrutiny.

He recalled his final face-to-face with Alpha (if one could concede his even having a face):

'Nothing can be kept from us. Ever. Anywhere in the universe. If we project trajectories with spatiotemporal efficacy, we can quite literally wander the cosmos without leaving this tiny sphere drifting through infinity.'

If they can use these micro-micro-sub-atomics as their 'eyes,' I'm certain I can do the same. Actually I did achieve this somewhat during my last healing process.

An idea struck him. A fascinating, dangerous idea, but an irresistible one and possibly the advantage he sorely needed in his upcoming confrontation with the Kosmians.

Then another, more immediate idea came to him as well.

He smiled to himself.

It would seem the Doctor is right. I should spend more time in bed.

Acting on his second idea, he squeezed the little bulb that rested bedside. Jake entered immediately.

"Jake I need a few things. Some may be difficult."

"Captain Phil, you are under a strict bed-rest injunction. You are not that far removed from death yet, so I suggest you respect it."

"Right Jake. Thank you. Now would you get me a data pad so I may prepare the list for you? I also need a good bottle of Ganti Scotch. Considering you and HERB are effectively in command of this vessel, isn't it odd that I be ordering you about?"

"Would you prefer someone else Captain Phil?"

Phil smiled. "No one else Jake. No one. And don't call me Captain Phil ... makes you sound like some sort of deep-south share-cropper, when such things still existed."

"If you will excuse sir, I will fetch the pad and the Scotch. Anything to eat sir?"

"Yes. Thank you. If you can arrange it I would really enjoy three or four live Red Snapper."

Jake shuddered inwardly, while his expression never faltered. "I will do my best."

***

Phil patted lips, chin and neck with an immaculate linen napkin and then turned his attentions to hands. "That was delicious Jake. Thank you."

"You're most welcome sir. Interestingly, the central kitchen rescued a large aquarium of live fish, especially for you. I have no idea how they knew of your specific predilection."

"Nor I. But please extend my thanks. Now Jake, here is the list of the items I need." Phil extended the pad to Jake.

Jake scrolled through the list, eyebrows rising higher and higher. "This will take quite some time sir."

"When is the support ship from Kosmas due in?"

"It is expected in one-point-five days."

"I see. Then we will have some delay as they re-provision and overhaul us?"

"Indeed. The latest statement is twelve days."

"That long?"

"I'm afraid so sir. We may also require two to three days for testing and shakedown. But that is not yet confirmed. It is quite possible the repairs may be of such quality we can confidently resume immediately.

"There will however, be some time lost in the buildup to .51 light-speed if we are to adhere to our schedule."

"Why?"

"Forward velocity was somewhat diminished as a result of our damages and we experienced measurable course deviation due to uneven explosive decompression of Out-World. All the same, we are certain we can regain .51 in but a few days."

"And our estimated time to Kosmas?"

"When we are up to speed and on course, add an additional one hundred and seventy-eight days."

"So ... that makes us roughly two hundred days out?"

"Right sir."

"I still have my pebble?"

"Pebble sir?"

"Yes. It was with my clothing from Shark Bay."

"Oh. Is that what that is? Yes. It's in a small, black wooden box on your desk."

"Excellent. I will need the items listed on that pad in no less than two hundred and ten days. I assume I will be fit long before that."

"I hope so sir. I will start on the list straightaway."

"Thank you Jake. And Jake ... the items on that list are *EYES ONLY* and *MISSION CRITICAL*. If possible, try to avoid acquiring no more than one item from any given source at any given time."

"Aye sir."

"We don't have an unlimited number of sources, but I'll give it my best shot."

Deliverance

WHEN HELP ARRIVED, it proved to be a resounding non-event.

The recovery vessel itself was a gargantuan leaden sphere with no markings, or distinguishing features whatsoever. It docked at the enormous in-load access-port, without heraldry, or any formalities other than the technical minutiae requisite in a vessel-to-vessel coupling at 3.5–7ths light-speed.

In fact, considering the ship's autonomic systems, the crew was bewilderingly superfluous. Captain Carr, senior ship's officers, and the majority of Gauntlet's compliment were gathered at the entry glade where Phil was first captivated by the wonders of Gauntlet.

After nearly half an hour, the huge airlock was unsealed and majestically yawed opened for the first time in nearly seventeen years.

The subsequent, breathless, near terrifying interval, awaiting the wonders of life beyond imagining was … well it was damned disappointing.

With a very smooth, very quiet movement of indecipherable mechanics, a very small grey, gun-mettle sphere entered Gauntlet.

Without delay the tiny automaton floated up to Captain Carr. Without preliminaries, it addressed him.

"Captain Carr, we have been ordered to provide the repairs and replenishments required by the Interstellar-Sphere Gauntlet."

"Excellent. You are most welcome. How can we …"

"With your permission we will commence."

"Certainly. You have our …"

Without comment the diminutive orb moved away faster than human eyes could record.

Then it began.

Dozens of similar gray spheres sped aboard Gauntlet.

Ship's stores were scrupulously restored. The rancid mess created by Phil's maelstrom lost its smell and gradually initiated the tedious process of retreatment. Mechanical systems were suddenly a deafening cacophony of twisting and screeching howls.

The Webberian Sea, as though Moses himself were amongst them, rose alarmingly. Huge swells engulfed its banks—miraculously never overflowing. Sea spouts the size of tornados of incredible energy sprang from everywhere.

The cacophony wore on without abate, twenty-four hours a day. At the end of twelve days, the ship's compliment was exhausted, nerves jangled, nearly at wits end.

On the thirteenth day, the small sphere appeared before Philip. "Captain. We have completed our repairs. Do you concur sir?"

Phil addressed his communicator. "XO?"

"Yes sir."

"Ship's status?"

"Status was reported in detail just moments ago. All systems report five-by-five."

"No additional testing or shakedown necessary?"

"No sir."

"Thrusters and heading?"

"We are on course 185.63325 29.89598611."

"Velocity?"

". 50785 and increasing steadily."

Phil turned back to the little gray sphere. "I concur. Your work has been amaze …"

All the maintenance drones exited as quickly as they had appeared and within moments the access bay was closed and sealed and the huge gray sphere moved away at breathtaking speed.

Phil considered the situation for a moment, speaking into his communicator. "Alright XO. How 'bout a drink?"

Phil could hear the broad smile in the man's voice. "Absolutely sir."

In Range

COMMUNICATIONS WITH *KOSMAS*, sporadic until now, suddenly sprang to life with welcomes from thousands of races, status, ETA, docking and orbiting coordinates, detailed human requirements and hundreds of schedules.

Near overwhelming, yet all in all, a most cordial beginning. Seventy crewmen we delegated just to handle and action communications augmented by ship's intelligent systems.

Phil ordered permanent night conditions, and the entire crew watched in fascination, as *Kosmas* grew large at blinding speed, despite their radically reduced velocity.

Kosmas grew to an unbelievable giant commanding the entire sky. Phil reckoned it to be roughly the same size as Saturn without the deadly extra-planetary fields. A nearly nonexistent magnetosphere. Radiation emissions dwarfed by those of Jupiter. Due to its highly cribiform composition—a capricious anomaly of planetary accretion—geology borne of smaller sister planets.

Phil devoted hours struggling to adequately describe the swift approaching object. Monstrous in size. Every shade and nuance of color imaginable. Lights in regular columns advancing towards the planet's surface until they were lost in the glow of a million columns of light converging at *Kosmas* ground level. Everything was light and graceful pylons ranging out one hundred thousand kilometers in every direction ... exploding into a titanic, glowing, cosmic sea urchin the circumference of an solar gas giant.

The most colossal construct imaginable and a source of inconceivable intimidation for Phil.

He searched for a metaphor. Some imaginable object of comparable form and grandeur. A Christmas ornament the size of Neptune? Titanic crystals grown in zero gravity, refracted by the pure white light of a giant Class F star? The incredible chandeliers of the Winter Palace in St Petersburg? An enormous three-dimensional fractal? A fourth dimensional fractal finally perceived? None began to approach the grandeur before him.

Phil sat alone at the Captain's Station on the vast Command Bridge. All systems were on automatic waiting final docking instructions, which would then divert full control to Kosmas Central Control.

"HERB. What exactly are we seeing?"

"Those are life sphere vessels that brought the Quaestors to this planet. They provide the living environment to maintain each life form in comfort, whatever their native ambience may be. All creatures, whatever their nature and amelioration, ultimately need the solace of their home world."

"That's interesting. I was under the impression we would be required to vacate Gauntlet in favor of accommodations on Kosmas."

"Not at all. Not only would that be impractical by doubling the necessary capacity of Kosmas, it would subject arriving species to undue inconvenience."

"Strange I didn't realize that, or even question it. Has our friend QASI been busy again?"

Overlooking Phil's observation HERB continued. "Many sphere are similar to *Gauntlet,* although their propulsion systems are, by-and-large, far more powerful."

"Why is that?"

"Humans do not enjoy the same inertial robustness as the majority of galactic specie."

"I see."

"Available materials on Earth were also highly limited. Earth is not the treasure trove of minerals and natural resources humans believe it to be."

"Really? How would you describe it then?"

"I trust you will not be offended by this?"

"I doubt it."

"Earth would generally be described as a wilderness and an incredibly smelly, marginally propitious, swamp."

"Oh no. That doesn't offend in the least." His sarcasm was not lost on HERB. "So the same would apply to Gauntlet?"

"I'm afraid so Captain."

"We'll just have to be damned careful who we invite over for supper."

"I'm sorry sir?"

"Proceed HERB."

"The most advanced vessels are elsewhere, imperceptible to human acuity. Even were such numina not beyond your perception, they exist beyond your comprehension."

"Vessels fashioned of such stuff that they are invisible?"

"Not invisible Philip. Simply not visible to *you*. You were making marginal progress in that direction as part of your study of Higgs Fields, back on Earth, if you recall."

Phil was captivated.

Interstellar vehicles beyond my cognition …

"How many such wonders?" he whispered.

"Last count: 49,293"

"My God. And I will be communicating with such creatures?"

"With those who can and will communicate with you Philip."

"I see. Therein lies the challenge."

"And the joy Philip. The joy."

Feeling inspired, hugely diffident, and of recent development: Audacious

Phil gripped the arms of the Captain's chair.

Now is the time!

***

Phil hurried from the Command Bridge to his Residence. Upon retrieving his beloved pebble he navigated his rugged all terrain PM directly to Shark Bay. He literally tore off his clothes and dove into the dark water.

When he was settled on the bottom there was just enough light to make out the small pebble he'd placed before him. Environment Control had been cajoled a few years ago into producing *moon-glow*, as they had always provided *sun-glow*. Life aboard Gauntlet had been duly enriched. Tonight *moon-glow* had the auspicious aspect of weakly illuminating Phil's tiny stone.

Soon he was effortlessly diving into the infinite depths of the stone at near light-speed. He immediately sought out the unmistakable signature of a cardinal formation. He felt they were old friends now. Maybe in some curious way, they were.

As he assumed the lead position he spoke to them as a wing commander would his attack force—as the familiar team they had become—although he had no illusions about their comprehension in any manner.

Or perhaps he was fearfully wrong?

Nonetheless, the act clarified his mind and fostered a warm familiarity with some of the most basic building blocks of existence itself. Phil was not only learning the nature of reality, he was becoming intimate with such. He was learning to love the cosmos themselves.

"Today we will not reticulate. We will deviate, but we will not seek permanence of azimuth. Today we come in peace. Today we voyage. Today we explore. I will lead you. You will be my wings and my eyes and together we will quest worlds and creatures beyond wonder."

Phil smoothly guided his formation out of the sea, traversing Gauntlet and effortlessly passing through the shell of the huge sphere.

My God. Alpha was right. Synergy with these particles is near magic. I can actually see. I can see everything.

He saw Kosmas far to his right, so he banked the formation to starboard towards the colossal construct.

Within seconds he entered the first of forty-five million titanic spheres, most of which easily dwarfed Gauntlet.

He then plunged into a cataract of such alien strangeness it would tax his sanity for as long as he would endure life.

✳✳✳

Three days later he awakened at the bottom of the sea where he had started; and in point of fact had never left.

The sea was unharmed. He was unharmed. All was calm. No cataclysm this time.

Wonderful.

Realizing where he was, he realized where he had been. And he had been … everywhere. He'd seen it all. He remembered it all. He remembered *everything*! None had seen him, or sensed him, or tracked him in any way. Such power! Such ascendancy!

The wonders he had witnessed defied description. Not just beyond description, but far beyond …

Then it exploded in his mind like a massive sledge.

Ohmy … ohmygod, ohmygod … OHMYGOD!

His reason was slipping away like seawater through his fingers. He must get to the surface, to something human, something of home, something familiar … and fast … or he would become irrevocably mad, beyond human contact. Beyond even his own prowess to endure.

Despite his training and strength, he couldn't assimilate, or believe, or understand, or live with what he had seen. He wanted to weep and scream and bellow and descry the impossible strangeness.

I've got … I've got … I've got to g-get out of here.

He struggled to his feet and searched desperately for a large stone. Then he sought with equal urgency his treasured pebble, although he well knew he was losing valuable time.

Burdened with both stone and pebble, he trudged the sea bottom aimlessly. In his addled condition he was certain the pebble would help keep his sanity for a time. It would comfort him. The large stone would keep him anchored to the bottom, allowing him the negative buoyancy to effectively walk. For some bizarre reason, simply swimming never occurred to him.

He was totally unaware where the shoreline lay, where Ganti City could be, or where help and human succor might be found. He was quickly losing memory of where and why he was seeking anything. He had now completely lost sight of his impending insanity, his swiftly approaching death by massive mental trauma, his loss of perspective. Even his will to live. He wasn't prepared to die; he simply was unaware of, and unconcerned by his imminent demise. It was as if some super-virulent form of

Alzheimer's suddenly overwhelmed him. Panic did somehow linger however, an icy presence in his gut that might yet save his life.

After nearly twenty-seven hours and no small amount of luck, he arose from the sea, not far from the city. _September Morn_ daubed with dark-reddish-brown dementia, within a razor's edge of certain death.

The entire crew and compliment of Gauntlet had been searching for their Captain and so were greatly relieved to discover him, albeit naked and catatonic on the narrow ribbon of beach, between moorings, just below city center. As there was no evidence of physical injury, six crewmen carried him directly to his Residence, alerting Dr. Singe along the way.

***

"Captain? Can you hear me? This is Dr. Singe. Are you all right? Are you hurt? Can you hear me Captain? Please say something." After several moments "Say anything goddamnit. What in hell has happened to you? Where have you been? What have you been doing?" Constantly saving him had grown tedious and frustrating, even though he was Captain. "Captain. Talk to me!"

No reaction.

After several minutes devoted to examination, Dr. Singe spoke to his medical team over his shoulder. "What we have here is category U on the AVPU Standard Scale. Entirely unresponsive. No response to pain. No eye, voice or motor movement; and we haven't the slightest idea what induced this state. I believe it is evident this reaction was provoked more by an emotional, or even cerebral shock, as opposed to physical trauma."

"On what do you base that Doctor?"

The Doctor made no effort to keep sarcasm from his voice. "Well, for one thing there is absolutely no evidence of physical trauma. For another, the Captain appears to be aware of his surroundings and those in his proximity. He simply cannot respond due to some unknown factor. Our resident psychologist, Dr. Hampton—Singe nodded to his colleague—suggests deep physiological distress. I agree. At the same time we cannot overlook a physiological source and associated treatments."

"What are your instructions Doctor?"

Dr. Singe concentrated for several moments, formulating a complex series of cascading procedures. If a given treatment produced no result, a subsequent remedy would be standing by.

He addressed his team.

"We will begin with standard resuscitation procedures. We'll start with intubation and ventilation and certainly rehydration. After that, Nurse, I want you to prepare for intravenous thiamin and glucose injections. Ensure we administer thiamine first."

"Thiamin first Doctor?"

"Glucose can provoke Wernicke's encephalopathy if malnutrition participates in the pathology. I suspect the Captain has taken no nourishment or sweet water in some time."

"Does the Captain require sweet water?"

"That's a question we've wrestled with for some time. Blood analysis indicated he does; and I believe we should accept that hypothesis until a compelling counter-factor arises. If the prognosis remains negative we will initiate trials with naloxone, or flumazenil, whichever we have in inventory. Either one is low risk, producing a rapid response.

"I hope surgical intervention will not be necessary. However, we must not overlook the possibility of a subdural hematoma, despite the lack of any obvious physical trauma. Prep the rooms for that as well nurse, and have anticonvulsants standing by. I favor the tried and true medications, so I'm ordering Carbamazepine, or Oxcarbazepine, or Eslicarbazepine, whichever we have in stock."

Dr. Singe peered up at his team.

"Proceed with preparations at once, meantime I'm going to administer a few good hard slaps."

With that, he began slapping the Captain violently, knocking his head from side to side continuously, producing angry red finger marks. Most of his team was clearly shocked by such treatment, markedly compounded, as he was their Captain.

Over and over again with each blow he bellowed, "Wake up Captain! Wake up damnit!"

The Doctor drew his arm back, cocking at the elbow for another powerful blow. As his palm shot towards Phil's face, another hand shot out at blinding speed, taking the Doctor's arm in a vice grip. The Doctor froze, as did his team.

The hand belonged to Phil.

Without comment, emotion, or even regard, he rose and walked leadenly from the room.

Dr. Singe rose to follow Phil from the room, as he did so he turned to his team "I will be alone with the Captain, but remain in this area in case further treatment is needed and keep all preparations on hot standby. Please ask the Executive Officer to join us."

Phil had seated himself in the enormous reception room he rarely employed. He merely sat. Eyes unseeing, not moving a muscle, hardly even breathing.

Singe quietly sat beside. The XO joined them in short order.

"Captain, can you tell us what happened?"

"No." Phil's voice was a blank wall, no emotion, or even sentience.

"If you don't mind my asking, why?"

Phil sat silently for quite some time, seemingly pondering the question.

Finally he whispered "I uh … well … I uh … just don't have the words."

The XO leaned in. "Sir, I must ask you this. I hope you understand. Do you consider yourself fit for command?"

Phil's face took on a melancholy, wistful countenance. His lips described an ironic half-smile. Without comment he reached in his robe's pocket and withdrew his cherished pebble.

He began to study it with an intensity of such fierceness, inclining his head forward, then left, then right. The Doctor and the XO suspected he was most certainly unbalanced. He drew the stone closer, his face distorted with an obsessive, frightening concentration, terrible to observe.

To their shock and horror his lower lip began to tremble, his eyes closed, his nose began to drip, and a single tear made an erratic track down his cheek seeking out his chin.

Phil lowered his head, nearly to his lap and then returned his treasured pebble to his robe. His hands fell to his sides, now ending in fists so tightly clenched they trembled. Clearly he was desperately trying to cling to sanity.

Ultimately the trembling subsided, along with a huge ragged sigh. Phil drew himself upright and arrow-straight.

He looked around the room and at the two men and spoke into his DIT. "Jake."

"Sir?"

"Jake, will you arrange for a two live Red Snappers and good bottle of white wine?"

"With the greatest of pleasure sir."

"And please bring in a pitcher of iced-water now."

Phil regarded the two men with a cordial smile.

"Thank you for your assistance gentlemen. I apologize for these new difficulties, but I assure you this was an exceptionally critical element in this mission."

The Doctor and the XO tacitly nodded their acceptance.

"After lunch I will be at my position on the Command Bridge and we will proceed with our mission. Dismissed."

Destinatio

FROM THE CAPTAIN'S lonely position on the Command Bridge, Phil marveled at the gargantuan planetary construct growing monstrously larger with each approaching second.

Thus enthralled, he considered the fantastic nature of their mission and his fitness to command such an enterprise.

***

This endeavor has cost mankind …
Mankind.
The most incalculable price.
The greatest sorrow.
The greatest pain.
Never shall there be such pain again.
This was done for me.
And what of me?
I live.
I've recovered fully in body and mind.
Several times in fact.
I've commanded an interstellar crossing, light-years in duration.
I have faithfully preserved my crew and my ship.
I have fathered five-dozen extraordinary children and banished—damn near killed—exactly half of them.

I've evolved unto Verteror, which I'm told constitutes the most singular being in the galaxy—perhaps in all the Cosmos.

I've overcome QASI and the QAVL, and defeated their dark designs.

Creatures millions of years our senior.

I've thoroughly explored that colossal planet presently dominating the endless sky of this spheriscope, and somehow preserved my sanity.

That was … difficult.

I pray the crew fares as well.

Perhaps we can formulate a less traumatic introduction to such a mind-bending alien concord.

I have never undergone such a trial.

Never such pain and uncertainty.

Ultimately now, I am ready to face them.

All of them.

***

He had learned to appreciate just what tens of millions of worlds truly portend

Daunting beyond credent

Yet he was confident

Confident to be a citizen worthy of worlds infinite and eternal

He was still but a motile spark adrift in an endless universe

A tiny flicker dancing above an infinite flame

But he was growing

With each second he grew

With each minute, hour, day, he grew

With each new challenge he grew

With each profound torment he grew

What limits such growth?

Nothing in this Universe

Or beyond

He would be Colossus

He will stride the Cosmos

He would ascent to the Eternal

He was growing

My how he was growing …

Glossary of Names & Terms

ANUMEN: [anomalous Numen] Unforeseen advances in the power or spirit—the emergence of latent abilities inherent to a hopefully evolved human species.

Apotheosis: ironically endemic to a legacy fostered by millennia of man's savagery. An ancient and all-too-often unsavory race.

AAM: Accelerated Anthropogenic Metabolizers, an exceptional enzyme inductor that excites an especially speedy metabolic process, triggering metrignosiculation within one hour

Aiy: Aiyana (Aiy) Atsila a former girlfriend of Phil, who was enticed into betraying Oneiro, ultimately provoking a devastating world war, and nearly ending her life in the most gruesome of circumstance

Anne Jones (Dr.): Former Director of the Art Department on Oneiro and one of Phil's longtime loves

Apotheosis—Late Latin *apotheosis* "deification," from Greek *apotheosis*, from *apotheoun* "deify, make (someone) a god," from *Apo*—special use of this prefix, meaning, here, "change" + *theos* "god" Deification of a human. Glorification. The apex and greatest period of a person's life

ASC: Abandon-Ship-Craft

AVPU Standard Scale: Alert, Voice, Pain, Unresponsive. A means of quantifying and describing catatonia-like states

Bayronatae: Physically solid OBJECTS or BEINGS (corporeal) having tangible mass comprised of coherent matter such as neutrons and protons

Bayrontonic-nBayrontonic: See _Matergy_

Bussard Drive: Also known as the Bussard ramjet. A novel approach to inter-stellar propulsion. Human innovation of the Drive occurred in 1960 by physicist Robert Bussard, employing a ramjet capable of extreme velocities, based upon a considerable EM field operating as a scoop to concentrate and compress hydrogen (not necessarily limited to hydrogen) from ambient interstellar matter

Chib-Erd: Aiy's affectionate sobriquet for Phil, literally interpreted as 'shit-bird'

Craig Webber (Dr.): An exceptional scientist who founded Oneiro and the remarkable genetics that took fruition there. In one respect he was Phil's father. Phil was his heir, inheriting the island of Oneiro and a formidable fortune

DIT: Digital Interface Transceiver

Edward McKnight: Phil's butler and friend on Earth

Eos: Greek goddess of the dawn. The name Dr. Webber bestowed upon an incipient cellular life form he produced and was in the midst of perfecting at the time of his death

EVA: Extra-vehicular activity

FOND shower: A normal shower, enriched with Kosmas Serum to near in-stantly flush Foreign Organic & Non-organic Detritus (FOND) from throughout the body eliminating disease, impurities, infections and materi-ally extending life

GAEA: _Gauntlet_ Administrative Engineering Anthromorph. An acronym taken from Greek mythology: Gaea the Earth Goddess. On Gauntlet

GAEA is the automated system that looks after nearly all aspects of ship's systems, telemetry, navigation, defenses and upkeep

Gauntlet Bar: A chocolate bar containing massive amounts of AAM (Accelerated Anthropogenic Metabolizers) as well as detailed training on the operation of Gauntlet, matriculated in less than an hour

GENITOR: A Kosmian expression (one of millions of such appellations throughout the galaxy) designating the force deemed to be the creator of the universe, not necessarily implying any theological connotation

GRB: Gamma Ray Burst. Thought to be possibly the most powerful explosions in the universe, second only to the Big Bang itself—probably attributable to the collapse of especially colossal stars and the intense, possibly sporadic, radiation release associated with such an event

Heisenberg Uncertainty Principle: A concept developed by physicist Werner Heisenberg in the 1930's, which remains generally accepted and ontologically enduring unto today. It stipulates *if the precise position of a subatomic particle is known, its velocity and direction cannot be accurately measured*, which applies equally to its corollary. In effect, the principle implies that the physical act of observing a particle somehow alters the particle's locus, celerity, or azimuth.
$[/\backslash X * /\backslash P \geq h / (4 * pi)]$

Heliosphere: A titanic sort of 'bubble' (roughly analogous to planetary magnetosphere energized by photonic energy) comprised essentially of pressures from the solar wind

HE-SAM: High Explosive—Surface to Air Missile. Materials that propagate an explosive event exceeding the speed of sound are considered high explosive

Howard Doyle: A highly skilled Intelligence Officer who worked for Phil on several occasions throughout pre-launch Earth

Ian McGregor: A murderous insurgent saboteur reporting to a sinister and rapacious middle-eastern conglomerate high in the Atlas Mountains of Morocco, responsible for igniting the worldwide conflagration which virtually destroyed human civilization

JAEKEL: An exceptionally advanced and deadly all terrain submarine developed and built on Oneiro, skippered by Phil during their decisive underwater battles voyaging from Oneiro to Mount Anastasios Island, in order to flee a dying Earth aboard Gauntlet, thereby honoring their pledge to Kosmas and mankind to excogitate amongst the stars in the company of the most advanced species in the galaxy

Kpzmik-Dast: [Greek: Cosmic-Dust] A cosmic cloud, light years across, comprised of beings, probably from another galaxy, incorporating into its nebula advanced specie from all over the Milky Way. These beings are the primary motivators in recruiting Philip Carr by whatever means available.

Kosmas: An all-inclusive agnomen applied to the vast number of specie engaged in research on Kosmas Kentrikos

Kosmas Kentrikos: A dark planet, having literally no albedo, engineered to accommodate the tens of thousands of specialized environmental spheres (such as Gauntlet) needed to survive a common planetary locus (translated Cosmic Central), some seven light years from Earth—orbiting the star Gilese 581—an anomalously active red dwarf in the constellation Libra

Lander: An Oneirion expression referring to people who inhabit the mainland

Matergy: As particles approach infinite granularity it becomes impossible to distinguish their nature, as whether matter or energy. This condition persists no matter the sophistication of the observer or instrumentation. Hence the name

Mesonatae: Ethereal mass-less OBJECTS or BEINGS formed of articulated Solar Energetic Particles (SEPs) such as electrons, photons and selected subatomic ions, as well as selected HZE ions (Hilfen Zur Erziehung or High-Z High Energy) defined as high energy nucleic particles comprised of galactic cosmic rays (GCRs) which eclipse a given energy threshold

Metrignosiculation: A method matriculating knowledge based on the intake of nutrition, first developed decades earlier by Dr. Webber on Oneiro

Mike Auslander: Acting President of Oneiro in Phil's absence

PM: People Mover. Very small, very quiet and clean, one or two man chariots powered by Gauntlet's electrical broadcasting facility

Pseudogene confunction: An alliance between Pseudogenes, which in fact are segments of DNA resembling a gene, having no genetic function

QASI: QASI QaQAYdun46—QAVL Ambassador to Earth and close friend of Phil until his precipitous departure in the voyage to Kosmas

QAVL: A race millions of years older than man, comprised of pure organized energy. They observe progress on millions of worlds on behalf of Kosmas, and have been observing Earth for three million years. The QAVL discovered Phil, as well as the phenomenal, near instantaneous rise of the Kosmas language amongst Oneirons. This prompted their construction of Gauntlet, ignition of a global Armageddon and the subsequent departure of 200 Oneirons to Kosmas Kentrikos

Qadyme: Companion of the QAVL

QAVLGate: A hybrid zero-energy transport system using QAVL frictionless materials in conjunction with Newtonian gravitational dynamics

QAVL Document: A fourteen-million page treatise, developed by the QAVL to educate sufficiently advanced populations on the known nature of the universe

Quaestor: A delegate to the *Kosmian Collegium.* Kosmas literally has no equivalent to a governing council. However, the *Collegium* counsels the studies and research on Kosmas. (Quaestor: L. [kwĕs'tər, kwē'stər] fr. quaestus 'one who asks questions')

Rhona: Rhona Grishall, Director of Advanced AI Heuristic Systems Design, challenged Phil as the war broke out on Earth, making a profound impression on him

Resumptive reticulation: A colossal thermo-baric force produced when a particle resumes its course after an induced diversion (thus far only by a Verteror)

Seekers: Races appointed by the *Kosmian Collegium* to comb the galaxy in search of species qualified to join Kosmas, by virtue of their acquisition of the *Kosmian* language, indicating a suitable degree and intelligence, knowledge and civilization.
The QAVL are currently the principal Seekers

SNA: Subatomic Nucleic Apperception. Infinitely miniscule sub-sub-sub-sub atomic particles which descend in size literally unto infinity. SNA executes literally every event in the universe, no matter how colossal, or infinitesimally trivial. SNA contains all the knowledge and every event in the universe, which is intelligible to beings capable of perceiving and interpreting SNA. Such beings may virtually traverse the known universe as well. Every point of knowledge, time and space, past, present and future is available to those capable of SNA divination

Spheriscope: A revolutionary technology perfected on Oneiro wherein a highly advanced periscope is capable of instantly transforming any enclosed area, a room, a submarine, an aircraft, or an entire space craft into transparency, thereby creating a perfectly faithful illusion of the ambience, or any other ambience given a sufficiently faithful record

SOP: [Military] Standing Operating Procedure

T-MAAM: A Gaunti slang acronym for Trans-Mega-AAM, AAM as in Accelerated Anthropogenic Metabolizers

Verteror: The rarest beings in the galaxy (perhaps the universe) capable of re-directing the azimuth of a subatomic particle. Every Verteror for the preceding ten million years died in this pursuit. Philip Carr is the only extant Verteror in the known universe at this time

Weltschmerz: [German] *World-pain* or *world-weariness*, is a concept introduced by the German author Jean Richter, describing the feeling experienced by humans who realize the real world will never be in accord with man's perception, or aspiration

WOF Module: Water, Oxygen, Food processor installed aboard an ASC

Yang: The light force in the Yin-Yang duality

Yin: In Chinese Taoist philosophy Yin represents the dark force in the Yin-Yang interrelated duality

9 781942 899594